HOSTAGE

JAMIE DOWARD

Constable • London

CONSTABLE

First published in Great Britain in 2016 by Constable

This paperback edition published in Great Britain in 2017 by Constable

1 3 5 7 9 8 6 4 2

A CIP catalogue record for this book
is available from the British Library.

ISBN 978-1-47211-557-7 (paperback)

Typeset in Bembo by Photoprint, Torquay
Printed and bound in Great Britain by
CPI Group (UK) Ltd, Croydon CR0 4YY

Papers used by Constable are from well-managed forests and other
responsible sources

MIX
Paper from
responsible sources
FSC
www.fsc.org   FSC® C104740

Constable
is an imprint of
Little, Brown Book Group
Carmelite House
50 Victoria Embankment
London EC4Y 0DZ

An Hachette UK Company
www.hachette.co.uk

www.littlebrown.co.uk

For my brothers, Will and Nick

Chapter 1

In the final desperate moments of a journey viewed in flash-back, a life of few lingering memories, hardly any touched by joy, there came a moment of terrifying clarity. He'd run out of options. His ordeal was over. He was over.

The metallic-grey duct tape binding the man's legs and hands made anything more than the slightest movement impossible. His neck was secured to the car's steering-wheel with a bicycle D lock. Metal around flesh, man and machine fused as one. No escape.

Through a thin tear in his blindfold he was able to make out a fragment of the car's floor: pedals, a stained rubber mat, nothing more. The garage, or whatever barely used building his coffin of a car was parked in, had no windows. The only illumination came from a skylight, its glass burned brown by the sun. It was a place of deep shadows. The man could hear the growl of traffic beyond the building's walls. Some sort of fetish device, a ball attached to a choker round his neck, was stuffed into his mouth. They'd laughed when they'd attached it. He could still hear the laughter now, competing with the furious baseline of his blood pumping through his body. His head throbbed. His heart seemed to

1

be beating inside his brain: two vital organs competing to see which could explode first.

The man tried to head-butt the steering-wheel to sound the horn but his neck was held too tightly by the lock. His eyes burned from the pepper spray his assailants had used to blind him when he'd opened the door. The oven had been on when they'd attacked him, he remembered. He wondered if it was still on. There was no point worrying about it now, though. There was no point in worrying about anything any more.

The carbon monoxide filling the inside of the car was clouding the man's brain. The tremble of the exhaust as it spewed the gas into the rubber pipe tucked through the car's left front window suggested to him that he was imprisoned in an old vehicle, a wreck, perhaps. So he was going to die in scrap metal. The irony. Him, a Porsche owner. Changed his car as regularly as other men changed girlfriends. He didn't have a girlfriend. Never had.

How'd they found him? His brain was too confused by the fumes to make the connections but it was most likely that they'd hacked his email, traced his encrypted messages through protected servers secreted halfway round the planet and back again until one spring day they'd ended up at the door of his home, a huge top-floor penthouse flat in a converted Victorian school in Battersea.

'Nice place,' one of his attackers had remarked, as they'd dragged him to their car to lock him in its boot. 'Kind of ironic, I guess. You living where you do. You sick bastard.'

The man could tell from the way they spoke that his assailants were going to kill him. They were free with their talk, confident that he would never have the opportunity of recounting their conversations to the police. He could make out most of what they were saying even when trussed up in the boot. Humdrum stuff, mostly. The need to get some new shoes (Why for me? the man had wondered), fill up the car, buy some food. They could have been two men driving to a football match or to a pub for a few quiet ones, a chance to put the world to rights.

He wondered if they'd found the others. If so, well, that was something else they had over him. He'd never known any of the others. That was how the network functioned. You couldn't trade if there was a chance you'd be traced. The network endured only if everything, absolutely everything, was kept secret. Its members hid behind countless pseudonyms, protected handles scattered across Dark Net computer systems that knew how to keep secrets.

And yet, still, they'd found him. The man swallowed several times, felt the cold steel of the bike lock on his throat. The blood rushing in his ears was becoming deafening. The sound reminded him of a holiday in the South of France, when he'd rented a house near a fast-flowing river. He'd hidden himself away. No internet. An attempt to cleanse himself. It had lasted just days, the cleanliness. He couldn't escape his addiction. There was a taste of metal in his mouth. The man felt polluted. He was going to leave the world contaminated.

If his attackers hadn't found the others they'd probably go looking for them. They seemed driven by a belief that they were dispensing justice. Fools. There was no such thing as justice – the man had learned as much when he was a child. When it had all started. Evil begets evil. That's why nothing would ever change. Everything was cyclical.

'Make as much noise as you like,' they'd encouraged him, when they'd locked him into the car, a dank pillowcase over his head, the makeshift blindfold wrapped tightly around his eyes.

At that moment he'd felt like a prisoner of war: hooded, terrified, ready to promise anything. 'I'll go to the police,' he'd told them. 'Let them deal with me.' He'd offered them money, of course. Everything he had. But they'd just shaken their heads.

'You're all right,' one had said, in an accent that came from the banks of the Mersey. 'Put your chequebook away. That's not how we want you to pay. Your money's not needed.'

There was something of the forces about the pair of them, the man thought. They were both powerfully built, looked like they kept in shape. He'd made that much out as he'd opened his front door, as they'd hit him with the spray, as they'd rushed him in his hall. Yes, he thought, his brain now just a patchwork of shadows, they were probably ex-military. Trained killers spoiling for a new battle. Violence was a form of kinetic energy. It couldn't be destroyed, only transferred.

The shadows clouding his vision were starting to join up to form one long expanse of blackness. The man's brain was shutting down. He tried not to breathe. Everything was becoming laboured, sluggish. His actions, his thoughts, his fears were all crumbling. This is the end, he thought. This is the end. He was fifty-three and it was only the previous year that he'd left details for his funeral with his solicitor. There was no close family to instruct. He was going to be cremated. Soon all that would remain of him was dust and, on powerful computer systems run out of heavily protected server farms buried below the perma-frost in a remote part of Scandinavia, the tens of thousands of images he'd traded. It was not much of a legacy. Much of his collection wasn't even that exotic now. You could get anything over the internet. You could find anyone to do anything no questions asked, for the right price. The Philippines, Russia, some of the more remote former Soviet states. There was no shortage of supply. Everyone had a video camera, these days, and many were prepared to share the most terrible images with a connected world. Children were an online commodity, like music.

Outside, the man heard the hush of rain on the asphalt roof of the building. He wondered how long it would be before someone found his body. Maybe never. Maybe they'd torch the place. His mind flickered back to his earlier thoughts. Why, why, why?

Why not?

Why?

Maybe they'd been abused themselves. Yes, that might offer an explanation. Biblical. An eye for an eye. Or maybe they'd been abusers. Possible. Maybe they'd abused prisoners when they'd been in the army. Tortured them in some hot fucked-up place that made the news only when a car bomb exploded in a marketplace and the death toll hit a cricket score. Plausible. It didn't matter. They'd found him: that was all that mattered. They'd joined the dots.

The man let out a long, deep sigh, one that it seemed he'd been saving up for a long time. In his half-dead state he still wondered about the shoes. Why'd they put some cheap shoes on him? Slip-ons, too. He'd never worn slip-ons in his life. His mind wandered back to his childhood. A door. A study beyond. That was where it had started. A single knock on the study door and the word 'Come' intoned regally.

The man had thought he was lucky to be around when the internet arrived. He'd considered it his salvation, a device that could sate his appetites, feed his limitless addiction. But it had done for him in the end. It had exposed him, ultimately, shared his addiction with others, made him part of a pattern that could be identified. He hadn't been able to hide after all. They'd traced him through it.

The man tasted salt water in his mouth. The pillowcase over his head was soaked through. He'd been crying, he discovered. He'd been crying but had been too scared, too lost, to notice.

He could hear the gentle sound of children laughing. It was coming from the car's speakers. It sounded like it had been recorded in a city park. Excited shrieks and whoops competed with the gentle thud of small feet pounding tarmac: the sounds of innocence and freedom.

Another deep, deep sigh. The man got it. He got what they were doing. They wanted him to reflect. Well, he wasn't going to give them that. He tried to drown out the voices. He focused on his earliest memories. But all he could see was the door. A big green heavy door that dwarfed him. If he'd never knocked on that door then things would have been very different. He wouldn't have entered the room. He wouldn't have been polluted. That was the problem with doors. They allowed you to enter but they could also prevent you leaving. He'd been in the same room all of his life, the man realized. It was his final thought.

Chapter 2

Geneva really needed a better airport, Adams thought. The city billed itself as an international financial centre, a vast, sprawling temple to Mammon, but he'd seen better airports in developing countries. On half the incoming flights you had to be bussed to the terminal. The queues through security were monstrous, inhumane. As for the restaurants, they wouldn't even hold their own against those in some half-dead mall back in his native Michigan.

No, Adams thought, give him Berlin or Paris any time. Madrid, wonderful, bankrupt Madrid. Oslo. Copenhagen. Christ, he'd settle for Helsinki. It came to something when Finland was preferable to where you were. And Geneva itself was hardly any better. You could learn everything about the city riding one of the moving walkways through its airport. Every backlit advert was for an expensive watch or a private bank offering bespoke tax-avoidance services. The ads spoke of a city obsessed with the ultimate, unresolvable trade-off: time versus money. Tick tock, tick tock, tick tock.

No, next time, Adams told himself, he'd get someone else from the Agency to make the trip from its European head-quarters outside Rome. He was getting too old for short visits. Once, a younger version of himself would have found such journeys exotic. The CIA was one hell of a way to see the world, older colleagues had promised him when he'd been starting out. Right. One hell of a way. But it was all bullshit, he'd learned. Being a spook was just one hell of a way to see airports, that was all. And he really hated airports. You didn't know where you stood with them. They were transitory places, nodes that didn't obey time zones, that existed somewhere between nation states, cultures, eras even. Hermetically sealed by scanners, secured by electronic barriers and patrolled by heavily armed police, they were scrutinized by a million CCTV cameras. Airports, Adams thought, were basically prisons for the free.

He dragged his heavily padded body past giant TV screens reporting rolling news stories. Or, rather, news story. It had been leading the bulletins for the last three days: the online ransoming of a hundred American and British gas refinery workers seized at a plant in North Africa. The terrorist group holding them was threatening a mass execution if a $100 million ransom wasn't paid. It was encouraging people to donate online to save the hostages. What was the world coming to, Adams thought, when terrorists were using the internet to crowdsource ransom money? The kidnappers had already executed a handful of prisoners. And now they were gunning for a world first. Either they'd make a fortune or they'd commit a spectacular. And the macabre beauty, Adams appreciated, was that the Western world, the players, the big nations, had all been completely circumvented. The Agency had no say in what was going to happen. Its only hope was to find the hostage-takers, a brigade led by a fanatic who had become rich smuggling guns, oil, drugs, tobacco across the Sahara. Impossible, Adams knew. The Agency hadn't been able to find the target in the three years they'd spent looking for him. They were fighting too many threats on too many fronts with limited resources and too few people. Tick tock, tick tock, tick tock.

Adams exited the airport and made his way to a nearby hotel. The narrow windows in its grey stone walls made him think of arrow slits in medieval castles. The little goodwill that had survived his journey was close to evaporating. He looked up at the building, could almost feel its weight crushing his shoulders. It was more like a bank than a hotel. But, then, the same could be said for half the buildings in Geneva. Well, at least it wasn't Zürich . . .

Inside the hotel, the impossible happened: Adams's mood soured further. He had to remind himself that things could be a lot worse, that he could be in Yemen or Saudi or Syria or some horrible, stifling flea-pit in sub-Saharan Africa. At least the hotel had air-con, minibars and adult films. One hell of a way to see the world . . .

He caught the lift up to his room on the fifth floor, slid his key card into the door and entered. Falcone was waiting for him inside. Adams's asset looked pleased with himself.

'Thought I'd let myself in.' Falcone's New Jersey accent was still as thick as ever. It was almost like he was acting out where he was from, Adams thought. He was emphasizing his provenance, as if he lacked confidence in himself. Understandable, really. Falcone was immersed in a borderless world where organized crime met terrorism. He probably didn't know who he was any more. He'd had a couple of kids by a couple of wives, Adams seemed to remember. Or maybe that had been someone else doing a similar line of work for the Agency. Adams avoided getting to know too much about his assets. They were just tools, he told himself. Tools that could be replaced. Eventually. He nodded at

Falcone, thought about making small-talk and gave up on the idea. Maybe Geneva was infecting him. He was in no mood to waste time. Tick tock, tick tock, tick tock. Better get straight down to business. He threw his small metal suitcase onto the double bed. 'Lot of product shipping across Sudan, I hear,' he said. 'Seems a pretty new development.'

'You hear right.'

'So?' Adams performed his usual ritual when he found himself in a strange hotel. He placed a small framed photograph of his wife and son next to his bed. He glanced down at the two most important people in his life and felt his mood lift a little. His family lived in a safe, free country because of people like him. That was why he had to put up with places like Geneva. He was protecting them and, by extension, everyone like them, everyone who mattered. Everyone good. In the modern world sometimes you had to travel far to protect those nearest to you.

'So it seems that some Chinese investors have built a tobacco plant out there in the Republic,' Falcone drawled. 'Yes, I know, I know, another one. Cigarettes for the black-market. They're all fakes, of course. Knock-off Lucky Sixes and Uncle Sams, both Empress brands. Much of it then finds its way back into Europe and Russia. Seems pretty lucrative for all concerned. Government gets a nice cut from sales. It's buying the president an awful lot of Kalashnikovs to use against the rebels.'

'And?'

'And if you're asking me what I suggest you do then I suggest at the moment you do nothing. The deal's been quietly sanctioned by the Chinese government. My sources tell me they're going to get some oil concessions out of this, maybe some rare earth minerals, too. The Sudanese government's pretty weak and wants their support. They need the Chinese money to buy the guns to keep the rebels in check. Leave it all alone and don't meddle. Tobacco is buying some kind of stalemate. Only ones losing out seem to be Empress and they're not shouting about it. They never do when counterfeit product is involved. They've got way too many skeletons in their closet to start kicking off about this sort of stuff. They spend a fortune shipping their product around the world so they can avoid paying tax. Empress won't want people focusing on this. Not the Swiss way.'

'Fine.' Adams shook his head. 'Never understand why big tobacco's based here. Monaco I get – it's got the sea – but here . . . Jesus.' He gestured out of the window. 'I thought the Swiss were obsessed with clean air. All these fucking mountains within a fifty-minute drive from Geneva and yet what they really seem keen on is filling people's lungs with smoke. Kind of skewed.'

'You know why,' Falcone said, yawning. 'They're multinationals, structured so their national subsidiaries can be as autonomous as possible. That way Head Office can allow them to get on with things without asking too many difficult questions. Just like the banks. That way they got deniability if things get messy in a particular country. But they still got to base their headquarters somewhere. So why not base yourself in a tax haven? Switzerland is tobacco HQ now. Makes perfect sense. Useful for keeping overheads down, too. Hey, that reminds me, you seen what Marathon is up to in Tanzania?' Falcone opened the minibar, helped himself to a beer. He offered one to Adams.

'Bit early in the day.'

'I'm on New Jersey time,' Falcone said. 'Currently it's five o'clock in my head.'

11

'It's always five o'clock in your head. And it's not five o'clock in New Jersey. More like seven in the morning.'

Falcone laughed. 'Yeah, well, don't knock vices. Keep me in a job. Cheers.' He raised his bottle.

Adams looked at Falcone and saw someone who'd never finished making the transition to adulthood, someone who needed the imprimatur of being a CIA asset to make them feel they'd grown up. The Agency couldn't function without such people, and Adams appreciated that. Half of its employees were men with fragile egos and a poorly developed sense of self. The intelligence world was a magnet for the truly insecure. He nodded at Falcone, who was lying on his back now, an unlit cigarette between his lips. 'What were you saying about Marathon? Been on a big buying spree, I hear.'

'Right,' Falcone mumbled. His unlit cigarette moved back and forth like a conductor's baton as he talked. 'But get this, it's not just companies they're buying. It's entire countries now. They've turned Tanzania into a tobacco state. Bribed the government to offer farmers grants so they stop growing normal crops and start growing tobacco.'

'Fair enough. It's a free market.'

Falcone snorted. 'Yeah, but once they start growing tobacco for Marathon they've got to use its recommended pesticides and fertilizers. All provided by a Marathon subsidiary based in Switzerland. And, of course, after a couple of years they start hiking prices for all their crop treatments. Pretty neat, hey? You got to hand it to big tobacco. Practically invented slavery and now it's doing it all again but this time they dress it up as a force for good and hold an entire nation hostage.'

Adams sat down on the bed, reached for a bottle of water on a nearby table, poured some down his throat. He removed his glasses and polished them with a cloth. Something about the act of wiping away the smears on the lenses calmed him. Falcone's broad grin was unsettling. Adams had no time for smiles. They were not a currency recognized by the Agency. 'Enough with the geography lessons,' he said. 'We both know why I'm really here. We've got much bigger fucking problems than whether a tobacco giant is screwing some third-world country. I need to know how Raptor is working out. Roscoe tells me shit. It's been six months now. Time for an urgent assessment. And I do mean urgent. People are getting edgy. Investors turning up the heat. You seen the TV, right? We're going to witness a mass slaying soon. Everyone in the Agency wants answers. Fuck, I can't stand watching the news any more. Every day, it's the ransom story. We need a result. I'm not asking for miracles, Falcone, but I need something. Energy companies putting huge pressure on Congress to sort out a rescue. President getting edgy. He doesn't want to go out soaked in blood. And, as for our new director, this is pretty much top of his in-tray. He's not across Raptor yet. But he's on my case twenty-four seven about the hostages. And I'm too old to do twenty-four seven.'

Falcone sat up, belched, took another swig of beer. 'Well, the good news is that Raptor may work. I could have told you all this in an email.'

Adams allowed himself a deep breath, gestured around the room. 'You know we can't discuss this sort of shit unless it's face-to-face. It's too fucking sensitive, for a ton of reasons I'm figuring you must understand. Go on.'

Falcone swirled beer around his mouth. 'I'm hearing that Raptor's electronic watermarking is damn near perfect. Had my doubts but it's real cute. When Roscoe was banging on about embedding radio frequency identification tags the size of a grain of rice in the lid of cigarette packs, I thought,

13

Fuck, we're through the looking glass here. But, turns out Roscoe is onto something. Those tags, there're tens of thousands of little beacons sending out secret microwave signals that our guys can pick up with the right equipment. And, believe me, we have the right equipment. Should do, given the money invested in Raptor. Fuck, I reckon Raptor's budget must now be what the US spends on prostate-cancer drugs each year. No wonder Roscoe's jumpy. He needs a return, especially as I hear he's planning on floating Raptor soon. But, still, this is going to take time. Serious time.'

Adams struggled to control his breathing. 'But you're telling me Raptor really works? That you've got guys on the ground tracing this? This is not some wind-up by an asset who thinks I'm too stupid to find out he's bullshitting me?'

Falcone spat the unlit cigarette onto the floor. 'No, no bullshit. Raptor's working. Tell Roscoe and his investors to quit worrying. Raptor's got the potential to be huge. We can use it to trace product halfway around the known universe and beyond if we want. We know where it's coming from, where it's going to. You'll be able to trace your man Al-Boktorah. You just got to make sure the energy companies cut Congress and the president some slack for a while longer. Use back channels to tell them to go easy with their demands for action. The technology's still suffering teething problems. But one day soon you'll be able to follow that yellow brick road and find him at the end.'

'How long we talking before these problems are ironed out?'

'I reckon five, maybe six.'

'Days?'

'Months.'

'Shit. Seriously?' Adams felt like he'd just been punched.

'Maybe a bit less but I don't think it's realistic to believe that they can all be sorted out before then. You wait for Raptor to locate your target and you're going to have a lot of dead hostages on your hands.'

'So Roscoe's just been peddling shit.'

Falcone gave a heavy New Jersey laugh. 'So what's new?'

'Guess Scott is going to have something to say about it all once he gets his head around it,' Adams muttered. 'I won't hold my breath, though. Take him two years to find where the bodies are buried.' He replaced his glasses and looked at Falcone through blue, bloodshot eyes. With his neatly parted grey hair and pristine white shirt bulging over a torso that hadn't seen a gym in years, Adams looked like a salesman who'd spent too long on the road. But, then, that was what he often told people he did for a living. 'I'm in sales,' he'd tell them. 'I sell insurance.'

It was the truth, in an oblique way. Security was a form of insurance. But now Adams had come to grasp in grim, brilliant clarity that he really was in sales. The CIA's main hope in locating America's most wanted man lay in an unproven technology developed by a renegade arm of the Agency that wasn't interested in saving lives but making billions. Politicians were no longer running the Agency: big business had the whip hand. No one seemed to have noticed when or how the transition had occurred but somewhere along the line terrorism had become just another marketing opportunity for every Palo Alto venture capitalist with a hundred million to spare. Fuck it, Adams thought, it wouldn't be long before the big Silicon Valley firms were providing national security just like everything else. They were already experimenting with drones, for Christ's sake . . . 'So, we're fucked,' he muttered. 'Raptor's just not going to find him in time.'

Falcone gave another big-bellied laugh. He cracked open a second beer, rubbed the bottle neck on a large, hooked nose that had been broken at least twice. 'Don't worry yourself so much.'

Adams wondered why Falcone just didn't get the urgency of the situation. 'Come on, you know there's a file somewhere that some senator or other has got. Most of the world is going to find out that we built Al-Boktorah. And if he goes ahead with his mass execution, that day is coming sooner rather than later. You won't believe the pressure the Agency is under. So many different parties want a result on this.' He reached for a beer. Falcone was right: it was five o'clock somewhere. Suddenly he felt very tired. He popped the top off the bottle, sipped his Coors, ran his tongue around lips that seemed to be permanently dry from spending too long in air-conditioned planes. He clinked his bottle against Falcone's. 'Why you grinning so much anyway?'

Falcone reached into his jacket pocket and pulled out a grainy black and white photograph. He handed it to Adams. 'Ta da.'

Adams tried to speak but he could emit only a short grunt. He felt like he'd been punched. Again.

'I guess maybe I should have shown you this at the beginning,' Falcone said. 'Would have saved you a lot of anguish. This was taken six days ago.'

Adams stared at the image. 'No,' he muttered. 'No, no, no.' He looked at Falcone. 'This can't be true. It's a fake, yeah?'

'Nope. It's definitely genuine. That's your man Al-Boktorah. Seems sly old Roscoe has got himself an insurance policy because he knows Raptor isn't going to deliver. He's got an asset on the inside tracking our man wherever he goes. Guess Roscoe don't want too many knowing that. Would be pretty damaging for the credibility of Raptor if it turned out it was one of Al-Boktorah's lieutenants who gave him up rather than a technology Roscoe and his buddies have spent hundreds of millions on.'

'Fuck,' Adams said. 'Roscoe know you know this?'

'Yeah. Not sure the asset trusts Roscoe completely. He put out some feelers to me and we arranged to meet. Our man's got a large family and he wants out. When we bring him in he'll need a new ID for him and his family, a new home, new job, car, dog, probably, you name it. He needs his old self completely erased. Major exercise. But it'll be worth it, I'm sure you agree.'

'Right,' Adams muttered. 'I hear you. The hostages?'

'Asset says they're being held in a cave some twenty miles from where Al-Boktorah's headquarters are based. Makes sense, I guess. Keep them better hidden that way. Asset says Al-Boktorah's brigade would be prepared to do a deal to release them if their man was taken out. They'd want money but they'd be prepared to state a ransom hadn't been paid.'

Adams stared at the photograph of Al-Boktorah. He felt twenty years younger. His lungs seemed to double in size. He could breathe in vast quantities of life-affirming oxygen blown down from the pristine snow-capped Alps. Maybe Geneva wasn't so bad after all. He turned to the photo of his wife and child and gave them a triumphal nod.

It was the last image burned into his retina. The bomb blast could be heard over in the city's financial district. It was three days before the ruins of the hotel stopped smoking. The atomic clock in its foyer was recovered unscathed. Emergency crews heard it ticking under the rubble as they searched for the dead. Tick tock, tick tock, tick tock.

17

Chapter 3

'He was found at low tide. Andrew Wade. Chartered surveyor. Married. Three kids. Cause of death, drowning.'

Sorrenson stared at the body. It was laid out on a table underneath a white sheet, like some pre-prepared wedding buffet. 'And you think that?'

Williamson tutted. 'I'm a pathologist not a probing DCI like you, Sorrenson, but, for what it's worth, yes, I think there is a high probability that Mr Wade's murder could be related to the other.'

Sorrenson counted the beads of sweat on Williamson's forehead. Nine. Working under the fierce lights needed for the forensic examination of a cadaver was harsh. No wonder he looked so spent. He was in a state of permanent dehydration. 'How do you get to that conclusion?'

Williamson pointed at the small metal table beside the body.

'Christ,' Sorrenson said, as his eyes located the slip-on shoes. 'Same make, same size, I take it?'

'Right. Size eleven. Far, far too big for the deceased. Makes no sense that he was wearing them. Just like our other murder victim, found dead in that smoke-filled wreck of a car.'

Sorrenson looked back at the body. 'And Simm tells me he was found in a casket?'

'I believe, Sorrenson, that the correct term in the UK is "coffin". Only our American friends use the word "casket", but yes. He was alive when he was placed in the coffin. Someone had positioned it out on the mudflats, near to the oyster beds up the coast. Tied it down with rope and chains and secured it to some rocks half buried in the mud. Then the tide came in and, well, you can appreciate that it was a pretty horrible end for Mr Wade. Terrifying, really. It wouldn't have been quick.'

'He,' said Sorrenson, 'or maybe they. The killers, I mean. Seems like they're big into slow deaths.'

Williamson nodded. 'It's pretty methodical, the way they go about things. The one in the car, the unfortunate Mr Gavin Hayes, would have taken a good while to die, too.' He held up a key-ring with no keys. 'This was in one of his pockets.'

Sorrenson examined the small piece of black leather. It was just a typical key-ring, the sort you saw on rotating stands outside countless gift shops in countless British holi-day resorts. There was some sort of image etched into it with gold leaf. Or, at least, there had been. The salt water had eroded most of it. Christ knows what it had done to the corpse. Sorrenson didn't want to see. He was getting too old for death and he had plenty of imagination. 'I don't get it.'

'I'm not sure any of us does, Sorrenson. But if you're asking me which castle is on the fob then, with the usual provisos that we're all prone to error and can only ever give at best an approximation of the truth, et cetera, et cetera, then I'd say it was Tintagel.'

'Tintagel?'

'Oh, come, Sorrenson. You must know your Arthurian myths.'

'King Arthur and his Round Table?'

'Merlin, too. The key-ring seems to have been placed in Mr Wade's shirt pocket deliberately. Just like that miniature bottle of brandy – sorry, cognac – that had been glued with great care to the dashboard of the wreck in which we found the late Mr Hayes of Battersea. Now, I may not be an expert on the human condition, Sorrenson, but I would imagine someone, somewhere, is trying to tell you something. Even if the message is the product of a deeply disturbed mind or, as you have already suggested, minds.'

Sorrenson shook his head in disbelief. 'Statistically there aren't enough people on this stretch of coast for us to have a couple of linked killings.'

Williamson attempted a laugh. 'You should brush up on your history, Sorrenson. This coastline has been one seething bed of unsettled scores for centuries, millennia even. Goths, Saxons, Romans, Normans. All very unpleasant. And then, of course, back when Napoleon was threatening, your throat would have been slit if people thought you were tipping the wink to the Revenue men. Free trade thrived on silence. You can't have people talking. Bad for business.'

Sorrenson closed his eyes. The harsh lights were burning into his skull. 'The shoes could be a coincidence. What's your money on?'

Williamson shrugged. 'I'm not a gambling man, Sorrenson. You're not going to examine the deceased?'

'Is it necessary?'

'Necessary, no. Just thought you might be curious.'

Sorrenson swallowed hard. 'Right.' He approached the corpse, pulled back the sheet, and looked down at the bluish-grey skin of a recently drowned man, less than a decade older than himself. He stared at it, trying to imagine what it would have been like when its heart had been beating. 'Horrible way to go.'

'They both were,' Williamson said.

'Presumably that's the point. Someone wanted them to suffer.'

'Which would imply that someone knew something about them, maybe about what they did or had done,' Williamson murmured. 'I mean . . .'

'Afternoon.' A younger voice, one that didn't belong in a morgue. 'Sorry, couldn't stay away.' The red-headed man nodded at the detective and the pathologist, ripped the ring pull on a can of Coke and took a swig.

Sorrenson and Williamson stared at Simm. The junior detective was unsurprised to see they weren't smiling. It was a generational thing, police humour, he was realizing. It didn't cross age boundaries well. 'Sorry,' he muttered. 'Dumb thing to say.'

Sorrenson nodded. 'Simm, meet Andrew Wade, the deceased.'

Simm walked up to the body. 'This is the drowning one, right? Found in a casket?'

'In the UK we call them coffins,' Williamson muttered. 'Unless, of course, we've been watching too many American television detective shows.'

'Right,' Simm said. 'Same difference. Still drowned in a box.'

Sorrenson scratched his grey stubble. He wondered where the junior detective would be in five years' time when the novelty of death had worn off. A long way from the coast, probably. A long way from the police, certainly. The grind

21

just wasn't worth it. The force was already asking too much of its younger recruits. It could just about cope with normal crime but anything epic or unusual, how it responded to that sort of challenge, well, it was in the gift of the gods, these days. Murder was unusual. Serial murders were off the chain.

'Shoes,' Sorrenson said. 'We'll start with the shoes.'

She didn't need him to say what he did for a living. It was almost as if Kate was seeing her old self in abstract. There was something closed about the man. He stood very still, feet planted, arms at his sides. But his eyes betrayed what he was trying to keep buried below the surface, an anxiety, a fear of not being in control of things. They darted around the office. He was a man looking for targets. A man looking for enemies.

She gestured for him to take the chair in front of her desk but he chose to remain standing. Taut and hard-faced, he was almost preternaturally thin. He reminded her of a heron. He clearly preferred looking down at her, head cocked slightly to one side. Typical, she thought. Where would they be without their innate sense of superiority? Halfway to human, probably.

The man faced a dilemma, she knew. He couldn't decide where she stood on things. That was the problem with former members of the service. They were off the leash, semi-feral. You could threaten their pensions, blackmail them with the Official Secrets Act but, ultimately, they were outside the world of MI5 groupthink. 'What story did you tell them at Reception?' she said.

'Reception had gone home. I told your security guards that I'm with Customs, come to share some intelligence on black–market smuggling. Flashed them some ID. That did the trick. They were not exactly curious fellows. You might need to think about changing that.' The man waved an HMRC badge at her.

Interesting, she thought. He'd gone to some trouble to disguise his real job. A preposterous exercise, completely unnecessary. But, then, Five did love the subterfuge, the mendacity. Lies were its major currency. Still, it was a strange one. The man had chosen to wear a mask. He was trying to disguise his identity. He wanted to protect something or someone. Maybe his employer, maybe himself. There was something there. A vulnerability.

'Customs,' she said, glancing down at her watch. 'Well, I guess it's nearly plausible. Although it's eight in the evening. Not sure Customs work those hours. Sadly, they're very much nine-to-five operators, I've come to learn. No real incentive to burn the midnight oil, you see, those in the public sector. The overtime's not great and, unlike some people, they have lives outside their work.' She smiled at the man. 'You might need to work on your back story next time you visit Smith and Webb. Or you could just pick up the phone and call, like normal people do.'

The man said nothing, just stared at her intensely. Other agents had looked at her in the same way when she'd been seconded to the service. Maybe it was something to do with her height – she was nearly six foot tall – and that she wore her dark curly hair long and loose. She stuck out far too much. She would have made a lousy agent in the field. She could never blend in. She pointed up at the man. 'Five, right?'

He nodded.

'Figures,' she muttered. 'You all have the same aura, you know that? It's a mix of arrogance and fear. Must come from having all that confidential information in your head. Thrilling but toxic. Some of it must slosh out every now and then.'

The heron remained silent. His eyes continued to dart round the office, at its expensive furniture, its limited-edition prints, the polished wooden floor that predated the industrial revolution. She knew what he was thinking: This is what you get if you leave. This is what the green pastures look like for ex-MI5 agents. This is what you get when you move from the public to the private world.

She studied the man closely. He was about five foot ten, early forties, no wedding ring, but he was sporting the almost obligatory signet ring worn by agents of his age and gender, confirmation that he came from a family that pursued foxes and was able to trace its lineage back to the Norman invasion. Neatly clipped hair, skin untroubled by stubble. He could pass for an estate manager or a vet, she thought. But, then, they all could, his sort. It was as if they were bred in some Whitehall basement to be as unobtrusive as possible. It was an issue. In the hyper-modern world, the majority of agents still being churned out by Five were becoming exotic in their resolute, fallible blandness. While the rest of the world was intermingling, becoming ever more blended, interesting, fluid, Five's agents were starting to seem glaringly white, privileged and dangerously, dangerously dull. The service was almost the last bastion of the public-school-educated white male. But not for much longer. You looked at the eyes and saw something there, something troubling that was far from dull. You saw a man who knew that he was a threatened species, who wondered where his future lay. She felt a pang of kinship.

'Can't see what Five want with a visit to the seaside,' she said. 'Spot of convalescing? The air down here can be pretty cleansing in April. Whips straight across the bleak North Sea all the way down from Scandinavia. Restorative.'

'Callow sent me.'

So, then, her former employer definitely wanted something from her, if Callow was involved. 'How is the fat deputy controller?'

'Still fat, still chain-smoking. He's a heart attack in the making. Talks about his retirement like he believes it's going to happen. Says he's going to go and live in Provence or somewhere and renovate a *mas*, whatever that is. I think he's deluding himself. He's too institutionalized. He'll drop dead the moment he leaves the service. He should have got out long ago.'

She was surprised. The disclosures seemed unforced and thoughtful and were clearly genuinely held beliefs. She was being softened up. 'Yes, I think you're right about Callow. I'm not sure that he really wants to leave anyway. And he's too old, too proud, to do something like this.' She gestured around her office. 'But he's still too young to tend his *potager* or whatever the French call their allotments.'

A grey face peered round the office door. The voice was high-pitched, wheezing. 'You're busy, Miss Pendragon. I'm so sorry to interrupt.'

'No worries, Mr Cole.'

'I'll come back when you're free.'

'Thank you. That would be helpful.'

The face disappeared.

25

'Urgent matter?' The man afforded Kate a well-practised half-smile.

'Do you have a name?'

'Fawcett. Peter Fawcett.'

'Quite original.'

'It's my real name, not that I expect you to believe me.'

She considered his answer. It didn't appear to be an outright lie. She became even more suspicious. Just what was it she had that Five wanted? She gestured at an empty chair in front of her desk. 'Peter Fawcett, please take a seat. You're making me uncomfortable standing up.'

He sat down. She gestured at the pot on her desk. 'Coffee? I've just made a fresh cafetière.'

'Thank you. Black, no sugar,' Fawcett said. 'Looks like you're expecting a long night. Perhaps it's to do with the matter that your colleague, Mr Cole, your head of compliance, wanted to discuss with you just now.'

She poured the coffee. Presumably Fawcett wanted her to understand something. He'd clearly been briefed on Smith and Webb's senior personnel or he wouldn't have known Cole's role within the company. So, then, Five had scoped the UK's largest tobacco company. Things were becoming clearer. She felt conflicting emotions. The service believed she could be of use to it in her current job. But Five wasn't her employer any more. She owed it nothing. Yet still it had come back and was knocking on her door, and going to extraordinarily contrived, almost comical lengths not to be observed doing it.

'Mr Cole is a diligent man,' she said carefully. 'He takes his work very seriously. He's always concerned about things, always anxious. I think it comes from years of smoking his company's products, then trying to give up. He's always craving nicotine. As a result he's permanently stressed.'

'Maybe,' Fawcett said. 'Or maybe he's been watching too much news on television. Foreign news. Dreadful things happening in the desert. Just when you think we've reached the plateau when it comes to atrocities, something new comes along.'

'I have no idea about Mr Cole's viewing habits.'

Fawcett sipped his coffee. 'Tastes good.'

'One of the perks of working here. We get free bags of Colombian coffee. Mr Cole likes his company's cigarettes. I like its coffee. We all have our vices.'

'You have any others?' Fawcett looked at her meaningfully. His words hung in the air. Kate struggled not to cross her arms. He'd obviously read her file, personally shaken hands with all the skeletons in her cupboard. He would have read all her psychological assessments. He would know about her dead father. He would know about her dead husband. He knew more about her than almost anyone alive yet he was a complete stranger. She hated the asymmetry between them. 'I run,' she said quietly. 'I lose myself in running.'

'Well, that seems pretty harmless,' Fawcett observed. 'Nothing to fear there, then. Nothing to fear at all.' He took another sip of coffee. 'I think I might be addicted to caffeine. This is one of Smith and Webb's own brands, I take it? I must get some.'

'They've been buying up food and beverage companies over the last couple of decades. Insurance against the possibility that people might stop smoking. It was a crazy diversification strategy that they're now trying to unwind.'

'Well, they were right in a sense,' Fawcett said. 'Smoking rates are falling in Europe. Just the rest of the world where it's ballooning. Places where tobacco isn't taxed very heavily. Places where tobacco isn't taxed at all in some cases. Like some of the more unloved parts of the Middle East and Africa. Business is booming.'

She stared at Fawcett. She wasn't going to make his life easy for him. 'It's a complex area, distribution. Smith and Webb are at the forefront of introducing innovative ways of tracking their product to make sure all duties are paid.'

'Spoken like someone who's worked for the company for years,' Fawcett snapped. 'Tell me, how long did it take to learn that mantra?'

Kate felt herself redden. It was true. She hadn't meant to sound like a company spokeswoman. She'd been working for Smith and Webb for almost nine months and hadn't realized how deeply she'd assimilated its culture. It had rubbed up against her assiduously, unobtrusively, so that she hadn't noticed the quiet way it had been moulding her. Fawcett had provided her with an embarrassing reality check, a reminder of how institutions, companies, agencies, religions, ideologies governed. What must it be like for those who'd been with the company for years? Employees who'd started out as trainees straight from university and were now lashed to the company mast, too dependent on its pay, its perks, its pension to break free. Such people were biddable. They were nothing without the corporate teat. 'Fair point. I'm quite new to this. Still finding the transition from public to private tricky going. It's a whole new language that you have to learn.'

'I could imagine that completing the journey would be quite difficult,' Fawcett said acidly. 'Of course, you never really make it, you do know that, don't you? You never truly get from A to B. There will always be a part of you left back where you started. In your case, the oh-so-quaint, well-meaning public sector.'

Her shoulders tensed. Danger, danger, danger. She knew what was coming. Some sort of offer was going to be made, an exchange of sorts. In time. But Fawcett was shrewd. He was clearly in no rush. He sipped his coffee, attempted a thin smile, allowed the seconds to drag on.

'You make it sound like all ex-spooks suffer from some form of Stockholm syndrome,' she said quietly. 'Like we're hostages who end up bonding with our captors.'

'I wouldn't put it quite as dramatically as that,' Fawcett said.

'So how would you put it?'

'Just that people like us know the importance of taking sides. That you can't be in the middle of things. You can't be on the shoreline. You're either in the sea or on the land. Otherwise you're too exposed. Vulnerable from both directions. You know that. That's why you'll always be one of us. You know you're either with us or against us.'

'You seem very sure of that.'

Fawcett changed the subject. 'Did you know that during the war cigarettes were a form of money in prisoner-of-war camps?'

She said nothing. Fawcett's words had got to her. The world was far more complicated than he was making out. In his mind it was all about stark choices. And yet something about what he had said resonated. If it came down to it, if she was on the shoreline and she had to make the call, she knew that she would choose a side. She knew which side too.

'Yes, I read a book on it,' Fawcett continued. 'Very interesting. No one had any money, but they did have Red

Cross-issue cigarettes. So tobacco became a form of tender, far more coveted than real money, which couldn't buy anything. Not very much has changed since then, I would suggest.'

'Except we're not at war,' she said coldly.

'I rather think that depends on which side of this desk you're sitting. If you're on my side, I'd say we are. An ugly, complicated war being fought on many fronts, far too many for our liking. But on your side, Ms Pendragon, well, perhaps things are considerably clearer. I envy you. You know where you are in business. You're either partners with someone or rivals. But in our line of work, intelligence, things are fluid, as you know.' Fawcett fiddled with his signet ring. 'Friends can become foes. Friends can let you down. Relationships, old alliances don't just disintegrate, they rebound on you and sometimes come back with force. That can be unfortunate.' He seemed to think about saying something, then sighed. 'Either way, Ms Pendragon, forgive me for telling you what I'm sure you've learned during your relatively brief time with your new employer, but even today cigarettes are still a powerful alternative currency. They can be exchanged for anything and are pretty much untraceable, unlike money sent through bank accounts. And once you've created an illicit tobacco-distribution network, well, you can use it to distribute anything. Guns, bombs, bombers. One long conveyor-belt of menace. Your late father understood this.'

A low shot. 'I'm fully aware of my father's work for the service. I don't need history lessons from you.'

But Fawcett persisted: 'Cutting the purse strings of the IRA, clamping down on their trade in contraband, was his speciality. You have to speculate how much more damage he would have done them if he hadn't died so early.'

'No,' she said. 'You don't. The past is the past. I don't go there. I haven't for a very long time.'

Fawcett shook his head. 'I think you do. We all do.' He pointed at the walls painted an expensive Georgian blue. 'Is it worth it?'

'Is what worth it?'

'Is taking the corporate shilling worth leaving the service?'

'I was never with the service.'

'Yes, yes, I know, I know,' Fawcett said impatiently. 'You were just on secondment. You were never one of us. And yet you're legendary, Ms Pendragon. You drove a car onto a runway and aimed it at a Gulfstream jet. You prevented an attack on a nuclear installation and saved a CIA-run bank from implosion, which would have taken half of the banking sector down with it, according to some of the more febrile gossips in the service. Whether true or not, all agree it was the most exciting thing anyone in the Agency had done since the Berlin Wall came down. I heard they begged you to stay. And yet you chose to leave. I reckon you regret it more than you let on – leaving, I mean. At least you knew where you stood, back then. Tell you the truth, I don't think you're cut out for the tobacco trade, working for a venerable company like Smith and Webb that made its money from tobacco plantations in the American south. Awkward, knowing that your employer and your pension pot got fat on the forced labour of long-dead slaves. You must have trouble sleeping.'

She stood up, her eyes flashing. She was a good two inches taller than Fawcett and she felt better for being able to look down at him. She wanted to reclaim control of the situation, of the space around her. He was pathetic, the man in front of her. But, then, they were all pathetic, she reminded herself. All of them, with their stupid games and rituals and coded, clipped manners. God knew how they treated their wives, their children. Did they even have any true friends? She remembered why she'd left, why she'd never really joined. She'd left because she didn't want to become like them. It was true, institutions governed. Spend long enough in one and you would absorb its culture. It would mould you, like a cult, like a terrorist cell. It would think for you if you weren't careful. 'I think we're done,' she said.

Fawcett got to his feet, made a theatrical point of assessing her figure. Too theatrical she thought. Clumsy. Something wasn't right there. He nodded several times to himself, as if in approval. There was a hint of a leer on his face. 'Well, then. We're done. But you know the form, Ms Pendragon.'

Kate played dumb. 'The form?'

'You know you have something we want.'

'You might be wanting to trade but I'm not playing.'

'One of your colleagues said that and we took him at his word. We left him alone and didn't trouble him again. But eventually he came round.'

'Then you can grant the same courtesy to me and take me at my word.'

'Fine.' Fawcett straightened his tie. 'We'll respect your wishes just as we respected those of your colleague.'

'Do. Now leave.' She indicated the door.

'Aren't you curious?'

'I take it you mean curious about which of my colleagues you have on your books?'

'Correct.'

Again she waved at the door. 'No.'

'I had you down as someone with a healthy curiosity.'

'Then you had me wrong.'

Fawcett moved to the door and paused. His eyes darted around her office a final time.

'I'll see myself out. Thanks for the tip about Customs, by the way. I'll work on my back story some more for next time.' His eyes locked with hers, an agent and ex-agent joined in an unblinking union, the public and private worlds melding. The heron smiled tightly. 'And there will be a next time.'

Chapter 4

He walked among gnarled dark oaks and shimmering silver birch, wondering where the spring had gone. It was a May evening but summer had come early. Rain had been absent for weeks and the scrub underfoot felt tinder dry. One spark was all it would take to turn the wood into a giant firewall. The blaze would be seen all the way along the coast, some three miles away. There was a dustiness in the air that made him think of fields after harvesting. In his mind he practised what he was going to say. He'd rehearsed it, whittled it down into something bland, easy-on-the-ear.

'I'm as broad-minded as the next man,' he'd tell them. 'But you know how people talk in this town. Stories get told. They travel. There have been complaints. If you could just . . .' Yes, he thought. It sounded slightly formal but it would do. They would get the message and move on. Find another location. Somewhere else they wouldn't be interrupted. There were plenty of locations along the coast where they could continue unobserved.

The policeman searched the ground for traces of their licentiousness. But there was nothing to incriminate them. No rubbish. No discarded cigarette butts, used prophylactics or empty bottles. Just a few tyre marks in the bone-dry soil at the centre of the copse where, he'd learned from salacious reports in the local newspaper, they liked to park their cars.

He looked around him. It was a good place to fuck. The copse offered protection from prying eyes. The cars could face each other in a round, like circled wagons in old Westerns. Still, though, it was a strange one, what people got up to in their spare time. The policeman was barely into his twenties and considered himself enthusiastic when it came to sex but he struggled to understand the motivation. With strangers, too. Some people.

It seemed absurd that he should have been dragged into it. But here he was, almost seven on a May evening, steering his gangly six-foot-three frame through the wood. He felt awkward, unsure of himself. It had been complaints from runners who used the trails through the wood that had triggered it all. The runners had said nothing at first. But eventually the meetings between the two groups had become habitual and clumsy jokes quickly soured into petty resentment, then anger. The runners felt as if they'd been invaded. The scrub above the coast, the woods looking down onto the sea, the hills above the town: that was their territory.

The runners were not slow in spreading stories around the area. And the local paper was not slow in reporting the 'shocking open air orgies'. Neither was the local council slow in demanding action from the police commissioner. The police commissioner was not slow in ringing the chief inspector. The chief inspector was not slow in demanding action from his superintendent. The superintendent, a middle-aged man, two years off his pension, was not slow in farming out responsibility for the matter to the young policeman, who was barely more useful to a community than a postbox in the senior man's privately-held opinion.

'This is more your type of thing,' the super told him. 'A young person's thing. I'm sure the internet is to blame. You never got this sort of thing before computers.'

The young policeman tried not to be judgemental. Everyone needed a vice. That was how the world moved. Unsteadily, on a crutch. He sat down under the branches of a centuries-old tree that hadn't known a saw in its life, and prepared to wait for the strange sect to arrive. He'd learned that they came every third Thursday of the month. Regular as clockwork. The first Thursday, too, in the summer months.

As his eyes adjusted to the gloom created by the dense, untended branches above him, the policeman discovered he wasn't alone. A man at the other side of the copse was watching him, leaning back against a tree and yawning. He had an astonishing number of teeth.

Perhaps he was one of them, the policeman thought. Yes, that would make sense. Why else would someone be in the wood on their own at that time of day? He got to his feet and stumbled across the dusty earth towards the figure. Rays of evening sunshine drilled through the trees, sending brilliant shards of light slicing through the gloom. 'Evening,' he called. 'I wonder if I – I wonder if I could have a word. Now, I'm as broad-minded—'

His thoughtfully crafted opening sentence came to an abrupt end. The policeman vomited, the poorly masticated remains of a tuna and sweetcorn sandwich splattering his shoes. He tried to wipe his mouth but his hands hung limply at his sides. Mumbling nonsensically, he fumbled in his pocket for his mobile phone, a flare to summon the lifeboats.

He couldn't stop looking at the other man's eyes. Or, rather, the holes where they had been. He tried to count the burn marks on the man's face, scores of thumbnail gouges red raw and putrefying. But there were just too many. Too much horror to take in. The man's mouth was stretched wide open in an ugly leer. Crammed into his mouth were packets worth of cigarette butts. All one brand, the policeman saw, through blurred eyes: Double Jeopardy – you could tell by the gold filters. The policeman stared at the corpse. It was too much for anyone to comprehend. He tried to punch numbers into his phone but dropped it, fell to his knees and folded himself into a ball, arms clasped round his shins. He wanted to make himself as small as possible. It was many minutes before he uttered anything like a recognizable sentence, hours before he stopped shaking.

He'd seen bodies before, of course. Bodies of elderly relatives whose time had come; a motorcyclist crushed by a truck; a wispy-haired pensioner, who'd fallen in a shopping centre, her skull, thin as an eggshell, too weak to protect her brain. But he would never forget the stubbed-out victim, as he came to think of the man. Years later the policeman, the remnants of him at least, would dwell on the horror of the man's final hours. He would indulge in grotesque speculation about the pain the man had experienced in the final minutes of his life. He would try to understand the terror that came with realizing that some things were worse than death. In the dark, quiet hours of a winter's morning, when the world itself seemed to have died, such regular feats of imagination left him exhausted, terrified.

The policeman looked at the body, at the horrifically deliberate way in which it had been arranged. So much thought had gone into ending the man's life. So, he thought. Another. They'd found another.

★ ★ ★

'Smoking kills.'

Sorrenson said nothing, allowed himself several deep breaths.

'I said, "Smoking kills."'

'I heard you the first time, Simm.' Sorrenson gazed around the wood. The trees were being assaulted by the flash of cameras and the static of police radios. 'Very droll. If it doesn't work out for you as a detective you can always turn to comedy. Pays better and you don't have to spend your days dealing with this.' He pointed at the figure in front of them. They stared at the crumpled body, illuminated by arc lights, the face lolling forward as if the neck had snapped, the flesh reduced to a mass of craters turning from red to black. A forensic team in white suits was sealing off the wood, wrapping the copse in yellow tape, like some sort of grotesque Christmas decoration. Powerful searchlights combed the dark periphery of the wood. Sniffer dogs nosed the scrubland under the trees, their handlers shouting occasional encouragement. The wood had been a crime scene for almost four hours yet it seemed to Sorrenson as if they had been there years. It was as if his younger colleagues were an army bedding in for a long fight, half excited, half scared witless. Sorrenson could live without excitement. He'd had enough of it.

'You've got to admit, though, it's one hell of a way to go,' Simm said. He ran a hand through his wiry red hair. 'One hell of a way. I mean, Jesus, this is one for the record books or something. Poor bastard must have been praying for death. What a fucking mess. There are some sick fucks out there. To go to those efforts, tie him to a tree, then burn him all those times . . . That takes application, that does. He must have done something to really piss someone off. Do you think it's related to the others?'

'Maybe,' Sorrenson said. He thought about the policeman. He'd been with the body for almost two hours before he'd phoned it in, paralysed by fear. Simm, on the other hand, seemed inured to the horror. Excited, even. They took all sorts, the police.

'Maybe?' Simm said. 'Definitely, more like.'

Sorrenson looked up at the sky, hoping to see something familiar above, but it wasn't a night for stars. There was a near full moon. Far too much illumination above the earth. 'Maybe,' he muttered. He could almost feel his grey hairs multiplying. He felt as if he was ageing rapidly. There was a permanent tightness in his chest that had not been there the year before. A physical warning sign: careful, slow down, danger ahead.

'Shit,' Simm said. 'If this is related to the other two, we'll be on the ten o'clock news.'

Sorrenson wondered when the novelty of death had become lost on him. He'd been in the police twenty-one years, joined up when he was twenty-three, and he'd lost count of the number of bodies he'd seen. Bodies whose owners' lives had been ended prematurely, usually with blunt or bladed instruments. That was the thing about being in the police. You only got to see the victims of feuds and spent loves, the unlucky and the vulnerable. You got to witness no good deaths. The endings were always brutal and squalid and, after a while, they all melded into one.

Until now.

Simm was right, Sorrenson thought. The coast was becoming news. Death was relatively unusual in a place where few people lived. And when it came in triplicate that

JAMIE DOWARD

made it even rarer, a freak show that had just rolled into
town. In his stretch of the country, the bit that fell away into
the Channel, almost all murders were domestics. The odd
Kent gangland feud erupted now and then but it was nothing like the seventies. Homicide on the coast erred towards
the perfunctory. But now violence was becoming inflation-
ary. It was shifting through the gears. He pointed at the body
being gently freed from the tree and lowered into a special
plastic container. He studied the scene for several seconds.
Then he looked at Simm. 'The chief constable has been
informed, right?'

'I think so.'

'You think so,' Sorrenson said slowly. He scratched the
grey-white stubble threatening to invade the hollows of his
cheeks. He was surprised by the gauntness of his face. He'd
lost weight, too much. Maybe he'd come back too early. A
few months' more convalescing might have been a good
idea. 'You'd better know so, Simm. You hear me?' Sorrenson
nodded at the throng of police swarming through the wood.
'Someone here is going to get a nice tip fee from the papers
very shortly. This story will be everywhere soon. You don't
want Morrison to find out about it for the first time when
he clicks on his iPad.'

'Right,' Simm said. 'I'll make the call.'

'You do that.'

'This your first serial killing, Sorrenson?'

'Be careful. We don't know what we've got here.'
Sorrenson jerked his thumb at the figure coming towards
them. 'So?'

'So, Sorrenson, I'm quite pissed off,' Williamson said.

Sorrenson laughed. 'We keeping you from some assigna-
tion, Brian?'

'I wish, Sorrenson, I dearly wish. But no.'

'So what is it, then?'

'It's this other forensic team coming from London. I mean honestly, Sorrenson, it's really taking the piss.'

'News to me.'

'Well, we've only just found out ourselves. Phoned the deceased's details through to the relevant agencies and the next thing we know the Yard are all over us.'

'What's the Met's angle on it?' Sorrenson said.

'I was rather hoping you'd tell me that,' Williamson said. 'Maybe save us both some time. There's no point in us being called out if someone else is leading on it. We're stretched as it is. It's like they don't trust us to do a competent job. Can't have people losing confidence in the justice system.'

'Looks like it's a bit late for that,' Sorrenson said, his eyes on the body. 'I think someone lost faith in the justice system some time ago.'

'Well, Sorrenson, I know the deceased was a tobacconist but I hardly think that's a reason for torturing him. While I wouldn't condone such behaviour . . .'

'What's the deceased's name?' Simm said.

'Well, we believe, from the documents on his person, credit cards, driving licence, all subject to confirmation from loved ones, relatives, et cetera, et cetera, that he is a Mr Antony Carrington. No *h* in the Antony.'

'And he ran a newsagent's?' Simm said.

Williamson shook his head. 'That was my attempt at a joke, Detective. When I say he was a tobacconist what I really mean was that he worked for big tobacco.'

'Doing what?' Sorrenson asked.

'Well, it seems he worked in distribution. It sounds dull but actually Mr Carrington was responsible for overseeing the shipment of billions of Smith and Webb's finest cigarettes around the world. A modern-day Sir Walter Raleigh distributing tobacco God knows where. The unfortunate Mr Antony-without-an-*h* Carrington has probably done more to advance cancer than almost anyone in Britain. Not an accolade that he will have enjoyed taking to his grave. But, then, I imagine he had other things on his mind in the long, tortured hours before he finally died.'

'Smith and Webb. My partner . . .' Sorrenson was conscious of how strange it felt to be referring to Kate. He might as well have been talking about having a second head, it sounded so alien coming from his mouth. 'My partner works for them,' he said flatly.

'So does half the population around here, Sorrenson,' Williamson told him. 'They're one of the biggest employers on the coast, these days. Got their own business park just out of Folkestone. Very smart it is, so I'm told. And, of course, they own many of the decent Georgian buildings along the coast. There's money in addiction. So your wife is a tobacconist, too.' Williamson pointed at the body being loaded into an ambulance and tutted. 'Let's hope this isn't catching.'

'I said partner, not wife, and she's freelance. She advises them on security issues: risk, counterfeit products, black-market exports, all that sort of stuff. You don't want any of it ending up in the wrong hands.'

'Well, I would expect she's remunerated handsomely for her expertise,' Williamson said. 'Watch out, Sorrenson. Having a partner like that could leave an impoverished detective chief inspector feeling quite emasculated.'

Sorrenson approached the ambulance, noting its brilliantly lit interior. The dead didn't need illumination.

'I used to picnic here with my wife,' Williamson called.

'The third, I recall. It's quite famous. The world's first passenger steam train ran up through it. They needed winding
machines to bring the carriages up from the coast because
the incline is so steep up here. The water to feed their steam
engines came from specially built ponds, which are still here.
There's an old winding wheel next to them too, I think.
You should bring your wife, sorry, partner, Sorrenson. It's
enchanting when the bluebells are out. Very life-affirming.'

'I'll make a note of it. She's still getting used to living
down here. Too much exposure to nature might unsettle her.
It's a bit different from London. The lack of diesel fumes
might—' Sorrenson stopped. A powerful car engine purred
through the trees. The pathologist and the two detectives
watched the BMW drive slowly towards them, its headlights
off so as not to blind the forensics team combing the wood.

'Here comes Scotland Yard,' Williamson muttered.

Sorrenson glanced back into the ambulance. Something
about the body was puzzling him. The man had been wearing a suit, expensive by the look of it, but no tie. There was
nothing strange in that, Sorrenson conceded. It was the
default outfit for most young executives, these days. But, still,
something jarred: the shoes. Reluctantly he advanced
towards the corpse and examined its feet. Yes, black slip-ons.
Judging by the way they were nearly slipping off the dead
man, they were a couple of sizes too large.

'Yes,' Williamson agreed. 'I had noticed. Someone does
seem to be trying to get some sort of message across.'

'Christ,' Sorrenson said. So, a clear link to the other two
killings. But they were all men and there had been no sexual
assault. There was no obvious connection.

Sorrenson walked towards the BMW. He peered hard into
the driver's side but could make out only a dark, squat shape

behind the wheel. Whoever was inside was in no hurry to get out. There was the efficient whir of an electric window. Sorrenson nodded at the driver. 'So, not the Yard, then,' he said.

'Not, strictly speaking, the Yard, no,' Callow said, his face wreathed in cigarette smoke. 'Last time I saw you, Sorrenson, was at McLure's memorial service. Guess we both thought we wouldn't be seeing each other again. How are the war wounds? Scars healing?'

'I'm doing OK.' Callow's sudden appearance had thrown him. What was the deputy director of MI5 doing at a murder scene? There was no obvious national security dimension, yet clearly the service suspected something that he didn't. A troubling night had become more so.

'Kate OK?' Callow said. 'You're together now, I understand.' His voice was gruff but not unfriendly.

Sorrenson said nothing. He didn't want the service intruding on his personal or his professional life. He wanted to keep as distant from men in suits and London as possible.

'Get in,' Callow said.

Sorrenson hesitated, then approached the passenger door.

'But just before you do,' Callow added, 'understand that this conversation is not happening and has never happened. This car has never been in this wood. This car does not exist. You hear me? This car is dark matter.'

Sorrenson got in.

Frenchie's face split for a fourth time. He fell back into the dust, hardly making a sound. His assailant stood over him, looking down at his devastating handiwork. The assailant wished he had a gun. Then he could kill himself. He'd just beaten unconscious a man he didn't know for no reason other than self-preservation. He started to weep, sobs that came from somewhere deep down and from long ago.

Two of the hooded captors walked over to Frenchie, kicked him a couple of times in the stomach. One of the pair bent down, spat on the lifeless figure. No response. 'Frenchie, you still with us?' one shouted, in a Black Country accent. He turned to the other man. 'Nah, think he's gone.' He pointed to the sobbing man. 'You hit him well good, bro, you know? He must have had like a soft skull or something. Fucking lame, really, the way he went down.' He threw a packet of cigarettes at the other captor. 'Here you go. Don't say I don't pay up, bro. What'll we do about him?' He pointed at the crumpled body, then gazed at the wide-eyed faces of the near hundred hostages kneeling around them in a circle, arms tied to their legs. 'Rude to stare, boys. Rude to stare. Let that be a lesson to you. You got to fight to the death if we pick you. Only way you're going to survive. And, remember, we give you better rations if you fight well for us. None of this Algerian shit. Chocolate. We got KitKats, we got Twix, we got Snickers.' He started laughing, pointed at a couple of the faces staring hard at the ground. 'Oi, look at me, you two. Could be your turn next, Yoda and Chewy. That'll be a good fight. You look well fierce, Chewy.'

'Where'd you get those names from anyway?' the other captor said.

'They look like 'em, innit?'

'Fucking don't know when you last saw *Star Wars*, bro, but they look nothing like them.'

'Whatever, bro. Frenchie was a shit name anyways. He wasn't even fucking French. His passport said he was from Belgium or some shit place.'

45

'Same fucking difference.'

'Whatever. What's the time?'

'Coming up to six.'

'We got to make the video,' the other captor said. 'Update the blog for our fans.' He nodded at the hostages. 'Who wants to send a message home to their loved ones? What about you, Yoda? You got like a kind of sad face. People going to be generous when they see you on the internet.'

Chapter 5

'Forgive me for not standing up.' Webster rocked back in his wheelchair to gain a better view of a man he knew well but had never met. Brandon Scott had been head of the CIA for only a few months but his journey to King Spook was well documented. The scion of a heavyweight banking family, and a former member of the US water-polo team, great things were expected of him. So far he'd delivered. A decorated veteran who'd been US ambassador to the UN, newspaper profiles suggested the White House beckoned. Still only in his late forties, Scott was handsome in a dated JFK way. His lack of intelligence experience, which had been attractive to a president seeking a new broom, was seen as the only obstacle on his journey towards a coruscating future.

'I was sorry to hear about the loss of one of your station chiefs in Geneva,' Webster said.

Scott jerked his head up and down vigorously. 'A big loss. Had to break the news to his wife and kid personally. Their faces . . .' He scanned Webster's office for something that might give him a handle on his opposite number. It was noon and the sound of angry traffic crawling down the Embankment filtered across the room.

Webster could tell what his opposite number was thinking. Scott's accommodation during his student days at
Harvard had probably been more spacious. 'I expect your
office is somewhat larger,' Webster said, following the visitor's
gaze.

Scott did his best to sound sincere. 'About the same. My
predecessor now, he really did have a big office. But then we
had some consultants in and there were suggestions that it
might be better for Agency morale if all offices were pretty
much the same size. Less hierarchical, they said. More col-
legiate. There was a need for a symbolic gesture, I guess. Put
everyone on a more equal footing. Fewer chiefs, more . . .
Well, you get the picture.'

Scott was clearly a pragmatist, Webster thought. That was
how he'd got the top job. The Agency had been almost
ruined by a succession of directors who'd wanted to leave
their mark. There had been concerns that the CIA was
becoming some sort of cult, the way it had been bent to
their philosophies. And everyone knew how cults ended: in
a fireball surrounded by DEA snipers and a thousand camera
crews. 'I'm relieved to learn that even the mighty Central
Intelligence Agency isn't immune to the ghastly foibles of
management-think,' he said. 'We had something similar happen here but it was dressed up as efficiency savings.'

'Cutbacks?'

Webster sighed. 'The only story in town, these days, I'm
afraid, Mr Scott. The security service's budget was once
protected by some sort of nuclear-bombproof covenant.
Now it's fair game, just like everything else. The only part
of us that gets a rise these days is cyber. The government
seems to have an open chequebook for funding cyber security. They're terrified of some outfit launching a cyber

Nine/Eleven or some such scenario, taking out the National Grid's computer systems or hijacking the banking world's critical infrastructure. Anything that might hurt business. It's just a shame we're having to fight terrorists in the real world as well as online.'

'I get it,' Scott grunted. 'Chinese and Russians, they crawl everywhere. Call me Brandon, by the way. I'm sorry it's taken a while for me to come and introduce myself. I'm doing a sweep of our major allies, getting to know you all. We have some good intel we can share with you on the Chinese hacking teams. They're always crawling over our defence contractors, who get pretty jumpy about it. Shouty too. They got powerful lobbyists who can make my life pretty difficult in Congress if I don't take them seriously.'

Webster nodded. 'Thank you, Brandon. Any help would be well received here. But you didn't just come here to show your face and experience the delights of London in June.'

Scott hesitated. There was no point in pretending otherwise. 'I know things haven't been great between our two agencies on an operational level. That stuff with Higgs Bank last year, the stuff you warned us about, you shouldn't have had to do that. We should have seen that Higgs was being manipulated. Hell, we kind of half knew it but didn't really appreciate what was happening. We dropped the ball. History will one day record that the CIA ran a dodgy bank that nearly turned into another Lehman Brothers. No wonder my predecessor had to leave. They said he retired, of course, but, well, I don't think there's an agent anywhere in the world who believes that.'

Webster shrugged. 'Well, here's to a new era of mutual trust and intelligence-sharing.'

The two men looked at each other, doing their best to

appear sincere and serious but disinclined to sustain the lie for any longer than necessary.

'On which point I need to make a request for assistance, Mr Webster.'

'Paul, please.'

'We need some help, Paul. You know what's happening in the Sahara. We're trying to avoid a mass slaying. We need to find Al-Boktorah. We've heard he's hiding money in tax havens in your British territories, like Cayman and the BVI. We wondered if . . . you could shed any light on which accounts are his. It could help us trace him.'

Webster was surprised at the bluntness of the request. They must really be desperate. He wasn't unsympathetic. But he was powerless to help. 'I'm sorry but that request would be a matter for the Treasury, Brandon,' he said. Webster read the irritation on Scott's face. 'For what it's worth, it makes our lives more difficult, too. It's regrettable that these havens exist, more so that we facilitate them.'

'I hear you. It's all just, you know, becoming more urgent now.' Scott gestured at the large plasma TV in the corner of Webster's office. The sound was off but a rolling news channel was showing pictures of Al-Boktorah's captives. Webster wondered which Scott feared more: that the hostages would be killed or that benevolent, outraged people around the world would stump up the ransom and Al-Boktorah would get his $100 million. Either way the CIA would be shown to be impotent. No wonder Scott talked of urgency. He was in danger of heading an agency that was about to become a global irrelevance.

'I do understand,' Webster said, staring at the screen. 'We clearly have a mutual interest in locating him. He's holding our citizens too.'

'Right,' Scott said. He really needed Webster to come on board. But, Jesus, the man was hardly saying anything. The Brits could be laconic. They made the Finns seem garrulous sometimes. He tried a different approach. 'Our station chief, the one killed in Geneva, he'd been tracing Al-Boktorah's tobacco-distribution network. We figured that if we followed the cigarettes we'd find him eventually. Our man had an asset who was proving useful. We lost him in the blast as well. Major setback for the Agency. Not helpful, especially now. You'll be aware that the president wants some quick wins at the moment. He's sliding in the polls, not that it really matters to him. But the election's only nineteen months away. OK, he's a lame duck but he wants to hand over to someone on his own side. Unlikely, the way the mood of the country is turning. Bagging Al-Boktorah would be a useful counter-punch. Earn the Agency some much-needed points when its stock has fallen so far, too. That's what I'm interested in. Restoring our reputation in Washington, then the rest of the world.'

Webster turned away from the television screen to the much younger man in front of him. He was conscious of the huge personal and professional differences between them. 'Do you have any idea who was behind the Geneva bombing?'

Scott leaned back in his chair. 'Well, we're pretty sure our man was the target. The bomb went off in the empty room next to his, suggesting someone knew where he was. That sort of high-value intel, well, you fill in the blanks. You've got to have a lot of eyes and ears to be able to pinpoint something like that.'

'So you suspect another state's security agency? That would be a disturbing development. Bombing a US agent

51

in a major European city when you know there will be civilian casualties? Pretty much unprecedented in my experience.'

'Yeah, it is. But no one else would have the ability to get that information about our man and his whereabouts.'

'The asset, could he have talked?'

'Maybe,' Scott said. 'We're checking but we're dubious. He'd been run for years and was real careful. No, the way we see it, that intel had to have been harvested using electronic interception and code decryption. Pretty much only two state actors capable of that sort of thing.'

'You mean we're back to our friends the Chinese and the Russians?'

'Yeah,' Scott replied. 'Like I said earlier, they crawl everywhere. Of course, we've been briefing that it's the work of some Al-Qaeda affiliate, targeting financial capitals in the West as part of a new terror campaign. Putting it about that it's part of their plan to degrade international capitalism and beat ISIL in the PR stakes or some such crap. It's been well received, the line we've been spinning. You see the *Reporter* three weeks ago? They swallowed the story and put it on their front page. Bought us some useful cover. Last thing we want anyone to know is that we had an agent in that building. Swiss would start asking all sorts of awkward questions. And we kind of need them onside as much as possible. There's a load of their bank accounts we're interested in.'

Webster rocked back and forth in his wheelchair several times. 'But what's in it for them, the Chinese or the Russians? It's not their style. They're rational actors. They don't want to start the Third World War. The Russians have got enough problems as it is and the Chinese don't need to bomb anything to get their way. They just buy their way out of trouble.'

Scott shrugged. 'Maybe you have a point. We're still looking into it. I'm not saying it was sanctioned by their governments but you know as well as I do that some parts of their security services have sort of claimed UDI. They're rogue actors, not rational, these guys. They're very cosy with state-owned big-business interests. Chinese and Russian firms have been doing well out of trading with Al-Boktorah. He was buying a lot of arms from the Chinese. Russian oil and gas firms doing nicely every time he blows up a refinery in Algeria. A lot of people have an interest in ensuring that he stays in the energy-disruption business, even if he doesn't realize it. Maybe someone was looking out for him. They know we're trying to track him and they take out our top man responsible for bringing him in. Sounds pretty plausible to me.'

Webster's face remained blank, but Scott knew he would suspect the other, unspoken, reason why the Agency was so desperate to find Al-Boktorah. Webster had been in the British security service for more than twenty-five years. He'd made his name degrading the IRA, Scott knew, from the briefings he'd read. The IRA had controlled the smuggling of cigarettes between the Irish Republic and Northern Ireland. Disrupting the distribution network had been a major focus for the British security service. In intelligence circles it was open knowledge that the CIA had helped build up Al-Boktorah, believing him to be a useful ally in a fractious part of Africa, only for the relationship to implode when his brigade discovered that hostage-taking was even more lucrative than smuggling. In the beginning the energy companies had always paid the ransom for their captured employees, but Western governments were now making it difficult for them to do so, threatening to jail executives of firms that wrote big cheques. Al-Boktorah had merely tweaked the business model. He was bypassing the energy concerns and going straight to the global public. He was nothing if not entrepreneurial.

It was almost funny, Scott thought. For all their combined efforts to keep their citizens safe, to destroy the financial networks that powered terrorist cells, to prevent the trafficking across borders of oil, arms and drugs, for everything they did to keep their enemies at bay, the huge expansion in the use of drones, surveillance, intelligence-gathering, very little seemed to change. Security was just constant iteration of the same old themes, played out over time. History was a carousel ride. Stay on long enough and you'd see the same things coming around again. Webster would know that better than anyone. No wonder he looked so tired. He'd been watching the same film for the last decade. Scott wondered whether to ask about the wheelchair, then thought again. It would be in a briefing somewhere.

'So, why'd you sign up to all this anyhow?' Scott gestured around the office, at its pastel walls and undemanding water-colour paintings that had the unthreatening feel of a conference-hotel room somewhere in Mitteleuropa.

'Oh, the usual,' Webster said.

'Which is?'

'A belief that what we're doing is right and important. That this is how things have to be. The irrefutable argument that we need a security service. Hobbes, if you must know.'

'Hobbes?'

'The philosopher. Seventeenth century. Came up with the idea of the social contract. In a state of nature, man's life is nasty, brutish and short. But if he agrees to observe certain boundaries, obey certain laws, then he in return gains the protection of a state or government and enjoys a more secure life.'

'I hear you.' Scott got up from the desk and walked over to one of the three windows on the far wall of Webster's office overlooking the Thames. It was an overcast day and rain was threatening but people were swarming down the Embankment in their shirt sleeves and summer dresses. From above they seemed untroubled, a sprawling, chaotic, energetic mass of humanity. He turned back to Webster. 'So, you think that we're still meeting our side of the contract? That we're keeping our people safe?'

Webster looked at the man: Scott would probably be out of his job within three years and might, if the rumours were true, end up as the most powerful man in the world. 'No,' he murmured. 'Increasingly the answer is no.'

'I was very sorry to hear about Mr Carrington. Grisly business. Maybe the coast isn't such a good place for convalescing after all.'

Kate glanced up from her desk. Fawcett was being ushered into her office by a security guard. 'Twice in little more than two months you pay a visit to the coast, Mr Fawcett. We can't seem to keep you away.'

'Indeed. I'm beginning to become quite familiar with your security guards. I think they remembered me from my last visit.'

'You told them you were from Customs again, I take it?'
'Correct.'

God, the man was condescending. Condescending and clearly wanting something from her. She knew what it was. She watched the news. There was only one story: Al-Boktorah – or Mr Double Jeopardy, as the press was calling him, such was his command of the illicit tobacco trade. He had a near monopoly on it across the Sahara, bringing it into the narco states in West Africa, then transporting it across the continent. Track the tobacco and you'd find Al-Boktorah. Then special forces could do the rest.

But she was going to have to disappoint Fawcett. As she'd learned in the nine months she'd been working for Smith and Webb, tracing its product was impossible. There were so many parties between the company and the smoker that you just couldn't join the dots. A part of her – a part she didn't want to acknowledge or discuss with superiors like Cole – had come to the conclusion that her employer had deliberately scattered the dots as far apart as possible, using a bewildering number of outside organizations to make transparency impossible. Cole seemed reluctant to discuss the issue whenever she brought it up. And now the one man who could have shed light on the Byzantine nature of what was happening had been found dead, turned into a human ashtray.

Kate leaned forward across her desk, joined her hands together, rested her chin on top of the arc formed by her fingers. 'What's your interest in Carrington? Thought Five was interested only in national security, not perfunctory matters like murder.' She already knew the answer. Just as she'd worked out why Five was interested in her. She had the unnerving sense of having read the script. She just needed Fawcett to read it aloud.

Fawcett sat down on the chair in front of her desk. 'It has

been known for national security and mundane murder to overlap. Perhaps this is one such case.'

So she'd been correct. Five had an interest in Carrington. But how far had it got with him? It was difficult to work out what it could have offered to make him an asset. He had been well paid and had seemed fairly happy, if a little solitary. She uncoupled her hands and sat back in her chair. Whatever it was it wasn't money. 'So what did you have on him? How'd you bend him?'

'Oh, come on,' Fawcett snapped. 'The "what" is no concern of yours. The "how" I can do. We got our friends in the New Zealand intelligence services, not as much of an oxymoron as you might expect, to intercept his emails. You know the drill. You know how it's done. We use them to . . . examine people we're interested in over here, their electronic communications, so we can get round the need for warrants and horribly bureaucratic things like that.'

Anger was slopping around inside Kate. 'Listen to yourself. You're boasting about how you get around the law like other people boast about how much their house is worth or something. You have no right.'

'We do when it comes down to issues of national security.'

'Oh, please, that's what you always say and it's meaningless. It's your get out-of-jail-free card. Allows you to tell yourself that you're one of the good guys when you look in the mirror.'

'Maybe,' Fawcett said quietly. 'Maybe not. The first rule of any nation, its only rule perhaps, is to protect its citizens. You know that. Certain things, certain freedoms, certain rights cannot be protected if some of us don't have that licence. And trust me, Mr Carrington wasn't one of the good guys even though he was working for us.' He bent down from his chair and retrieved a thin metal suitcase. 'But enough of this. And now, Ms Pendragon, the moment we've both been waiting for. Drumroll, please.' Fawcett's long, thin fingers danced on the desk top.

Kate shook her head. 'I'm not going to help you. Tell Webster, tell Callow, they'll need to find someone else.'

'Perhaps. Perhaps not.'

Out of the suitcase Fawcett pulled two manilla folders. He pushed one across the desk. 'When I say issues of national security this is what I mean.'

She looked at it. Even touching it would be toxic. She would be contaminated by its contents, made privy to something dreadful, something devastating. Whatever was inside the folder couldn't be buried once she'd opened it. She kept both hands gripping the edge of the desk. That way nothing was going to happen. That way she remained in control.

'And this second folder here,' Fawcett murmured, 'is what we're prepared to trade. Sanctioned by Webster himself, no less.' He picked it up and flourished it in the air.

Kate continued gripping the desk. She felt as if she could snap it with her bare hands. 'Let me get this straight. The head of MI5 has sanctioned a trade with an ex-employee?'

'Correct,' Fawcett said.

'Pretty unusual.'

'I would say unprecedented.' Fawcett pushed the second folder across the desk.

She felt her left hand edge across to it. Her fingers brushed it. 'What is this?'

'Open it and find out. You're naturally curious, that's why you're one of us. Go on, open it. Otherwise you'll never know.'

'No, no trade.'

'You still think about him?'

'Who?'

'You know who. Your father. They say he would have ended up running the service if . . . well, if things had worked out differently.'

She wasn't going to play. She didn't want to be dragged into their games.

'I'm sure you do,' Fawcett said. 'Too many things don't make sense about his death. Must make it difficult having that horrible curiosity eating away at you. Difficult to put things to bed. If I harboured doubts about how my father had died, I'd do pretty much all I could to get to the truth. Go on, open it. A taste of what we're offering. A fraction of the real story.'

She'd underestimated him. There was a hardness to Fawcett, a calculated brutality that came from somewhere deep within, a place of trauma and resentment. They'd clearly picked the right man for the job. Some of the chinless wonders who populated the corridors of Five would just have made her laugh if they'd tried to bring her in. But Fawcett had got to her. His hooks had pierced her skin. They were reeling her closer.

He stood up, smoothing the front of his trousers in a well-practised manner. 'Goodnight, Ms Pendragon,' he said. 'I do hope we'll be meeting again soon.' Another nod. Another fake leer.

She bit her lip, looked down at the two folders. She knew what she would find in the one in her left hand. There was only one thing Five possessed that would interest her. And, of course, it wouldn't be much. Just a fraction, as Fawcett had said, a hint of what might be revealed, if she agreed to help. She picked up the second folder, weighed both in her hands. She was drunk on questions. Was one worth the other? How could you work out the conversion rate? How much was the truth worth, anyway?

Chapter 6

Several of the Georgian houses a short stroll from Victoria station were graced with blue plaques denoting that some-one famous, or possibly just moneyed and philanthropic, had once lived in them. A tourist would be forgiven for think-ing that the imposing row of properties was still inhabited by the rich and the fortunate. But they were no longer homes. Each had its shutters closed downstairs. Through the windows of their upstairs rooms, shelves of folders could be glimpsed. Few people ever entered or left the buildings. No milkmen or online delivery companies stopped there. Children were strangers to them. They were as sombre as graves. Only the small brass plaques beside the doors indicated that the fine houses were actually businesses. The presence of CCTV cameras suggested that their occupants took security matters seriously.

Closer inspection of the brass plaques revealed that the businesses had names like Sparrowhawk Investigations, Controlled Threats, Global Risk Solutions, Black River Intelligence.

The man who stopped at the last of these buildings, which had a plaque that bore the initials OSI, had clearly been to the property many times. He'd walked along the street head down, barely acknowledging his surroundings. Outside the house he punched a keypad on the front door and pushed at the sound of a buzzer. Inside he didn't acknowledge the elderly secretary behind the desk. Instead he walked up the expensively carpeted stairs and, on the first floor, entered a room that seemed to have changed little since the Boer War. Stern-faced generals glowered down from burnished paintings. The room was a rich dark red, the colour of empire.

He padded across the thick carpet towards a figure with sandy hair, who was wearing thin wire spectacles. The figure was sitting behind a large, polished wooden desk on which an ashtray cradled two burning cigarettes. The man took one of the cigarettes and inhaled deeply. 'Good of you to have lit one for me, Matthews.'

Matthews picked up the remaining cigarette and put it to his lips. 'All part of the service. I know you find the walk from Victoria upsetting, Metcalf. The reward of one of your company's comforting, stress-releasing products is the least I can provide.'

'Glad to see what Smith and Webb's retainer fee is paying for,' Metcalf responded. 'At fifty thousand pounds a month, you're going to have to light us a lot of cigarettes. Or get a more attractive secretary. That one looks like she's been smoking too many of our products. The lines etched on that face. Makes me shudder every time I come here. She looks like you've been employing her since Suez.'

Matthews blew smoke from his mouth. 'I'm only fifty-two, Metcalf. But in our line of business it doesn't pay to employ young people. Far too garrulous. And, besides, I think you're getting value for money. Nobody at Smith and Webb seems to be complaining.'

Metcalf coughed. 'That's because virtually no one knows you exist. You should thank fuck for Limassol, Matthews. If we couldn't hide our payments to you via Cyprus we couldn't employ you. If our shareholders found out we had you on retainer we'd both be looking for work.'

'Yes,' Matthews said. 'People forget just how accommodating tax havens are. Capitalism couldn't flourish without them. They make all the ugly necessary things possible.'

Metcalf ground out his cigarette, wondering if Matthews was being deliberately fatuous.

He never enjoyed visiting the man, who was just another Oxbridge public-school product.

Typical ex-spook. Never missed an opportunity to namecheck his previous employer.

Metcalf had left school at fifteen. Every year the chip on his shoulder grew bigger. 'You seen the papers?' he said.

'Most of them. Terrible business.'

Metcalf glanced around the room. 'Are we safe?'

'Safe as can be expected,' Matthews said. 'Room was swept this morning as per . . . We've got jammers on, of course. Perhaps it might be advisable not to be too explicit.'

'Right.' Metcalf sat down. Lights from the chandelier bounced off his polished head, mottled with sun spots. His forehead was a series of creases and he had the gaunt, cadaverous face of a man who smoked forty a day. He lit a second cigarette procured from a silver case that he'd removed from an inner pocket of his jacket. 'I've been head of security with Smith and Webb for almost fifteen years now and I've never seen the board so jumpy. Carrington's death is an excuse for everyone to crawl over the company. It's open season. It's hitting the share price. Police have been in our HQ for days now.'

'He was tortured, so it said in the papers,' Matthews said, taking a cigarette from Metcalf's proffered case.

'Mmm.'

'All violence is a breakdown of the political process,' Matthews said quietly. 'That's drilled into you early on when you join Six. But the torture aspect is interesting. Suggests some political dimension to it.'

'Well, I think we can agree that the political process in this case has well and truly broken down,' Metcalf said. He sucked heavily on his cigarette. The ritual inhalation of smoke soothed him. He was a man who still didn't know himself. There had been no time for self-discovery. Smith and Webb had dominated his life. The tobacco trade was a difficult one to leave. It immersed you because it had to. It couldn't afford to lose staff. They would just leave and spill their secrets and that would be damaging. Big tobacco had to keep its people close.

'Grisly stuff,' Matthews said. 'Torture. A lot of burns. Must have been agony. You torture people for two reasons. Either you hate them and want them to suffer. Or you need them to reveal something that they'd rather keep hidden.'

Metcalf blew smoke up towards the chandelier. 'Makes sense, what you're saying.' He looked hard at Matthews, tapping the table with a finger several times for emphasis. 'It's the latter that worries me. And it's the latter that we pay you to worry about.'

Matthews sighed. He had been out of MI6 for four years, with a CBE and an extensive network of similarly employed ex-colleagues to show for his efforts. But despite his lucrative new job in corporate intelligence, he was not nearly as comfortable in the present as the past. There had been much more purpose about his old self. There had been better definition. Things were cleaner and clearer back then. The new self, the new older one, was still feeling its way through the world he'd elected to enter. It was exciting on many different levels – professional, financial, emotional – that was for sure. But it was complex and carried multiple risks. There would be collisions if he wasn't careful. He gazed at Metcalf, at the tired grey husk of a man in front of him. Less than a decade separated them but Metcalf looked like he'd been born long before the war. He wasn't a good advert for smoking. Matthews was not going to end up like him. 'So,' he said, 'what do you want me to do? Find Carrington's killer?'

Metcalf looked shocked. 'Christ, no. Find him? What good would that do anyone? No, I want you to find out what Carrington knew. What he found out or did or said that made someone want to . . . kill him in such a way. I want to make sure it's got nothing to do with us. Or if it has that we're protected. You know how vulnerable we could be on this. I'm sure I don't need to spell it out.'

Matthews nodded slowly. 'Did he have any known enemies at work?'

Metcalf exhaled furiously. 'How the fuck should I know? That's your job. Read his emails, check his texts and all that. Which reminds me . . .'

'Which reminds you,' Matthews said. 'How is she doing?'

Metcalf nodded. 'You read my mind. Or my emails.'

'Well, I've read hers and there's not much to go on. She and Cole still seem to be discussing what they cryptically refer to as "distribution issues" but I've no idea if it's anything that should trouble you or would have troubled the late Mr Carrington. Read her texts, too. You know she's seeing a local detective? Man called Sorrenson.'

Metcalf shook his head. 'News to me.'

'They seem quite taken with each other. Some of the messages are what we might describe as on the racy side of things.'

'Enough.' Metcalf put his hand up, as if he were trying to stop traffic. He wasn't good at the personal. He'd had only one meaningful relationship in his life and that was with his employer. He half joked that his ashes would have to be scattered in the company offices when he died. Sooner rather than later, probably, the way he was going. They could just pour him into one of the ashtrays outside Smith and Webb's revolving doors so he could end up mixed with his employer's product. He should give up, really. Never too late.

'You still concerned she's a plant?' Matthews said. 'You really think she's talking to Five?'

Metcalf crushed his cigarette in the ashtray. He looked closely at the ash, as if he could divine something in it. Yes, better give up. He'd get some patches. Or maybe try those e-cigarettes everyone seemed to be talking about. He coughed several times. 'Maybe. Given her past.' He was conscious that he'd lowered his voice. He frowned at the other man, a judge passing sentence. He wanted Matthews to understand something. 'People like that don't change.'

'People like that?'

'Ex-spooks. You lot. You're all still spooks, really. You never shed your skin.'

'That's what you believe?'

Metcalf peered at the generals in the paintings and felt a stab of irritation, powerful as toothache. Look at them! The stupid old fools, blindly fighting for Queen and country. The modern world was a lot more complicated than the past. Companies were having to fight on so many fronts if they were to survive, provide jobs for their employees, profits for their shareholders. You had to go right to the margins of what was permissible, perhaps sometimes beyond, if you were to endure. That was the nature of modern business. The lines between legal and illegal were literally paper thin, the decree of some bureaucrat or judge. 'Yes,' he said, his eyes still fixed on the generals, 'I do.'

'Well, I'm different,' Matthews said.

'Yes,' Metcalf murmured. There was sarcasm in his voice. 'But then you're an exception, Matthews. You know whose side you're on. The person who pays you.'

She was still finding her way around the house. Each day a room would reveal a new secret. The way a window sucked in the light over the sea in the morning; the creak of a floorboard if she stood on it in a certain way; the sound of the wind scraping across the deck. It was as if the house was sharing its private knowledge, a bid to lure her into staying. She was spending more and more time in Sorrenson's house and less at her apartment in London. The coast was becoming an all-consuming distraction. It snared her like a wrecking light. She needed to be careful. She could end up smashed into a thousand pieces.

In the darkened kitchen, illuminated only by candles, her hands worked quickly, methodically. Slicing the onion she imagined she was cutting another layer off Fawcett and his kind. Chop, chop, chop. Within seconds there was nothing left of Fawcett, just layers and layers of translucent flesh. Yes, she thought, that would be good. Strip Fawcett right down to his cellular level. Get down to the fundamentals. Then you'd see what he was really like. She thought of Carrington.

How had Fawcett turned him? And what exactly had the service wanted him for?

She heard Sorrenson pad across the deck. He grinned at her through the window. 'Power's gone, I take it. Or are you feeling romantic?'

'The former, sadly for you.'

He came through the door, walked up behind her and put his arms around her waist. 'Smells good.'

'Me or the food?'

'Both.'

'Fish stew. Got the fish from that town up the coast from here. I left my running belt in London and thought I might find another there but no chance. Fish, yes. Running accessories, no. Quaint place, though.'

'Aye. But it's a bit fake, you know. Half of the fish comes in on trawlers from Scotland and Devon. They pass it off as local produce to stupid Londoners come down for the day. People got no idea where it's coming from, you know.'

Kate nodded. She knew. Food, tobacco, drugs. People rarely questioned the provenance of anything. Just so long as it kept coming. 'Local paper's carrying some fairly gory reports about the murder.'

'Still? It's been a couple of weeks.'

'Still.'

'Well, I guess it is pretty big. Especially for down here.'

'You making any progress?'

Sorrenson hesitated. The pause wasn't lost on her. They were both aware of the invisible wall between them. He was investigating her company. There was only so much he could share. 'No,' he said. He knew he had to give her something. To lock her out would mean he doubted her. 'If anything we're going backwards.'

68

'How do you mean?'

Sorrenson considered his options. What was it to be? The truth, the partial truth or a lie? It had to be the truth. Anything else would suggest he didn't trust her. There could be no future for them then. 'It's all been complicated by the second investigation team.'

She looked closely at him. 'Second?'

He paused, thought for a couple of seconds. 'The Yard,' he said slowly. 'Or its counter-terrorism unit. They're reporting everything back to your old employer. I'm sure you'll find this out in time, if you don't know already.' He waited for her to respond, but she kept staring out of the window to the sea. In the distance buoys on the horizon blinked green and red. 'I'm aware that they're taking an interest in the murder,' she said. 'Not quite sure why. Their interest could be misplaced.'

'Maybe. Can't figure out why they might think that Carrington's murder had anything to do with national security.' Sorrenson remembered what Williamson had said. 'I mean, he was just a tobacconist.'

She went back to chopping the onion. They hadn't been together long but she knew when he didn't mean what he said. He was clearly carrying something around that made him uncomfortable. 'Who's helming it for Five, then?' She tried to sound casual but they were both straying into dangerous waters.

'Your friend Callow's taking an interest.'

'Right.'

'He came to see me, the night after the body was found. When we had the wood cordoned off and it was one big crime scene. Drove down from London on his own. It was all very discreet.'

She struggled to keep her voice level. 'And you didn't think to tell me this until now?'

'Of course I thought of it. But you know what they're like. They insist on getting people to keep their secrets. And, besides, I thought you . . .'

'What?'

'I thought you knew. I mean, I figured they would have been in touch. I didn't want to make a complicated situation any more complicated.'

It was a fair comment, she thought. 'So what did he say?'

'Not a lot. He just explained that Carrington was someone they'd been interested in for some time and that the nature of his death suggested to them that it could be an issue of national security.'

'That was the phrase they used, "national security"?'

'Yes.'

She weighed up what to say next. She had information to trade. Just her thoughts, really, but it was probably worth saying. 'You know what he did, Carrington?'

'Distribution.'

'Yes. He oversaw the movement of all, and I do stress all, of our product. He was pretty much the only person in the company who understood our distribution network. We often use third parties to move the goods. They ship them on to fourth and fifth parties.'

'Quite a network. Complicated. Why not use your own people?'

'If you want my opinion it's made deliberately complicated. Makes things hard to trace and diminishes the accountability of the producer if the product falls into the wrong hands, like, say, organized criminal gangs or terrorists. The company can say that's the fault of the third parties, not them. And, of course, they still make their profits. Just means they keep all the nasty stuff at arm's-length.'

'Useful. So . . .'

'So Carrington was an expert on the networks. We paid him for his contacts, the middle men who could move massive amounts of product around the world. It's not illegal but it doesn't look good up close. System's set up to ensure product gets into the hands of even the most unsavoury types. We all know about Mr Double Jeopardy holding the hostages out in the Sahara.'

'But why is Five worried about what happens in Africa or the Middle East?'

There was a sudden purring sound as the cooker came back to life. The kitchen was bathed in light and the sea, visible through the windows in the half-light of the evening, disappeared into darkness. Kate started filleting a fat, glistening mackerel. She ran the knife under its skin, down its backbone. The action felt alien, brutal and satisfying. 'Five has a saying: "Britain is only three missed meals away from revolution."'

'Meaning?'

'Meaning that if people have to go without the basic things in life, if only for a short time, they become uncontrollable. That's when government falls, when people doubt its ability to protect them. When people hear the phrase "national security" they think about bombs and hooded men with AK47s. But if you really want to damage a country, if you want to threaten its national security, you take out its critical infrastructure, cut off its energy supplies.' She reached for a second fish, slid the blade into the skin. The action would once have repulsed her. Not any more. 'Think about it. We've just had a blackout for three hours.

Imagine what would happen in this country if it had been three weeks. What terrifies Five is not terrorism. Ultimately it can cope with fatalities. If anything, that makes it stronger – people value it then. What it can't cope with is being found out.'

'Found out?'

'Right. It can't afford for people to realize that it's not up to the job. That, ultimately, it's unable to protect the state. If people ever grasped that, it would die. For Five, maintaining the illusion it's in control is becoming more and more difficult in a globalized world where seemingly unrelated events abroad can make for big problems at home. When Five sees someone seizing British oil interests in Africa, it doesn't only fear a threat to this country's energy security, it fears a threat to its existence.'

The quayside glistened with salt rain. Puddles in the worn flagstones along the harbour wall shimmered under arc lights. It was late in the night – or the beginning of the day if you worked the boats. The high tide that would lift the dredgers from the heavy mud of the harbour floor was still hours off. There was a calmness in the air. The harbour was as untroubled as a village cemetery.

On the far side of the quay a man in a lumberjack shirt and jeans patterned with diesel stains crouched over a fishing net. He ran his fingers through the holes, nodding his approval as he went. Yes, it would do. He'd like to see them escape once snared. He would haul the fish up, a horde of silver blades stolen from the sea, their mouths gaping with astonishment at the unfairness of being caught. The man smiled to himself. The sea delivered bounty. Fish were just one of its gifts to him – almost a byproduct, really. Cover.

He made to stand up but never got off his knees. The metal pipe smashed into the back of his skull, almost taking his head clean off. He fell into the harbour, his head, then his limbs, hitting the rig of his trawler. He was dead before the slime claimed him.

His two assailants looked down from the quayside.

'I thought he might have made a noise. Some sort of groan or something.'

'Didn't have time. Bosh. Straight out.'

'Do you think the tide'll take him out?'

'Nah. The trawler crews will be here soon. They'll spot him. Look, the gulls have already.'

Two fat herring gulls tentatively approached. They stopped next to the corpse, now half submerged in the wet mud. One tapped at an outstretched arm with its red-tipped beak, as if trying to establish whether it was a suitable food source. The other joined in: tap, tap, tap.

'No respect, those birds,' one of the men said. 'Shameful behaviour.'

'It's late,' the other man said, yawning.

'No, it's early.'

'Same difference.'

'How long before Plod turns up, do you reckon?'

'He's busy at the moment, Plod. Got a lot on his hands.'

'Yeah, I read about that.'

'Horrible, that murder in the wood above here. Really grim.'

'It's a dangerous world out there. No one's safe.'

The two men laughed.

Chapter 7

Scott looked around the private dining room, at the oak-panelled walls that seemed to be as old as the Constitution. It was big enough to take twenty diners but there were only two of them in the room. Five serving staff waited outside, statues that could be activated at the push of a button. Scott was grateful for the privacy. Being seen sharing a steak dinner with Washington's most powerful lobbyist wouldn't play well in certain quarters. People would start asking too many questions. Scott didn't need that kind of gossip. Not so early into his job. Not before he'd begun his political journey. People could talk then. Not before.

'You come here much?' Ailes grunted at Scott.

'Never. Heard a lot about it. They say more political decisions get made here than in the west wing.'

Ailes stuffed most of a bread roll into his mouth. 'Figured as much. You look like you're keeping yourself in good shape. People'll be reassured by that. No one likes a fat warrior. You stick with the programme.'

If they were intended to be a compliment, in Scott's mind Ailes's words sounded like criticism.

'But I wouldn't set too much store by what people say,'

Ailes said. 'This place is good for steak, not pork-barrel politics.'

There was still a hint of Texan in Ailes's accent. Scott had read somewhere that he'd been born in Dallas. His father had been a janitor, his mother a secretary. It had been an inauspicious start for the young Ailes, who'd started out selling propane straight from high school. His employer liked to cultivate local politicians. When Ailes made the shift from sales to community relations, he was given responsibility for dining useful legislators. Apex Propane had done well out of the relationship. A lot of state contracts for propane ended up going to the company. Ailes had learned on the job. He understood what people wanted, what they feared. To be a good lobbyist you have to be a good psychologist, he liked to say. 'Get inside their minds, then you got 'em.' And now look at him. He was the high priest of Washington, a long way from the Lone Star state. The capital city was his altar. Political careers were regularly sacrificed on his instruction. Any senator or congressman who failed to back legislation pushed by Ailes's energy and defence clients soon found that the money pipes gushing donations to their political action committees dried up. Ailes was the biggest hawk in a city of big hawks. He prided himself on the description but objected to the other epithet regularly attached to his name. 'People say I'm a neocon,' he often said. 'There's nothing neo about me. I'm a fossil. Born with oil in my veins. Cut me, I bleed black blood.'

Ailes was fond of playing the dinosaur. He made a thing of portraying himself as being on the brink of extinction, an old-school Washington power-broker. But Scott was under no illusions. When he looked at Ailes's sweating, jowly face, the strange comb-over thing he'd done with his hair, he saw the largest carnivore in the city. Ailes might be a dying breed but that only made him more dangerous. Scott took a sip of his wine, tried not to grimace. French. He'd have preferred a beer. The former soldier in him would never be seen drinking wine. But, then, he was no longer a soldier, he reminded himself. He was a player. And that was why he needed Ailes. That was why he needed to throw the lobbyist some red meat, give him something to feed back to his clients. Something secret. Something unimportant. Something that would help the pair of them get off on the right footing. And there was only one story a man representing energy interests was following right at that moment.

'So I was over talking to the Brits,' Scott said. 'I say talking to them, more like we were having two different discussions. I've been to see their main man, Webster. Christ, they can be stubborn when they want to be, the Brits. They're not doing much to help us trace Al-Boktorah. I'm a bit surprised. British companies got big interests in oil and gas in the Sahara. They need that fuel. Half their nuclear plants are mothballed because they're too old, North Sea oil is drying up and they aren't fracking. They don't want to buy from Russia. Places like Algeria are only going to become more important to them. And still they're not co-operating with us. So much for the special relationship.'

Ailes lathered a chunk of steak in its Roquefort sauce. He wondered whether Scott was retarded. Their first conversation, and the director of the CIA was giving him stuff that could have been culled from the inside pages of the *Post*. He remembered his conversation with Roscoe, the favour he'd been asked. It was time to fire an early shot across the bows. Ailes knew all about Scott's political aspirations. The new CIA director needed some urgent context. 'A lot of people will be unhappy to receive that information,' he said. 'Energy companies don't like crises and they don't like losing employees. Their insurance premiums go through the roof.' He cut himself a second thick square of blackened meat from his T-bone, stabbed it with a fork. 'These people have long memories when it comes round to elections.' Ailes contemplated Scott over the top of his wine glass. 'You really don't want to make them pissed.'

Scott looked down at his meal. It was untouched. He tried to summon his appetite but it had fled the scene of battle. There was something about Ailes that was numbing every one of his senses. He was like a dark star, sucking up all matter. 'I know that people want to see a result,' he said cautiously. 'But there's only so much we can do here.'

Eighteen stone of Ailes examined thirteen stone of Scott. The lobbyist drained almost half a glass of wine, then patted his lips with a linen napkin. The pupils in his eyes gleamed black. Scott found himself thinking of sharks in formaldehyde. 'Tell me,' Ailes said, 'you got Roscoe and the ISG involved in this?'

Scott looked over at the fake fire burning in the fake grate and experienced a minor epiphany: one way to solve the global energy crisis would be for Washington's high-end steak houses to go easy on the *faux*-flames. But, then, he understood how the elite on Capitol Hill liked their fires. It brought out something primeval in them, reminded them they'd once been hunters chasing prey. He examined his plate. No, it was no good: he had no appetite to consume a dead animal. He felt more hunted than hunter. Scott realized that Ailes was staring at him. 'Sorry. What d'you just say?'

Retarded and deaf, Ailes thought. Just what the CIA

needed. He pointed his knife at Scott. 'I said, you got Roscoe and his Intelligence Support Group in on this?'

Scott was surprised by the question. Why did Ailes think the hunt for Al-Boktorah was an ISG concern? As far as he could tell, the group was little more than a technology play, a chance for spooks to learn what geeks could do for them, how they could help the Agency understand the way terrorists talked to each other, the methods they used to groom new recruits online, that sort of stuff. Maybe Ailes wasn't as plugged in as he'd imagined. Maybe he was spending too long chewing on the carcasses and not enough time listening. 'The ISG aren't involved in this, no,' Scott said. 'This is not about one of their investments. This is far outside their remit.'

'Right,' Ailes said. 'Whatever you say. I guess you'd know if they were involved.' He picked up his T-bone and gnawed on it. 'I mean, that would be a given, presumably.'

Scott felt uneasy. Ailes was more interested in his steak than him. He'd come second to chargrilled meat. That didn't feel good.

The hostages were led out from the cave blindfolded, chained together two by two.

Around twenty of their captors stood a few metres away from them, looking on, silently, under a dark desert sky punctured by stars and the occasional tracking arc of a satellite. Many of the hostages were shaking. Two or three had dropped to their knees only to be dragged back to their feet, urgently, by the others.

'You know the rules,' one captor shouted, in a Canadian accent. 'You go to ground, you're going to stay on the ground. You ain't getting up again.' He approached the long line of hostages. 'People think we were born in caves or something. That we don't know shit. Well, we might not believe in all your crusader crap but we believe people have choices. You can choose to be an infidel. Or you can choose not to. Right now, though, we need one of you to choose to be a martyr. That's how reasonable we are. We're going to allow you hundred or so guys to decide among yourselves who's going to get a bullet. We need to get the world to dig deep, people. So one of you had better step forward. What about you, Yoda? I hear Chewy licked you in a fight the other day. Seems to me you ain't got long anyway. You be doing your bros a favour . . .'

She looked out into the empty corridor, then returned to her office and locked the door. For once Kate was grateful that the open-plan concept had yet to fire the imagination of Smith and Webb. True, its newly-built headquarters, the public face of the company, was all about communicating space and light but it was just a façade. The real workings of the company went on in the numerous Georgian properties it owned along the coast. Anonymous, sturdy, sepulchral, they kept their secrets well.

From a drawer in her desk she removed the two manilla folders. She stared at them for several minutes, as if she could divine their contents before reading them. She sighed, poured herself a coffee and opened the first folder. Yes, there it was. An intelligence report. Fairly comprehensive. No sources credited but it appeared pretty authoritative. She would have been impressed by the diligent work that had gone into it, if she'd called it in at the service.

Much of it she already suspected. The report discussed how large volumes of tobacco were entering the West African narco states before being shipped to Mali and Niger, and on to countries like Algeria along the old Spice Route across the Sahara, ending up in the hands of third parties with close links to terrorist interests. Much of the product was manufactured by her employer.

She recalled what Fawcett had said: 'Dreadful things happening in the desert.' It was the epic scale of what was happening that was truly shocking. The tobacco trade had assumed truly sinister proportions under the report's forensic analysis. The irony was not lost on her. People had spent so long obsessing about the war on drugs that they'd failed to see how a legal drug was threatening to do far more damage to global security than heroin or cocaine. Like Fawcett had said, tobacco was a currency.

She felt a deep sense of revulsion towards her employer. There was shame, too, and an ugly, bubbling anger directed mainly at herself. She hadn't gone into her job blind. She'd done her due diligence. She'd asked questions. That was what she was paid to do. But it was clear that her employer's product was soaked in blood. So much of it was ending up in the hands of terrorists, chiefly the Al-Boktorah brigade. It was hard not to believe that senior people in Smith and Webb were unaware of what was happening. As the anonymous author of the report observed in a rare break from its tinder-dry narrative: 'Smoking kills.'

The report noted that one of Al-Boktorah's recent attacks had closed an oil refinery, causing its Anglo-American owner's share price to haemorrhage. In the interim, the shortfall meant Britain had to source more oil and gas from elsewhere, Russia most likely. Hardly the most Anglophile of suppliers at the best of times. And it wasn't the best of times.

She read on. Al-Boktorah seemed to have an impregnable franchise fusing terror and trade. The more chaos he trailed across the sub-Saharan region the more he controlled it, the more powerful he became, the more weapons he could buy, the more disciples he could recruit from Europe and North America, and the more he could dominate the unpoliced, unobserved corner of Africa where he ran everything from drugs to guns.

She had to force herself to slow down, remind herself to question everything. Intelligence could be wrong, she knew. The contents of just one report had to be treated with suspicion. People made money peddling fabrications to the intelligence services. Countries had been invaded on the ramblings of hucksters trading thick lies for six-figure sums. She found herself thinking about Carrington. Presumably he'd been integral to the report's composition. He would have been the only person in the company capable of joining the dots.

There was a blank card with a mobile number scrawled in blue pen at the bottom of the file. She typed it into her mobile phone and pressed save. She ripped up the card and took satisfaction in watching its shredded remains rain down into her wastepaper basket. She reached for the second file and pulled it towards her. It moved slowly across her desk, as if it was dragging chains.

Chapter 8

Sorrenson left his car and walked up the steep shingle path that hugged the thin strip of shoreline dividing the sea from the salt marshes inland. A low early-morning sun burned into his eyes, bleaching the path and the sea beyond so that all he could see was a fierce, all-encompassing brightness that allowed no shadows. Sorrenson squinted at a figure up ahead. He made out a series of small ponds, each barely larger than a tennis court. He raised his hand in greeting. 'Billy Davey?'

'You the detective that phoned earlier?'

'Yes.'

'Here, take this.'

Davey threw Sorrenson an empty black bucket, scrambled down onto the bank of one of the ponds and began uncoiling a series of rubber pipes. Somewhere nearby a generator kicked into life. In the distance, Sorrenson could hear the rattle of a train. He surveyed the lonely spit of land. It was almost desert, little more than scrub, a place that would one day be claimed by the sea. Towering over the ponds, the remains of a Norman keep maintained its thousand-year watch for invaders. Further down the coast, Sorrenson could make out the forty-year-old tower block that lorded it over Margate.

'Here, give me that back.' Davey took the bucket from Sorrenson. 'It's about Jack, I take it?'

Sorrenson nodded. 'Mr Gaunt was a business partner of yours?'

Davey laughed. 'Of sorts. Had a lot of fingers in a lot of pies, Jack Gaunt. My business was just one of many he was involved in.'

'Involved in?'

'Aye, involved. Some days.'

Sorrenson took in the man in front of him and concluded that it was unlikely there was a Mrs Davey. He was wearing a dirty jumper that poked out under a ripped cagoule held together with masking tape. His rubber boots were caked with mud and his wispy grey hair danced jigs in the wind. 'You live up here alone?' Sorrenson said.

Davey spat at the ground. 'Got three dogs. That's enough.'

'Right.'

They walked past a series of ponds, dark pools of water fed by black, winding pipes that resembled snakes sliding down riverbanks. Sorrenson looked down into the water and saw hundreds of small oysters the size of coins. Davey pointed at them. 'For every thousand or so oysters we try to grow, only two or three have a hope of making it to adulthood. And then most of them will get eaten by starfish or catch a disease. Every oyster you eat is a miracle, a triumph of hope over despair. Remember that next time you swallow one, won't you?'

'I'm not sure I could afford them on my salary,' Sorrenson said. He walked over to a battered Land Rover Defender parked on a slope above the ponds. There are nation states

83

younger than this car, he thought. He gestured at the ponds. 'You make a living from this?'

'Depends what you mean by a living. There's no money in rearing oysters from sprat.'

'Sprat?'

Davey sighed the long, hard sigh of someone who'd had to explain themselves many times before. 'Oyster spawn. Trust me, Detective, there are easier ways of making a living. That's what Jack thought, any road. And in that at least I think he was correct.'

'Mr Gaunt was a fisherman, too?'

'Yeah, had his own boat. And, like I said, he did a few other things, too.'

'Such as?'

Davey shrugged. 'Fishing trips. Ran excursions to the Maunsell Forts out there.' He pointed at the rusting installations on the horizon. 'Popular with the history crowd, those trips. Very busy taking people out to see them, Jack Gaunt was.'

There was the deafening sound of shearing air. Three army helicopters swept across the waves in a triangle formation. Aerial sharks. The two men watched them swoop down the coast.

'One long militarized zone this stretch of the coast,' Davey said. 'Always has been. They trialled the bouncing bomb down here. Further down the coast there's a First World War wreck loaded with cluster munitions. Potential bomb, that thing. Take out most of the coast if it went off. They still test explosives over in the estuary. Not a lot's changed in the last seventy years since they were in use.' Davey pointed out to sea. 'Those Maunsell Forts out there brought down thirty V1s in the Second World War.'

Sorrenson stared out at the forts then went back to the ponds, the pipes, the water tanks, the rotting wooden huts, the drainage ditches. It was a vision of the post-apocalypse, a place where the desperate tried to grow protein in a denuded world. 'When did you last see Mr Gaunt?'

'Four or five days ago. They say his skull was smashed in.'

'His body was found in the harbour three days ago. I can't comment on Mr Gaunt's wounds.'

'So, then, it was murder?'

'Officially, we're saying we're keeping an open mind but foul play looks likely, yes. I'm sorry to be the bearer of bad news.'

Davey grunted. 'Don't be, not on my account. Gaunt was a business partner but not a friend. Owned a third of this oyster hatchery but that was the extent of our relationship. Not sure anyone liked Gaunt, really. Had no family to speak of. He was a bit of an outsider. Not born round here. Came down from London decades ago and never left.'

'So what did Mr Gaunt do in regard to your business together?'

'Not much. He'd lay down the sprat on the reefs offshore, so they could fatten up. Fair play to him, he was a grafter when it came to that. Went out in all weathers.'

Sorrenson looked out to sea and the forts. 'Did he have any enemies?'

Davey laughed. 'A lot of angry husbands. Jack was always putting it around. Women were his vice. Married women especially. He was quite the charmer. Had to be because they couldn't have been after him for his looks. Yeah, you want to find who did him in, start with all the cuckolded husbands in Kent. Tell them to form an orderly queue.'

Sorrenson turned back to Davey, a man who seemed part tramp, part biblical prophet. The coast was kind to eccentrics, he thought. It gave them space. 'I'll be off,' he said. He handed Davey his card and began to walk towards his car. 'I'll send someone to take a statement later in the week. Anything occurs to you, well, you have my number.'

'Right,' Davey called after him. 'About time someone discovered the truth about Jack Gaunt. Modern-day pirate, him. Just as well he wasn't born in the free-trade era. He'd have ended up going the way of any smuggler who couldn't bribe the Customs men, swinging on a gibbet.'

But Sorrenson heard none of that. It was drowned by the whir of blades as the three helicopters swarmed back along the coast, their blurred shadows ripping across the sea, like yachts racing towards the horizon.

According to the specialist internet tracking agencies, the first article went virtually unnoticed for almost fourteen days. It had resided quietly in a corner of the web, waiting for the other articles to join it, when they would fuse together to create an explosion that was greater than the sum of their parts. Some three thousand words long and with accompanying documents, the first article was written in a manner that suggested its author had a journalistic background, or at least pretensions to write for the racier news magazines. The second and third articles, shorter but equally incendiary, seemed to confirm the suspicion.

All three pieces might have gone unnoticed for years, possibly for ever, if journalists on national newspapers hadn't received emails containing links to the website on which the articles had been posted. Even then, not one of the papers was interested. The stories could not be substantiated and were too risky to print. If they turned out to be untrue the libel bills would be crippling.

But the articles, analysing in forensic detail how third-party agencies used by Smith and Webb were working with terrorist groups to ship billions of cigarettes around the world, found a following.

Bloggers, whose servers were located outside the UK and therefore immune to its libel laws, were quick to reproduce them. Century-old defamation laws were defenceless against the smuggling of devastating information down fat broad-band pipes. Questions were soon being asked in Parliament, allowing national newspapers to report the extraordinary allegations without fear of being sued.

The finest City PR firms were unable to protect Smith and Webb. Metcalf seemed to haunt the company HQ, like a modern-day Richelieu, patrolling its corridors as if his mere presence could protect his employer from further harm. Smith and Webb's share price had almost halved in a matter of days. Talk of a cut-price takeover hung in the air. City spread-betting firms started giving odds on how long the company's chief executive would remain in his job.

Kate wondered if Five was behind the articles. At one level it made sense. It would force Smith and Webb to make drastic changes, now that the truth had been flushed out into the open. But it wasn't how the security service operated. It was too obvious and far too clumsy. Strategically it made little sense. Five would want something more, substantially more, than simply the disruption of a black-market network that was funnelling profits to terrorist groups. It thought like the Vatican. It contemplated the future in terms of decades, not weeks.

No, she thought, if anything it felt more like something the CIA might do. The Agency was notorious for setting up magazines, campaigns and front groups to promote its aims around the world. Sometimes it made no secret of its involvement. At others it was reluctant to take the credit.

The day the fifth article appeared, Kate found Cole secreted in his darkened office. She worried that he was ill. His head shook slightly; his breathing was laboured; he was ashen-faced; a patina of sweat clung to his receding hairline. When he did speak, she could smell spirits on his breath. She felt as if she was in some hospital ward, visiting a terminally ill patient.

'The board want us to make a presentation,' Cole muttered. He pointed at his laptop. 'They want to know how much of this stuff checks out.'

Kate urged herself not to laugh. 'Now they ask. How are we supposed to know? This person's better informed than we are. He has shipping documents and details of trans-African cargo movements that we didn't even know existed. There are wire transfers coming straight out of Limassol and Tortola and Zug and God knows where else. The more you study this stuff the more you get lost in the complexity. I mean—'

Cole had flipped his laptop around to show her the screen. 'You seen that our man has broken cover? The person posting this stuff has used his latest to identify himself. Gives his name as Gary Grant.'

'Yes, I'd noticed. A Google search suggests he's a former US civil-liberties lawyer turned crusading journalist. Lives in Puerto Rico now. Someone somewhere is feeding him some good stuff.'

'Mmm,' Cole murmured. 'But why reveal yourself as the writer of the articles?'

'Why not? There's a strong public interest in what he's doing. And he probably wants the attention.' She thought about Carrington. Could he have been the source of the stories? What would have been in it for him? Kate stared at the photo of Grant attached to the article. He was in his early thirties. Fresh-faced, in a preppy American way. He seemed eager, zealous. He has no idea what he's done, she thought. He has no idea what he has unleashed. She hoped his house in Central America was secure.

'I'll get something prepared for the board tonight,' she said. 'I presume Metcalf will be calling in whatever private security firm Smith and Webb has on retainer but I'll collate what we know internally. But I need to run first. My brain's scrambled. I really need to exercise.'

Cole gazed at her doubtfully. She noticed a thin line of sweat had formed above his dark pencil moustache, the only part of his face that still seemed alive. He really didn't look well. She needed to say something. 'Are you OK?'

'Fine, fine,' Cole muttered. 'A cold, nothing more. You're going for a run right now? You really need to run?'

'Yes.' She wanted to put miles between herself and her corrosive employer. She needed clarity. She needed to know who she was, who she wasn't. She needed to know which side she was on.

Chapter 9

They were sitting in a café, the early-morning sunlight greeted by a cacophony of gulls screeching. The two detectives had the place to themselves. The rest of Margate had hit the snooze button.

'So I took a statement from Billy Davey like you asked,' Simm said.

Sorrenson stirred his coffee. 'Good.'

'He could talk for Britain. I got a lecture on shellfish, then Britain in the war, then the perils of the Common Market and finally one on the origins of what he called the free trade.'

'And what's that?'

'What they used to call smuggling, back in the Napoleonic times. Everyone was at it down on this strip of coast apparently. Entire fortunes were made bringing in French brandy. Cut a deal to get the Customs men to turn a blind eye and no one was the wiser.'

Sorrenson took a bite of his bacon sandwich. 'I'll look forward to reading your account of the interview, Simm. Seems like I might learn something.'

The junior detective swigged from his can of Coke. His bloodshot eyes and grey skin suggested he was in the throes of a virulent hangover. 'I'm just glad we don't have him down as a murder suspect,' he mumbled. 'Questioning him would be a fucking nightmare. Tape machine would go into meltdown.'

'How do we know Davey's not a suspect?' Sorrenson put down his sandwich and sipped his coffee. Outside the café, the sun was coming up fast. Soon the beach, the colour of bone, would turn gold. Sorrenson loved the rapid trans-formation of the town, his town, when the sun came out. He loved the way the light re-energized what, only seconds before, had been tired old buildings, places, people. He understood why Turner had spent so much time in Margate. It wasn't the healing powers of its famed waters. It was the light, the irrepressible power of illumination. Light was a life force. The only currency that mattered.

'Davey was on a cross-Channel ferry at the time of the murder, doing a booze cruise,' Simm said. 'Not sure how that squares with his anti-Common Market views but there you go. There's CCTV footage of him driving his van onto the boat. Forensics have confirmed it. He couldn't have killed Gaunt. Ten video cameras say he was somewhere between Britain and France when it happened. Can't argue with that.'

Sorrenson looked out through the café window. Out to sea a huge container ship was making its way towards the Thames estuary following a trade route that had first been piloted hundreds of years ago. He couldn't take his eyes off the vessel. It dominated the horizon, a metal fortress on the waves, neither of the sea nor of the land but something in between. It was its own state obeying its own laws. One day the ship would be ripped apart for scrap, providing the sea didn't claim it first. But then another would replace it and another after that. 'No,' he said. 'You can't argue with that.'

'Yoda, you want a blindfold? Don't say we don't give you no choices.'

The American energy contractor, a father to three, four years off retirement, shook his head. He stared at the ground, refused to look up. It was all he could do not to fall to his knees. He closed his eyes. He just wanted it over. He just wanted the darkness.

How many times had poached chicken made an appearance in his career? Webster attempted the maths. After Northern Ireland, he'd been based in Five's headquarters for a quarter of a century. During that time he'd had to attend at least one lunch a week with a minister or senior Whitehall official or a visiting security chief or a retiring colleague or even, a nod to the service's fake attempts at openness, an editor of a national newspaper. The number of lunches had rocketed up as he'd progressed through the ranks. So, then, a conservative total came to well over a thousand lunches. And it was nearly always poached chicken. Bland, unremarkable, non-threatening poached chicken, a meal that seemed to have been created so as not to draw attention to itself. Yes, Webster thought, Five's default signature dish was well chosen. He sipped his sparkling water and studied the guest list for that day's lunch with the new home secretary. The usual faces. The head of the Joint Intelligence Advisory Committee; the Cabinet Office's director of resilience; the Yard's head of counter-terrorism; his opposite number from Six. It was a sign of the times, Webster thought. In a shrunken, globalized world, overseas problems quickly washed up at your own door. Dealing with them at source prevented blowback, went the thinking in fashionable intelligence circles. He himself was dubious. Half the time it seemed the UK's efforts to calm a situation overseas served only to inflame it. The consequences weren't often immediately apparent. But they became so in the longer term. The robust interrogation techniques that the intelligence services and their allies had employed in places like Kenya, Somalia, Pakistan, Afghanistan, Yemen, Libya and Iraq seemed only to make the damaged, angry young men who flocked to them even angrier. These people were hybrids, Webster had decided. They were neither of the West nor of the countries in which they fought. There was something deeply medieval in the way they thought but something profoundly modern in their dispassionate approach to industrialized slaughter. Their rootlessness made them difficult to confront. They had ownership of very little. You couldn't bargain, threaten, cajole or bribe them. No, give him the Cold War or Northern Ireland any day, Webster thought. There was no such nihilism a generation ago. There was no great tide of human bombs.

And no pressure to adopt the latest inane concept imported from the business world, either. Somewhere in the last couple of decades, Webster struggled to work out exactly when, the security services had become infected with the belief that they needed to think more like companies. They needed to be lean and efficient and strategic, and cling to a raft of insincere, meaningless aspirations. You couldn't argue with such thinking, Webster knew. You'd be portrayed as some sort of intelligence Luddite if you questioned its logic. You'd be marked down as resistant to change or some other horrible HR term. Today's security service was all about embracing concepts such as fluidity and adaptability. It was all about keeping up with the latest intelligence trends. Webster pitied the new generation of recruits. They spent so much time digesting manuals outlining the service's corporate culture that they were often unable to focus on their core jobs. Still, it would take a brave man to stand up to fashionable thinking. A younger man. Webster was not young. He was ancient in spook terms. Very much what the business manuals would call a legacy case. On his way out. Another year or two and then some sort of retirement. God knew what he'd do. He was dreading the moment, dreading the isolation hurtling towards him.

Until then, Webster knew that he had to be, as the manuals would probably put it, on message. Inviting his counterpart from Six was his way of telegraphing that he understood this, that he understood the world was shrinking, that he was comfortable with fashionable thinking. And, anyway, a good working relationship with Six was vital. Even Webster conceded that much. Five and Six were increasingly swapping personnel as fashionable thinking and cutbacks collided. Threats were colliding too. Webster glanced at the television screen. The hostage crisis in the desert continued to dominate the news. How long, he thought, before the killing begins?

There was a knock at the door. Callow shuffled into the room, nodded and started fiddling with an electronic cigarette. He glanced up, caught Webster watching him curiously. 'Apparently it's a cessation aid,' Callow mumbled. 'The only thing it's cessating is my will to live. It's all too complicated. Talking of smoking . . .' He waved at the television screen and handed Webster a folder. 'This is what we know. What we definitely know. Can't see the Americans being very interested in it.'

Webster pulled a single sheet of paper from the folder and frowned. 'Seriously?'

'Seriously.'

'This is all there is? This is how much we've got on Al-Boktorah's financial network?'

'Yes,' Callow murmured. 'Better hope that Fawcett pulls his finger out. He's going to have to be very persuasive.'

Chapter 10

'How is France?'

'Like it always is,' Douglas said. 'The bit I know, anyway. The bit above Paris that no one wants to visit unless they're interested in the dead of two world wars. It's grey, it's flat and it's drizzly. It's Belgium, basically.'

Roscoe's chromatic glasses darkened as the sun disappeared behind grey clouds racing across the London sky, strips of cumulus desperate to escape the city, make it to the coast. 'So, pretty much like here, then? This city's not so hot either, you know. You're better off in France. At least they know how to do steak and *frites* correctly, even if they do prefer to serve their meat rare.'

'Yeah, I'm getting a taste for it,' Douglas drawled. 'Bit of blood in my meat, I mean. You should try it. Really feel like you're eating something that's barely dead.'

'You're going native. You be careful. You spend much time thinking like the French and we'll have you down as an enemy of freedom.'

Douglas shook his head. 'No danger of that. I spend half my time in an American cemetery, remember? I get to see the sacrifices that have been made every day. I know whose side I'm on.'

The two men were sitting in Regent's Park. Rain threatened. In front of them two cricket teams were preparing to do battle on a recently mown pitch. The smell of cut grass filled the air. Douglas gestured at the cricketers. 'There's talk of taking this game to the US, you know. Getting some of their biggest professional teams playing in the States. A way of building up the brand, I guess.'

'It'll never catch on,' Roscoe said. 'We don't need some Brit export. We don't need to take their shit. We've got our own version of this game and it's a lot more enjoyable. Jesus Christ, what will they throw at us next? Rugby? When will the Brits realize no one wants what they've got any more? They're not the future. They're just trading on old glories. They're fucking spent. And still they poke their nose in when it's not needed. They should know by now to leave the important stuff to us. They're not running the world any more. Barely running themselves, these days. Took me ages to get here. Fucking bus strikes. The whole city was gridlocked. What kind of country can still be bossed around by unions anyway?'

Douglas said nothing. He was used to Roscoe's outbursts. His boss had read too many business manuals. Somewhere along the line, Roscoe had come to equate strong leadership with the need for naked displays of fury. It was predictable, Douglas figured. Most of Roscoe's tech icons had volcanic tempers. Where they led, Roscoe followed. Once the likes of Roscoe, ambitious senior Agency personnel, would have found professional inspiration in the biographies of great warriors. Now it was whoever was fashionable in Silicon Valley on any particular day.

A thwack caused by the collision of leather and willow. The two men looked over at the cricket match. The batsmen were running furiously between the wickets.

'Jesus,' Roscoe muttered. 'If this game didn't exist you wouldn't invent it, right? You know you can watch these things for five days – five whole fucking days, there are marriages that haven't lasted that long – and no one wins? Imagine that. You invest five days of your life in watching something and that's the kind of return you get. A big fat nothing. Britain is not a results-driven country, Douglas. Hasn't been for two centuries. It's just happy to get by. And that's why it's fucked.'

He stared across the cricket pitch at the garden behind the US ambassador's house bordering the park. Who would want that job? he wondered. The ambassadorship was just a sop to some generous friend of the president. No, give him Palo Alto any day. Give him the West Coast. That was where the future lay. That was where the whole world looked now. Not Washington. The West Coast was where Roscoe hunted, where he made his killings. Not that many people even inside the Agency were aware of his exploits. Roscoe's Intelligence Support Group had so few personnel that barely anyone in the CIA knew what it did. But its budget and its remit were substantial. The ISG was the venture-capital arm of the CIA, its large cash reserves funnelled into any companies, banks, consultancies or start-ups that the Agency thought might be useful to it one day. Half of Silicon Valley had benefited from the ISG's largesse some time in the last decade, Roscoe joked. It was only a partial exaggeration.

Not that many of the companies were aware that they had the CIA as a sleeping partner. That would be toxic for their brand. The big search engines had never been able to shrug off accusations that the US intelligence services had a stake in them. Even the merest whiff of CIA money made people suspicious. And that wasn't what the ISG wanted. It wanted people at their most trusting. Hence the need for total secrecy. This suited Roscoe and it gave his unit huge licence. As so few people knew it existed, the group couldn't be held to account. 'We're the real spooks,' Roscoe liked to tell his colleagues. 'The real phantoms. We ghost from place to place taking care of things, rolling out the bridges so someone else can roll in the tanks.'

Its total anonymity made the ISG useful to the CIA. It could do things 'off grid', as Roscoe put it. Things the Agency could never risk being involved in. Things that went far, far beyond the ISG's original remit. 'We can go far outside the box,' Roscoe often said.

Size mattered. Big, flabby business had it all wrong, Roscoe observed. You don't need to be a nine-hundred-pound gorilla. Sometimes the smallest things, a virus, say, had the biggest impact, simply because you never saw them coming.

And his unit could be proactive, too. Or, at least, that was how Roscoe saw it. It could read which way the political wind was blowing. It knew what sort of projects played well in Washington, what would get big business reaching for its chequebooks. No one understood the strange symbiosis that existed between the spooks' world and the military-industrial complex better than Roscoe. It explained why a grateful Agency had granted his unit near total autonomy for the nineteen years it had existed.

It helped that the CIA was obsessed with the threat of Chinese spies in its midst. It was a fear Roscoe exploited as he sought ever larger funds for the ISG to invest in technology plays. They made useful people to blame, the Chinese, Roscoe had learned. They always had. Right back to the turn of the twentieth century. But they were no longer bearded men with opium pipes: they were rogue business interests with super-computers licensed by the Chinese Communist Party to penetrate the darkest recesses of the West's military-industrial complex. The CIA saw them everywhere, pouring out of fat optic-fibre pipes and stealing everything. The Agency was paranoid to the point of distraction. It was a dangerous myopia, Roscoe appreciated. But it was one that he was more than willing to exploit.

Shouts from the cricket pitch. A wicket had fallen. Roscoe looked at his watch. 'Time for us to form a reception committee. Going to take hours to get to Brize Norton now most of London's at a standstill. What's it say on the manifest?'

'The usual. The plane's carrying three senior intelligence officers. No one else.'

Roscoe nodded. 'Good. Where's it come from? That black site in Poland?'

'No, Romania,' Douglas said. 'We're not using Poland any more. Change of government. They started asking too many questions.'

'You heard from our man on the plane?'

'Yeah,' Douglas said. 'I still don't trust him. Why use someone outside the ISG? Why use a lame Brit?'

'You know why. The more distance we can put on this the better. And we got the Brit in our pocket. He wants his big fat pay day. Him and his boyfriend.'

'Fucking fags.'

'Easy, Douglas. This isn't the eighties.'

'You know I don't trust that Matthews. Might check him out. His kind, they operate differently.'

'Like I said, this isn't the eighties.'

'Fucking shame. Things were a lot easier then. No oversight. People up the chain going to ask a lot of questions
soon. You'd better be prepared for that, Roscoe. They're
going to want to know how an asset in our protection ended
up dead.'

'Let them ask,' Roscoe said. 'No one will have any useful
answers. How we going to do it?'

'Combination of injections. Mixes alcohol and cocaine to
form a compound that triggers a massive adrenal rush.
Induces a heart attack. We've done it a couple of times
before. Mossad uses it a lot. It's pretty quick. No fingerprints.
Death attributed to natural causes.'

'Good,' Roscoe responded. 'Dumb fuck should never have
approached Falcone. If he hadn't started shooting his mouth
off, threatening to escalate this all the way up the chain, we
could have looked after him.'

'Guess he didn't trust us.'

'Guess he was right.'

'Turns out we're in luck. Sort of.'

'The shoes, you mean?'

Simm nodded. His thick, red hair bounced up and down.
'Yeah, the manufacturer says they're new stock so only a few
hundred pairs have been distributed so far – and all to just
one chain of discount retailers.'

Sorrenson stabbed a poached egg with his knife. He was
going to have to be careful. His cholesterol levels were on
the high side, according to his last medical. Go light on the
meat and dairy, they'd told him. Easier said than done, now
that the café he frequented on Margate's seafront had
switched from being his second office to his main office. It

101

was better for briefings than the police station, which was now little more than a building site. The merger of several police districts had meant more and more officers were being shunted into fewer and fewer stations. The result was a lot of walls being knocked down and a clutch of angry coppers deafened by buzz-saws and pneumatic drills. The station resembled one giant crime scene. There was tape everywhere, telling you where you could and couldn't go. Dust furred doorframes, radiators, skirting-boards. It had become attritional, the never-ending renovation. It was the builders versus the police and the builders were winning.

'What size feet was our man Carrington?' Sorrenson said.

'Eight,' Simm replied. 'But, like the other two, he was wearing cheap slip-ons far too large for him. Size elevens. Weird.'

'Just one of the many weird ones about this,' Sorrenson said. 'That suit Carrington was wearing cost two thousand quid, yet he was wearing twenty-pound shoes.'

'Maybe he just liked the style.'

Sorrenson contemplated Simm. 'Your wife enjoys shopping?'

'Right.'

'Well, then, do some domestic detection, Simm. Ask her if she'd match twenty-quid shoes with a two-grand dress.'

'Yeah, fair point.'

Sorrenson wiped his mouth with a napkin. 'No, someone's definitely trying to tell us something. Not many people take size eleven.'

'They've sold thirty-three pairs across their network of stores.'

'Should be easy to find, then.'

'We've traced the sales from sixteen stores so far, and matched the shoes to their owners. Thank fuck for credit cards. Got four more stores to go. But maybe we're in luck already.' Simm pushed a grainy black and white photograph across the Formica table, negotiating its path through the ketchup and vinegar bottles and past the paper-napkin dispenser.

Sorrenson reached for the image. 'What's this? Brian sharing more CCTV footage with us?'

Simm shook his head. 'No, I pulled this. It's from a store in Ashford. We believe this person bought several pairs of the size elevens. Paid cash.'

Sorrenson studied the photograph. It was little more than a collection of shadows. The figure, a man most probably, seemed to be wearing a baseball cap. 'Good work, Simm. You going to get Brian to enhance it?'

'Yeah.'

'Well, good luck with that one. Let's hope he's on a bit of a promise the day you ask him. Any news on the other investigation?'

'We've been pulling in some of Gaunt's acquaintances. Not getting much back. Apparently he was a bit of a smuggler. Well, more than a bit. That was his main livelihood. Not sure whether there's anything in it. Sounds kind of far-fetched. Don't know what he was smuggling either. Drugs boys say he wasn't known to them. The National Crime Agency's never heard of him. If he was smuggling, it was low-grade, low-key stuff. Little more than a cottage indus-try, I'd guess. Different from that guy.' Simm pointed at the television screen in the corner of the café, Al-Boktorah's face scowled at them.

Sorrenson looked out of the café window across the beach to the sea. On the horizon he could see scores of wind turbines refusing to turn in a windless sky. They wouldn't be producing much power that day or for most of the week, according to the forecasters. The national grid would need to look elsewhere to keep the nation's kettles boiling. He shifted his gaze further east, to the two clusters of Maunsell Forts guarding the mouth of the estuary, the point where the Thames fused with the sea, where salt water met sky. Up close the forts must be huge, he thought. They were castles built in corroding metal, each the size of a multi-storey car park. He handed the photograph back to Simm. 'We need a boat,' he said.

'Mr Zetouin? Welcome to England.' Douglas indicated that the thin, dark-eyed man should take the back seat and pulled the people-carrier's door shut behind him. 'Good flight? Bitch flying out of Diego Garcia, I know. Weather can play havoc with flight plans.' He examined the man sitting across from him on the other side of a small, retractable table. He was older than Douglas had expected. He'd thought his sort, terrorists basically, were all in their twenties, but Zetouin was in his mid-forties. Still, you didn't get to occupy his position in Al-Boktorah's empire without putting in some serious years. If you weren't any good, you wouldn't survive. Terrorist franchises were as Darwinian as any tech giant when it came to personnel retention.

'You want water?' Douglas asked.

Zetouin shook his head. He stared out of the window.

'OK, going to be one of those journeys, then,' Douglas said. 'Suit yourself.'

The vehicle sped off through the Oxfordshire country-side. Zetouin couldn't take his eyes off the world blurring past outside. Everything was so lush and green. It was a paradise. When he was moved to France he'd insist on a house in the country. He'd milk them, the idiots. They had no idea who they were bringing in, where his loyalties lay. They saw him as a solution not a threat. So trusting. So short-sighted. That was Americans for you. Dumb. Very dumb. He was going to betray them and they were going to reward him handsomely for doing it.

A few miles out of Brize Norton the people-carrier turned into a small country lane and pulled to a halt. The door slid back. Two other men wearing sunglasses piled in on either side of Zetouin and pushed him into the middle of the back seat. He looked at Douglas. 'Why we stop?'

Douglas laughed. 'Why we stop? We all got to stop some time, amigo.' He nodded at the two other men. They grabbed Zetouin's arms, held him firmly. He kicked out but his two captors wrapped their legs round his so that he was completely immobile. His eyes grew wide. He shook his head from side to side, trying to head-butt the men. Douglas leaned forward, rolled the left arm of Zetouin's T-shirt up a fraction and sank a hypodermic needle into his arm. Zetouin gasped.

Douglas pulled the needle out and immediately jabbed in a second. Zetouin started to shake violently. Spittle formed at the sides of his mouth. He let out a low, pained groan. His head slumped forward. For a second or two his fingers continued to flex and then they went still.

Douglas grinned at the other two men. 'Don't mix drugs and drink. Really bad combination. Can be fatal. One of the most common causes of heart attacks, these days.' He found his phone, hit a pre-dial. 'It's done,' he said. He glanced at his companions, pointed at Zetouin. 'Now we've got to get him to a hotel. Leave him for some maid to find. Guess it was inevitable, really. First taste of freedom and he goes on a drink–and–drugs binge. Some people, they got no control.'

Chapter 11

She was forty minutes into her run when she saw him. He was at the far end of the peninsula yet she recognized him from half a mile away. Fawcett looked out of place in his dark blue suit, an alien predator imported to keep a native species down. He stood on the very edge of the shoreline staring out at the sea. Reluctantly, she ran towards him. He was sporting a sun-tan, she noticed.

'You run here a lot?' Fawcett said, as she approached. She followed his gaze along the bleak stretch of coast. In the distance glowered the hulking mass of a nuclear power station. Yellow flowers poked through the dunes of shingle. 'Strange old place,' Fawcett continued. 'Bet you can't get a decent espresso for miles.'

Kate stood contemplating him, hands on hips, gently stretching. She felt a stab of irritation. Her run had been interrupted. Fawcett was an invader, one she'd been expecting for several weeks. 'I like it here,' she said. 'You can run for miles without seeing anyone. It's good to get out of London. Gives you perspective. Helps you understand what's important.'

Fawcett reached into his jacket pocket and pulled out a packet of cigarettes. He produced a lighter, shielding his cigarette from the breeze blowing in off the Channel.

'You should give up,' she said. 'They're very bad for you.'
'They keep you in a job. You should be grateful.' He blew
smoke into the clean peninsula air, appraising her black running leggings, her body-hugging pale blue vest. He looked
at the GPS watch on her wrist, the sculpted water-bottle in
her hand, the fluorescent yellow running shoes that seemed
to belong in the future. He looked at her long black curly
hair, scraped back into a ponytail. He looked at the sweat
forming on her top lip, then cast his frame of vision lower,
to her midriff, between her leggings and her vest. He looked
at every part of her. She was conscious that her pierced belly
button was glinting in the sunlight. Fawcett nodded at the
supertankers out on the horizon and exhaled enthusiastically.
'I was in naval intelligence before I joined the service. That
was an eye-opener. You'd always wonder what was hidden
away in the boats passing through our waters. People think
of the internet as unregulated. It's nothing compared with
the oceans. Now, they really are ungovernable. I've come to
think of the sea as the first world wide web. Everything flows
across it, everything that matters anyway.'

Two seagulls screamed overhead, chased each other out to
sea. The sun disappeared behind a solitary cloud. In an
instant the dazzling sea turned a dark green.

'I guess your father would have understood that,' Fawcett
murmured. 'The importance of trade, I mean.'

Neat, she thought. She'd wondered how long it would be
before Fawcett dredged up her father again. Perhaps he'd do
the double and bring her dead husband into it, too.

'I take it you read your father's file?' he said.

She edged forward a couple of feet, so that she could
face him square on. They were standing on a shingle dune
that peaked some six feet above the beach. She had two

inches on him, but he had more than two stone on her, she reckoned. Still, she fancied her chances. For a second she thought about hitting Fawcett in the face, the satisfaction that would come from watching him spill down the shingle. In her mind, she heard him crumple against the shore, saw the blood pour from his mouth. She took three deep breaths and promised herself another eight miles of running once he'd left. 'I wouldn't call it a file,' she said. 'It was a few pages, that was all.'

Fawcett's cold blue eyes rested on her piercing, then combed back up her body to her face. 'There could be more.'

She should have hit him while she had the chance. But it was too late. He was too far away from her now. 'You expect me to be grateful for the scraps you're throwing me?' she said.

The sun returned from behind the cloud. Fawcett squinted out to sea, his neat blond hair ruffled in the breeze. 'Calm down, Ms Pendragon.'

'Don't be so fucking condescending.'

'I apologize. It's to be expected.'

'Expected?' Just what was it about Fawcett? His entire manner seemed to have been borrowed from another era. The thirties, maybe. He was so clipped and inscrutable. He should have been a butler.

Fawcett shrugged, exhaled. 'Your internal quarterly assessments when you were with the service indicated that your type are prone to losing control.'

'My type?'

'Your type, Ms Pendragon, is apparently classed as displaying weak personality behaviours. Due to a lack of parameters early on, when you were a child. Means you

109

grow up not knowing where the boundaries are. Understandable, really, given that your father was away so much, spending all that time working undercover in Northern Ireland. Find a reckless person and an absent father's not far behind.'

Kate felt her hands clench into fists. No amount of running would take away the overwhelming urge she had to inflict extreme and urgent violence on the man standing near her.

'Yes,' Fawcett continued. 'Children who know no boundaries end up much more likely to be sexually promiscuous later on as adults, so the shrinks say.' He glanced back at her piercing. 'There may be nothing in it, though. Just a theory.'

She turned away. 'We're done, right? You've come down here and said your piece. Now you can go back to London and report that you tried.' She started walking back up the beach. She could feel the warm sun skimming across the sea, radiating the shingle. It could still be a good day, she told herself. It could still be a good day. 'It's people like you who remind me why I never joined the service, Fawcett,' she called back to him. 'You're just pathetic public-school boys playing stupid games so that you can feel important when you turn out the lights each night. Christ knows what your type must be. I'd love to see your assessments.'

'Featherblade,' Fawcett shouted. She kept walking. 'Your father's codename was Featherblade.'

Kate stopped and turned. Fawcett was now some fifty yards away. He was holding a sheet of paper above his head. 'This here is solid, I promise,' he shouted. 'It's yours, regardless of whether you choose to help us. After this I'll leave and you won't see me again, if that's what you want. I give you my word. But consider this a peace offering.'

She hesitated. Her gaze shifted past Fawcett to a sea shimmering under a sun that she knew would die one day. When the world was plunged into darkness only the sea would remain. It was laughable, humanity's frantic, confused efforts to leave even the smallest imprint on a narrative sweeping across billions of years. Why, ultimately, did it bother? Why the effort? She stared down at Fawcett, as if the force of her glare could barrel him into the sea, send him crashing across the waves. He stood looking up at her, head cocked to one side, a man who seemed to belong in a past that was not his own.

'I feel we've rather got off on the wrong foot,' Fawcett shouted up to her. 'It's not great admitting this but we are truly desperate. You really could make a difference, you know. Your expertise could help us.'

She continued staring down at him, counted to twenty, then looked back out to sea. One day it would all be over. Why try to do anything? Only she already knew the answer. She'd known it for days.

Scott examined himself in the large gilt-framed mirror that covered most of the far wall of his sizeable Washington office. He congratulated himself on the decision to have his teeth whitened. Yes, it was true what his wife said: he really had stolen JFK's smile. But maybe it was about time to go a little easier on the hair dye. A few streaks of grey might be politic, Scott thought. Give him some gravitas. Not too much, though. He was in no rush to acknowledge his own mortality.

Blue or red tie? Blue. More sober. The colour of the current administration, perhaps one day his own. He picked at his teeth with his thumbnail, something he did when he was anxious. It was his first appearance before the Senate Intelligence Committee and he wanted to make a good impression. He'd met all the members privately, of course, and the meeting was behind closed doors for reasons of national security. But how his appearance was received would filter all the way to 1600 Pennsylvania Avenue.

Scott's phone buzzed, the signal for him to make his way to the committee hearing room. Two blonde female assistants met him outside his office, pulling small black suitcases containing reams of classified briefing notes.

'They're mainly going to want to talk about what's going down in Algeria,' one of the assistants said. They entered the underground tunnel that connected Scott's office to the Senate.

Scott stopped abruptly. 'Mainly? What else is there to talk about right now?'

'They like to throw curve balls,' one of the assistants murmured. 'Some of them do anyway. The "awkwards", we call them.' She looked at her colleague. 'Maybe four of the twelve on the committee are awkwards. Depends on the weather.' Both flashed Scott perfect smiles.

Yes, he thought, the teeth whitening had been a good idea. You needed enhanced enamel in Washington. 'So then, come on, throw me a curve ball.'

The looks exchanged between his two assistants weren't lost on Scott. He'd read their CVs before agreeing to hire them. They both had Wharton MBAs. Their antennae were sensing danger. 'So?'

Another exchange of looks.

'Come on, clock's ticking.'

The two assistants nodded at each other. 'Flight plans or budget plans?' one said.

'Which should cause us the most concern?' Scott muttered.

They shrugged. Scott looked at his watch and then at the two suitcases. 'We'll do flight plans first,' he said.

Metcalf walked through Admiralty Arch and headed down the Mall towards Buckingham Palace. Just before St James's Palace he turned right and steered himself up the centuries-old streets in the direction of Smyths. Metcalf was a member of several London clubs but Smyths was the preferred venue for his more discreet meetings. One advantage of Smyths was that half of its members couldn't hear what was being said at the table next to them. Say what you like about the rich, Metcalf thought, but they really did live longer. The ones in Smyths went on for aeons until they were so infirm they could hardly function at all. And yet somehow every morning they materialized through the ether to idle their days away in the club's fusty dining rooms and library. Metcalf despised them. His lack of schooling and university education meant he was always an outsider to them. The club had accepted him only after strings had been pulled by a grateful former director of Smith and Webb. There had been a spot of bother involving the director's car and a collision with a pedestrian. Metcalf had been on the scene quickly. They'd never found the car. The pedestrian had purchased a villa in Spain with the compensation.

Metcalf walked past the booth at the club's impressive front entrance, nodded to the porter on duty and made his way into the billiards room. Two tables were set up ready for a game but the room was empty, except for one corner where Matthews was sitting in a green leather chair nursing a gin and tonic.

The two men acknowledged each other. Metcalf pulled up a chair, then muttered an order for a whisky and soda to a waiter who appeared at his shoulder.

'I took the liberty of signing myself in as your guest,' Matthews said. He raised his glass to Metcalf, who kept his eyes trained on the departing waiter until he was a safe distance away.

'This is a disaster on a truly epic scale,' Metcalf said. 'I take it you know Dunbar has resigned?' He picked up a copy of that day's *Evening Standard* from a nearby table and lobbed it at Matthews.

'Yes,' Matthews said. 'It had not escaped my attention that Smith and Webb is now in the embarrassing position of being *sans* chairman.'

'The City pages are full of it. Apparently our distribution network is now the subject of multiple investigations by security services around the world. That fucking blogger. All the stuff he's putting out there linking us to terrorism is hammering Smith and Webb.'

The waiter brought over the whisky and soda. Metcalf drained it, then immediately ordered a second. 'And some nuts,' he bellowed, as an afterthought.

'I think you need to calm down,' Matthews said. 'Ease up on the drink. Get a bit of perspective.'

Veins on Metcalf's head throbbed. He flashed a sour look at Matthews. 'Easy for you to say. You're not in the mouth of this thing. It's going to devour us.'

Matthews sipped his gin. He was alarmed to discover that his drink was playing host to a slice of lemon. No one, no one sane anyway, put lemon slices in gin and tonic, Matthews thought. It was lime every time. Christ, the country was going to the dogs when even its most venerable members-only club couldn't serve a simple drink correctly. He thought about requesting membership just so that he could complain. But, no, he'd stick with the Carlton and the RAC, the usual haunts of the ex-spook community. Better for networking, and it would keep him out of Metcalf's orbit. It didn't pay to mix too closely with clients. You needed to establish barriers.

'Well, it seems to me you're pretty close to the end of the horror story,' he said. 'You'll fire a few employees as scapegoats and everything will blow over. You'll get a new chairman and the share price will bounce back. The City will fall in love with you again – after all, your product is quite literally addictive – and in twelve months all of this will be forgotten. Every company has crises. You'll pull through and come back stronger. They'll take out Al-Boktorah some time soon. End game.'

Metcalf took a large gulp of his drink. 'That won't stop the security service and fuck knows who else crawling all over us, trying to fathom how our product has been ending up in the hands of a fucking terrorist network in Algeria that's about to execute a hundred British and American hostages. You heard the news this morning? They killed two last night just to generate some more publicity, get a few thousand more soft touches around the world to stump up for the online ransom. People are pointing the finger at us, claiming we've got blood on our hands. Half of Al-Boktorah's profits are apparently coming from the tobacco trade.'

Metcalf leaned forwards. There was drink on his breath. He must have been drinking before he'd entered the club, Matthews realized.

'Let's be clear here,' Metcalf hissed. 'We both know that Smith and Webb's distribution network has been designed to ensure its products can be shipped to whoever, wherever, no questions asked, so it can avoid unnecessary and unhelpful complications, like sanctions and taxes. We're not unique in using third parties and tax havens to facilitate these things. Far from it. Every tobacco firm works in the same way. Christ, every company needs to operate on the margins of the law, exploit the loopholes, stay one step ahead of the regulators. That's how they remain competitive. If we didn't do it, we'd die. That's how our business model has functioned for hundreds of years. That's how it will continue to function. But now this terrorism angle has truly fucked us.' Metcalf finished his second drink, threw peanuts down his throat. 'And I care about this company. I'm not going to let it be destroyed. I've worked too hard for it to end like this, being held hostage to some fucking blogger letting all our secrets leach out across the internet. How the fuck did he get all that information anyway? Chinese hackers trying to bash the share price, make us vulnerable to a takeover?'

Matthews took another sip of his gin as he studied the oil painting of a pop-eyed former club president hanging on a far wall. He fished the lemon wedge out of the remains of his drink and deposited it on the table. He thought for a few seconds. Metcalf would probably work it out in time. He'd probably locate the source of the leaks. But even the source didn't know how the files had come his way, didn't know that by leaking them he was furthering the interests of Matthews's Chinese client. The way Matthews saw it, he'd

116

just tapped into one man's growing sense of injustice. He'd read the man's emails. He knew there was a latent anger that could be exploited. He'd merely provided the gun and the ammunition. It had been the other man who had pulled the trigger, pushed all the damaging intel out there. Well, the other man would now have to deal with the consequences. Matthews had no obligation to protect him. It was time for him to prove his worth to Smith and Webb, earn his retainer, as Metcalf would put it. He leaned closer to Metcalf, trying not to breathe in his alcohol fumes. 'I think you need to look closer to home,' he said.

Chapter 12

Their skins, once smooth and gunmetal grey, were flaking red with rust. Salt water was doing its best to devour them. What the Luftwaffe had failed to bomb into oblivion, the sea would take in time. But that day would be centuries off, Sorrenson could see. The Maunsell Forts were still standing strong, 750-ton heavyweights, implacable in the face of everything the North Sea could throw at them.

The forts were truly huge. Dour cathedrals forged out of metal. They'd been relieved of their Bofors guns, but otherwise they remained largely intact. Only the odd daub of graffiti, a reminder of when they'd played host to a pirate radio station, suggested that they'd been touched by the second half of the twentieth century.

Even now there was no mistaking the forts' military intent. They'd been designed with one thing in mind: to keep others out. Had it been worth the huge effort, Sorrenson wondered, the massive amount of manpower that had gone into their construction? Someone, somewhere, must have done an assessment after the war. Thirty V1s brought down in their time didn't sound that much in the grand scheme of things. But, still, Sorrenson figured, there would be people alive, the grandsons and granddaughters of those the downed rockets would have killed, who owed their existence to the forts. That had to count for something.

The launch pulled up alongside the first fort. Ropes were thrown, the boat secured. A small team of police, Customs and coastguard ascended a rusting ladder covered with sea-gull droppings. Sorrenson found the ladder cold to the touch, despite it being midsummer. He looked down at the waves buffeting the launch below. It would have been a terrible deployment, being confined to the forts. They really were just giant metal cans in the cold North Sea. You would have been on them for weeks before you got any leave, with little to do other than to fish off the side and wait for the next wave of terror, the next swarm of German bombers. He looked again at the waves, parcels of energy crossing what once they'd called the German Sea. He thought about his distant relatives in Norway. Whenever he looked at the sea he felt a connection to them, a connection to a past he'd never known. He felt – and he was embarrassed to put it into such a clumsy word – he felt a sense of universality; that he was somehow connected to everyone, everything, every era. A stupid thing to think, he told himself. A powerful thing to think. He continued to climb the cold metal ladder up into the fort.

'That a Birmingham accent?'

The hooded man broke off from speaking to his fellow captor and gazed at the tethered hostages squatting in the dirt, like factory-farmed chickens. The cave was dark, lit only by a couple of arc lights powered by a mobile generator that made a violent humming sound. He couldn't see which of them had spoken. 'What if it is?'

119

'Just asking,' the voice said, in a thick West Midlands accent. 'Sounds like we might be from the same place.'

The hooded man laughed, gripping his Kalashnikov tighter. 'Don't try to tell me we're the same, bro. We're not the same. You and me, we're very different.'

'Alum Rock, right? I reckon you're from Alum Rock. I might know people you know.'

The hooded man muttered something to the other captor. 'You come out here,' he said. 'I want to see you.' A figure shuffled across the dirt towards him. An Asian guy in his thirties. 'What's all this Alum Rock shit?' the hooded man said. 'Why you giving us all this I-know-people-you-know shit? You think we're going to bond or something? You think where we're from makes any difference to how I think? You think I'm going to go soft, give you an easy time cos we been to the same Nando's or something?'

'Just saying,' the hostage mumbled. He tried to raise his hands imploringly but they were tied to his legs. 'Sorry,' he said. 'Dumb thing to say.'

'Too fucking right.' The hooded man stared down at the figure in front of him. Slowly, very slowly, he raised his assault rifle.

'No, man, no,' one of the other captors hissed. 'Not here, bro. Put the gun down, bro. Time'll come. Then you can pull the trigger. You can do all of 'em in time.'

The hooded man nodded. 'You count yourself lucky, Alum Rock Man. You still worth more to us alive than dead. You better pray you stay that way.'

The Smoke. Even now, long after the industrial smog had lifted, it was still a suitable name for the capital. Kate could

120

feel London re-entering her lungs, taste the diesel fumes in her mouth. It was only when you returned that you appreciated London in all its foul, corrupting omnipotence.

She walked down past Parliament, past the sturdy metal barriers designed to repel suicide trucks from blowing up the nation's legislators, and made her way towards Five's headquarters overlooking the Thames. The traffic snarling down by the river seemed deafening. Funny, she'd never noticed it when she'd lived in the city. The crowds, too. They'd always sort of morphed into the background, like moving wallpaper. But now London was a stranger to her. Or, rather, she was a stranger to London. The best part of a year on the coast had made her view the city as some sort of ant colony, a place that obeyed a maddening, chaotic logic, a secret, guarded code known only to its citizens. And she was no longer one of them. She was an alien.

She paused at a bus stop and looked at an advert. 'Our security is your priority,' read the Transport for London notice, warning people about suspicious packages. Such posters seemed to have mushroomed in recent years. It was the same with the trains and tubes. Every journey came with a recorded warning urging people to be vigilant. The capital had been placed on a permanent state of alert. The cynical would say that it helped the security services if people were fearful. It made them more pliant, willing to tolerate well-intentioned transgressions. Viewed in this light, scaring people was little more than a PR exercise waged by the security apparatus to justify its existence. Fear was the currency the service traded in. It would disappear if people stopped being scared.

But it was easy to be cynical, she conceded. You forgot

how tightly cities packed people in when you were on the coast. You forgot how the urban world was an easy target for catastrophe. Millions of fish in a barrel. One person could visit untold destruction on many. You forgot all this when there was just the sky and the sea and the shore.

It had been unsettling, staying in her Clerkenwell apartment the night before. The place was familiar, but it no longer seemed her own. She'd ransacked it for photos of her parents, letters from her dead husband. She'd found his medals and wound the ribbons tightly around her fingers, as if the simple act of constriction would bring her closer to him, to her old self. Maybe it was time to sell the apartment, she'd thought. A new start. Let go of the past. Embrace all the clichés.

She entered Five's bombproof security doors, then waited until the bored-looking security guards waved her through. On the other side, she deposited her handbag on the conveyor-belt running through the X-ray machine. She turned to find Fawcett waiting for her. 'Thought I'd come and get you personally.'

'Thanks, that's . . .' She willed herself not to complete the sentence, the kneejerk response people always made in such situations. She wasn't going to tell Fawcett that he was kind.

'Shall we?' He gestured towards the lifts. As they walked she felt comforted that nothing had changed since she'd left. There were still posters advertising subsidized childcare for staff, and sponsorship pleas from Five's many enthusiastic triathletes; the canteen's daily menu was posted on a pillar near the lifts; there was a flier promoting the next performance of the service's choir, the blandly named King's Singers. No, she thought, nothing had changed at all. The patina of normality was pervasive. It stretched throughout the building, lingered on every surface. It was only once you were beyond the corridors that the pretence, the much-needed artifice, became difficult to maintain. Your work, what you saw, what you were tasked with doing, well, no amount of subsidized crèches and charity concerts could distract you from the overwhelming truth that your job was more than your job. You could never just leave your work at work. You carried it with you always, like the memory of a dead parent.

They exited the lift and approached Webster's office. Outside, Fawcett knocked on the door three times, then ushered her in. The head of MI5 was behind his desk, rocking gently back and forth in his wheelchair. Never a good sign, she'd come to learn. Webster attempted a smile, was about to say something when a deep, hacking cough cut him short.

'Sorry,' Callow muttered, walking in from the roof terrace outside Webster's office. 'Needed a nicotine fix.' He smiled at her. 'Good to see you. I was beginning to fear that you'd given up on us.'

'I had.'

'Please, take a seat.' Webster pointed at a sofa near his desk. Fawcett and Callow pulled up a couple of easy chairs. The contrived attempt at informality made her feel as if she'd been sucked into a mid-morning television programme. She almost laughed at the absurdity of it all. Then she looked at Webster and saw the face of someone much older than he was. Webster had aged a decade in the year she'd been away. He was clearly exhausted.

'Geneva,' Webster began, then turned to Callow. 'You explain. You're deeper into this than me.'

Callow chucked nicotine gum into his mouth. 'You read about that bombing in Geneva a while back, right? Took out the hotel near the airport?'

'Difficult not to. It was all over the papers. Some AQ offshoot blamed, right? Focused on bringing terror to European financial districts?'

'Right,' Callow agreed. 'Only that story was a crock of shit. CIA black-ops stuff, the usual. They leaked it to give them cover.'

'Namely?'

'Well, we believe they thought it was better to blame some mad, bad towel heads than allow the truth to get out.'

'And the truth is?'

'The truth is the Americans have a different theory,' Callow said. 'They believe the bombing was targeted at them. They think it was designed to take out a CIA station chief and an asset who were close to establishing Al-Boktorah's exact location. They were both in the hotel. They'd been working on the op for a couple of years, cultivating a major informant network. Both were killed in the explosion. Four civilians also died. Twelve injured. It was a big setback for the Agency. Not that you'd know it from reading the papers.'

Nearby Big Ben struck three.

'A big setback for the hundred hostages Al-Boktorah's about to execute, too,' Kate murmured. 'Seems like their best hope ended in the rubble of a Swiss hotel.'

'There's also a political dimension to all this,' Callow said. 'A presidential election's in the offing. The CIA are under huge pressure to deliver quick wins. The outgoing president wants a head on a plate and soon. He wants his legacy shored up. Keeps talking about the fourth quarter of a basketball game being the most important. He wants to smooth the way for his successor. He wants Al-Boktorah taken out.'

'Right.' Kate was distracted. She couldn't stop staring at a watercolour painting behind Webster's desk. It was of a fisherman casting into a river. Early morning, probably. The hand that had painted it wasn't particularly gifted. She stared at it for several more seconds. Yes, she thought, it reminded her of a similar picture she'd seen somewhere else. A vague memory took shape, then became distinct. An uneasy feeling started to take hold of her. She interrogated the memory. The uneasy feeling was now close to smothering her. Yes, there was something about the painting, something sickeningly familiar. She knew where she'd seen the other. No, it couldn't be . . . Just a coincidence, surely. Had to be. But . . . She sighed heavily and leaned back into the sofa. She closed her eyes and spoke in a low, emotionless voice. 'The headhunter you put me in touch with when I left. She wasn't really a headhunter, was she?'

She opened her eyes and scrutinized the three men closely. They exchanged glances, remained silent. It was enough of an admission. She cursed herself. She should have known. Of course, it had all been too easy. One phone call, her CV emailed to an anonymous office behind Victoria station, an interview with a woman who looked like she'd rather be judging at Crufts and, hey presto, a well-paid job doing something vaguely interesting that would at least tide her over until she knew what to do with the rest of her life.

She remembered again what Fawcett had said. She remembered, too, the thin smirk on his lips as he'd said it.

'Is taking the corporate shilling worth leaving the service?' Bastards. That was how they all thought. Once you were in you were in. You would never leave. Or, rather, the service would never leave you.

'How did you . . . ?' She started again. 'Why did you . . . ? Oh, never mind.'

They'd gamed her. Right from the start. 'We'll put you in touch with a specialist recruitment consultancy,' the head of HR had told her when she'd left Five. 'They're very discreet. They specialize in finding people like you high-calibre security personnel, jobs that match your unique talents. The private sector is crying out for former intelligence agents. Fantastic perks. The pensions are tremendous.'

She looked at the three of them and shook her head slowly. She felt as if she'd been robbed. She closed her eyes, ran her hands through her hair. 'Anything else you want to tell me? I don't really think there's any part of me left that Five hasn't gamed. Maybe my relationship? You set that one up too?'

'I need a break,' Callow muttered. 'I need to get some smoke into my lungs.' He looked at Fawcett. 'You can come and keep me company on the terrace.'

The two men left Kate staring hard at Webster. She was conscious that she was experiencing a familiar feeling, one that she'd had before several times in his presence. She had a strong desire to attack a man in a wheelchair.

Webster pressed a button and mumbled, 'Four coffees, please, Jane,' into a small microphone on his desk. Outside, the bell of Big Ben struck half past three. For the first time Kate became aware of a ticking sound, then saw a small carriage clock on a mahogany sideboard.

Webster followed her gaze. 'Embarrassing but true, I'm afraid. You used to get one after ten years' service. John Lewis vouchers, these days. Much more popular.' He turned back to her. 'We're running out of time. We're not the French or the Italians. We don't pay ransoms. Our options are rather limited. This is not a zero sum game, intelligence. It is messy, fluid and awkward. We need the Americans' help. Increasingly so. But they're stretched, too. They're closing some of their military bases over here. Even superpowers are having to cut their cloth accordingly in these leaner times. The prime minister has made it clear in private briefings to me that he sees threats to our overseas energy interests as a threat to national security. If the lights go out in this country there will be chaos. You saw how Britain was paralysed by the riots a couple of years ago. Now multiply that by ten. This is why Downing Street has made it clear that finding Al-Boktorah must be considered the most urgent priority for the security and intelligence services. That is why we need to help the Americans find him. We can't take him out ourselves. We just don't have that capability. Not any more.'

'So?'

Webster seemed uncomfortable. 'Now that Geneva's ended their best bet of finding Al-Boktorah, the Americans are trying to trace him through his finances. They believe much of his money passes through British tax havens and have asked for our co-operation. But those places are unbiddable. We have little means of legally forcing them to divulge anything to us. It's a ludicrous, terrible situation but we are where we are. We had hoped that unpicking the finances of his cigarette-smuggling network might lead us to him. An old idea but a good one. That's why we'd cultivated Carrington . . .'

'Cultivated?'

Webster ignored her interruption. 'And that's why we pulled some strings to put you into your position. We thought you could help us on this, if we really needed it. We've done similar things in the past. Had a lot of people we thought might be sympathetic to us put into jobs in South Africa during apartheid. Most of them we never tapped up but a few proved useful. But, well, this strategy's pretty much come to a dead end on this occasion. Literally with respect to Carrington. As I said, we're running out of time on it. We need a result. Whatever it takes. We can't afford the Americans to think we're not doing all we can to play ball. There's already accusations coming out of Washington that we don't take security seriously enough. Some generals are complaining we're not spending enough of our GDP on defence. We need to win the Americans back. Even if that means we have to find some . . . exotic solutions. Perhaps by using trusted third parties who don't work for the service . . . Do you understand?'

She understood. Five wanted plausible deniability if anything went wrong. It didn't want its fingerprints anywhere near anything grubby. It needed someone who was neither of it nor an outsider. She inclined her head ever so slightly.

'There's something else,' Webster said awkwardly. His eyes remained fixed on his desk. 'I believe Fawcett offered something in return for your help. The file we have on your father's death. A form of barter, as it were. Crude, I know, and not something that would be considered best practice, or whatever ghastly phrase is now in vogue in the service manual, but, well, it will come out one day and end up in the archives at Kew so, for what it's worth, here it is.' He handed her a brown folder. 'Your father was a great man. He always will be.'

Chapter 13

They found Gary Grant's body on the deck behind his rented house. The head was caved in. The police reckoned the fourth blow had been the fatal one. A small bloodstained rock, discovered nearby, was quickly identified as the murder weapon. The man's hands had been bound behind his head and there was evidence that he'd been forced to kneel before he was killed. There was dust on his knees, indicating that he'd held the position for some time.

But the police weren't really interested in the hows and the whys of Grant's murder. It was a body. Another body. They'd plenty of those. Their report, shared with the US ambassador to Puerto Rico, suggested robbery as the primary motive. It wasn't so unusual. Many of the beachfront condos in the area had been broken into in recent months although, true, none had ended in a killing. Grant must have disturbed the robbers, the police suggested. They were probably high on crack and as angry as hornets. They wouldn't have been thinking straight. The use of the rock suggested it wasn't pre-meditated. They'd just grabbed the nearest thing to hand when he'd confronted them.

The ambassador arranged for Grant's body to be flown back to the US, along with some of his possessions. His digital camera, his books and his seventies' turntable were returned to his parents. But not everything completed the journey successfully. His computer was missing, along with a number of encrypted hard drives and USB sticks.

No one was charged with the crime and the murder didn't venture beyond page seven of the local press for fear of its impact on the tourist trade. In time, prestigious US magazines and several British broadsheets took more of an interest, devoting thousands of words to speculation that Grant had been killed before he'd filed his most explosive article, a comprehensive demolition job, forensically dissecting how Smith and Webb's tobacco had benefited terrorist groups. Columnists pontificated on whether Grant would have remained alive if he hadn't chosen to publicize himself, turning his journalism into a personal brand. It was dangerous when the messenger threatened to become bigger than the story, they suggested. Made them visible. Brought them a lot of enemies, people keen to trace them.

In death, Grant divided opinion. To some he was a hero, a truth-teller who'd paid the ultimate price for whistle-blowing. For others he was a narcissist who fell in love with the online self he'd created.

Few believed that the police had called the murder right. It was rare for robberies to end in a killing, most agreed. So there had to be more to it. Sometimes the most obvious stories were just too prosaic, too implausible. Sometimes they weren't.

The two robbers who'd been high on crack when they'd murdered Grant were themselves killed weeks later in a squabble over drugs.

There was no more damaging drip-feed of stories. But it was too late for Smith and Webb. Within days the company succumbed to a humiliating cut-price takeover from China's Marathon tobacco.

Years later Grant's parents created a scholarship in his honour. Each year it handed ten thousand dollars to a crusading journalist judged to have spoken truth to power. It was their way of keeping their son alive, they explained. They were proud of him, of what he'd achieved. The Grants became increasingly reclusive in their grief, hiding away in their impressive antebellum mansion just outside New Orleans. Grant's father, a wine grower, had inherited the property from his father, who'd inherited it from his father. Grant had grown up enjoying fat vistas of well-tended vineyards, whose full-bodied, sun-kissed product had ensured he'd never have to worry about finding a proper job with a monthly pay cheque.

Tourists would sometimes stop by to take photos of the Grants' property. The family had thought of building a website to tell people a little about their home's history. But they knew its secret, the one buried under the vines. It had once been the largest tobacco plantation in the American south. They couldn't tell their mansion's story without admitting its epic role in slavery. The Grants decided against the website. Some truths were best left buried.

She read it several times, sitting in the brilliant sunshine warming the well-swept steps of the small church in Smith Square, a short walk from Five's headquarters. Initially Kate thought the document was a fake. It was only a photocopy, after all. Such things could easily be invented. The security service was skilled in making the official look unofficial, the unofficial official. It operated in the world where truth and lies collided. It knew how to bend things, people.

Gradually, though, she became convinced she was reading something that the service had never wanted to come out, not for a good half-century at least. Not until those still alive had been reduced to ash or bone. The document was a first-person account in spidery handwriting that made some of it difficult to read. On occasions she was forced to choose her own words to insert into the narrative to make it flow. It made for an unsettling exercise, her intervention in the text. It seemed to bind her to it. Spools of yarn tying her ever more tightly to the truth of long-faded words.

She gave a deep, trembling laugh that caused her to wrap herself defensively into a foetal position on the church steps as she tried to stop the spasm of her ribs and shoulders. The truth was not amusing, not in the least. But she couldn't stop herself laughing. The great irony, the one thing she'd never believed, was that her father really had died in a car crash. The most implausibly plausible explanation was what had actually happened.

There'd been no set-up, no sinister forces at work. It had not been made to look like a traffic accident. It had been a traffic accident. One day her father's car had left the road near to a small loch close to the Giant's Causeway and had hit a tree at more than 60 m.p.h. He'd died almost instantly.

As far as she could tell, the account had been written shortly after her father's death by another agent or perhaps some undercover police officer or soldier who'd known him well. The man was clearly someone in whom her father had confided.

There had been a woman. Kate's father had been her lover and had got her pregnant. The woman was from a Catholic family with close links to the Provos. She was twelve weeks gone when she walked into the loch near the Causeway and drowned herself. The account explained that Kate's father had been left devastated. He'd wanted out but he'd been under huge pressure to maintain his false identity and he'd started drinking heavily. Loose-lipped, sodden with remorse, he'd told his story to a priest. The family had found out. There was an ultimatum. The British businessman had to pay. They'd have a word with the Provos and he'd end up in a bog with a bullet in the back of his head. Or he could do the honourable thing and save them a bullet, spare his wife back home the knowledge of his betrayal. Her father had outlined the bare facts of it all to whoever had written up the account. He'd confided that he was going to throw a wreath into the loch, then turn his car into a deadly weapon.

Kate's first reaction, when she'd managed to control her sobbing, was not to think about her father but her mother. Shortly before her death, when she was racked with pain, high on opiates, her mother had hinted that she suspected something about her husband's past. Maybe she'd known the whole truth and had spent years shielding her daughter from it, Kate thought. The service, too, had played its part in burying everything, presumably keen to spare itself embarrassment. She thought about a remark Webster had once made about her father's death: 'Almost too perfect to be an accident.' Maybe he'd been trying to tell her all along. She returned to the document, the scrawled words. The dull tone that permeated the narrative. Could Webster have written it? Possibly. Certainly he had known all about it. It didn't really matter either way.

She reached for her phone to ring Sorrenson. She really wanted to see him. She needed to get out of London.

A shadow blocked out the sun. She could smell cigarette smoke. She looked up at Fawcett, her eyes filled with tears. He still had his tan, she noticed distractedly.

'So,' he said. 'Now you know.'

Sorrenson felt the vibration in his jacket and reached for his phone. Around him on the Maunsell Fort, a team of police officers was searching a rusting warren of corridors, sleeping quarters, messes, ops rooms and munition silos. He read the text. It was unlike Kate to be asking where he was. She wasn't the sort. Something was up. He made his way back towards the ladder and the launch.

'You're leaving?' Simm shouted.

'Something's come up,' Sorrenson shouted back. 'My partner . . .' He stopped. It still seemed strange to be calling her that. 'My partner,' he repeated. 'She's been taken ill. I've got to get back. You can deal with this.'

'Fine,' Simm said. 'But before you go, just come and have a butcher's below. Un-fucking-believable.'

They descended a badly-rusting metal ladder that looked as if it could give way at any moment. It was dark at the bottom but there was enough light to make out rust-coloured pools of water and the odd faded letter or number stencilled on the walls. Along a corridor Sorrenson could hear voices and see the sweep of powerful torches. He walked towards the lights and found himself in a large room that he guessed had been sleeping quarters. The room was entirely empty except for one thing. From floor to ceiling it was packed with tens of thousands of cigarette cartons.

'There's four other rooms like this,' Simm said. 'The fort could keep half the nation in cancer sticks for months.'

'How many, do you estimate?'

Simm ran a torch up and down the stacks of cartons. 'I dunno. We're talking millions of cigarettes. Beyond that, hard to say at the moment. And that's before we get to the other forts. Good chance we'll find more.'

'All the same make?' Simm grunted. 'Mostly Double Jeopardy, the luxury product from Smith and Webb. Some others. But all Smith and Webb.'

'Double Jeopardy,' Sorrenson said. 'That was the brand used to turn Carrington into a giant ashtray, right?'

'Yeah. So I guess the rumours were true, then. Our man Gaunt was a smuggler. Pretty successful one, too.'

'I'm not sure you'd call this smuggling,' Sorrenson said. 'More like thieving on a fairly massive scale. I take it these are genuine?'

'The coding seems to check out,' Simm said. 'Looks like they're legit.'

'So if they're not counterfeit they're stolen. Or, to put it another way, they've been diverted. But how could you divert this much product without anyone noticing? Must have been done by someone in the company. Gaunt had help. Someone on the inside. Round up Gaunt's dredger pals. We know a few people had it in for him. Now his operation's been closed down maybe they'll be more likely to talk.'

'Right,' Simm said. 'Guess it's going to be a busy day at the office for your partner when she recovers.'

Sorrenson stared at Simm. 'Recovers?'

'You just said she was ill. When she finds out Gaunt wasn't interested in the Maunsell Forts because he was a history buff but because he was using it to siphon off tons of her company's product, she's going to have to start a whole new investigation.'

For a second or so Sorrenson struggled to understand what Simm was saying. He glanced down at his watch. 'Right, my partner,' he said. 'I've got to go, see how she is.' He took a final look at the towers of cartons, skyscrapers of addiction, a city of cigarettes. The image was surreal. Sorrenson's smoking days were long behind him. He couldn't understand what he'd seen in it. It had been a ritual as much as anything. The snap of the cellophane as you broke open a new pack; the sweet smell of tobacco that immediately hit you when you popped the lid; the tearing of the silver foil to liberate the cigarettes. If only you didn't have to smoke the things, Sorrenson thought, cigarettes would be pretty attractive. Addictive, even. He went back along the corridor, towards the rusting metal ladder. He felt as if he was walking among ghosts, making the same short journey that others had made in a different time, when everything was at stake, when everything was to lose, when people knew, truly knew, who their enemies were, what terror really was.

He was about to climb the steps, head back into the comfort of the warm afternoon sun, when something stopped him. He gripped a rail running along the corridor, felt the coolness of rust-corroded metal on skin. Something wasn't right. Something didn't make sense. Something was missing. Something very obvious was missing. Sorrenson turned round and walked back towards the sleeping quarters. The thing about rituals, he realized, was that you never really forgot them.

Chapter 14

'Apologies for turning up unannounced. I was over here on other things and thought I'd just look in again, say hi.'

Webster wondered how long he'd have to make small-talk before the head of the CIA divulged the real purpose of his visit.

'Other things, Brandon?' Webster said. 'Coffee?'

Scott hesitated. Five's coffee was appalling. He wasn't even sure it was coffee, truth be told. Still, never start a conversation on a negative. He'd read that in some management guru's book. 'Thanks,' he muttered.

Webster buzzed his intercom and ordered two coffees. He looked back at Scott. 'You answered only one of my questions.'

'I know.'

'So?'

'So,' Scott said. 'Do you want to have this conversation, Paul? Do you really want to know about the other things?'

'Sounds like it might be important.'

Scott shook his head. 'I'm cleaning something up. A mess not of my own making, I assure you.'

'Something here?'

'That's right. Something here.'

'I see,' Webster said. 'Then do we need this conversation recorded? Will we benefit from having a transcript of it in years to come, when people are asking awkward questions about whatever it is you've been cleaning up over here?'

Scott rocked back and forth in his chair. Webster knew a distressed man when he saw one. It was like looking in a mirror.

Scott sighed. 'Look, Paul, I'm new and I'm trying to sort some things out. Don't get all official on me now. Please. No transcripts. Don't want some senator on the intel committee grabbing himself some more bullets to use on me. They've got plenty of those. That's why I'm over here cleaning things up.'

'Yes, I heard about your appearance before the committee. News filters across the Atlantic eventually.'

'Crazy how a confidential briefing is suddenly known to everyone. It was a fucking drive-by shooting. Those senators were just out to score cheap points by asking obscure questions that, of course, I wasn't going to be able to answer. Do they really think I have the time to drill down into that sort of detail? How granular do they expect me to get? If they want to know about the flight paths of certain planes leased by companies used by the Agency then they should request the logs themselves. Stop asking me about it and let me get on with the job. They're not interested in national security, those people. They just like the feeling that comes from working the Agency over, giving it a good shakedown. Makes 'em feel powerful. Hey, I read your man Hobbes, by the way. Helped me crystallize my thinking on all of this. Considered sending a copy of his book to those jokers on the intel committee. If they read it, they might understand they've got obligations, too.'

'I would imagine they're busy people,' Webster said. 'As much as I'm sure that they'd benefit from reading seven hundred pages of seventeenth-century political philosophy, I rather feel you'd be wasting your time.'

There was a knock at the door. The CIA chief watched as Webster's secretary brought in the coffee. 'She been with you long?' he asked, after she'd gone.

'Decades,' Webster said.

'That's impressive. My lot, well, they're gone in a couple of shakes. It's like, boom, they're out of here. The Agency's so vast they keep pinballing from job to job. God knows where half my staff end up. The private sector mainly, making a stack of cash.'

'Staff retention is something of an issue for us, too,' Webster murmured. 'But I rather think we're getting away from the subject.' He looked at Scott expectantly.

'OK, OK, I hear you. But I'm not sure you knowing any of this really helps you. And, please, no transcripts. Not for this one. So, we've recently ghosted someone through the UK. Through Brize Norton. It's a military airport so, obviously, no one's going to be able to trace the plane, unlike some of the other airports we've used in the past. Normally we just use it to bring in the ambassador or embassy staff. It's all legal. Only this one time, just one time a few weeks ago, we brought in an asset and it would be kind of awkward if that information got out and then you expressed some sort of . . . surprise at what had gone down. I'm trying to be as straight as I can with you on this. New era of transparency and all that. I stress that he was an intelligence asset, not a detainee. And the plane's operated by a front company working out of Kentucky so the Agency's got no fingerprints on this but, still, we can't take any chances – we can't risk souring our relationship with our most trusted ally. If people thought we were still operating rendition flights, there aren't enough guns in the world to defend the Agency from the assault that would follow.'

Webster shook his head. 'I still don't fancy your chances of keeping it concealed. Someone will make the connection somehow, some time. You know, these days, for a couple of dollars, you can buy an app that allows you to track planes. Even if you can't identify one you can still see where it's been flying. Builds up a pattern. People follow the routes from obscure airport to obscure airport and work things out.'

'Well, exactly. As soon as I saw the flight manifest I knew I had to inform you. But Paul, like I said, this was just a one-off. It would be devastating for the Agency if one recent mistake were to result in it being flamed.'

'Why now?' Webster asked. 'Why bring this guy across now?'

Irritation flashed across Scott's face. 'Uh, well, a thousand reasons, but mainly because he was sucking up a lot of recruits across north Africa for Al-Boktorah, so my people tell me. Some day those guys will pitch up at our door. Your door, maybe. Better to act now.'

Webster sipped his coffee, looked at the painting of the fisherman on his wall. 'Quite a catch. Must have taken some doing, landing that target.'

Scott nodded. 'Been working on it for months, my people say.'

The reference to 'my people' wasn't lost on Webster. 'And you knew about the operation?' he said. 'Or have you just been briefed by your people?'

Scott hesitated.

Webster allowed the silence to fester. 'I see,' he said. 'Maybe this is one of the problems of running a fluid organization whose staff are always moving around. Makes things difficult to track. I'm sure the management consultants would have a view on this.'

'Well,' Scott said, 'our hand was forced, my people tell me. Like I said, we had to move fast if we were going to bring him in.'

A siren raced down the Embankment, screaming into Webster's office. 'Five storeys up and bombproof glass for the windows and still that noise gets in,' Webster observed. 'Sometimes we forget we're as much a part of the outside world as everyone else. There are rules that have to be obeyed. Otherwise, it's chaos. Hobbes would understand.'

'I can cope with chaos,' Scott said. 'Chaos, I'd settle for. We've got skin in the game if there's noise. It's the silence I don't like. Once you've heard the silence after a bomb blast you never forget it.'

Webster eased back in his wheelchair to afford himself a better view of his opposite number, of a man scrambling to work out his relationship with the organization that he ran. The CIA had spent three hundred thousand man hours ensuring its operatives weren't breaking the law when it came to rendering terrorist suspects around the world so that they could be interrogated at black sites. Or, to put it another way, the CIA had spent three hundred thousand man hours ensuring its operatives could do things that wouldn't end with them being embarrassed in an international court of law. As a result, some people within the Agency had clearly come to believe that it was accountable to no one. There was no oversight, no comeback on its actions. It had created the law. Therefore only it could pass judgement on itself. The

Agency was a giant drone hovering above the world, ready to dispense its own version of immediate justice at the push of a button. It deflected ugly questions as if it was King Kong swatting away biplanes circling the Empire State Building. And if people wanted to disagree, there were plenty of accommodating countries that could take them. North Korea, Somalia, Afghanistan. They could take their pick. People had to understand that the reason they were free was because an agency like the CIA was prepared to go to extreme lengths to protect them.

'And where is your detainee now?' Webster asked. 'I rather hope he isn't on British soil still. It's one thing to transport a detainee through the country, another to hold him here. That could complicate things.'

Scott scratched his cheek with a heavily bitten nail. He looked at the older man in the wheelchair and wondered why it was that he didn't feel superior to him any more. The man couldn't stand, for Christ's sake. And yet Scott felt deeply uneasy. They thought they were so superior, the Brits. But they didn't have even a twentieth of the problems that the CIA was facing. They didn't have the Hydra-headed monster that was Washington breathing down their necks, the huge political apparatus, the lobbyists, the energy companies, the military industrial complex, all demanding results, all with vested interests, most of them conflicting. No wonder some days he felt he couldn't breathe. The monster had him in a bear hug from which there was no escape. Gradually the air was being squeezed from his lungs until soon there would be none left. Running the world's most powerful intelligence organization was a job he'd believed he'd been destined for. But he wasn't running the CIA, Scott had started to realize. It was running him. He contemplated his untouched coffee. 'Well,' he said quietly, conscious that the monster's huge arms were now threatening to crush his ribcage, cause bone to shatter vital organs, 'things have changed a bit. The game has changed a bit.'

Webster said nothing, counted to five, then looked up at the ex-Marine in front of him. He saw a man who was still a soldier, a man who feared enemies everywhere. 'I wouldn't call it a game,' Webster said.

Simm walked through the crowded café, ordered something at the counter, then sat down at Sorrenson's usual table. He was wearing a soaking black mac that smelt of summer rain. 'Cats and dogs out there. Can hardly see the sea today. Not a lot of fun for those on holiday down here. Good news for cafés, though. No one wants to be outside when it's like this.'

Sorrenson smiled. 'I like it when it's like this. Cleansing.'

'Tell that to the grockles out there. They haven't come to the Marbella of Kent for the rain.' Simm opened a brown leather satchel and produced a sheaf of papers.

'Station still a mess?' Sorrenson asked.

Simm laughed. 'It's going to be months before it's all finished. I don't think we'll ever get rid of the dust.' He examined his fingernails. 'It seems to get everywhere.' He handed Sorrenson the papers. 'Accounts. Billy Davey's oyster hatchery.'

Sorrenson ran his eye up and down the figures. 'So . . .'

'So, then, not a healthy company. Been losing money for years. But you can see in the last couple it started losing a lot more. Rustling.'

'What?'

'It was a victim of oyster rustling. Rivals were taking its oysters off the beds out at sea. No insurance so Davey was forced to take the hit every time.'

Sorrenson shook his head. 'Oyster rustling. Christ, didn't know there was such a thing! It must be pretty rare if you can't get insurance for it.'

'It must have been a pretty lucrative crime. Think about it. Zero traceability on product. You can't barcode an oyster.'

Sorrenson stirred his third coffee of the morning. 'No.'

'Just saying, that's all.'

Sorrenson took a sip. 'The thing I don't get is how you would know where they were.'

'What? The beds?'

'Right. Presumably, that's a guarded secret. One of these wild oysters costs, what, three or four pounds in a London restaurant? You've got hundreds of thousands in beds out under the waves, you're going to want to keep that information protected. Once it leaks out, people can find them. Then you're in trouble.'

'Yeah, that makes sense. They'd won awards, the oysters. Half of them around here are imported from Ireland and the West Country and hardly see the Channel. But these ones, Natives they're called, they spend years down there. Get them nice and fattened up. Premium product, apparently. They have their own sort of brand, like Dom Pérignon Champagne or something. One of the old boys down the harbour was telling me some Russian ambassador once sent some back to the Kremlin on a submarine because they tasted that good.'

'So someone knew their real value and where to look,' Sorrenson said.

'Gaunt?'

'My money would be on him. He owned, what, a third of the business? If he steals from it, he's just making sure he's maximizing his return.'

Simm nodded. 'Local dredgermen say Davey was offered a good sum for the business a few months back. Scottish shellfish firm looking to diversify. But Gaunt wouldn't let him sell. Hardly surprising if it gave him cover for his other interests and he was stealing all the oysters anyway.'

'Could just be dredger talk.'

'Yeah, could be.' Simm took a napkin from the chrome dispenser and tore it slowly into strips. 'But seems there's a clear motive. It's something to go on. He's hardly upset at Gaunt's passing.'

'I'm sure some of Kent's finest criminal underworld would have been happy to oblige him for the right price,' Sorrenson said. He finished his coffee. 'Either way, seems Gaunt was quite the entrepreneur. He knew where the money was to be made. Premium products. Oysters, luxury-brand cigarettes. He aimed high. Must have had a pretty good distribution network to sell it all on.'

Simm's breakfast arrived. He stabbed a fried egg with a burned sausage. 'Seems to me that the coast hasn't changed so much. Still one big smuggling strip. You got good access to the sea, anything's possible.'

Sorrenson looked past Simm and out through the café window. The sun was taking back the sky after the storm. Mothers were once again pushing buggies outside. Half an hour more, and the storm's legacy would have disappeared, save for a coolness in the air. Yes, Sorrenson thought, storms were good. Violence could be cleansing. It washed things away, allowed for a new start. 'Get Davey,' he said. 'Bring him in. And try to find an interrogation room that's not covered with dust.'

'Right,' Simm mumbled, though a mouthful of food. He swept baked beans across his plate with a knife. 'Williamson asked me to give you this.' He handed Sorrenson a packet of cigarettes.

'Double Jeopardy. From the forts?'

Simm nodded and attacked a slice of fried bread. Sorrenson found himself fearing for the younger man's cholesterol levels.

'Williamson ran the checks like you asked.'

'And?'

'And you're right. There is something different about them. And it's not just that the packets aren't wrapped in cellophane.'

'So?'

Simm speared a mushroom with his fork and introduced it to a piece of bacon. He waved it at Sorrenson. 'Talk to Williamson. He tried to explain it to me but I couldn't follow what he was saying. Something out of science fiction. Went right over my head.'

The hooded man prodded the sleeper with the muzzle of his assault rifle. His victim squirmed, then let out a cry.

'Sorry, Chewy. Feel bad about waking you. But I just thought you'd want to know your pal Yoda's gone viral, man. He's got like more than a million clicks on YouTube. That is huge.'

The man started crying and rolled his body away so that his back was to his captors. Tears dripped onto dust.

147

'Some people,' the hooded man muttered. 'They never thankful. His homie becomes a celeb and he just lies there and cries.' Again, he prodded the man with his gun. 'Million clicks, man. He's going to live for ever now. People digging deep to save you guys. You should be grateful, man, grateful it was his head we blew off his body, not yours. You hear what I saying?'

Chapter 15

Matthews stalked past the headstones, numbed by the hushed solemnity of the place. It was something to do with the numbers, of course. So many demanded total silence. Tens of thousands of pristine graves in tragic perfect row upon tragic perfect row. There was a pitiful symmetry to it, he thought. Everything in the cemetery was orderly, dignified and profoundly humbling. The grass around the stones had been reverentially trimmed and was a moss-free, verdant carpet. The tall trees forming a protective enclave around the graves were majestic and alien, imported from the fallen's homeland. Only the occasional, almost imperceptible movement of a bird high up on a branch spoke of movement, of life continuing.

So many had given their lives taking back northern France, Matthews thought, and the unpalatable but irrefutable truth was that it had all been worth it, the mass, industrialized slaughter. The American servicemen, the Rangers, the Engineers, the Marines, all of those buried in the cemetery had paid the ultimate price on D-Day. But their country had reaped the benefits while it had taken decades for the wounds of an eviscerated Europe to heal.

The Second World War had turned the US into the only credible superpower. People often forgot the good that could come from war, Matthews thought. They focused only on the body count. They didn't see how conflict made things possible. That was civilians for you. Far too myopic, far too squeamish. They needed to brush up on their history, understand the necessary violence that had forged the Empire and allowed Britain to win two world wars. Then maybe they wouldn't be so judgemental. They would see opportunities. He thought of his lover. Fawcett understood that. It was one of the many beliefs they shared. An understanding that only wealth made things possible.

The former MI6 officer watched the man in the thin beige raincoat and reflective sunglasses walking towards him. Typical American spook, he thought. It was like they always had to wear a uniform.

'Thanks for coming,' the man grunted. 'Appreciate you making the effort.'

'I've been summoned to some strange meeting places in my time but this must be in the top ten.'

The man had the mandatory crewcut of all CIA spooks working in the field, Matthews thought. Brown bristles turning grey. They must breed them somewhere.

'Yeah, not my choice,' the man said. 'Apologies for the inconvenience but I was in Paris so the ISG sent me up here. Thought it was a good place to talk. Quiet. Discreet. You're on American soil now, Mr Matthews. Please don't forget that.' The man gestured around him. 'This, all of this, is US of A. You're not in France, you're not in Europe now. No matter what the maps say. You understand?'

Matthews understood how things worked. You could take liberties in unobserved places. MI6 had found it was much easier to interrogate suspects if they did it in locations that obeyed few local or national laws. Such places were the spooks' equivalent of tax havens. Necessary, unobservable, untraceable. Spying, like business, worked best in the shadows: out-of-sight, undetectable, unrestricted. But, still, the American's hectoring tone was annoying. Matthews forced himself to remember what was at stake. A major pay day. They were so close now. He wasn't going to do anything that would jeopardize that. Well, nothing the Americans would find out about anyway. His limited intelligence-sharing with his rather more exotic client would remain buried. It was a free market. Information flowed to those prepared to pay. The Americans would be naive if they thought he worked just for them. His job for them was simple: ensure Raptor ran smoothly. Iron out the kinks along the way. Anything else, well, that was a bonus.

The spook gestured ahead of him. 'Shall we?'

They started walking through the stones, white as baby teeth, and came to a glade with a polished wooden bench. A thin drizzle was descending. Matthews envied the other man his raincoat. They sat down and watched a snake of largely elderly German tourists file silently past the graves, heads bowed slightly, a pilgrimage of quiet apology. Thin men with neatly clipped beards, large women with short hair in slacks and sandals. A few gangly teenagers, giants compared to the adults, the stunted people who'd grown up on war rations.

'And still they come,' Matthews murmured.

'People don't get tired of coming here,' the other man said. He had a deep Midwest accent that seemed vaguely familiar to Matthews. 'People from all nations. They want to pay tribute. Still. They want to learn.'

'Learn what?' Matthews found himself asking. He hadn't meant to form the question. It had just slipped out. It didn't pay to play the interrogator.

'Learn how we kicked ass, of course,' the man said. 'Learn how the Land of the Free saved your beaten-up old Europe. The usual narrative. The one we, the victors, wrote.'

Matthews presumed he was being ironic but it was difficult to tell. Behind his shades the man's face was inscrutable.

'Yes, people who come here, they want to learn how this all happened,' the man continued, pointing at the stones. 'Brings it home to you when you see all these names, all these dead. Makes you realize we've got to keep honouring their memory and stay vigilant. Defend the same freedoms they fought for. Makes you understand the sacrifices that have to be made. The difficult decisions that have to be taken.'

'Sacrifices?'

The man turned to Matthews. 'Yeah. The necessary sacrifices. Sometimes certain things need to get . . . overlooked, if you get me. If things are going to get done, I mean.'

'I take it you're referring to . . .'

'Yeah. Those things. They're things, not people, the ones that your two little friends took care of. The world's a better place without them.'

'I agree,' Matthews said. The drizzle started to ease off. He felt clammy, uncomfortable. He ran a finger under his collar. He was sure it was almost cutting off the oxygen to his brain. 'Has it been worth it?' he asked. 'What we've done, has it . . . bought you cover? It's quite a body count.'

'You know I'm not going to answer that. But Raptor's still on track, if that's what you mean. Float's still going to happen in the timetable agreed. Roscoe sends his regards by

152

the way.' The man turned to Matthews and removed his sunglasses. 'So, here we are again.'

'Again?' Matthews struggled, but then he got there. Kenya. Of course. They'd met in Kenya when they'd been interviewing suspected jihadis trying to get into Somalia. The CIA and MI6 had kept the suspects in old shipping containers without light or fresh air. Every so often they'd drag one out and interview him in the suite of a local hotel after he'd been brutalized by the Kenyan intelligence service. The switch from being held in a fetid, dark prison, forty men in each container, standing room only, to a plush, luxurious room where they were offered fruit and iced water had been one of the agencies' better tricks. People who were expecting to be broken by brutal interrogation snapped just as quickly when they were disarmed by being well treated. They'd turned a few of the recruits that way. Not enough, but some. The operation had been quite a success until some of those they'd tried to recruit had returned to their own countries with tales of mistreatment and betrayal by their own intelligence services. They were fighting on behalf of an Islamic state against an aggressor, they said. They had no desire to turn Britain into a caliphate. Why were they being treated like terrorists? There'd been a modicum of outrage from human-rights groups and the whole operation had been wound up or, rather, handed back to the Kenyans to deal with on their own terms.

'I take it you remember me?' the man said.

'Douglas,' Matthews said, nodding. 'Agent Douglas. Well, it really is a small world.'

'Too small,' Douglas said. 'We could all use a bit more space, I reckon. It's getting too easy for everything, everyone to join up. That lot flowing in and out of Somalia being a case in point. They were ending up all over the place. Could do with stretching things out more, if you ask me. Creating a bit more distance between things, people, places, ideologies.'

'Well, that's the modern world for you,' Matthews responded. 'We're all connected now.'

Douglas flipped open a cigarette case that doubled as an ashtray. He offered the case to Matthews.

'Thanks,' Matthews said, reaching inside his jacket for his lighter. 'Double Jeopardy. My brand.'

'You and half the world. That's why it's Al-Boktorah's favourite currency.' Douglas inspected the ex-British agent next to him, his face reddened by gin, his ludicrous linen suit. The man was a walking anachronism. His wardrobe belonged to a different era. His face, too. That was the problem with the British, Douglas thought. They would never learn to let go of their empire.

'I guess you'll be glad when he's gone,' Matthews said.

'Yeah,' Douglas said quietly. 'I guess. The CIA doesn't want people knowing it created Al-Boktorah. It would be embarrassing if Congress started asking questions the next time the Agency went looking for more funding. Make the Iran-Contra deal look like a lemonade sale. But people don't understand that things were different back then. There was a reason the Agency threw a shitload of greenbacks at him, and that reason was we thought he was someone we could work with. Back then he was a crook, not a terrorist. He was a useful guy to have around. Helped us track arms shipments, drugs, the usual stuff, across the Sahara. He should have been happy with that deal, stayed clear of some ideology dredged up from the Crusades. I hope that's the last thought he has, when a drone takes him and his family out in a giant fireball.'

'It wouldn't be the first time the CIA built up some fanatic only to be betrayed by him,' Matthews said. He really couldn't help himself. 'There are some fairly spectacular precedents . . .'

They sat in silence for several minutes, two men whose best years were long gone, smoking reluctantly, looking out onto the massed ranks of the buried dead. The light drizzle resumed, sticking to their faces like sweat.

'You miss being in the field?' Douglas said.

'Not really, no. After a while one overseas posting blurred into another. This way I get to have more of a personal life.'

'Yeah,' Douglas said. 'I met your partner recently, just after he got back from a trip abroad. Taking care of something for us. Bringing someone back.'

'Right,' Matthews said hurriedly. 'He mentioned something briefly.' Matthews really didn't like people knowing anything about his personal life.

The quiet of the cemetery was smothering. The war tourists had gone back to their buses. The cafés of Arromanches would soon be doing a good trade serving *moules et frites* and frosted litre glasses of beer. Matthews wondered what would happen when the crowds stopped coming. It was unlikely that future generations would make the same pilgrimage to see where their great-grandfathers had been slain. They weren't going to be interested in the past. Anything pre-internet was just medieval, distant to the point of irrelevance.

'So, what do you want from me now?' Matthews said. 'You know I've . . . arranged for two more.'

155

'Good,' Douglas responded. 'That's good to hear.' He ran nicotined fingers through his crewcut. 'But I'm still worried.'

'About?'

'About someone working things out.'

Douglas's words drifted in the dank air. He ground out his cigarette, examined the butt between his finger and thumb. 'Can't risk anything leaking now. We're nearly there. Think about it: the world's first completely scalable track-and-trace network, one that allows you to monitor the movement of product right across the globe without anyone knowing you're doing it. Its potential is off the scale. No wonder it's protected by something like a million patents. Analysts reckon it will be valued at something north of seventy-five billion dollars when it IPOs.' He gazed out across the graves to the tall trees beyond. He nodded three times. 'So we need to be sure of ourselves. The whole Raptor operation could be compromised if people start crawling over things. We're just not sure who we can trust any more, you know? We need to close some things down. There are threats to Raptor everywhere. Places where we never imagined finding them. I mean, for instance, how do you think we'd react if we discovered that one of our chief assets, someone we've had on our payroll for some time, was working for another organization on the side?'

Matthews felt his collar tighten around his neck. He was struggling for words. 'Well, you'd need to be pretty sure you had the evidence to back up your suspicions,' he said feebly. 'Then perhaps . . .' He really should have brought a raincoat, he thought. The drizzle was penetrating his shirt now. He was soaked.

His head jerked back as his spine smashed against the bench. He looked down at his chest and saw crimson staining white linen. Funny, he hadn't even heard the gun being fired. The rows of white gravestones seemed to meld into one brilliant light. Matthews slumped forward with a little groan, an unlit cigarette between his fingers. A perfect bubble of blood had formed on his lips.

Douglas examined his companion, now as still and quiet as the cemetery around him. He nodded again, into the distance, at the unseen assassin. 'You can't try to play us off against others,' he said. 'You've got to pick a side. Us or the Chinese. Otherwise you get too conflicted. And then you end up dead.' He pulled out his mobile and looked over towards the trees. 'Nice shot,' he muttered into the mouthpiece. 'Now come and help me dispose of him.'

Chapter 16

Billy Davey leaned back in his plastic chair and looked at the two detectives in front of him. The sounds of banging and whirring metal blades cutting through brick came from outside the interrogation room.

Simm jabbed a finger at him. 'You should count yourself lucky. Listen to what our colleagues are doing to the other suspects next door.'

Sorrenson frowned at his colleague.

'I apologize,' Simm muttered. 'For the purposes of the tape I'd like to make clear that I was joking to Mr Davey.'

'Apology accepted,' Davey said.

'So, your business is in trouble, then,' Sorrenson said. 'Been losing a lot of money recently.'

Davey shrugged. 'Been a lean few years. I told you that much when I last met you.'

'Rustling,' Simm said.

'Rustling,' Davey agreed. 'Disease too. Herpes virus wiped a lot of my sprat out. Six million oysters gone, just like that.'

'Fuck,' Simm said. 'Really?'

Davey laughed. 'Don't worry, young lad. It's not catching. Bivalves suck up a lot of shit. Catch all sorts. You've got to really look after them. Like a shepherd protecting his flock.'

'Do shepherds carry metal piping?' Simm asked.

'Not the ones I know,' Davey muttered.

'How's your cellar?' Sorrenson asked.

'Cellar?'

'You went on a booze cruise, you told us, the night of Gaunt's murder, remember? You must have brought back a lot of wine.'

'Enough. I get thirsty.'

'What was the best bottle you brought back?' Simm asked.

'Dunno. Maybe a Bordeaux.'

'A Bordeaux,' Simm said mockingly. 'Anything more specific?'

'Look, young lad, I'll keep answering your questions but we both know I've got a perfect alibi. I was on a cross-Channel ferry when Gaunt was done in. You've got my van on CCTV. You can see me in the driving seat.'

'You got receipts for the wine?' Sorrenson said.

'Maybe. Dunno. Tend not to keep shit like that.'

'Which hypermarket did you go to?' Simm said.

Davey looked at the senior detective and then at his junior. 'The main one in Calais, down by the docks.'

'I'm a Côtes du Rhône man myself,' Sorrenson said. 'Too much of that Bordeaux is oaked for my liking.'

'Each to his own,' Davey said.

The sound of saws and hammers became deafening. 'Sorry about this,' Sorrenson shouted. 'It's the cutbacks. We're amalgamating police stations. Got to make more space in here.'

Davey nodded noncommittally.

'Yeah, we're all having to make efficiency savings,' Sorrenson continued. 'Some might call it cutting corners.' He looked hard at Davey. 'I don't cut corners, though.'

'Whatever you say.'

'Doesn't make me popular with my chief constable, but there you go.'

'Right,' Davey grunted.

'One of the things he moans about is the amount I spend on mobile-phone calls.'

'You the talkative kind, then?'

Sorrenson shook his head. 'You misunderstand me. Not making mobile-phone calls, tracking them. We have to pay a small fortune to the mobile networks to trace phone calls, you know. Who was phoning whom. When they were phoning them. Where they were phoning from. Those sort of things.'

Davey swallowed hard, shot a nervous glance at his perma-tanned solicitor sitting next to him. 'OK.'

'Yeah, cutbacks,' Sorrenson said. 'Take our forensics team. Always under pressure. Cut to the bone, forensics. The man in charge, friend of mine, he warned me mistakes will occur, given all the cutbacks. People will stop going the extra mile to get to the bottom of things. Well, turns out he was right. Our forensics lot went through the CCTV footage and, you know what, you're right, Billy. There is irrefutable evidence that you drove a van onto that ferry. Our forensics team stopped being so interested in the tapes after that. Handy for you, though. It's almost like you wanted to be seen getting on that ferry. A cynic might say you chose a location where it was impossible not to be seen. All those cameras monitoring your every move. There's no way they wouldn't capture you.'

'Well,' Davey said, 'think what you like. But don't reckon on getting me for doing Gaunt. I was nowhere near him. We agree on that.'

'True, but, like I said, I don't cut corners. We obtained your phone records. Shortly after the ferry sails we can see that a call is made on your mobile phone.' Sorrenson held up a piece of paper showing Davey's call log.

Davey glanced at his solicitor. She no longer looked bored. The gold bracelet on her right wrist jangled furiously as she scrawled notes. 'I think my phone might have been stolen around that time,' Davey mumbled.

'Sorry to hear that,' Sorrenson said. 'It can be very inconvenient.' He raised an eyebrow at Simm, who fiddled with something under the table.

'Did you get a replacement?' Sorrenson asked.

'What? Replacement phone? Yeah.'

A tinny sounding Beethoven's 'Ode to Joy' vied with the sound of hammers and electric saws.

'I think someone's trying to call you, Billy,' Simm said, putting his own phone on the table.

Davey pulled a phone out of his trouser pocket.

'For the purposes of the tape I'm asking Mr Davey to place his mobile phone on the table,' Sorrenson said. There was a patina of sweat on Davey's forehead. His mouth was doing its best not to become a snarl.

'The phone,' Simm said, pointing at the table. 'Your phone. Put it here, please.'

Davey placed the mobile on the dusty Formica in front of him. The two detectives, Davey and the solicitor stared at the device. Its screen was cracked. A strip of black electrical tape held it together. There was the odd splash of what looked like paint on its keypad. Sorrenson guessed that the phone was older than the millennium.

'I really think you should take that phone back to the

shop,' Simm said. 'You've been ripped off, there. I can't believe they gave you that as a replacement.'

'Chewy, man, good to see you made the cut.' Ten hooded captors trained their assault rifles on the far corner of the cave. There was the sound of someone being sick and of whispered, hurried conversations.

'No talking,' one of the captors shouted. 'You can say your goodbyes in your videos. Don't give 'em to your homies here. They only going to forget you, what you said. They got other things on their minds when you gone. Now you, the chosen ones, you move forward. We're going on a little journey.'

'I'm not coming.' A voice in the dark, close to breaking.

'That you, Chewy? Course you coming. You going to be in the front row. Starring role. You going to be more famous than your homie Yoda.'

There was the sound of more retching and of the Lord's Prayer being recited over and over again.

'You . . . have to shoot me here. I'm not coming.'

The captors started laughing. 'Come on, Chewy. You knew it was going to end like this. If you don't play ball now it'll just be a lot worse. Worse things than a bullet, Chewy, you know that. We could make you end up praying for a bullet.'

'Please . . . I have children. Four children. A wife . . .'

'So have lots of the others, Chewy. You ain't special. Now, come on, we got to roll. We need you outside before it gets too light. Don't want our friends above clocking our position now, right? All that fancy stuff up in the sky. Don't want them getting to play with that kit.'

★   ★   ★

162

The polished scarlet Stag looked out of place in the parched corn, like a bloodstain on a child's summer dress. A tractor toiling in a far-off field was the only sound competing with birdsong. The two men sucked up the near silence. They felt calm, rested and alive. It was as close to a perfect moment as they had known in their recent lives. They'd both been born in poverty-plagued cities in the north-west and even now, when they were in their late twenties and had seen something of the world, the absence of concrete, of noise, of man-made shadows was still a novelty. They'd experienced such places before, when they'd been sent overseas. But they'd been fighting then. They'd become so absorbed in the simple everyday act of not dying that they had ignored the alien landscape threatening to become their grave.

Now, though, they could relax. Appreciate things. After what they'd seen happen to some of their colleagues it was an achievement just to be alive and standing in a field on a late summer's day.

'Nice weather, Stevie,' one said. He was going to add 'for it' but stopped himself. It didn't really need saying.

'Dead right, Robbie.'

'You gave it a clean, I see.' Robbie pointed at the convertible, patted its canvas roof. 'Looks like it's come straight off a forecourt. You'd get some good wedge for this.'

'Carried a photo of it in my pocket when we were fighting Terry. Thought the least I could do was give it a wax.'

The two men lit cigarettes, enjoyed the sun of the September morning on their faces. The sky was a perfect blue. A haze hung above the ground. They watched a seagull circle in the air above them. 'Fat bastard,' Robbie said. 'Long way from the coast. Probably never even seen the sea. Just scavenges from tips.'

'Fat bastard,' Stevie said. 'That's what Atkinson used to call me.'

'He was one fucking tough sergeant,' Robbie said, shaking his head. 'He's going to go crazy now we're not in Afghanistan. He's not going to know what to do with himself with no Terry Taliban to play with. I wouldn't like to be his missus.'

The two men laughed, sucked heavily on their cigarettes. They watched the tractor make its way up and down the field.

'Looks an OK sort of life,' Robbie said. 'Farming, like. I fancied working outdoors when I came out. Applied to be a park ranger up in the Lakes. Didn't get it, mind. Long fucking queue for that sort of work.'

'Yeah, no shortage of ex-squaddies looking for work,' Stevie said. 'I had a job working private security for the big music festivals. That was outdoor. But, well, you know the rest. Lost it one day and . . .'

'Yeah. Difficult to calm down. Stay calm anyway.'

'You're just buzzing all the time, you know? And then, boom, you snap and the next thing you're in a fight with some stranger in a car park and his teeth are on the tarmac and you're being blamed for losing it and then they say they can't trust you to control it and . . .'

'Difficult to stay on top of things. Hold a job down when you're like that.'

'Fucking right,' Stevie said.

'They give you any advice or whatever after you left? You were, what, out a year before me?'

'Had a session with a careers adviser and that was it. Basically, he seemed to think I should sign up for another tour. I said, "Fuck that shit. I seen way too many from my camp go out and never come back. How'd you fancy getting potted fighting in a war you don't understand? How'd you like fighting without the right equipment? Do you even know what night goggles are? You ever even been in a Snatch Land Rover?" I think he understood where I was coming from after that.'

'I got made to watch an hour-long video,' Robbie said. '*How to Spot the Signs of PTSD*, it was called. Something like that, anyway. Fucking joke. It said I had to be careful as I'm someone who's going to take risks with things – I should never go anywhere near a motorbike or a fast car. Way too risky. I'd end up smashed across some dual carriageway. Told me to stay away from drugs and booze, too.' They laughed.

'Horrible way to go,' Stevie said. 'Dying in a car.'

They laughed again.

'There are worse ways to go,' Robbie said. 'You remember Davis?'

'Poor fucker,' Stevie said, pulling on his cigarette. 'Took fucking ages to die. I was thinking of slotting him myself, just to take his pain away, just to make him stop fucking screaming. Sitting there without his legs like that. Blood everywhere. Terry taking pot shots as we scrambled around in the dust trying to find cover. You could hear him on the radio after the IED went off, laughing his fucking head off.'

'You remember Mantel?' Robbie broke open a couple of beers, handed one to Stevie.

'Mental? Course. Hanged himself, didn't he, after he got back? From a tree in that forest near the barracks?'

'Yeah. Told me he never got over Davis. Couldn't see where the justice was. How come he survived and poor old Davis didn't? He was really fucked up by it. But, then, I reckon he was fucked up by it all even before he got there. He was one of them sorts. Looking for an excuse for a fight.'

'Well, guess we all feel like that a bit,' Stevie said, slurping his Grolsch. He enjoyed the buzz that came with the early-morning taste of lager. 'I mean, we wouldn't have, well, you know, started doing all this shit if we hadn't wanted to pick a fight with someone.'

'Yeah. But the difference between us and Mental is that we had a plan. Targets. I mean, there's not many worse than Terry but it's a war they started. Like our man said, they're the enemy. We took care of them because no one else had the bollocks. No fucker's going to cry over those dead bastards, that's for sure. I'd do it even if we weren't being paid to slot 'em. You saw the shit they had on their computers. Off the chain horrible.'

'How much we got left?' Stevie said.

'Around fifty, I reckon.'

'And, what, another thirty for the last two on the list?'

'That's what our man said,' Robbie said, patting the Stag and laughing. 'One we've just taken care of. Just leaves this fresh one to go and then we've done the five, as agreed. Our man's normally left us a message in the drop box by now. But I looked this morning on the computer and there's nothing. He's been a bit quiet in the last few days. Maybe he's gone abroad or something.'

'Maybe. You think we're ever going to work out what his angle is?'

Robbie shook his head. 'Posh Fuck? Fucking doubt it. I don't really care, to be honest. You remember the millions of emails, back and forth, back and forth, before we met up again after Kenya? All those questions he was asking after he found us on the PTSD forums? All those questions he kept asking about how he we felt about things? Took him fucking ages to get to the point. And then he'd only do it in person in the middle of some fucking wood in the dead of night. He's one careful cunt. Making sure his fingerprints are nowhere near any of this. But who fucking cares? He pays well and, like he told us, we're doing the nation a service. He's still clearly got spook links. How else would he have got all that shit on the ones we've done? Must have some clever people working for him, finding that shit. It's not like they just keep it in an easy-to-read folder on their computer. I reckon he's still with Six. He looks the fucking type with his stupid fucking white suits. What's that stuff called? The stuff his suits are made of?'

'Linnet?'

'Linnet. No, linen. Yeah, linen. Yeah, I reckon Linen's still with Six. Taking care of some stuff Six can't do.'

'Maybe,' Stevie said. 'Still don't get his angle. Not exactly a threat to national security, those types, even if they are a waste of a bullet. PM's not going to be out of a job if some kids in the Philippines or somewhere end up being raped on video cameras.'

'Yeah, but like Linen said, most of the gangs making those videos are trading the cash they make for drugs and guns. Not difficult to see them linking up with terrorists. Fucking lucrative, too. One big smuggling racket, kiddy-porn. People get addicted to that shit.'

Stevie blew smoke through his nostrils. He looked at the tractor again, admired its slow progress. Yeah, he thought, a farmer. That was what he should have been. That would have been a nice life. He took another swig from his can and turned it upside down.

'Do you think they'll find us in the end?' Robbie said.

'Hard to say. Not sure Plod will be too interested in hunting down paedo killers.'

'If they work out that's what they are.'

'Fucking should do,' Stevie said. 'Left enough clues. Pretty fucking gruesome deaths. Even Plod's got to see they're connected. I hope Plod works out the shoe thing.'

'Well, like I said when we started, doubt he's been to the Middle East.'

'Still, he's not that thick. He'll understand what an insult it is to steal a man's shoes over there. He could fucking Google it.'

'The things you learn in the army, hey?'

'Right,' Stevie agreed. 'Plod'll see the pattern. He'll get the message. He'll understand these are not good men.'

'Or women.'

'Or woman,' Robbie said, jerking a thumb towards the car's boot. 'Can't get my head around what a woman's doing mixed up in all this. In her fifties, too. I guess some of them are as sick as men. Maybe she was just selling it. Maybe that's how she made a living.'

'Or maybe she was just fucking sick. You can get women kiddy-fiddlers, you know. I reckon our friend in the boot here is one of them. She looks the sort.'

'Maybe.'

The two former soldiers were laughing again. The drink and the sun were getting to them. It had the makings of a good day, the sort of day that could go on for ever.

'Shame we have to stop at five, really,' Robbie said. 'We're doing a good job, taking out all this trash. There are thousands of others, probably, but we have no way of finding them without Linen's intel. They operate in their own separate cells, these people.'

'Like terrorists.'

'Bang on. Like terrorists. Not a lot of difference between them, when you think about it. Maybe kiddy-fiddlers are just a bit worse in most people's eyes. At least terrorists get themselves killed every now and then. Got a bit more respect for them, like.'

Robbie collected the empty beer cans and cigarette packets and put them into a plastic bag. They opened the car doors and climbed in. Robbie turned on the ignition and the Stag grumbled into life. 'Thought this might be appropriate,' he said. He slid a disc into the CD player. There was the sound of a jangling guitar.

'Funny,' Stevie said when he heard the opening bars of 'Stairway to Heaven'. 'Very funny.'

Chapter 17

Marijuana smoke drifted across shingle. A white man, shirt-less, with dreadlocks and a paunch spilling over faded denim shorts, was playing a cover of Bob Marley's 'Redemption Song' on a beaten-up guitar. There was the smell of meat cooking on disposable barbecues and the sound of children laughing.

Sorrenson walked up to the makeshift bar fashioned from a battered groyne and bought two beers. He returned to Kate, handed her a bottle, clinked his against hers. Along the shingled shoreline scores of tiny fires were framed by heaps of oyster shells.

'The lighting of the grotters,' Sorrenson said. 'They do it every year. Locals, I mean. In the past, the early Victorian era, I guess, dredgermen believed that if they lit a grotter before they took to sea they'd be protected. It was either that or pray to St James, patron saint of fishermen. And the dredgers weren't exactly a God-fearing mob.'

She was amused by the awkward way he was looking at her. It was clear he loved the ritual being observed on the beach. Clear, too, that he feared it wasn't something that she, who lived in one of London's most exclusive postcodes, would enjoy. She felt the need to reassure him. She pointed across the beach. 'Dredgermen would have needed all the help they could get. Have you seen the photos of the dredging crews on the pub walls around here? It's all scowls in sepia. A hard life. Not much easier now, I guess.'

'That's why some of them are choosing to diversify. The murder victim I was telling you about, Gaunt, the one running his illegal export business, he was a dredgerman of sorts. Maybe he should have lit himself a grotter or two before stealing your employer's product on a truly epic scale.'

She turned her gaze towards the sea. In the middle distance she could see the frames of the oyster beds poking out from the estuary mud, like giant millipedes. Beyond them, the water shimmered in the late-evening sun. 'I don't think a grotter would have saved him,' she said. 'From what you told me, a lot of people had it in for him.'

'His business partner's confessed to arranging the contract. Hired two lads from Kent, and they really were lads, just twenty and twenty-two, very well known to police. Guess how much he paid them?'

'The killers? Ten thousand?'

'Four.'

'Christ, deflation hits the world of contract killing just like everything else! You know we're going through lean times when that starts to happen.'

'Yes,' Sorrenson said. 'They're not exactly big-time, our killers. Unlike elsewhere. You've seen the news today, I take it?'

'Can't escape it. How many confirmed dead?'

'Twenty-five. Bodies all dumped in the desert. Mainly Americans from what they were saying on the news. All shot in the back of the head. That's something. I mean, at least it

would have been quick. The other way, well, Jesus, that's—'
He broke off, studied her face. 'Something wrong?'

She wanted to confide in him. But what could she say?
She wasn't even sure where to begin. She couldn't say anything about her work for Five. She pulled her knees up
under her chin and folded her hands across her shins. 'It's all
a bit tricky at the moment, that's all. There are things going
on that, well . . .'

'People pointing the finger at Smith and Webb, asking
how its cigarettes are ending up in the hands of the world's
most wanted man?'

She was grateful for the interruption. She hadn't been
sure how she was going to finish the sentence. 'Something
like that.'

'Your employer probably could shine some light on that,
I reckon.'

'How do you mean?'

'Well, you know I told you that none of the cigarette
packets out on the forts was wrapped in cellophane? Tens of
thousands of packets. Yet not one of them was wrapped.
Strange.'

'Yes, I guess.'

'I couldn't figure out what was going on. I mean, presumably they'd been diverted after they'd left the plant just
down from the coast here.'

'Agreed.'

'So somebody somewhere removed the cellophane. Why
do that? I was stumped until we took a pack apart. Had to
bring in a specialist forensics team to examine it. The sort
of people the Yard would normally use for counter-terror
stuff. Proper scientists. Chief wasn't happy about the expense
but there you go. They found it, though. But even they

struggled to work out what it was at first. Like something beamed down from the future.'

She was no longer sitting hunched up. Her legs were splayed out in front of her, as if she was ready to jump to her feet. 'So what did they find?'

'Well, it was tiny, and I mean really tiny. It was smaller than a grain of rice, a radio tag.'

She tried his words on for size, stress-testing them to see if they made sense. 'Radio tag,' she said slowly. 'Smaller than a grain of rice.' No, the words were alien, bordering on the nonsensical.

'Right. We did the same test on ten more packs. All had the tag inside them. RFIDs, they're called. Radio frequency identification tags. They're the coming thing, so the internet tells me. Huge potential. You can use them to track and trace anything anywhere. Big tech companies in Silicon Valley are throwing loads of money at RFIDs. Looks like your employer was testing some sort of prototype.' Sorrenson looked at Kate closely, studying her for a reaction.

She was confused. Which employer was he talking about? Either was plausible, yet Sorrenson might as well have been speaking Mandarin for all it meant to her.

'I'd guess from your reaction that—'

'That it's news to me. Yes.'

He heard the anger in her voice. It was buried deep but it was there. 'And would you have expected to know about it?'

She scooped up a handful of shingle, dropped it back onto the beach. She didn't have an answer. The more she was finding out about Smith and Webb, the more she doubted whether anyone in the company knew entirely what it was doing. It was Byzantine in structure. It was a corporation out of control. Relentless, greedy, all-consuming, omnipotent. Few blue-chip companies had its pedigree, its provenance, its history. It was a child born half a millennium ago that had never stopped growing. It was, in short, the British Empire's prodigal son. And now it was about to be adopted by the Chinese. Peel that onion, she thought. You won't find its core. Not then. Not now. Not ever. She stared out at the darkening sky, then counted the flashing buoys at sea. Five green, four red. Go trumps stop every time.

'We're not getting much help from your new owners when it comes to investigating the Carrington murder,' Sorrenson said. 'We've asked to see all his computer files but they're not exactly overwhelming us with their response. We've got his laptop, though. We're still interrogating it.'

'Not a big surprise. The deal hasn't been completed yet. These things take time to work through. Months if not years.'

They didn't speak for several minutes, watched the sky turn from purple to black, stars scatter over an inky, wave-less sea. He looked down at her hands, at the sticking plaster wrapped around one finger. It had been there for several weeks now. 'Difficult all this, isn't it?' he said quietly.

She nodded. 'There's stuff I want to say but I can't. It's horrible. There's this tension. There's you and your job and my job and . . .'

'And?' He wasn't going to let her trail off like that. She needed to finish the sentence. She owed him that.

'And I'm not quite sure where I belong, that's all. I'm try-ing to work out where I fit into this. *If* I fit into this.'

'This?'

'All of this.' She swept an arm across the beach and pointed out to sea. 'This.'

'And wearing that, what's that about?' Sorrenson said, indicating her finger.

She shrugged. 'I'm not sure. Actually, scrub that answer. I have no idea why I'm wearing it again. None whatsoever. It just feels right somehow.'

'A security blanket.'

She attempted a laugh. 'Something like that. Bit old for that sort of thing. But I'm beginning to think the day when I said, "I will," was the last time I exercised any form of control. Listen to me. You must think I'm properly, certifiably insane.'

Sorrenson drained his beer. 'No more than the rest of us. It's inevitable that you're going to end up fearing losing control. You spend all your life worrying about threats. You types see them everywhere.'

'Types?'

'Spooks or whatever you call yourselves.'

'Intelligence analysts.' She moved closer to him, reached for his hand, put her head on his shoulder.

He smelt her hair, her skin. If she were to leave him, Sorrenson thought, it would be her smell he would miss most. 'Hey, I nearly forgot,' he said. 'Bought you this. Got it off the net so it might be different from the one you had but I think it'll do the job.' He rummaged in a backpack, handed her a small brown cardboard box. 'You were saying the other day that you often left yours in London. Well, now you've got two so you can keep one down here.'

She took the box and opened it. She couldn't remember the last time someone had bought her something. She felt anxious, as if she was preparing for someone to play a trick on her. She ripped open the flaps, peered inside and felt her anxiety subside. She laughed. 'Thank you. Just what I

175

needed.' She held up the running belt complete with holsters for energy gels, water-bottles, keys.

'I think it comes with a few other things that you can attach,' Sorrenson said. He was clearly embarrassed.

She rummaged inside the box. 'So it does,' she said, laughing again.

'Well, you can't be too careful,' Sorrenson muttered. 'I hope you don't think I'm being over-protective. It just came with the belt, that's all. Don't think it's much use in Kent. Trail-running in the Rockies . . .'

'I don't think that at all. Thank you. You're very thoughtful.'

The sun was leaving the northern hemisphere. Late Bob Marley had been usurped by early Van Morrison. Oyster-catchers were out, using the cloak of dusk to comb the shingle. The tide was dragging the sea begrudgingly towards the horizon. Sorrenson pointed up towards the brightest of the stars. 'Venus,' he said.

'And that one?' She pointed to another.

'Easy. Betelgeuse.'

'That one?'

'Jupiter.'

She pointed to a fourth.

'Polaris. The North Star.'

'Those two?'

'Mizar and Alcor. Known as the Horse and the Rider.'

'How come you know so much astronomy?'

He was glad she wasn't looking directly at him. He didn't want her to see his embarrassment. 'Took up star-gazing when I was on my own. Not a lot of light pollution down here. You get some really dark skies on the coast. It made for an easy hobby, something to do when I got home. Kept me out of the pub. Gave me some useful perspective. Just how small we really are.'

She looked out to sea, at the flashing buoys guiding super-tankers, horizontal shards of light, towards London. The buoys seemed to be multiplying in the gathering darkness. Eight red versus five green, she counted. Stop, stop, stop, they said. Stay, stay, stay. She touched her bandaged ring. It wasn't just dredgermen who had their superstitions.

Sorrenson's phone rang. He examined the number flashing up on the screen. 'Simm. What is it?' He listened to his colleague for a few seconds. 'Jesus,' he said. 'Christ. Are you . . . I mean . . . OK, OK. Don't do anything. Seal it all off. Ring Williamson. I'm leaving now.' He dragged himself up off the shingle. 'It was so much easier before mobile phones. They couldn't track you down. I really don't want to leave but, well, I'll explain later.'

She broke away from him, pulled her knees back under her chin. 'Going to be a late one?'

'Very late.'

'Be seeing you, then.'

'Yeah.' He bent down to kiss her, then felt awkward and had second thoughts. He raised a hand, as if waving good-bye, let it drop to his side. He was out of practice, Sorrenson realized. He needed to relearn the protocols of farewell. 'See you later,' he said.

She wanted to tell him she was going away but she didn't have the words. She watched him pick his way through the grotters, a single shadow weaving through countless fires.

It was the absences. They jarred violently, sickeningly. In his mind, Sorrenson wanted to paint the most perfunctory of pictures, a man sitting down on a late summer's evening. Only his eyes wouldn't allow the image to be completed. They'd seen the terrible truth of things and they weren't going to allow the lie. 'Christ,' he murmured. 'Christ . . . it's so . . .' He gave up. There was nothing to be said. Words added nothing. They were redundant. The image was everything. That, Sorrenson presumed, was the point.

'They've just got to be connected. I mean . . . surely.' Simm pointed down the bridle path. 'I mean . . . got to be.'

'Christ,' Sorrenson repeated. He felt sick. The beer he'd had earlier was rushing back up into his mouth. He was like a teenager who'd drunk too much. So much for his Viking blood. It was all he could do not to throw up. He looked at the body, then at Simm, then back at the body. 'When did the call come in?'

'Just before six, couple of hours ago. Woman walking her dogs. Too shocked at the moment to give a statement. Shaking like she's having a fit. The old dear's going to be having nightmares for months. Her pacemaker's probably tripping out from overwork.'

'Show some respect,' Sorrenson growled. Up and down the sealed-off path police officers wearing white suits and head torches were crabbing their way over the caked earth on hands and knees. Sorrenson knew the path well. He'd run along it many times. In the winter it was almost a stream, a glistening snake sliding through marshy fields. But it was bone dry now. He could feel the hardness of the ground under his shoes. Dust on compacted mud. The trees bending over the path to form a near-perfect tunnel were shedding their leaves and it was still only August. Autumn would come early to the coast. The land was preparing to die. Normally, Sorrenson loved the change. It made for epic sunsets. But now he was no longer so keen on summer giving way. He needed it to hold the line. He needed things not to die: seasons, people, relationships. Everything.

He thought of the young officer who'd found Carrington. The lad was a complete mess. He'd be out of the force within three months, once the medics had concluded he was a wreck that couldn't be salvaged. PTSD. Poor sod. He was spent before he'd even begun. His job had asked too much of him too soon. No one of his age could cope with that sort of demand. 'We got an ID?' Sorrenson said.

Simm shook his head. 'No. It's a strange one. Nothing in his pockets. In his sixties, I reckon. Difficult without the eyes, though. I never realized how much you told someone's age from their eyes. It's fucking horrible, taking someone's eyes. Worse than the other ones, I reckon. Someone's got a sick sense of humour. There's one in the mouth, too, Williamson says.'

'What – a golf ball? Christ!'

'Yeah.'

They looked at the corpse. Where once there had been eyes there were two golf balls, both carefully arranged to display their logos. Sorrenson edged closer to the body, the urge to vomit almost overpowering. Maybe he wasn't so different from the young copper, he thought. He looked at the logos on the balls: Powerdrive. The brand meant nothing to him. He knew nothing about golf. He'd never seen the point of the game. He was with Twain: a good walk spoiled. 'And one in the mouth, you say?' Sorrenson struggled to stop himself retching. He didn't want Simm to think he was losing it.

'No, he didn't say so. I did,' Williamson was trudging up the path, his mouth muffled behind a white paper mask. He walked up to Sorrenson, removed his latex gloves.

179

Sorrenson allowed himself several deep breaths. Even several miles inland he thought he could smell the sea in the air. It felt cleansing, familiar, the stuff of childhood. 'Hope we're not keeping you from anything, Brian.'

'It's a Friday evening in late summer, Sorrenson. I had tickets for *As You Like It* at the Marlowe. It's going to the West End next, you know. People would kill for them. Sorry, rather inappropriate comment given the circumstances.'

Sorrenson pointed at the body. 'We thinking same killer as the rest?'

Williamson sighed theatrically. 'Maybe. I'm a scientist, Sorrenson, not a detective. It's your job to find the killer or killers. At least, that's what our contracts stipulate. Still, I'm sure in the future of multi-skilling policework things will become more fluid.'

'But?'

'But, on the early balance of probability, putting in place the necessary provisos that these are early days, and ceding the argument that, empirically speaking, we can never be a hundred per cent certain of anything, et cetera, et cetera, I would say that, yes, it's the same killer or killers.'

'What makes you so sure?' Simm said.

'Well, I would have thought that was fairly obvious, Detective. Statistically, it's unlikely that we've got four different torturers on our hands. Unless some sort of drug is finding its way into the east Kent water system and the entire coast has turned psychopathic.'

'How do you know this one was tortured?' Simm asked.

Williamson looked at the junior detective and stroked several of his chins. 'Because he was still alive when his eyeballs were removed. I'd say that constitutes torture, wouldn't you?'

180

There was the sound of retching.

'Easy, Sorrenson,' Williamson said. 'People will think you're losing it.'

Sorrenson wiped his mouth with a handkerchief. 'Something I ate.'

'Maybe an oyster,' Williamson suggested. 'I heard a load were found with a herpes virus. More common than you'd think, apparently.'

'Not really an oyster eater,' Sorrenson mumbled. He thought of Billy Davey and the price his shellfish fetched in London. 'I'm not paid enough to develop a taste for rich living.'

'Same could be said for our man here,' Williamson said.

'What makes you say that?' Sorrenson asked.

Williamson pointed at the body. 'Cheap clothes. Old jeans and a beaten-up cagoule. His hands are rough, suggesting he was familiar with manual labour. A few piss-poor tattoos, including those horrible little blue swallows, the ones ex-prisoners have done to show they've been inside. Doubt he was familiar with the near-elemental delights of swallowing a bivalve.'

Sorrenson tried not to think about the dead man's final minutes. 'Cheap clothes and rough hands?'

'Yes.' Williamson was about to elaborate but stopped when he heard panting. Four legs trailed two legs across the parched ground. He bent down, patted the passing sniffer dog and nodded at its handler. 'I'm sure we have fewer dogs than we used to. Perhaps our canine companions are victims of the cuts, along with everyone else.' He looked at Simm. 'Comes to something when even the force's dumbest members are feeling the pinch.'

181

Sorrenson read the flash of anger on Simm's face. Now was not the time for a row. 'What about the shoes?' he asked quickly.

'Cheap ones from what I can tell,' Williamson said.

Sorrenson walked towards the body. He didn't want to. He really didn't want to. But he needed to know. 'Black slip-ons, right?'

'Right,' Williamson shouted after him.

Sorrenson stopped a couple of feet from it. It was lying in front of a large holly bush, arms outstretched, legs in a V-shape. With its hideously transformed eyes and mouth, the corpse resembled a gruesome character dragged from the darker parts of a German fairytale. The shoes were cheap black slip-ons. And even from several feet away he could tell they were too large. He wouldn't stake his life on it but he would probably stake his home on them being size eleven.

He turned and went back along the bridle path. The sweep of torches, the muffled voices, the static from the police radios, it was all becoming terribly familiar. All that was missing was a dark BMW emerging from the gloom. Yes, that was all they needed, Sorrenson thought. More complications, another invasion of the coast. The world was shrinking. Even terrorist acts on another continent were threatening blowback in his remote part of the world, a place of salt-bleached scrub and dark skies.

'Do we know how our man died?' he asked.

'Tests still being conducted, awaiting toxicology results, but it's clearly a poisoning. You can tell by the foam around the mouth. He was made to swallow something unpleasant and, as he was dying, he had his eyes hacked out. We live in a horrible world, Sorrenson. A nasty, brutish and short one.'

Sorrenson's phone vibrated. He pulled it out of his pocket, looked at the text from Kate: *Gone back to London. Need to sort a few things. See you soon, I hope Kx.*

Hope, Sorrenson thought. Did she really hope she'd see him again? Unlikely. Rather, she was running away from him. She was deliberately putting distance between them. He shouldn't have gone on about the ring.

A police car, blue light flashing, siren off, crawled up the bridle path. Sorrenson looked out beyond the path to the dense, dark fields beyond. They were hop fields, he knew. Half the country's beer was flavoured with their flowers. Or at least it used to be. A lot of hops were imported from Poland and Romania now, he'd read somewhere. He wondered how long before the fields would be given over to something else. Biofuels, tobacco, even. Why here? Sorrenson wondered. Why four bodies in his corner of the world? He had a hunch: the places had been deliberately chosen. It suggested local knowledge. Someone had been to these places before. Well, that narrowed it down . . .

Sorrenson crouched down, traced four marks in the ground with a finger. He pulled a small torch from his pocket and shone it on the pattern in the dust. 'Patterns simplify,' he murmured, staring down at the marks. 'They illuminate, help people understand things more clearly. You see a pattern, you see connections, and it all starts to make sense. You feel reassured by patterns. But you can miss things in them. You see the big picture, you miss the small.'

'Right,' Simm said doubtfully.

Sorrenson pointed at the police car. 'Go and see what they want. They obviously can't be bothered to come to us.'

'I give him three years,' Williamson said, when Simm was out of earshot.

'He's not so bad,' Sorrenson said. 'He's a grafter. Asks the right questions. Who'd join up now? These days, you can earn more working in a coffee shop than when you're first on the beat.'

'Well, precisely,' Williamson said. 'If you pay peanuts . . .'

They watched Simm walk over to the vehicle and speak to its occupants. He came back, shaking his head.

'What?' Sorrenson said.

'Probably nothing but . . .'

'But?'

'Our man's a tobacconist, apparently. The tattoos are the giveaway. They match someone on the missing list. Runs a newsagent's down near Truro. *Ran* a newsagent's, I mean. More of a little cabin than a shop. Reported missing four days ago, according to Cornwall police. Andrew Hastings is his name.'

Williamson gave a hoot of laughter. 'Splendid. The plot thickens, Sorrenson. Looks like someone really does have it in for people in the tobacco trade. Maybe the cancer charities are getting militant. Perhaps the Royal College of Surgeons is developing some sort of provisional wing. Maybe this is just the beginning. Perhaps they'll start fire-bombing all the Georgian stately homes that were built with money from the slave trade.'

'Anything else?' Sorrenson said.

'He's got some form,' Simm said.

'Go on.'

'He's fifty-six, apparently. Did a three-year stretch a decade ago for a cash-in-transit raid. Suspected of several more. CID say they think he was involved in a dodgy vodka-smuggling racket. A gang was mixing pure ethanol with water and labelling it as premium, imported from Russia. That sort of stuff can kill you. Or make you go blind.' Simm hesitated. No, it was too easy. It was a gift. It had to be said. 'Guess our victim would know all about that now.'

Williamson and Sorrenson stared at him. The junior detective shrugged. One joke, one small joke, and this was how they reacted. God, they took themselves seriously, the older generation.

'Was he married?' Sorrenson said.

'No,' Simm muttered. 'No kids. None that we know of anyway. No significant other.'

Sorrenson remembered the line from a poem that had been running through his head for weeks: 'what will survive of us is love'. God knew what it was doing in his mind at that precise time. 'Find out if he was a member of anything, a club or society,' he said. 'Anything. Maybe he always drank in the same pub or went to the same bookie's. There's got to be something more to him than this. He's left some trace of himself somewhere.' He'd raised his voice, he realized. 'Someone must know something about him,' he said, this time more quietly.

'I'll get on to it.' Simm went back towards the police car. The guy behind the wheel would get his joke, he thought. They were about the same age. Maybe he'd give him a lift back. Leave the old guard alone with their solemn thoughts. They were like statues, Simm thought. Stern-faced, brooding. They ought to smile a bit more, especially given all the shit they were dealing with. You needed to laugh every once in a while.

Sorrenson was thinking about composing a text to Kate. It was too difficult. How could you say anything important in so few words? A connected world was an instant world. It encouraged brevity but not clarity. He scrambled up the bank of the bridle path and found himself in a long, dark alley between two rows of hops. He walked along the dense, fragrant corridor between the natural camouflage barriers through which nothing could penetrate, through which nothing could connect. He lay down on the bone-hard earth and stared up at the stars above.

Chapter 18

Kate stood outside the large, well-lit wooden door of her apartment block and tried to summon the courage to enter. She checked her watch. It was the middle of the night, and the snarl of the traffic some hundred metres away on Farringdon Road felt like an all-out aural assault. It would be days before she'd left the coast behind, was able to block out the incessant baseline roar of a capital city hurtling forwards into the twenty-first century, oblivious to everything but the urgent need for change.

She looked at the door for a fourth time, at the CCTV camera trained above, at the swipe-card sensor beside it, and still didn't move. It wasn't so much opening the door that bothered her. It was the act of closing it. Once she was back in her apartment, she'd be leaving her recent self behind, returning to an older version, one that she was less sure of but less excited by.

She found herself thinking back to a few hours before, to when she'd been on the beach surrounded by fires. She'd looked out across the estuary, at the horizontal blocks of light far out on the horizon, the huge cargo ships making their way from the Port of London. The image wouldn't leave her alone. She kept playing it over in her head, like a video. In her mind she studied it again. A sea at night. The horizon. Flashing buoys. Supertankers. Yes, that was all there was to it. A sea at night. The horizon . . . No, there was something else. Something she'd missed. The mushroom–like objects out to sea. The Maunsell Forts. She closed her eyes, examined the image. Yes, that was what was troubling her. At some stage the radio tags would have had to be hidden in the packets of cigarettes out on the forts before they were transferred to ships taking them to West Africa. That would be a sizeable operation. There weren't many organizations capable of facilitating that. It would take serious manpower and financing. She was sure it had nothing to do with her employer. So that meant . . .

Something smashed behind the door. There was the sound of someone swearing, then sobbing. Gently Kate pushed open the door to the lobby. A middle–aged woman was kneeling over some ceramic wreckage. Kate thought she recognized her. She'd moved into the block a couple of years ago. She was a barrister and part-time judge. Divorced. The woman looked up at Kate and shook her head. She had watery grey eyes and pale, blotchy skin. Even from several feet away, Kate could smell the drink. 'Are you OK?' she said.

The woman looked at her dully. She gestured at the shards of pottery on the tiled floor of the lobby. 'Teapot,' she muttered. 'Present from my daughter. Dropped it.' The words were slurred and, despite the tears, spoken with little emotion.

'Here, let me help you.' Kate knelt down and prepared to scoop up the shards. 'Do you know where she bought it? Perhaps you could get another.'

The woman attempted a shrug. 'No.'

'Was it expensive?'

188

The woman nodded. 'Antique. Staffordshire. They don't make it any more. Haven't for years.'

Kate regarded the small pile of debris. The smashed teapot was a concentric disaster zone. Outside the devastated dusty epicentre lay small pieces of gleaming china. She picked up a piece, made out several letters inked in blue. She examined several more, found the one she wanted. 'Look,' she said, pushing two pieces together, 'this is the name of the designer, etched on the base of the pot. Maybe you'll be able to find another now you know who made it. It's something to go on at least.'

The woman stared at her incredulously. She took the two pieces of broken china from Kate. She looked back at Kate, holding up the two pieces as if she was offering them for inspection. 'Thank you,' she murmured. 'You're right. It's something. It's a start.'

'I'll get a dustpan and brush,' Kate said, standing up. She made for the stairs up to her apartment but stopped abruptly. She looked down at the wreck of the drunken woman, kneeling among the wreckage of her daughter's shattered gift, desperately clutching the broken pieces.

'Look,' the woman said, showing Kate the two broken pieces pushed together. Her voice was almost child-like. 'I can find the designer. I can trace him.'

Kate stared at her. She was truly desperate. There were lots of desperate people out there, Kate understood. All desperate to find someone. She thought about ships at sea. She thought about strange technology hidden inside cigarette packets. She thought about Carrington. Yes. Suddenly she saw how it might all fit together. Out of the fragments she could make one smooth whole. It was a strange object to behold, though. At once familiar and unfamiliar, like the

189

egg of a strange, lost bird. If she was right, something some-where had gone very wrong. She needed to be sure.

Kate walked up the stairs to her apartment. With each step her thoughts assumed definition. She stood outside her door, turned the key, walked into her past life. She went over to her bedroom window, looked out across London at St Paul's, the Tate Modern, the Shard. She turned her gaze upwards to a sky hungrily devouring the city's unfettered light below. There were no stars.

'This is going to end up becoming a situation, Webster.'

So they weren't on first-name terms any more.

'You hear me OK? You're kind of silent.' Scott's voice boomed out of the speakerphone on Webster's desk.

Webster looked at Callow. The two men shook their heads.

'I presume this is about Brize Norton,' Webster said.

'You presume right. We told you in good faith we'd rendered . . . I mean moved our suspect through one of your airports. You wouldn't have known about any of this if we hadn't told you, and now I find out your ambassador is tak-ing this up with our Senate Intel Committee behind closed doors.'

'He's simply making the case that you cannot use British airspace for rendition. We are not making this case in pub-lic. I had no choice but to convey what you told me to our government. We report to them, not the other way round.'

'You are watching the news? Al-Boktorah's started killing the hostages. We've run out of time on this. You might not like what we've been doing but you must understand why we've been doing it. And this isn't rendition. This is . . .'

Whispers on the speakerphone. 'This is more complicated. But it isn't rendition. We weren't ghosting him against his will to a black site where he was interrogated out of sight of the law.'

Webster glanced at the carriage clock. Urgency, he thought. You could justify anything if it was urgent enough. Or at least find excuses for not weighing things up properly, ensuring protocols, laws, guidelines, rights were recognized. He looked at the clock again. Time was a commodity the security service had less and less of. One day, he promised himself, one day soon, he was going to throw the clock into the Thames. 'I was under the impression that you'd lifted him,' Webster said.

There was silence from Scott's end. Webster looked at Callow. Christ, his deputy seemed old. He remembered when Callow had joined the service in the early eighties. There was none of the younger man left in his older self. Callow would say the same about him, most probably.

'I . . . It turns out I was misinformed on that point,' Scott said, after a further silence. 'That was the account given to me at the time. That account has changed. The picture of what happened is a bit blurred. Our guy who helped bring him in died in the Geneva bombing. I'm still trying to piece together what happened exactly.'

'I see,' Webster said. 'That must be difficult.'

Scott's voice became more emollient. 'Look, this is a sensitive time for us to be accused of rendition even if it is behind closed doors. You've seen the way things kick off every time one of our drones takes out some terrorist in piss–poor places like Yemen. Everyone's saying the US shouldn't be intervening abroad. In an ideal world, things would be smoother. Agreed. Protocols would be obeyed. But we don't live in an ideal world, Webster. You know that. You understand that. We live in a world of beheadings and people being burned in cages and crucified. Sometimes you have to pick a side. Ask yourself this: are you with the bad guys or the good guys?'

Webster eased himself back in his wheelchair, looked once more at the carriage clock. Tick tock, tick tock. 'How useful was the intel from your asset anyway?' he said. 'Has he got you any closer to finding your target?' He could hear voices in the background. Scott was clearly being briefed. He seemed to have half the CIA in with him. 'It would be helpful if we knew something about him,' Webster continued. 'Then the next time I'm briefing the Intelligence and Security Committee I can at least emphasize the importance of the operation.'

'The asset,' Scott began, and stopped. Webster looked at Callow. Clearly something was wrong. The murmurs on the speakerphone were becoming frenetic. 'The asset,' Scott said. 'He was Al-Boktorah's head of logistics.'

'Where's he being debriefed?' Webster asked.

There was a long pause. 'He's not being debriefed anywhere. He's dead.'

The two captors kept their voices low. Sound travelled easily across the cave and they didn't want the hostages to learn anything about their future. Not that either captor had anything useful to impart. All they knew that the hostages didn't was that a series of pristine white Toyota pick-ups had pulled up three days before, apparently bringing new instructions. Not that the captors knew what they were. The brigade

192

wasn't good at sharing information. It knew that there was security in ignorance.

'I don't know, bro, just saying things feel different,' one captor muttered. 'Some of the brothers higher up than us, they saying something's coming. Talk about moving the hostages somewhere. Our man Al-Boktorah, he's got a plan. Big plan.'

'Heard that talk before, bro. But it's just talk, innit?'

'Maybe, bro. Maybe.'

'I'm bored.'

'You wanna play UFC?'

The two captors looked across at the hostages chained together in a corner of the cave. 'We used up all the good ones already,' one of them said. 'Can't play Ultimate Fighting Champion with this crowd. None of 'em any good. They just weak, bro. You put 'em in a ring and they fall over soon as. We should have kept Chewy and Yoda. They were well funny.'

'I hear you, bro. Crusaders, they're just lame. Maybe we should feed 'em up a bit. Then they might be tougher, last a bit longer.'

'We don't need 'em to last that much longer, bro. I hear the ransom's nearly paid.'

'Talk shit, bro. You know nothing. We never going to find out if it was paid or not.'

'We find out it's paid if they go free.'

'Like that's going to happen, bro. They dreamin' if they think they going to get out here alive. They only coming out with bullets in their heads.'

'When do you think?'

'Soon, bro, soon. Something's coming. I sense it.'

Chapter 19

The anger was slopping around inside her, threatening to spill. Bang, she could feel it smashing up against her ribs. She felt lethargic, lost. She hadn't run for two days and the need for movement was overwhelming. The plane journey had been long, dull and uncomfortable. Her hotel was character-less and without air-conditioning. She'd been glad to get out of her small, sticky room. But the midday heat didn't help. Belize City was a joyless ruin of a place. More shanty town than modern metropolis.

Maybe she'd been wrong to come. But there was a logic behind her decision to fly across the Atlantic to Central America. Callow had seen merit in her idea. He'd approved it, providing she agreed to one condition. And now here it was, strolling towards her, grinning. It was still sporting a tan, she noticed.

'Lovely day,' Fawcett said. 'Sorry I missed you at breakfast. Thought I'd take a stroll to get to know the place. Not as charming as I'd hoped it would be. That's the remnants of the empire for you.' He stopped in front of her and gave a sort of mock-bow that drew bored looks from the alcoholics lying around the treeless square. It was thirty-five degrees and muggy. Half-dead vehicles, US imports with dented bumpers and smashed-up wings, spluttered past them. A forlorn Union Jack hung limply from a flagpole in the centre of the square. Stray dogs, their eyes sunken, their bodies little more than ribcages, picked their way through the dust, noses to the ground, scavenging for scraps.

A crowd of fat, garishly attired American tourists, fresh off a cruise ship, were making their way around the square. Street hawkers were trying to entice them into buying fake designer clothes and crudely painted wooden toys. The tourists looked uneasy. They were a long way from the luxury of their ship. They clearly hadn't been prepared for such poverty. There were no cafés, no smartly dressed waiters, no flowers, no pavements even; nothing but rickety wooden shacks selling SIM cards, warm water and cigarettes. Belize City was unlikely to be the highlight of their cruise, Kate thought. It was hardly worth a photo.

And it was hardly how people would imagine a tax haven. None of the huge wealth flowing through Belize City was leaking out. The place was merely a conduit to bigger things. Money rushed through it without even a backward glance. It wasn't Geneva. It was the dirty end of tax avoidance, the bit the banks didn't show their premier clients in the brochures.

She looked up at the building in front of her, the reason for her journey. It resembled a small medical centre that had perhaps been built with foreign aid. Its large windows were reflective, its lines clean and modern. It was like nothing else around. Beside it, the other buildings were decrepit, forlorn.

'So that's where all the secrets are hidden,' Fawcett said, following her gaze. 'Belize House. Tens of thousands of offshore companies and trusts in there. All anonymous, of course.'

Kate wished she wasn't wearing sunglasses. She wanted Fawcett to see the look in her eyes. 'Thanks,' she said. 'I had no idea.'

He shrugged. 'Just making a point. It's not going to be easy dragging anything useful out of there. The people in that building don't have to play ball with any requests we make for assistance.'

Kate continued staring at the building. 'That's not why we're here.'

'I thought we were supposed to be tracking offshore companies and accounts used by Smith and Webb. We trace them and then we can unpick the network that ultimately supplies Al-Boktorah. We find who he's paying, they'll lead us to him. That's what you told Callow.'

Kate said nothing. The more she stared at the building the more out of place it seemed, a slice of the future crowbarred into a shabby past. 'The fundamental concern of any government is the protection of its citizens,' she said. 'That's what's drummed into us from day one. And yet successive governments allow Britain's overseas territories to facilitate epic money-laundering, arms-dealing, drug-trafficking, terrorism-financing, all via offshore trusts that no one can penetrate. It's like they're just turning their backs on any-thing that happens overseas – the things that matter, I mean, the networks that make all the bombings and killings pos-sible. Our governments aren't interested in changing the system – it's far too risky for them to attack the status quo. But they don't seem to understand how what happens out here will come back to haunt them, how everything is connected.'

'You said "they",' Fawcett said. 'You don't feel you're part of Her Majesty's government at the moment?'

She removed her sunglasses and looked at him. 'I don't feel connected to anything at the moment.'

He should have gone home. His wife was expecting him. The kids weren't sleeping too well. She could have used his support, even though they had, what, three or four nannies and helpers? But they'd talked about it, his responsibilities. No excuses. You couldn't blame the job for neglecting family. That's what they'd agreed before he'd gone for it. You couldn't focus on your public life at the expense of the private one.

But that was exactly what he was doing. Scott found he was craving the security of his office more and more. Or, rather, one of his offices, the political one, as he'd come to think of it. He spent more time in Washington than Langley, these days. That said it all, really.

He walked into the anonymous building, presented himself to security. He asked himself a familiar question: would I know this was the CIA's Washington office? No, he thought. The building was a study in blandness. It made for a strong contrast with the Agency's better-known headquarters. The CIA's Langley HQ looked more like a hospital in Scott's eyes. It was surrounded by trees and well-tended flowerbeds, and at night its huge glass frame was lit up like a twenty-first-century cathedral. But the building in which he now seemed to spend most of his time was an anonymous ivy-clad, red-brick construction that didn't appear in any of the tourist guidebooks. Nobody would be making a pilgrimage to it to learn about its pre-eminent role in defending the Land of the Free. Nobody would give it a second glance. Its windows were small and shuttered, and there was little in the way of security other than an obligatory CCTV camera. It sat squat behind a small parking lot, fenced off by iron railings and neat boxwood hedges. If asked, people would probably say the building was home to a boutique investment house or maybe a specialist insurer. It spoke of nothing. Unlike Langley, which was an exercise in semiotics. Langley, Scott appreciated, was all about using architecture to send a message. It spoke of an agency that was open, transparent, modern, sleek, alive. Langley had a Starbucks. Langley was one giant lie.

The older red-brick building, with its long dark corridors and poor lighting, a place of muffled conversations and unobserved footsteps on parquet flooring, was the real CIA. Inside there were no secretaries, no admin staff. It was the inner sanctum of the Agency, a place few would ever see. The place where the real decisions were made.

Scott entered his office, triggering sensors that activated the lights, startling him. He blinked a couple of times as he became accustomed to the light, then made eye contact with the large photograph of the president on his wall. The two men stared at each other. Jaws out, chests large. Scott thought he detected the ghost of a grin on the president's face. So, then, the most powerful man in the world knew Scott was after his job and was amused by the idea. The president knew the pitfalls that lay ahead for the spy: the sacrifices, political, professional, private, public, that would have to be made; the powerful people he would have to cultivate to mobilize an army.

Scott examined the various files on his desk. He hit a button on his computer and sampled the latest intel reports coming in from CIA stations around the world. He barely bothered glancing at the ones from the Middle East. They spoke of only one thing, the same thing they had spoken of for the last two years and would speak of for years to come: chaos. And you couldn't fight chaos. Scott had realized that much early on in the job. Chaos had no shape, no soft angles, no vulnerabilities. His hands worked across the keyboard until he found the report he was searching for. Another nine sightings of Al-Boktorah in the last three days, five from drones, four from sources on the ground. Another nine that they could add to the list of hundreds that had already been reported, none of which had been genuine. The desert wasn't going to give up Al-Boktorah easily. He would kill another twenty-five hostages before long. Or maybe the crowd-sourcing ransom would be raised and America's long-standing policy of not paying kidnappers would become redundant. The most powerful country in the world bypassed by a psychopath with a broadband connection. Scott thought about Adams, thought about Geneva. Their best chance lost in rubble. Christ, it was a mess. He thought about how Ailes had casually dropped the ISG into their conversation about the hunt for Al-Boktorah. Maybe he'd just been trying to demonstrate how connected he was to the Agency. It wasn't a surprise that someone as plugged in to the military industrial complex as Ailes knew about the group's existence.

But, still, the memory of the conversation troubled him. Scott knew less about the ISG than Ailes, and that level of ignorance was alarming. He thought about his recent experience in front of the Senate committee. The next one would be brutal if they found out what had happened to the asset who'd died in England. The one person who might have had the ability to link them to Al-Boktorah and he'd died on their watch, before he'd divulged what he knew.

A heart attack. What were the chances of that? The man had been only thirty-nine. Who had a heart attack so young? Well, Scott knew the answer to that one. He would, the way things were going. He was forty-five but some days his heart felt like it belonged to an eighty-five-year-old trucker who'd spent too long at the wheel, knocking back coffee and doughnuts.

His fingers danced over the keyboard, searching through electronic folders. He found the pathologist's report. Yes, there it was. Cause of death: heart attack. There was some suggestion that the man had been a heavy drinker and cocaine-user. Mixing alcohol and drugs had conspired to form a compound called cocaethylene that had made him susceptible to heart attacks. Pathologists' references to the compound in the deaths of young men were becoming more prevalent, Scott read. Who knew?

He scanned the dead asset's file. Dhia Zetouin. Petty criminal in Tunisia. His grandfather had fought against the French in the sixties. Zetouin had spent time in Paris. Radicalized by preachers in the city's *banlieues*. Renounced petty crime, drugs, drink. The usual stuff. Worked his way up to become a trusted middle man for Al-Boktorah, someone who ran his logistics operations. Shortly before his death, he'd been approached by a CIA asset and given a choice: help the Agency or it would leak intel that he and his family had been spying for the US. Zetouin had crumbled, agreed to the deal, providing the Agency gave him and his family guarantees that they'd be looked after. The claim had triggered an internal scramble at the Agency. The ISG had offered to bring him in. They could hire jets off budget so no questions would be asked. The clock was ticking. Someone somewhere in the Agency had taken the view that it made sense to allow Roscoe and his group to take control of the situation. And now the asset was dead. Maybe it was no loss. Scott tried to convince himself. Maybe Zetouin could join the bullshit pile along with all the false drone sightings the Agency kept processing.

Scott yawned. Was it late? No, not really. Only eleven. But he did feel tired, a tiredness that went right to the bones. Maybe it was time to return home. Nancy would give it to him with both barrels but it would be worse if he slept in the office. He made to shut down his computer, thought about doing a quick morale-boosting sweep of the building, see who else was working late. The Agency attracted a lot of obsessives, a lot of careerists, people who knew it wasn't an end but a beginning. People like him. People like Roscoe. They just differed in how they saw the beginning, that was all. Scott saw the Agency as a springboard for his political aspirations. Roscoe saw it as a technology play, a venture-capital firm that profited from selling protection in as many guises as possible. The ISG had a major deal coming up, Scott was aware. Some technology company it had built up was going to be floated on the stock market for billions. Good business for the ISG, for Roscoe, for the Agency probably. No wonder Ailes was taking such a close interest. It was a crucial time for the group and its investors. Scott hunted through his electronic files until he found the IPO pro-spectus. Company called Raptor, which had patented a technology called TracknTrace. He stared at the name. It didn't sound much to get excited about. He skimmed the prospectus. Some sort of micro-technology company that had perfected the use of inexpensive tiny radio transmitters that could be tracked anywhere. The uses of the technology

201

were manifold apparently. You could use it to monitor anything: products, packages, people probably.

Scott's fingers wavered over the buttons. He re-read the file on Zetouin. Something wasn't right. How many Islamists still mixed their drugs and drink? The file claimed the Agency had turned Zetouin. But Scott was sure he'd been briefed that Zetouin had approached them, offered to do a deal. Only one story could be true. Why the conflicting interpretations? And what was the asset anyway? A recruiter for Al-Boktorah, as he'd originally been told, or his head of logistics? The inconsistencies were worrying. Scott looked back at the president. He didn't feel tired now. He felt deeply uncomfortable. He ran a hand over his buzz-cut, then repeated the action, as if the friction would cause sparks to fly from his fingers. He checked the clock in the corner of his computer screen. He needed to talk to someone who could tell him what the president was thinking. Scott picked up the encrypted phone patched in directly to Langley. 'It's Scott, get me Jefferson,' he said. 'Actually, no, just get Jefferson here now. Send a car for him if you need to. Just get him here.'

Chapter 20

The two prostitutes, bleached-blonde hair in corn braids, huge gold rings jangling from their ears, were better at pool than they were at attracting customers. They'd been playing for more than an hour but no one wanted what they were selling. Kate didn't know whether to be happy or sad. The women were young, and despite the near-permanent presence of cigarettes in the corners of their mouths, they were fresh-faced and healthy-looking. Their teeth were movie-star white. Their eyes, dark brown like their skin, were playful, welcoming. They didn't belong in the bar, Kate thought. Its walls were peeling, its concrete floor cracked and dusty. A ceiling fan had given up working long ago. A long, thin neon light running between the pool tables provided the only illumination. Fly-paper hung from the ceiling. A crumpled black and white poster of a moody James Dean occupied one wall. The bar wasn't somewhere that time had forgotten; rather, it had never wanted to know. It was effectively a prison. The barman had locked the cage-like door behind them as soon as they'd entered.

'It's to protect you,' he'd mumbled. 'This way, no one can get you. Some people round here, they target tourists.'

'Charming place,' Fawcett said. 'Reminds me of somewhere else that I've been recently. That had a cage too.' He smirked at Kate, waited for her to respond.

'Somewhere hot?' she said.

'You could say that, yes.'

'Business or pleasure?'

Fawcett shrugged. 'Boating holiday, sort of.' He burst out laughing.

'Don't have you down as the boating sort, Fawcett. Far too energetic.'

'I'm a man of hidden talents. And, besides, it was a very big boat. It had a very large staff.' Fawcett was still laughing.

'Is that where you got your tan? Pale-skinned type like you should take care. I'd hate to see you burn.'

Fawcett looked as if he was going to say something, then shook his head. He ordered two beers, helping himself to some peanuts from a bowl on the bar. 'And some rum,' he murmured. 'Got to have some shots of rum. Built an empire on the back of rum. Well, that and sodomy and the lash, of course.' He cast a theatrically leery eye at the prostitutes, then turned back to Kate. 'That one's got a piercing just like you,' he said.

She'd almost forgotten the day when he'd confronted her down by the coast, when she'd been out running. She looked at him and felt abject pity. Pity that he was choosing to live a lie. The service would have no issue with his sexuality now. Decades ago, yes. But no longer. Yet he was doing everything he could to pretend that he was heterosexual. He was just pathetic. Somebody who was lost. The type was familiar to her. They were good cannon fodder for the security services. They'd had strong mothers, had gone to good schools and reasonable universities, and had passed through life never having to think or struggle for themselves. They were only half formed when they hit their thirties. They'd had no real experiences to mould them. No wonder, then, that they'd ended up in MI5. It provided them with all the answers. Protecting national security was an all-encompassing ideology. It didn't allow for nuance. You could build an identity out of that. She examined the prostitute. 'So what if she has?' she said.

'Just saying,' Fawcett said, knocking back a shot of clear rum. 'I've read your files. Your type is very interesting.'

'My type?'

'Your type.'

'And that is?'

'Weak types. Don't know boundaries. Makes you sexually promiscuous.'

Kate swigged her beer, looked at the excuse of an agent sitting at the bar beside her. She toyed with her wedding ring and thought of Sorrenson. She wished she'd said more before she'd left. Women's laughter filled the bar. Two men were talking to the prostitutes, offering to buy them drinks.

'Strange you never had children,' Fawcett said.

'Not that strange. Our line of work means we're moving around so much that by the time you stop it's too late.'

'Maybe.'

The prostitutes were dancing suggestively with each other. Their two male companions were applauding. 'I take it you don't have children,' she said.

'You take it right,' Fawcett said. 'Far too selfish.'

'Or maybe it's something deeper,' Kate said. She leaned towards him. 'Maybe you're scared, Fawcett. Maybe you think that the world's too fucked up to bring more children into it. It was manageable once, when we had an empire and a massive military complex. Now, though, we're just bit-part players on the world scene. There are terror franchises that have more power than we do. There are companies who have more power than we do. There are people who have more power than we do. The protection bit, the bit we're supposed to be good at, it's falling down, Fawcett. And who'd want to bring children into that kind of lawless world?'

The drink was getting to her. Stuff was bubbling up that should have been kept buried. Some of it was new even to her. Some of it was wearyingly familiar.

'Touché,' Fawcett muttered. 'So, Pendragon, the mask finally slips.' He mopped his forehead with a blue spotted handkerchief. 'Your words give you away. I see you for what you really are: a control freak. Well, I guess you're in good company. The security service is full of control freaks. We do like to control. Countries, people.'

There was a sharp crack of pool balls colliding. Fawcett offered up a lop-sided grin. He was quite drunk, Kate saw. He wasn't a good advert for national security. In his loose-lipped state he was fast becoming a liability. The idea intrigued her. 'So tell me about Carrington,' she said quietly. 'What do you know about Carrington? Did you control him?'

'No.'

'Tell me.'

'No.'

'Come on, Fawcett. Tell me.' There was anger in her voice now. She stood up, scraping her bar stool on the floor. The prostitutes and their admirers had stopped playing pool to watch the foreign couple have their row. It wasn't that unusual from their experience. Their city was a stopover for honeymooners making their way to the Cays, the luxury island resorts further up the coast. Tempers frayed on a young couple's first night in Belize City. It was usually down to the humidity and the poor drugs they'd been sold by hotel staff who knew they'd never see them again.

Fawcett rocked back and forth on his stool, drained the last of his beer, contemplated the floor. Kate bent closer so that she could whisper in his ear. 'Here's what I think, Fawcett. You found something on Carrington and you used it against him. You promised it would remain a secret if he played ball. You held him hostage.' She looked into his eyes, conscious that the prostitutes and their friends were still watching them. 'Well, then, how's that trade worked out for you, Fawcett? Got anything useful from it so far? Apart from a dead contact?'

He looked up at her, a sneer on his lips. 'You have no fucking idea how to play the game,' he slurred. 'No fucking idea at all. Your kind never do.'

'My kind?'

'Your kind. You know what I mean. You don't appreciate the trade-offs that have to be made, how to balance things. Sometimes you have to do ugly stuff if you want a result. But you don't get that. You want a clean conscience. Remember that next time they're scraping the entrails off the roof of a tube carriage. Your dead husband would understand.'

She rocked back on her feet, shocked. It took everything she had not to kick him off his chair and wipe the stupid grin off his sweaty face. 'That's how you justify everything, isn't it?' she hissed. 'You can get away with anything if you say it's a matter of national security.'

'Oh, fuck you,' Fawcett muttered. 'Change the record. I knew it was a mistake allowing you out here. And on a lie, too. Why didn't you just tell the truth? Why didn't you tell Callow you wanted to inspect the Belize shipping registry? Why the subterfuge? What's wrong? The real job's not exciting enough for you?'

'Says the man who lies for a living. Says the man who lies about who he really is. Like I tried to explain to you earlier, I needed to test a theory. I don't want people knowing what that theory is right now. I may be wrong. I don't want to set hares running. I need to be sure of things.'

She nodded at the mobile phone Fawcett had placed on the bar counter. 'Ring your boyfriend. Maybe he can talk some sense into you.' She was pleased to see his face redden with anger. She made for the locked exit, then turned. 'You're pathetic, you know that? Totally pathetic. Everything you do is built around lies, Fawcett. But I'm going to find out what you had on Carrington, I promise you that.'

A thin mist hung above the sea. Sheep's wool snagged on barbed wire. It was a calm, windless night, a good night for sleeping outside. But Sorrenson rarely slept outdoors now. He rarely slept, come to that. Maybe he was getting old. Or maybe he wasn't old enough, lost as he was in the strange no man's land of being unmarried and childless in his forties.

A man could get lost in that space, Sorrenson had come to realize. He'd half fantasized about speeding things up. Get straight to his fifties and be done with it all. No more worrying about starting a family, settling down. It would be too late by then. He could retire with his policeman's pension and a flimsy conviction that they hadn't all been wasted, what he would try to call his best years. It was more than some could say. But, true, it was less than he'd recently dared hope for. The future, Sorrenson thought, was going to drag.

He padded across the deck behind his house, bare feet on wood roughened by salt rain. He lit a hurricane lantern, sat down on an old lounger and gazed out across an ink-black sea. Yes, he thought, it would be a good night for sleeping in the open air, sucking up the ozone, feeling like you were returning to the beginning of things, the simple things.

The signs had all been there, of course. The return of the wedding ring to her finger. He could read her. He could see the doubts. He'd just chosen to ignore them. That was all. He'd been hoping for too much and she'd detected it, that faint, desperate murmur beating just below the surface. A burden. No wonder she was retreating. The decisions she made now could end up ruining the rest of her life. It wasn't like the pair of them were in their twenties and could live with the regrets. There were few second chances once you'd reached the halfway mark. Time became the ultimate commodity. Only you couldn't buy more of it; you couldn't steal more of it; you couldn't smuggle it. There was no black-market in time. Tick tock, tick tock, tick tock.

Sorrenson opened the glass door of the lantern, held his hand above the candle flame, felt the heat on his palm, saw the silhouette of his fingers against the deck. He thought of a hundred fires on a shore. You're an idiot, he told himself. The mawkishness would pass. All things would pass. He poured himself a second glass of Côtes du Rhône, thought about turning the radio on but gave up. The airwaves were just full of bad news, most of it coming out of Africa. Another twenty-five hostages dead. Some hints that a ransom was about to be paid to free the remaining fifty but nothing certain.

There was the low grumble of a car engine. He looked at his watch. Williamson was making good on his promise. He walked back into his house, through the darkened lounge, opened the front door to his colleague.

'Like what you've done with the place, Sorrenson,' Williamson said. 'It's got a sort of New England feel to it. Although I may be wrong as I can hardly see beyond my nose. Have you had a power cut?'

'Sorry, come in.' Sorrenson ushered Williamson inside. He switched on some lights. Williamson winced. 'Far too bright for such a late hour. Switch them off again. It'll make it easier to read the screen anyway.' He pointed at a laptop on a coffee-table. 'This the patient? Property of the late Mr Carrington, Antony without an *h*.'

'Yes.'

'Well, I'm a forensic scientist, not an IT worker. Tell me why I'm here. And make some coffee while you're at it. Strong coffee. I'm not used to being out of bed after midnight, these days. Except for prostate-related issues, of course.'

'Sure. Make yourself comfortable.' Sorrenson gestured at the laptop and headed for the kitchen. Williamson looked around the sparsely decorated lounge. A few photographs of somewhere cold, Scandinavia maybe; a small model of a wooden sailing boat; a brass telescope pointing out to the sea beyond the retractable windows; a bookshelf heavy on biography and military history; a hi-fi system that had last seen active service in the seventies.

'Your wife – sorry, your partner – is away, is she?' Williamson called. 'Or does she not live with you? Very fashionable that sort of thing nowadays, I read somewhere.

I was ahead of the curve on that. Many of my ex-wives don't live with me either.'

In the kitchen next door Sorrenson threw coffee into a pot, took the hissing kettle off the hob. 'She's away,' he called back.

'Anywhere nice?'

Sorrenson hesitated. 'I think so.'

'Right,' Williamson said, as Sorrenson came back into the room. He took the mug from the other man's outstretched hand. 'I can't wait to meet her.'

'Maybe. She's quite private. We're still, you know . . .'

'Finding your way. I understand, Sorrenson. You don't want to rush these things. Take it from someone who knows. Marry in haste, repent at leisure, et cetera, et cetera. Let's have a look at this thing.'

Williamson knelt in front of the laptop, pressed the on button, watched the device spring into life. 'They always seem so excited to be switched on, these things, don't they? One minute they're dead, the next it's, bam, we're awake, we're connected. I wish I had their enthusiasm, Sorrenson, I can tell you.' He typed away on the keypad. 'Of course, you could have brought this into the station. Then we could have drafted in some proper computer experts to interrogate it rather than leaving it to some clapped-out old roué with a passing interest in technology.' He sipped his coffee. 'You're a second-rate detective, Sorrenson, but a first-rate barista. This coffee is really rather good.'

Sorrenson refilled Williamson's mug. 'Kate brings the stuff back from work. One of the perks of the job, apparently. And you're right, we could have done this down at the station but you know what it's like. One giant building site.

Laptops, especially expensive laptops, go missing. Can't afford something as important as this to disappear.'

'I hear you, Sorrenson. Can't trust anyone, these days. I guess that's especially true for you. Don't give me that flannel about builders. Even I'm not stupid enough to buy it. I take it you don't want anyone to know you're interrogating this device?'

'Something like that.'

'Something like that. I see. Will you elaborate?'

'Instinct, that's all. A lot of people are interested in Carrington. I'd like to know why.'

'Our dear friends from London, you mean? The ones who've been crawling over Mr Carrington's cadaver?'

'Something like that.'

'Something like that, well . . .' Williamson inhaled deeply, let out a murmur of surprise. 'Well,' he repeated. 'Well, well, well.'

'What have we got?'

Williamson shook his head. 'I'm not sure you want to know. I'm certain you don't want to see. It's doing for the few parts of my brain that haven't been damaged by claret.'

'Really?'

'Really.'

Williamson flipped the laptop around so that Sorrenson could see the screen. It was displaying some sort of flowchart, scores of small boxes connected by arrows. 'Thank God for strong coffee,' he said. 'That's a lot of information to take in. The last time I saw something as complicated as that was in the Cavendish Laboratory in Cambridge and I was a single undergraduate with the world at his feet.'

Sorrenson studied the chart. 'Turks and Caicos, British Virgin Islands, Delaware, Jersey, Guernsey, Cyprus, Belize,

Panama, the Seychelles, the Isle of Man, the Cayman Islands, Antigua, Mauritius, Switzerland, Liechtenstein, the Marshall Islands, Nauru. I couldn't point to half of these places on a map. I mean, Delaware?'

'It's in the United States of America, Sorrenson. I believe it's America's own tax haven, the one they don't like to talk about. Rather like our Isle of Man. All the places on this chart are tax havens.'

'So, this is a sort of map that shows the network Carrington set up to help Smith and Webb evade tax?'

Williamson nodded. 'Tax havens don't just help people evade taxes. They also help people evade being seen. You've got a trust in a tax haven, you're guaranteed anonymity. Your fingerprints will be nowhere near it. Makes it almost impossible to follow the money.' He pointed at the screen. 'Rather clever when you look at it. Almost beautiful. Reminds me of the cerebral cortex, all the different connections.'

Sorrenson gazed through the retractable doors out to the sea. Towards the horizon he could see the lights of a cargo ship making its way towards Belgium or maybe Germany. A thin whisper of salmon grey was fattening over the waves. Dawn was coming. Gulls were screeching above the shoreline. It was another day, another beginning. Williamson yawned.

'If you get tired you can have the sofa,' Sorrenson said.

'It's just like being married,' Williamson observed.

Chapter 21

It was a nondescript wooden door with white paint blistered by the sun, a rusting latch that looked as if it would yield to a glare. She stood on the thin deck outside the single-storey house and took a deep breath. The smell of cooked meat wafted to her from next door. A passing bus sent dust rising into the air. Kate rapped on the door.

She heard footsteps. The door opened with a shudder. Its wooden frame had warped a thousand times in the heat. 'Can I help you?'

Kate had rehearsed her lines. She had to be quick. She was offering a trade and she had only seconds to make it. 'No, but I can help you.'

'Sorry, but I already have a Bible, if that's what you're selling.'

Kate held out a small package. 'In here you'll find a letter, a phone and ten thousand US dollars. My number is programmed into the phone. Read the letter. Another forty thousand if you'll give me the name of the companies that own the vessels listed and their directors. I know you can do that. You just have to go into your computer system. A few clicks on a keyboard and you'll make fifty thousand dollars. Meet me at the address at the bottom of the letter on the day and at the time given. The athletics stadium on the edge of the city. No one will follow you. It will be over in a matter of minutes. It's a genuine offer, and if you help me, I promise you won't be traced and you'll never see me again. It is a lot of money I'm offering for very little information.'

The woman shook her head vigorously. Her eyes flashed alarm. 'I'm sorry, I think you are confusing me with someone else.'

'I'm not, trust me. I know that you work at Belize House. I know that you have the power to examine all documents relating to any of the hundreds of thousands of companies and ships registered in Belize.'

The woman made to shut the door. Kate could hear a radio playing classical music inside the house. 'It helps,' she said quickly. 'Music, I mean. Classical especially. Stimulates their brains, helps them form connections. There's a lot of research that suggests it's the best thing you can do for your child.'

The door remained open. Kate studied the woman's face. It showed a fear of death, her own. Not because of what it meant for her but for what it meant to the child inside the house, the brain-damaged child listening to the radio. There was no husband. The child would be alone. That was why the mother was so scared. She feared failing. She feared not being able to protect her child. Only mothers truly understood what security was really about; how in the end the only thing that mattered was the security of their children, of the next generation, the future. Such knowledge made mothers powerful, strong, fearless. It also made them vulnerable. You could work with those emotions. The cynical would say you could exploit them. Yes, Kate thought, you could exploit them. Why dress it up as anything else?

The woman struck a match and lit a fat, filterless cigarette. Through the gap in the door she assessed the tall woman standing before her. She sounded British, not American. Not like the women on the soaps she watched on satellite television. The woman clearly didn't have children. You could tell by the eyes. She nodded several times to herself and then exhaled smoke. She picked a small fleck of tobacco from her teeth, rubbed it between her fingers. 'So you know about my child,' she said. 'You know about her condition. Well, then, you have clearly been busy.'

Kate held out the package. The woman didn't move. She looked into Kate's eyes, tilted her head to one side. Her skin was heavily lined and there were liver spots on her neck. Her arms were sturdy. Her stomach bulged through her faded old sundress. Thin trails of perspiration glistened in the furrows of her forehead. The woman had diabetes, Kate knew. The MI6 briefing she'd called in had been well researched. Clearly the intelligence agency had prepared for such a scenario in the past, considered how it could extract protected information from the most securely guarded tax havens, worked out that the best way forward was by targeting the vulnerable. And this woman was clearly very vulnerable. Hers had to be an exceedingly tough life; she was running out of options and knew it. There was no safety net to catch her if she fell. *When* she fell.

The woman reached out a hand and touched the package. Slowly her grip tightened around it. Kate did not let go. The woman would have to take the package from her hand. It had to be her decision. That was how the trade worked.

'You done this before?' the woman mumbled.

Kate shook her head. 'No.'

'First time in Belize?'

'Yes.'

The woman looked at Kate's hand, saw her wedding ring. 'Your husband know you're here?'

'My husband's dead.'

'I'm sorry to hear that.' She took the package from Kate's hand, shuffled back inside her home. Behind the closed door she clutched the small package close to her. She held it carefully, as if it was something sacred, a crucifix or rosary beads.

It had been two days since he'd died. Martinson, someone had said his name was. Geologist from Vancouver. He'd just rolled over in the night and stopped breathing. Now the smell was becoming unbearable. The other hostages tried to sleep away from the cadaver but there was only so much room in their corner of the cave. There was only so far they could go. Every time they looked at him they hated him. He'd died in his sleep. It was more, they knew, than they could hope for. The envy ate away inside them like cancer.

'Please move him,' they begged.

'Don't you worry,' they were told. 'You're all being moved soon.'

Sorrenson padded down the stairs and found Williamson hunched in front of Carrington's laptop. The pathologist didn't look up. 'I thought you were getting some sleep.'

'I tried, then gave up. Maybe all that coffee.'

'Me too,' Williamson said. 'Take it from me, it's not good for you, all that caffeine. I'm a failed scientist. I know of what I speak.' He went back to punching keys on the laptop.

217

'I think you'll want to look at this. But, be warned, you need a strong stomach.'

Sorrenson walked over to Williamson and stood behind him. 'More flow charts?'

'Not exactly.'

'Christ,' Sorrenson said, after a pause. At first his brain had been unable to confirm what he was seeing. It was as if he had no mental template to accommodate the horrific novelty of the images on the screen. His brain was starting from scratch on a steep, grotesque learning curve.

'We could get arrested for looking at this,' Williamson remarked. 'There's tons of it.'

'Close it down.'

'Really?'

Sorrenson nodded. He walked over to a wooden cabinet, pulled out a bottle of twelve-year-old malt whisky and poured double measures into coffee mugs. They sat drinking in silence for several minutes, haunted by what they'd seen.

Sorrenson spoke first. 'You've got kids, haven't you, Brian?'

'Four. By three women. Not something I'm particularly proud of.'

'Tell me, if that'd been done to your kids, how would you react?'

Williamson sipped his whisky. 'I suppose as a servant of the Crown, someone whose salary is paid for out of the criminal justice budget, I should say that I would be confident that the likes of you would do their job, Sorrenson, and that the perpetrators would be punished.'

'But?'

'But if that was my kids then, honestly, I don't think I'd

218

be able to stop myself trying to find that person and tearing them apart.'

Sorrenson drained his mug. 'That's what I thought. How do you even get hold of that stuff? I mean, surely you can be traced pretty easily if you go looking for that sort of material.'

'You'd be surprised. People forget that most of the internet is what they call the Dark Net, the unseen part that you can't find using search engines. You can buy special browsers that make you anonymous. If you have the right coded web addresses, you can find pretty much anything you like and it's almost untraceable. I read an article on it. Selling videos of child abuse is a big, big market apparently. For criminal gangs it's just another illegal commodity like drugs and guns.'

'Pull up the files for a second. Don't open them. I just want to see them.'

Williamson put down his mug and ran a finger over the laptop's mousepad.

'*Et voilà!*'

They stared at the files.

'Clearly a tobacco man through and through,' Williamson murmured. 'Uses the internet handle Double Jeopardy. There's a man who liked to take his work home with him.'

'What are these?' Sorrenson said. He pointed at several file icons in the right-hand corner of the screen.

Williamson yawned, peered at the screen and clicked on the icons. 'Well, I'm guessing and I can't be sure, usual provisos, but I would say these are the names of others with whom he's been trading images. These appear to have been supplied by someone called Kognac and these from someone called Powerdrive. Here's some more. Wizzard.

Teacherspetz. The spelling is almost as appalling as their contents. I mean—'

'Christ,' Sorrenson interrupted.

'What?'

'Don't you get it?'

'Get what?'

'The connection. The links between them. Carrington.
What was he found with? Cigarettes, lots of them. All
Double Jeopardy brand. Wade's body in the coffin had that
key-ring with a fob of Tintagel. Tintagel home to Merlin,
the Wizard. Hastings, the man with golf balls for eyes. The
balls were the Powerdrive brand. There was a miniature
bottle of cognac glued to the dashboard of the car. The dead,
they're all part of a network. That's what links them. They
were all trading with each other.'

'And – what? Someone found them?'

'Clearly.'

'Vigilantes? This is Kent, Sorrenson, not the Wild West.'

'Agreed. But this stuff really happens. There are people out
there hunting paedophiles. Some will take the law into their
own hands. And someone wanted us to make the connections, see them for what they were.'

'Well, why not just leave a note next to the victims, saying, "Paedophile"? Why the thing with the shoes? Why all
the horror?'

'I don't know. I really don't know.'

Williamson gestured at the screen. 'Well, just maybe you're
right, Sorrenson. Maybe some vigilantes are going around
identifying paedophiles and dispensing their own unique
form of painful justice. Perhaps they've lost faith in the
police to do things properly. Can't say I blame them. But, if
so, then you have another problem.'

'How do you mean?'

'There are five icons,' Williamson said. 'And so far you've only got four bodies. I mean, the fifth could be dead already but there may still be someone else out there. How far will you go to try to save someone like that? I mean, really, when it boils down to it, what's the life of a paedophile worth anyway?'

Sorrenson didn't have an answer.

'There's something else, too,' Williamson said. 'You really need to see Carrington's emails. The ones from his personal account. Hundreds and hundreds about some project called Raptor. From the tone of them it doesn't appear they were to someone in his company. Rather, Raptor was something he didn't want Smith and Webb to know about.'

'Raptor. Means nothing to me.'

'All the Raptor emails were to the same person, it appears.'

'Who?'

Williamson looked back at the laptop screen. 'No name, just an initial, F. I haven't read many but the ones exchanged towards the end are quite shrill in tone. Mr Carrington and Person F, as I choose to call him or her, were at odds over something. Seemed Carrington was unhappy with the way things were going and wanted nothing more to do with it.'

'Can you bundle them all up into a single file?' Sorrenson asked.

'Sure. Why so?'

'I just know somebody who'd be interested, that's all.'

'Somebody?'

'Somebodies.'

Chapter 22

Jefferson was a big man who'd done well out of acting small. He was over six feet five, weighed more than seventeen stone, and had been with the Agency since he'd graduated from Yale in the eighties. That sort of longevity in intelligence circles was rare, Scott appreciated. People only got to stick around for that long if they were ruthlessly unambitious and learned how to shrink themselves so they didn't make easy targets. And Jefferson was as ruthless, as calculating, as they came. He'd done well out of keeping his silence, never seeking promotion, playing the part of the loyal page to a succession of Agency directors. As a result, he'd become embedded in the architecture of the Agency, a man who knew where the bodies were buried and would never say. Jefferson was an omniscient fossil. He was head of White House relations for the CIA. It was his job to work out just how strained the relationship between the Agency and the president was at any given time.

Through his window Scott watched Jefferson's unflashy station wagon pull into the parking lot. The dawn had arrived. The perfectly-cut boxwood hedge in front of the building had assumed a lustrous waxy green that in Scott's eyes seemed faintly ludicrous. He'd come to think of the hedge, tended almost reverentially by some Mexican gardener on ten dollars an hour, as just about the only thing that had any shape and sense of order in the entire Agency.

He sank back in his seat, counted the 119 seconds he believed it would take for Jefferson to clear security and enter his office. He knew the duration of the short journey from the building's entrance to his desk off by heart – he'd performed it so many times. The transition from public to private took just under two minutes. It required an urgent shifting through the mental gears to go from the outside world to the heart of the CIA. He often experienced turbulence along the way.

'Good of you to come in,' Scott said, when Jefferson materialized in his office. He checked his watch: one minute twelve. Maybe the security detail on the front desk were becoming more efficient. Or maybe it was just early and they had little else to do. Maybe, Scott thought, he should stop worrying about the time so much. Difficult, though, given events. Tick tock, tick tock. 'Yeah, really good of you,' he repeated. 'Appreciate it.'

'Not a problem,' Jefferson said. He pulled two Styrofoam cups from a brown-paper bag and sat on a chair in front of Scott's desk. 'Thought you might use some caffeine.' He slid a cup across polished wood.

'Thank you,' Scott said. 'Thoughtful of you. And, yeah, I need something to keep me on my toes right now. Four months in, and the more I know, the more I realize how much I don't know about this Agency. I guess it takes years to penetrate the shadows, drill down to what's really going on.'

He waited for Jefferson to say something but the giant just nodded and sipped his coffee. Scott found himself staring at

Jefferson's huge hands. He should have been a linebacker, Scott thought, someone who could operate at the sharp end of defence, not an office-bound agent, a Gulliver tied down by bureaucracy. That was the problem with the Agency. It was just like any other organizational behemoth. It crushed the individual, encouraged group-think, lacked dynamism. It was like some sprawling banking empire. No one was quite sure where its centre lay. No one was quite sure who was in control. Jesus, Scott thought, I'm starting to sound like Roscoe.

'I'm learning about stuff, though,' he continued hurriedly. 'I'm learning about all our departments. The ISG, for example. A very successful operation, I'm given to understand. Never knew the CIA was so interested in tech. But it's all here. Every ISG investment. Hundreds of them.' He pointed at the computer screen on his desk. Another pause. It occurred to Scott that Jefferson might see him as an almost existential threat. He was an outsider trying to shake things up. But Jefferson, like many others high up in the Agency, had done well out of the status quo. He'd no interest in seeing things change.

'The ISG's got a good track record,' Jefferson said guardedly. 'Made a whole string of investments. Most of them work out in time. Some pay off real good. Jewel in the Agency crown, some like to say. Roscoe, anyway.'

'What about Raptor?' Scott said. 'You reckon its TracknTrace technology is a good play?'

Jefferson examined his Styrofoam cup, trying to discern the future of the CIA in his coffee dregs. His life had been built around one conviction: that his job, his only job, was to ensure the preservation of the Central Intelligence Agency. Personnel would come and go; directors would come and go; presidents would come and go. But the CIA would not, should not, could not come and go. A free world depended on its survival. You got rid of the Agency and there was nothing left to counter the Russians, the Chinese, the manifold threats emerging out of Africa and the Middle East. Scott would burn out in time but the threats would only intensify.

'I mean,' Scott continued, 'we're pouring all this money into it, this unit that seems accountable only to itself but has big names like Larry Ailes pushing a lot of investors' money at it. I'd just like to know our investment in the ISG is safe. By that I mean the American taxpayer. I'm sure you'll have heard some of the rumours swirling around about the ISG. I'd like to hear them, too. People's pensions depend on getting this sort of thing right. Your pension, for example. You're, what, two years shy of retirement?'

Jefferson gave a half-nod and crushed the Styrofoam cup in his hand. A small brown puddle formed on Scott's desk. Jefferson swore under his breath. 'I'm going outside for a smoke,' he said. 'Maybe two.'

'You do that,' Scott said. 'Then we'll talk.'

Jefferson nodded. He really needed a smoke. Almost as much as he needed to make a phone call.

Was it ten or eleven? Simm had lost count of the roundabouts he'd navigated in just the last fifteen minutes. He was on a dual carriageway that seemed unwilling to allow drivers to proceed in a straight line. It was always trying to spin them off somewhere else, to another part of the country. Maybe it was something to do with his location. The Midlands didn't really know where it was. Not north. Not south. It was a place you passed through. Simm found himself missing the coast. You knew where you were with the sea. You were aware of how limited you were in your choices. But now he was as far from the sea as he could be in his own country. He felt lost and uncertain. Perhaps it had been a bad idea to use his day off to test a hunch. It would have been difficult, though, to make the journey in work time. Sorrenson would have told him to get the local police to check it out. Then, if he was right, he'd get hardly any credit. He really hoped he was right. He needed some respect. He needed to show them what he could achieve if they just backed him, recognized his potential. Maybe he should get a haircut. His wild red hair sent out the wrong signals. Made him look like a chemistry teacher. Yes, a haircut would be good.

Simm checked the mile counter: 221 miles. That was a lot of distance to cover on a Ducati in one day. There had been strong headwinds coming up the M40, too. The ride, performed at speeds Simm hoped hadn't been clocked by cameras, had been one long attritional battle with the wind. He felt like a sheriff riding back into town after a long day in the saddle. Weary, sore, relieved that the tiresome journey would soon be over.

He took a left at yet another roundabout and found himself in an industrial estate, a quiet, unprepossessing place that was home to modern warehouses with corrugated metal roofs, approached by tidy roads untroubled by heavy traffic. He eased his flame-red bike into the parking space in front of a low-slung brick creation that seemed older than the surrounding buildings. A sign outside read: 'Stelling and Sons, specialists in Triumph renovations since 1970'.

He dismounted, removed his helmet and walked towards

the building. There were only four places in the UK that cared for Triumph Stags, he'd discovered, and only one of them specialized in resprays. Maybe, Simm thought, just maybe, he was going to hit pay dirt. Then they'd have to take notice of him back in Kent. His career would go into overdrive. It would accelerate faster than his Ducati. The roar would be heard all the way down the coast.

Webster looked up from his desk. Voices in the corridor outside his office. The gruff tones of Callow and the more polished Scottish accent of McKie, Five's director of risk assessment. Webster checked his watch. Just after seven on a Tuesday morning. It was a strange time for Callow to call a meeting. He wasn't one of the service's larks, unlike McKie. She was never out of the building. Either she was worried that the service would fall apart without her or she was worried that it wouldn't, Webster had come to learn. McKie had the sort of personality that couldn't cope if either scenario turned out to be true. She'd have his job one day soon, Webster was sure. He hoped that she'd feel the sacrifices she'd made in her personal life had been worth it. Unlikely, if his experience was anything to go by. The longer he spent in his job the more he understood its limitations, the impossible demands it made on him. Threats were growing exponentially in inverse proportion to the resources thrown at countering them. It was a strange, lonely, dispiriting place, the top of the mountain. The views were great but you struggled to breathe.

'Sorry,' Callow said, walking in without knocking, a lit cigarette in his hand. 'We both agreed this couldn't wait.' He gestured at McKie behind him.

Webster stared at Five's most senior female employee. He'd never seen her without make-up on. She looked like some-one he knew only from photographs. No, strike that, she looked like someone he didn't want to see at that time in the morning. Nothing good happened before ten. 'This must be serious if you're involved,' he murmured. 'Tell me, on a scale of one to ten, just how worried should I be at this precise moment in time?'

'I think I can say that, if we're right, it's a safe ten,' McKie said. She sat down on the sofa near to Webster's desk, yawned and put her hand to her mouth. 'Sorry. Not getting much sleep at the moment. Got a nine-month-old. They need so much looking after at this age. It's relentless.'

Callow ground out his cigarette in a pot plant. 'Yes,' he said, 'I would imagine it is.'

'You've both read my initial assessment?' McKie asked. She stifled another yawn.

Webster hesitated. Which assessment was she talking about? So many log-jammed his inbox that he couldn't be sure. Half of them, he'd learned, came to nothing anyway. But that didn't mean you could ignore them. It was the seemingly trivial reports you had to pay attention to. They were the ones that could explode, that could have you hauled before the Intelligence and Security Committee, subjected to myriad questions from MPs with no real under-standing of what Five was truly up against. Webster searched his memory for the correct file. Front companies in north London channelling money to the PKK? No, he didn't think so. Unusual movement of money through a Swiss bank's London subsidiary known to be used by an Al-Qaeda com-mander? Perhaps. Maybe the one about drones being used to spray some deadly chemical or other in a football stadium? No. There were just so many threats and so many assessments that everything blurred into one.

McKie recognized the blank look on Webster's face. 'The forensic linguistics analysis,' she said tentatively.

Webster shook his head. That one had been nowhere near the top of his thinking.

Callow came to his aid. 'We've been examining some emails exchanged between the asset we were running who worked for big tobacco and an unknown correspondent. The emails were about a project called Raptor. It seems our asset, Carrington, had intel that he wasn't sharing with us.'

'Remind me why we were running an asset who worked for a tobacco firm,' Webster muttered. 'Would have thought that was more one for Customs.'

Christ, Callow thought, Webster was losing it. They'd discussed it only a few days ago. He clearly had too much going on. He couldn't focus. 'We know a lot of the company's product ends up being smuggled halfway around the world to avoid taxes. Ultimately some of it ends up in the hands of various groups of interest to us, not least our friend the hostage-taker in the Sahara who's targeting our oil refineries. We figured that if we could unpick the financial transactions that were facilitating the movement of the product we could expose his financial network and, ultimately, degrade then destroy it.'

'Yes,' Webster said. 'Yes, I remember now. Our old friends degrade and destroy.' He leaned back in his chair, pointed at his deputy. 'Mr Carrington's death was rather macabre and dramatic, I recall. We could do without some febrile speculation linking us to this appearing on the net or somewhere equally unhinged . . . newspapers, for example.'

Callow drew on his cigarette. God, he loved tobacco. It was, he felt, about the only thing that never let him down. You really knew where you stood with a cigarette. 'I don't know. I've been following the police investigation closely. It appears he may have been targeted for reasons wholly unconnected either to what he did for a living or what he was doing for us.'

'Such as?'

Callow inhaled deeply, studied the remains of his cigarette, discarded in the plant pot. 'Carrington was a paedophile. Sometimes they get found out.'

'Evidently.' Webster drummed his fingers on his desk, then leaned forward slightly. 'I take it this . . . predilection was how we turned him.' He looked at McKie, conscious that he needed to choose his words carefully. He didn't want this conversation being recounted before the ISC. 'We discovered Mr Carrington's unusual interest and offered to cut him a deal?'

Callow was watching McKie. She really did seem very tired. He wondered how he'd look now if he and Marjorie had managed to have kids. Probably no different from how he did now. It was impossible for him to look any more clapped-out than he was, he reckoned. 'Something to that effect, yes,' he said.

'Something to that effect, yes,' Webster repeated slowly.

Callow found his hands wandering to his inside jacket pocket for his cigarettes only to discover that he already had a lit one in his hand. It was a bad sign when Webster started doing his schoolmaster routine. Flashes of irritation could quickly become major explosions. Webster didn't have a short fuse, that was one of his strengths, but when he went for it, his anger could be volcanic. Callow knew that he needed to plug the crater. 'It looked like it was working, the arrangement,' he said quickly. 'Carrington was feeding us enough stuff to suggest it was worth scaling up the operation. Names of third parties shipping product, front companies they used, that sort of intel. It was a good start. He provided us with a map of the tax havens they were using. That was when we decided to draft in Pendragon. We felt she might help confirm some of the stuff Carrington was giving us. There's always a concern with these types that they just tell us what they think we want to hear to get us off their backs.'

'Right,' Webster said. 'I remember. We exerted some pressure on the chairman.'

Callow exchanged glances with McKie. One of them was going to have to say the unsaid. McKie shrugged. 'We did apply some leverage, yes,' she said. 'Smith and Webb's chairman, Sir Alf Dunbar, was grateful for some discretion. He created the position.'

Webster pondered the answer. He looked at his two colleagues. 'Discretion?' he said blankly.

'Same interests as Carrington,' Callow muttered. 'Maybe not so, erm, graphic, but, well . . .'

'Christ,' Webster said. He nodded at Callow. 'It's like the seventies all over again. It made sense collecting this kind of stuff back then. We needed to know before the KGB found out and started blackmailing half the cabinet. But now, well . . . all this is more difficult to square. Spare me the details now but send me the files on this. I'll need to work out just what we can say the next time the ISC starts asking about this sort of stuff.'

'Right,' Callow said. It was all very well for Webster to develop a moral compass towards the end of his career, but he knew better than anyone that intelligence-gathering was dirty toil. If you wanted to find things that were buried you had to dig. And the ground was usually polluted.

'Who was handling Carrington?' Webster said.

'Fawcett,' Callow said. 'And . . .' He looked at McKie.

'We've subjected Carrington's emails discussing this project, Raptor, to a forensic linguistics test,' McKie said. Her tone was half apologetic, as if she was anticipating the damage she was about to inflict on Webster. 'And, well . . .' She trailed off. She wanted Webster to work it out for himself.

Webster allowed himself another shuffle back and forth in his wheelchair. He looked enviously at Callow smoking his cigarette. He'd have to remind him at some stage that MI5 had a strict no-smoking policy in the building. Maybe when things were a little calmer. So maybe never, then. 'I'm lost,' Webster said. 'I thought it was only the Home Office that used these linguistic tests, to prove whether someone claiming asylum came from whatever conflict zone they said they came from.'

'Normally that's correct,' McKie said. 'But we thought it worth a shot on this occasion. We couldn't trace the source of the emails to Carrington so forensic linguistics was pretty much all we had to go on. It made sense to consider whether they came from Fawcett as he was handling Carrington. If we could eliminate him, we could look elsewhere.'

'And?' Webster asked. He felt uncomfortable. He had a premonition of what was coming.

'And large numbers of words used by whoever was corresponding with Carrington are also used by Fawcett in his written quarterly psychological assessments. There is a significant correlation between the two. Statistically significant, I mean.'

'Are we certain about this, I mean really certain?' Webster said.

McKie looked at Callow for support.

'About as sure as we can be,' Callow said. 'Apparently Fawcett uses a lot of Americanisms in his written text.'

'Americanisms?' Webster looked confused.

'His correspondence uses American phrases, slang. It is consistent with someone who is American or at least spent a lot of time there. He might speak English but Fawcett writes American.'

Webster thought of what he knew about Fawcett. He was as British as they came. He had a signet ring. Webster was fairly sure Fawcett belonged to a hunt. No, there was no doubting which side of the Atlantic Fawcett was born on. The forensic linguistics test couldn't be trusted. 'It might not mean anything, though,' he said. 'All of this, I mean. Maybe Fawcett was just grooming the asset, gathering all the intel before delivering it to us, when he was confident he had something. It does happen.'

'Maybe,' Callow said.

'But unlikely,' McKie interjected. 'These emails are very detailed and cover a lengthy time frame, several months. More than enough for Fawcett to have reported something back up the line on this. It seems clear to me that, whatever Raptor was or is, Fawcett was not inclined to share his knowledge of it with us. We have to ask why.'

Webster stared hard at McKie. 'Where is Fawcett now?'

'Belize,' Callow said.

'Isn't that where Pendragon is?' Webster asked.

Callow nodded. 'Yes. She's gathering intel on a series of offshore trusts.' Webster seemed to shrink physically. He's getting old, Callow thought. He needs to get out.

'How long has Fawcett been with us?' Webster asked.

'Almost ten years,' McKie said.

'Quite a long time,' Webster said. 'Enough time for someone to know where they stand on things, where they fit in.'

'Maybe too long,' Callow said.

'Meaning?' Webster asked.

Callow shrugged. 'You spend long enough in any organization and there's a danger you can get disillusioned with it. Fawcett has hardly been rising up the ranks in recent years. Maybe he received a more attractive offer. You can't move in this city for Russian and Chinese spies, these days. They're mushrooming like Starbucks.'

They'd made the last eighty kilometres on foot, the first two hundred in a convoy of jeeps. Each of the forty-three Navy Seals was equipped for Armageddon. They carried three different types of automatic weapon and belts heavy with stun grenades and plastic explosive. They were more robots than soldiers, sculpted bodies zipped into temperature-controlled suits. They wore night goggles that turned the darkened desert into a green-tinged dawn. They spoke softly into mouthpieces that could pick up the faintest commands. Headsets moulded to their ears relayed instructions from analysts monitoring their movements thousands of miles away at the US embassy in Madagascar. Cameras mounted on their helmets were capable of detecting the infrared heat patterns of another human hundreds of yards in front of them.

The Seals were good adverts for the technology they were wearing. They were poster boys for a new kind of war. Conflict astronauts. Stealthy, silent, they stalked the Sahara, like ghosts in Purgatory. A star-scarred sky bore witness to their hard-won progress, made in boots whose lightweight design borrowed much from the latest trends in sportswear. Each Seal carried ten thousand dollars in gold, insurance if they needed to buy safe passage across an inhospitable desert.

Just before dawn they found the cave. As one they advanced towards it, in a V formation they had practised many times. Ahead of them their heat sensors made out two sentries some thirty metres apart. But no one else was around. The Seals were surprised. Clearly those in the cave weren't expecting to be found. Dumb. Very dumb.

For several minutes the Seals listened in to the sentries' snatched conversation, conducted over walkie-talkies and in a language they initially failed to recognize as English, such was the thickness of the accents. There were references to *Star Wars* and Birmingham, England, *Grand Theft Auto* and, as much as the Seals could make out, some sort of fast-food chicken franchise. They might as well have been speaking Arabic for all the sense they made. The Seals waited for their orders. They sucked on tubes connected to camel packs containing blended saline and sugar solutions that ensured they were perfectly fed and hydrated.

A crackle in their earpieces: 'This is Maiden. We have audio confirmation that there are English-speaking people inside the target. Repeat, we have audio confirmation. We are ready to proceed.'

'Time,' someone muttered. 'Good luck, people. Stay safe.'

With a soft double thud the two sentries were taken out by sniper rifle. The Seals surged forward, waves of khaki grey, their urgent movements tracked by satellite, their heart-rates monitored by a team of army medics in a military hospital in North Carolina. The Seals had studied the terrain for days before they'd entered the desert, less than twenty-four hours after a convoy of white Toyotas had been tracked by satellite heading towards the caves. The convoy had stuck out glaringly, like perfect white teeth in the mouth of an old, grey man. US military analysts were confident that the pickups had been destined for the UN only to have gone missing somewhere in Mali. It had been widely reported that they'd ended up in the hands of Al-Boktorah.

The Seals poured through the dark mouth of the cave, their goggles straining to turn blackness into green-grey, their guns raised in front of them, the beams of red lasers mounted to their scopes pointing the way. Once inside, through the fog billowing from their smoke grenades they made out a flickering computer screen, a diesel generator, a couple of trail bikes, bags of rice and flour, cans of kerosene and cooking oil. In one corner they saw a crumpled body. There were no hostages to be seen.

'What the fuck?' muttered one of the Seals. 'Where the . . . ?' He walked up to the computer, which was showing videos of the hostages pleading for the ransom to be paid. He gestured at one corner of the cave, at an old chest freezer almost the size of a small car. Someone had scrawled 'Villa' on its dented white metal side. Two of the Seals advanced. A handful of their colleagues fanned out around them. Others stood guard by the mouth of the cave.

More crackle on the headsets: 'This is Maiden. We don't have visual confirmation of the hostages. Repeat. No visual.'

The two Seals edged closer to the freezer. One of them lifted the lid and immediately dived back. The Seals started firing wildly at the man emerging from the freezer, his eyes wild, a grin fixed on a joke that only he understood. 'Surprise,' he screamed. 'Crusaders, we've been—' He did not complete the sentence. His face was quickly turned to a

236

pulp. Most of his brain decorated the cave wall. His near-headless body fell forward onto the cave floor. It was only then that the Seals saw the detonator strapped to his hand, the pin removed.

'This is Maiden, abort, abort, abort.'

They needed no instruction. The Seals turned, rushed towards the cave mouth, towards the light of the coming dawn. But the light was nothing compared to that which was behind them now as the explosives in the freezer ignited. The light became all-encompassing, a sun starting life. The sun roared towards the mouth of the cave. And then it was free.

Chapter 23

Even from a distance the two men's body language wasn't difficult to read. One of them just stared at the table, refusing eye contact with the other. It was clear that he had no interest in being where he was.

'So,' Scott said, 'The Raptor project sounds a real impressive proposition. I've been reading the prospectus for the TracknTrace technology. I can see why most of Wall Street wants in on its IPO. Lot of money to be made floating this kind of tech play, so they say. Billions. Going to be the biggest flotation since before the Lehman's collapse. No wonder everyone's taking an interest in this. It's a sign of how far the US has bounced back, Raptor. Need to get this one away safely. Lot of investors looking for a return.'

Roscoe grunted something indecipherable. As far as he was concerned, Raptor was his responsibility. Scott needed to keep his nose out of ISG business. The group made good money for the Agency, providing the Agency left it alone. It was a commercial operation; it would be ruined if spooks started intervening. None of Scott's predecessors had bothered with the ISG. Scott shouldn't go breaking with tradition.

'Sorry,' Scott said, 'didn't catch what you just said.'

'You're right,' Roscoe said, 'Raptor's going to be huge. Going to be a great result for the Agency.' His tone was sarcastic. If Scott thought he could use his nice-teacher routine he'd have to think again. Roscoe could see him coming a mile off. He wasn't beholden to Scott but he knew he had to be careful. The king needed to feel that he was in control. It didn't pay to shatter his illusions. Roscoe's eyes darted around the diner. It was more of a burger bar, really, and at eight in the morning there were few people eating. It was like some sort of late-night speakeasy captured in a Hopper painting, a dark cavern of a place that had only a cursory understanding of illumination. It wasn't the sort of place Roscoe expected Scott to eat in. And it certainly wasn't the sort of place where he'd expect to be discussing Raptor. Discussion about Raptor belonged only in the fine dining rooms of investment banks, not in some dimly-lit place where you could order fries at any hour of the day. Roscoe guessed that was the point. Scott clearly wanted the conversation to be had on neutral ground. He relaxed a little. If Scott really had something on him they wouldn't be having the conversation in a burger bar. An army of CIA lawyers would be surrounding them.

'You want something to eat?' Scott asked, as a waitress appeared out of the darkness.

Roscoe shook his head. 'Just coffee.'

Scott read the waitress's name badge. 'Two coffees and a Danish, Mo.' He flashed a smile that came from the future. Everywhere he went, Scott practised his man-of-the-people schtick. A familiarity with the blue-collar worker would come in useful when he ran for public office. He turned back to Roscoe. 'I had dinner with Ailes recently. He was asking about the ISG.'

'He's got a lot of clients who invest with us,' Roscoe said. 'Understandable that he wants to know what the ISG is up to.'

'I was surprised he knew the ISG was part of the Agency. I thought no one would invest in its start-ups if they realized they were CIA. Guess I was naive.'

Roscoe shrugged. 'It's not good for the little man to know that, no. I mean the retail investors, the sort who buy a few thousand shares a year. The great American public. But it's not a problem if the big banks know. They can keep secrets. For them, the CIA isn't toxic, it's an opportunity. Whatever the Agency does has political consequences. Banks know that it offers possibilities. They want to be paddling in the same swamp as us.'

The waitress deposited the coffees and the pastry. Scott flashed her a second smile. He waited for her to walk back into the darkness. 'Possibilities?'

'Correct,' Roscoe said. 'It's a symbiotic relationship. We develop stuff, they invest; we use that money to develop more stuff; they invest more. That's how the military industrial complex works. That's how it has always worked. But I don't need to tell you this. I'm sure your meeting with Ailes would have convinced you of it.' Roscoe eyed Scott sullenly. Now was not the time for the head of the CIA to go anti-business. Everyone knew Scott saw the Agency as a stepping-stone for what he anticipated would become a coruscating political career. If he wanted to end up on Pennsylvania Avenue then he was going to need big players, like Ailes, who could hook him up with the major donors. He needed the banks. He needed the defence contractors. He needed big oil. Christ, he even needed big tobacco. So, no, Roscoe wasn't going to allow Scott to turn incredulous and high-minded all of a sudden. That would be insane. He had to understand that the Agency was one corner of the triangle. The other two were the worlds of politics and big business. The triangle existed only because of all three corners. They were equal angles creating a perfect three-lined shape. Each side was nothing without the other two. Had the useless fuck Ailes not impressed even that on him?

Scott sipped his coffee, bit into the Danish and instantly felt guilty. Sugared, doughy products were something of a novelty but he'd ordered one just to reinforce his man-of-the-people credentials with the waitress. He'd go to the gym later, he told himself. 'Tell me what happened with Zetouin,' he said. 'I thought you guys were looking after him.'

'We were.' Roscoe snorted. 'We brought him back on a jet after debriefing him on an aircraft carrier off Diego Garcia.'

'We?'

Roscoe cracked his knuckles. 'We used a third party. Trusted agent from another security service to oversee the operation. No fingerprints.'

Scott wondered where his agency would be if it wasn't allowed to outsource its war on terror to anonymous corporations. Permanently in front of the Senate Intelligence Committee probably. 'It was a Brit, one of their security service? They're the only ones who can get onto the island apart from ourselves.'

'Right,' Roscoe said. 'Don't worry, this isn't going to blow up in your face.'

Scott felt like laughing. 'I think it already has, Roscoe. I think we've got some major fucking consequences to deal with. I'm not sure you understand how much shit is coming the Agency's way because of all this.'

'Relax,' Roscoe said. 'No one's going to know. Zetouin was an unimportant intel asset whom no one knew about. And now he's a dead unimportant intel asset whom no one knew about. His body's been taken care of. He no longer exists. Find something else to panic about.'

'You don't get this,' Scott said. 'There's a trail. It's a mess.'

'These things happen sometimes. We made sure he was comfortable and then we got him back to Britain, ready to move him to his new life in France with his wife and family, and then he had a cardiac arrest. Go figure.'

Scott was struck by Roscoe's lack of concern. But then he remembered what he'd read about Roscoe in his files. Roscoe saw the beauty in systems, not people. He was fifty-one and had worked for an IT servicing company for years before joining the CIA. The company had won a multi-million-dollar contract servicing the National Security Agency and Roscoe had been drafted in to oversee a project helping it collaborate with its German equivalent, the BND. He'd helped establish a series of black boxes outside Frankfurt that sucked up terabytes of communications data. Roscoe was credited with providing intel on two Islamist sleeper cells operating out of Hamburg. One had been plotting a bombing campaign in Strasbourg. Promotion soon followed, then a leap to the CIA, where he'd embraced free-market economics with the enthusiasm of Milton Friedman. Only markets could solve problems, Roscoe had told the Agency. They connected capital to the brightest minds. Put the two together and the Agency would be unstoppable. All you needed to do was get the Agency thinking like a corporation. It needed the profit motive. That was what would get its juices flowing, not some archaic belief in the fundamental need to protect its citizens. That was a given. No, if it was to compete with the best, and in this Roscoe included terrorists, it needed to introduce incentives. It needed to recalibrate the risk-reward ratio. Roscoe had convinced many in the Agency. But not Scott. Not yet anyway. Roscoe needed to prove himself.

'Still, it was unusual for our man to die like that,' Scott said. 'Don't really understand why moving him was handled by the ISG, anyway. It seems far outside your remit. Long way from Silicon Valley. Long way from Wall Street. I think if I'd been across it I would have questioned it.'

'We've used IT companies to render suspects many times in the past,' Roscoe muttered. 'If we pay them for their services no one really knows what those services are. Is it building us a new computer firewall system? Or is it transporting someone below the radar? No one knows. And this is no different. If the ISG takes care of it, it's off the books and outsourced to our Brit friend. No paper trail. We're protected. Our man Zetouin is protected, too, because no one can track him. Unless someone informs another country that we've been using one of their airports to move him. That sort of defeats the object and makes our life much, much more difficult. That fucks everything.'

Scott heard the venom in Roscoe's voice, and wasn't going to have some jumped-up techno-nerd tell him how things were. Roscoe might think of himself as the CIA's saviour but he wasn't infallible. Even markets could fail. 'Got to obey protocols, these days, you know that, Roscoe. We can't afford to be the subject of another million-page Senate Intelligence Committee report. We can't afford for people to point the finger at us again, say we're shipping people halfway round the world to God knows where so they can be waterboarded at black sites out of sight of the law. There would be catastrophic damage to the Agency. No one's going to give us a second chance now. We wouldn't recover if people thought we hadn't learned from our recent past. From now on, we have to be straight on these things. Ensure all of our processes are in order.'

'Processes?'

'Right,' Scott said. 'I'm realizing there's not enough clarity inside the Agency. People don't know where they stand on things. I'll give you an example. One minute I'm being informed that we lifted Zetouin because he was a major recruiting sergeant for Al-Boktorah. Then I learn that that wasn't his USP at all. He was, in fact, some sort of logistics expert who could provide detailed intel on our target's location. One minute I'm being told we turned Zetouin, put pressure on him and his family to come over; the next I learn that he approached us and asked to cut a deal. At first I thought we brought him out of DG. Now I hear we used some Brit third party. You know, Roscoe, with the exception that we can both agree Zetouin is dead, not a lot else about him holds together. That's kind of worrying to me.'

Roscoe liberated a toothpick from a dispenser on the table, broke it in half and pressed the point into his thumb. He focused on the mild pain as a momentary distraction while he collected his thoughts. Scott was new. He didn't understand how things worked in the Agency. He saw it as monolithic and answerable only to him. All he was interested in was the politics of a situation, how they might affect his ambitions. He didn't understand the damage he risked doing to the ISG, to its investments. He didn't understand that, in the second decade of the twenty-first century, business trumped politics every time. You wanted a successful CIA, you needed a wealthy one. Scott didn't understand that powerful people out there would take an extremely dim view if he impeded the roll-out of technologies that would make the United States a safer place. Scott would understand all of this in time. Roscoe would get Ailes to talk to him again. It clearly hadn't worked the first time.

'When Zetouin appeared there was a lot of confusion,' Roscoe said. 'No one knew if he was genuine. People were trying to figure him out. Maybe he was some sort of plant. Lots of angles were being discussed so it's understandable not everything about what was coming out of Algeria makes perfect sense. But I hear you. We're going to be Snow White from now on.'

Even in the gloom of the diner, Roscoe could feel Scott's eyes boring into him.

You'll ensure his family are looked after, of course,' Scott said.

'Of course.'

'Good to hear,' Scott said. 'But not so good for us. They may talk one day. You thought about that? Maybe they'll hire some lawyers to start digging.'

'I said we'd take care of them.'

'Maybe it'll be enough. But what have we got to show for this? We've got nothing. The asset died before he was able to give us the intel on Al-Boktorah's location. That was unfortunate. Kind of clumsy to lose an asset like that at such a crucial moment.' Scott waited for Roscoe to say something but nothing came back. 'Yes, first Adams, then Zetouin,' he continued. 'This hunt is costing us dear. We just lost fifteen fucking Navy Seals in the desert. If the public ever find out about that fuck-up, someone's going to get crucified. I've got a president breathing down my neck. I've got Congress baying for blood and I've got a lot of angry, deeply pissed energy contractors who are demanding to know why we haven't got boots on the ground in Saharan Africa, turning the entire fucking desert into a battleground that will attract every ISIL and Al-Qaeda and Boko Haram sympathizer for a thousand miles around. And you know what, Roscoe? I don't really have any answers for these people. I've got nothing to give them. Zip. Now, can you help me out on this? You got a bone I can throw them?'

Roscoe drained his coffee. So, then, it was time to push the button. Jefferson had warned him that Scott would want impressing. It was time to impress. Roscoe would have preferred to make the great reveal a little further down the line, when they had it all nailed down and things could be polished up nice and bright so that they dazzled and distracted. That way no one would see the flaws or notice that the technology was far from the finished product. But, still, there really was no point in holding back now. Investors were impatient. They wanted a float and they wanted a spectacular. At some point in the next few days, Raptor's PR offensive would have to start. Scores of laser guided AGM 114 Hellfire missiles would rain down in the Sahara. That was how the perfect triangle of politics, business and defence worked. That was how it had always worked. It would provide a spectacular coup for the Agency. Then perhaps Scott would leave the ISG alone, concentrate on his political ambitions and stop asking awkward questions.

Roscoe leaned back in his chair, studied Scott's face in the gloom of the diner. 'Turns out you're in luck. We've got something we can give you, something the big tech investors call a paradigm shift.'

'And what do you call it?' Scott said.

Roscoe looked around the diner for the waitress. He needed another coffee. 'Al–Boktorah's head on a plate.'

Scott allowed himself a deep breath. 'And how can you be certain that you're going to deliver that?'

Roscoe was grateful for the darkness engulfing him. He really didn't enjoy lying under illumination. His face would give him away far too easily. 'Raptor,' he said quietly. 'Raptor traced him. We know where he's hiding. Raptor's been tracking him for weeks and is going to unleash hell in the desert.'

Chapter 24

The derelict stadium was an anti-building site. Everything inside it had been destroyed, dismantled, dismembered. Its all-weather running track was now a dusty path strewn with rubble and rubbish. The eight polyurethane lanes that had formed a synthetic orange moat between the stadium's stands and the grass oval at its centre had been ripped up long ago. The rubberized track, along with the sky-blue plastic seats in the stands, had found their way to the shanty towns outside Belize City, where they formed improvised walls and roofs. The grass centre was now just caked mud littered with the debris of burned-out motorbikes and rusting cars.

Kate surveyed the scene with a mixture of incredulity and shame. She had to remind herself that billions of dollars passed through Belize every day, that it was a conduit facilitating tax evasion on a truly epic scale. It was a long way from Monaco, say, or Grand Cayman. There were no Ferraris racing down the country' pot-holed roads, no Gucci concessions in its crumbling department stores, no luxury private yachts in its small, uncared-for harbours. Belize was not a good advert for the Commonwealth, for the spoils of empire.

Still, the remnants of a track were better than no track. A lot better. When you needed to run, really needed to run, anywhere was a billion times better than nowhere. And she really needed to run. Something was troubling her, gnawing away, making her restless, unfocused, angry. She couldn't trace the source, wasn't even close to locating it. She knew only that it was there, somewhere inside her, lurking, feverish. She needed the clarity that only running could bring, the feel of late-evening sun on bare limbs, sweat on her upper lip. She needed to feel alive. She needed to feel lost. She needed to feel in control. She needed the million different, often contradictory emotions that only running could give her.

She contemplated stretching but was too desperate to begin. Every minute delayed was a minute wasted. She'd told Fawcett she was going to arrive at the stadium early so that she could get in an hour's running. By the end of her hour, she hoped to have some idea of what was troubling her, at least identify its shape.

She set off, slowly at first, allowing her feet to become familiar with the dust and rubble. Two laps in, and she felt she was hitting her stride. Her arms moved freely. She felt balanced and in control. Her lungs seemed to enlarge and her breathing became strong and steady. I could run like this for ever, she thought. I could keep running round and round and round with no one ever seeing me. I would never stop moving. I would never get caught. It was only when you stopped that you became vulnerable, became a target.

Four, five, six laps. She wondered what Fawcett would think when he arrived. There would probably be some deliberately tactless comment about her running shorts and vest, a contrived attempt at a leer. She didn't care. She was oblivious to everything, impregnable.

Seven, eight, nine, ten. A gentle wind on her face, the sound of commuter traffic on the dual carriageway a mile away. Her running was sure and light. She barely made a sound, her feet skimming across the dust. The stadium was now almost completely dark. The moon seemed to have given up on Belize, just like everything else. The night sky was a vast, sad blackness; there was little light pollution filtering up. Belize City wasn't a place that made great demands on electricity. It couldn't afford power.

Eleven, twelve, thirteen, fourteen laps. So, then, three and a half miles in. Another twenty and she'd call it a day. The endorphins were kicking in, stronger than usual. Perhaps it was because she hadn't run for days. Perhaps it was the novelty of running in a stadium, even if it was a venue that had died long ago. Perhaps it was simply the connection it allowed with the past, a journey back to childhood, when the very act of running was something unbounded, something joyous. Yes, that was probably it, she thought. Running allowed you to wind back the clock, to return to your former half-formed self, when the world seemed less corrupted, more enchanted, more innocent.

Fifteen, sixteen, seventeen, eighteen laps. A fleck of white in the corner of her eye. She shifted her focus and the moment, the oblivion, was gone. Yes, there he was, the heron in his white linen suit. Even from a distance his ridiculous teak-stained tan stood out. Her phone vibrated somewhere inside her running belt. She pulled out the mobile, studied the email from Sorrenson: *Thought you might find this useful.* Cryptic. She clicked on the attachment and scanned the reams of emails between Carrington and some other unidentified person. Terse, gnomic sentences pinged back and forth in cyberspace referring to something called Raptor. The name meant nothing to her but it clearly had meant a lot to Carrington. What was so important about Raptor? There was another email from Callow asking her to call him. She'd several missed calls from him, she saw. Well, they would have to wait. Reluctantly she jogged towards Fawcett. She felt the anger rise within her again. She hadn't run nearly far enough.

Fawcett watched her approach. He could feel the weight of the serrated knife in his jacket pocket. He'd given some thought as to how he was going to kill the stupid bitch. A gunshot might be heard. But a blade was silent and quick, and he could make it look like a botched robbery. The stadium was next to the sea. She wouldn't be found for days, maybe never. Protein for barracudas and nurse sharks. Unpleasant, unwanted but necessary. Pendragon should never have come to Belize, never attempted to test her idiotic hunch by examining the shipping register. A link could be established, he was aware. There was only the slightest chance that she would make the connection but she still posed a threat. They couldn't take the risk. She was in danger of ruining everything.

Fawcett knew that he wasn't a psychopath. He wasn't a cold-blooded killer. He wasn't without remorse for what he was about to do, send Pendragon the way of her father, the way of her husband. He was simply a pragmatist. Someone who had taken a view of the future and decided which side to back. Unlike Matthews. The idiot, thinking he could work for more than one client. His lover had been too greedy. He could be replaced. No, Fawcett thought, collateral damage

251

was unfortunate but inevitable. Even precision-guided laser-targeted drone strikes produced civilian casualties.

'You're early,' Kate said.

'Thought I'd come and get a handle on what this running fix is all about. Nice outfit. Becoming, though it leaves little to the imagination. Perhaps that's the point.' Fawcett attempted a leer.

She shook her head. Now was not the time to confront Fawcett about his fake heterosexuality. There were therapists in Hampstead who would be able to retire on the proceeds of that conversation. 'She should be here soon. We get the intel and then we go home.'

'What – no R and R? Belize has some magnificent Mayan temples, you know.'

'Another time.'

'Seriously?'

'Seriously. I've had my fill of this country already. It's a disgrace, the condition we've left it in. So much for the Commonwealth.'

'Spoken like a true prole, Pendragon.'

Kate gestured around the stadium. 'Look at it, Fawcett. Just look at it. This is supposed to be the country's national athletics stadium. Says it all. I don't need to see some Mayan temples to find out what a ruined civilization looks like.'

'But see what you'd be missing.' Fawcett reached into his jacket pocket, took a step closer towards her, pulled out a small travel guide. On its cover was a pyramid half claimed by jungle. 'Here, take a look. It really is extraordinary what the Mayans achieved.'

Reluctantly she moved closer, held out a hand. 'Honestly, Fawcett, we have better things . . .' She felt a sharp pain as she rolled over on broken concrete, twisted an ankle. She

252

cursed herself for not looking down, resisted the urgent need to vomit. She wouldn't be able to run for weeks. For a second she thought she would lose her balance and fall to the ground. She groaned quietly. The pain continued to swell. It was only then that she realized she'd witnessed the flash of a blade, now nothing more than a memory. It was only then that she became conscious that the knife's teeth had scythed into her, shredding skin and clavicle. It was only then that it seemed all of her breath had been stolen from her body. She gave another low, deep groan, dropped to her knees. Her right arm crabbed its way across her body, searched for the newly-formed valley in her flesh. The wound burned like acid. She fell forward in the dust and rolled over, her back to Fawcett, sobbing, moaning. She tried to suck humid air into empty lungs. The shock of the assault, its randomness, flooded her mind with contradictory impulses. Rest, run, rest, run.

She tried to form words but none came. The stadium seemed to spin. Shapes melded into each other. She could taste dust in her mouth. An overwhelming sense of powerlessness seized her. She couldn't move. She had no more journeys to make.

'Sorry,' Fawcett said. 'It should really have been quicker than this. If you hadn't . . . stumbled, well, it would all be over by now. Annoying. For both of us.' He stood looking down at her, his tanned face a frown. 'Please believe me, I'm not enjoying this. If there had been another way, I'd have taken it. But, well . . .' He gestured around him at the dead stadium. 'You should never have come to Belize. A violent country, has been since it stopped being British Honduras. When will small countries understand that they can't make it alone these days, hey?'

He continued to stare down at her. When he spoke next his voice was low and flat. 'I guess Five will have to investigate your death but it's a robbery, plain and simple. Maybe they'll review their protocols or something equally tedious. I guess I'll be interviewed. A bore.'

She tried to laugh but no sound came from her lips. She rolled herself round to look at him, turning her head from side to side, trying to make the spinning stop. She stared up at him dully. It was hard to focus. The pain flowing from the burning wound was now close to consuming her. Fawcett continued to watch her, his head angled to one side, a bird on a riverbank sizing up a fish.

'Right,' he said. 'Let's get this over with, put you out of your misery. I'm sorry if I sound curt, uncaring. I'm just not familiar with . . . well, this.' He dropped to his knees, held the knife over her. 'This is all a bit dramatic . . . You may want to avert your eyes. Can't be pleasant. But it'll be over soon. Promise.'

She closed her eyes, anticipated the intense pain and the darkness to come. She was barely conscious. Only the burning wound seemed to prevent her slipping away. Would he attack her neck or her heart? Both probably. It would help, she figured, if her body was mutilated so that she was seen to be a victim of a frenzied attack. A couple of knife wounds would suggest a deliberate murder, something purposeful about her extinction. But a punctured corpse, well, people wouldn't ask so many questions. Her death would be dismissed as just another example of the random violence men meted out to women every day. Regrettable but not unusual. The savagery of the assault would conceal the real motive for her death. A hundred stab wounds would hide the truth revealed by just one.

In her semi-comatose state, the thought seemed to jolt her awake. She was about to become a murder victim and she didn't know why. It made no sense. She was no threat to Fawcett. And yet . . .

Light in the darkness. Her closed eyes saw a hundred fires. She felt air rush into her lungs. What was it that Fawcett feared about her? She had to be edging closer to something, something that truly terrified him, if it were exposed. She opened her eyes, turned every atom of her being into the construction of a single word. 'Raptor,' she whispered. She closed her eyes again. A hundred fires became two hundred.

'Raptor,' Fawcett repeated slowly, warily. He clapped his hands together, repeated the word, this time mockingly. 'Do continue.' Kate kept her eyes shut, shook her head gently. She forced her lips into a smile. Fawcett jumped to his feet, kicked her hard in the right leg. His words were clipped and sour. 'I said, do continue. Please don't make this any harder than it is already. It's all rather . . . unbecoming.'

Kate groaned, tried to nod. She pointed up at Fawcett, then curled her forefinger, beckoned him to come in close. 'Here,' she breathed. 'Come here.' Two hundred fires had become four hundred. Fawcett sighed, sank to his knees, bent close to her mouth. 'Raptor,' she whispered. 'I've seen the emails to Carrington. I know you didn't want Five to know about Raptor. I've worked out why. Others will work out why. You can kill me but they're going to find you, Fawcett. You're not going to be able to hide from them.'

She felt spittle on her face as Fawcett spat angry, incomprehensible words. She'd got to him, got under his stupid teak-toned skin. Just where'd he got that tan?

'You know only a fraction of the truth,' Fawcett hissed. 'If you knew more, you'd never have got yourself killed like

255

this. You wouldn't have left yourself so exposed, Pendragon. You'd probably understand my motivation, too, the decisions I've had to make, ones that flaky fucks like Callow and Webster would never understand. It's all about the long game, about how we can achieve a lasting security, not some quick win that'll come undone in a matter of years. There are fundamental positions at stake here. Any serious person who has studied the situation understands that we have to take sides.'

He stretched out a hand, ran it through her hair, adjusted his position so that he was kneeling slightly behind her. 'Now, I know I sound melodramatic, but it really is time for you to take your half-formed theories with you to the grave. This ugly scene has gone on far too long, I'm sure you'll agree.' Four hundred fires became eight hundred. Kate saw a beach at night. She smelt marijuana smoke wafting on the breeze, heard the strum of a guitar. Grotters on the shingle, stars above. She saw Betelgeuse, she saw Polaris. Her right hand flashed across her chest, located the canister on her gel belt. There was the sound of yielding Velcro as she liberated the pressurized container. She aimed it upwards, depressed the button, felt the rush as ten fluid ounces of capsaicin-laced bear spray rained upwards into Fawcett's face. The entire action had been performed in a heartbeat, as if she'd been rehearsing it all her life.

'Bitch, fucking bitch,' Fawcett hissed. 'Fucking . . . fuck, fuck.' His hands clawed his streaming eyes. He let out a deep, bestial scream, a wounded fox, stammered some words that were slurred, unintelligible.

Kate rolled onto her side, scrambled across the dust, her hands scouring the debris. She sensed Fawcett stumbling towards her on his knees, heard his sobs of rage. He was close. Very close. She spun around, the best part of a brick in her right hand. He lunged towards her, knife ready to plunge, eyes streaming, incoherent invective spewing from his lips. The brick connected with his right temple, sent him reeling backwards onto his knees. He crumpled to the ground, his linen suit now sepia from the dust.

The sudden silence was alarming. She forced herself to crawl back towards Fawcett, shocked to find that a second brick was in her hand. She could see that his chest was moving. The knife was still clutched in his right hand. She edged closer, reached out for the blade. With a scream Fawcett sat upright, whipped the knife away from her outstretched hand, lunged towards her. She brought the brick up fast, straight into his jaw, heard the crunch of bone and the shatter of enamel. For several seconds, Fawcett remained in an upright sitting position, blood pouring from his nose, his mouth, eyes staring blankly at her. Another silence, another absence of noise after extreme violence. She waited, unsure of her next movement. Her breathing came in short, fast gulps. She was thirsty for air. She needed to flee the scene. Only she couldn't move. There was something hypnotic about watching Fawcett, about witnessing the damage she'd done to him. 'Fawcett,' she began. She couldn't think what to say next. We'll get you patched up? Was that even plausible? Should she summon help from the embassy? Maybe go and flag down a car on the highway? She felt paralysed. She had no options. Motion, the one thing her entire wounded body craved, was being denied her. She was conscious that she was trembling, conscious that she was still holding the brick. Fawcett gave a tiny nod of his head. His right arm sprang back robotically, knife poised. There were bubbles of blood on his lips. He made a half-attempt at another lunge towards her. It was enough. It was a provocative act, a refusal to surrender. There would be no ceasefire. A million synapses fired across her brain. She smashed the brick into his face, fell towards him, into him. The two of them slumped backwards into the dirt. She'd passed the point of no return. Better that he was finished now. He wasn't going to survive, not in any useful way. She brought the brick down onto his head, screamed as his skull shattered as easily as an egg. Blood was spattered up her arms. Something red and jelly-like stuck to her wrist, like a leech. She couldn't look at it. It was too vivid, too grotesque.

Another silence broken only by the barking of a stray dog and the odd rumble of a truck on the highway nearby. It was over. Fawcett was over.

For more than an hour she didn't move. The acid burn of the wound was unrelenting. The night was warm but she couldn't stop shivering. She sat next to Fawcett, fascinated by the results of her destruction. She wondered what had happened to the woman who'd been supposed to show up. Fawcett must have contacted her, told her the deal was off. She stared down at the body, a heap of dirty white linen surrounded by a halo of blood, light in the dark. So, she thought, I'm a killer now. I'll always be a killer. From now on my life will be divided into two parts: before I killed and after. The thought didn't trouble her as much as she'd supposed. Maybe it was the trauma. Perhaps the guilt, the remorse, would come later. Or perhaps it would never come, a strange absence, an ache that would stay with her for the rest of her life. She couldn't decide which scenario was more likely. She couldn't decide which was worse.

Reluctantly she found her phone. She had no desire to contact anyone. As far as she was concerned the night could last for ever. She feared light. She feared the questions to come. But they'd need Six's help to take care of things. Callow could arrange that. Somebody could be despatched from the embassy to clean things up. Fawcett's body could be taken home in a diplomatic bag, if they moved quickly. She looked down at his tanned corpse.

'Was it worth it?' she muttered. Instinctively her hand snaked through the rubble, across the bloody dust until it came to rest on Fawcett's shattered skull. With a quick jerk of her fingers she freed a small clump of his blood-matted hair, zipped it up inside her running belt. She tried to stand but was too weak to move. She curled herself into a ball, held her mobile next to her face, punched some buttons. She closed her eyes, saw a thousand fires.

Chapter 25

He was stumbling over his script. The words just wouldn't come out right. He'd talked about the West, how it was to blame for his situation, their situations. All of the remaining hostages. But then he couldn't remember what to say next. Something about a ransom. Something about how people around the world held his fate in their hands. Something.

The man stared into the camera, dumbstruck at the prospect of being outside for the first time in weeks. The desert was so vast, he thought. It was an entire universe. No one would ever find their bodies in such a huge expanse of nothing. How long did bones last? Would they remain preserved under shifting mountains of sand or would they be quickly whittled down to nothing by the constant friction?

He tried but he couldn't help it. The man thought about his family back home in Aberdeen, about what they'd be doing at that moment. Friday night. Fish and chips, if he was at home. Cod all round, except for his wife, who preferred plaice. Then, if it was light, maybe he'd go and kick a ball around with his two sons in the road outside their house until Martha, their mother, called them in for a bath. They'd play again the next day, he'd promise them. It was the only way he could get them out of the street. Football mad, those two. Scotland for ever. If their enthusiasm for the sport remained undimmed, they'd have to get used to a lot of disappointment in their lives. The man choked back tears. He should have stayed on the rigs, never taken the job in Algeria. But jobs were drying up in the North Sea. No one was investing because of the falling oil price. He'd had no choice. You had to go where the money was. He'd done it for Martha and the kids. He'd been trying to provide for them. A normal, honest, everyday man, who now had a bomb for a necklace.

Encouraged by the hooded men behind the camera, he tried to find the words but they wouldn't come. He slumped forward into the sand, tried to bury his face deep into the ground, as if he could somehow bore down into the earth, away from them, away from the horror.

The two employees of big tobacco sat on the large wooden seat and looked across the estuary. The tide was so far out that the sea seemed to be in danger of disappearing beyond the horizon. Where there had once been saltwater there was now only wet mud and the rotting skeleton of a long-dead yawl.

A fierce wind whipped across the shoreline. Storm clouds were rolling in across the Channel. Gulls screeched in the dusk, looping back on themselves as they battled the gusts that riffled through the shingle, chopping the waves into jagged snow-capped mountains.

'Pace?' one of the men said, reading the word carved into the back of the seat.

The other man turned his head, examined the inscription. 'Peace. *Pace* is Italian for peace. This is a peace bench. Built to commemorate some peace campaigner who lived in the town years ago. Dead now.'

'Right.'

The other man looked at the dark green hills on the other side of the estuary, at the long strip of white sand below them. 'Nice way to be remembered. I wouldn't mind that.'

Metcalf turned to Cole and shook his head very slowly. He lit a cigarette. 'Not much of a memorial, some bench that'll rot and be crapped on by gulls.'

Cole felt as if his entire body would crumble at any minute. The cancer now owned him completely. He was aware that he was contemplating the shoreline for what might be the final time. He wished the tide would bring the sea back, for one last goodbye. 'Does anything really endure?' he murmured. 'I mean, really live on.'

Metcalf watched the approach of a fat gull, its yellow beak urgently pecking the ground. There was a swagger about the bird that he found unsettling. It wasn't scared of him. 'You're getting philosophical in your old age,' he said.

Cole could make out the odd light moving across the dark hills. People were driving home. It seemed a nice place to live, the isle in the middle of the estuary. If he had his time again maybe he'd look at buying a home there. The early-evening light above it was mesmerizing.

'I'm heading for the exit,' Cole said quietly. 'Cancer. Week or two at best.' He nodded at the cigarette in Metcalf's hand. 'You should quit. Very bad for you. You should quit Smith and Webb, too, Metcalf. Retire. Go and see something of the world.'

Metcalf ground out his cigarette beneath his foot, lit another. He stared at the gull; its yellow eyes seemed to be judging him. 'I've never really been interested in abroad. Smith and Webb is my world.'

'Well, trust me, you don't want to get to the end of the road and just have years of service for a tobacco giant to look back on. You see things with much more clarity towards the end of the film.'

Metcalf sucked on his cigarette. 'That why you did it?'

Cole reached into his jacket pocket, pulled out a vial of painkillers, popped two into his mouth. 'I'm not really sure. It was opportunistic. Someone fed me the files. Don't know who, don't know why. I just passed them on. I'd like to think I'd have done it if I hadn't been dying. But maybe not. It's liberating, though. The end. I'm no longer a wage slave. Don't have to worry about my pension any more. I can take risks.'

'And what do you think you've achieved?' Metcalf hissed. 'What have you got to show for betraying your employer?'

'Not much. Easier to look at myself in the mirror, maybe. Even though I really do look like death.'

'You think it was some sort of noble act, what you did? Feeding all that stuff to that blogger? You must have known we'd be able to work out it was you.'

Cole shook his head. 'I don't know. I don't really care. But Smith and Webb, it was an empire out of control, Metcalf. It needed reining in. It needed to understand that there are consequences to its actions. Its products had become the preferred currency for terrorists. Smith and Webb deliberately engineered a system to make sure its product ended up in the hands of anyone just so long as they could pay. And look how that worked out. A bloodbath in the desert. Our employer has helped bring that about. We helped bring that about.'

'You think the new Chinese owners will do things differently?' Metcalf snorted. 'You've been signed off work ill for the last month or so and you don't know anything. But I can tell you nothing has changed since they arrived. Nothing. Do you really think anything is going to change in the future?'

'Probably not. But at least people are going to be asking questions of them now. It's something to leave behind.'

'It's nothing,' Metcalf said. 'Fucking nothing. You're about to hit the exit and you've got nothing to show for it. You're a dying man who's aiming for sainthood, Cole. Well, you've fucked it. Chinese will sell to anyone. Terrorists included.' Metcalf stood up, threw his cigarette in the direction of a gull. 'I take it you won't be coming back to work?'

'Right.'

'I'm not coming to your funeral, Cole.'

'Never asked you to.'

Metcalf glowered at his colleague. He felt impotent and full of rage. Cole was a coward. Anyone could make a stand when they had nothing left to lose. He'd come close to destroying one of Britain's – no, one of the empire's most successful companies. It was an act of wanton vandalism. Tens of thousands of people owed their livelihoods to Smith and Webb. There was no moral high ground in the business world. Every company was tainted, ultimately. That was how the system operated. Cole was an idiot to make an example of just one corporation, to single it out for his own special form of justice. 'Are you going for burial or cremation?' Metcalf snarled.

'Cremation. Ashes going to be scattered here, around this bench.'

'Good. I'll come back and piss on it when you're dead.'

'You do that. I'll be long gone. Your problem, Metcalf, is that you won't. You'll be stuck fighting fires, trying to shore up a crumbling kingdom. They won't find your body under the rubble.'

'Save your breath, dying man. Might keep you alive a few painful days longer.' Metcalf walked across the beach, aware that he was being watched by more than twenty gulls. Ugly, ugly birds, he thought. He knelt down, scooped up some shingle, threw it at them. 'Fucking take this!' he yelled.

Cole didn't watch him go. He remained gazing out over the estuary, at the brilliant strip of white sand on the other side. In front of him, in pools of saltwater left by a departing sea, flame-tinged clouds burned like fires.

Scott had expected to meet resistance but not on such a scale. The power of the apathy being directed towards him was crippling. He was experiencing an unusual troubling sensation. He found himself plagued with self-doubt. Standing in the bombproof bunker, deep in the bowels of the CIA's Langley headquarters, he felt as if he were on trial. He was an innocent man, pleading for the scales to fall from the eyes of others, but no one in the court believed him, or at least cared whether he was guilty or not. Rather, they'd already chosen to condemn him. The judge was donning his black cap.

The hostility from both sides manifested itself in long, awkward silences and a blanket refusal to make eye contact with him. Scott realized he had no allies. The defence chiefs and his fellow spooks viewed him as a politician, someone who would blame them when people got round to asking the difficult questions once the smoke had cleared. Both sides feared that he was more than capable of smashing things up to advance himself. He was isolated. Iconoclasts couldn't count on the support of others, Scott was learning. Demolition was lonely work. Even if the public didn't know, everyone in the room was all too aware of what had happened to the Seals . . .

Scott looked up from his notes, then returned to the grainy satellite image projected on the screen behind him. He poured himself a glass of water, took a deep gulp that seemed to make him only thirstier. Maybe he'd drunk too much the night before. But he was so tired all the time and alcohol smoothed things down, made exhaustion manageable, knocked the edges off things. He was conscious that fifty pairs of eyes were staring at him. He should have stuck a firing target on his face, made things easy for them. He'd never seen so much khaki in one room. Never encountered so much cynicism towards his side either. Understandable. The generals and the spooks were never going to find any common ground. Each side saw the other as a threat, a robber of resources, of presidential attention, of Congressional goodwill, of glory. Only one empire could rule in such an attritional world. Both sides wanted it to be them. 'I guess you have questions,' he said, after he'd completed a short prepared speech that had taken around four minutes to deliver and five hours to compose. The inevitable hand went up. Scott's self-doubt ballooned: Kominski. Not a great start.

'Tell me, what exactly are we looking at?'

Scott wondered how someone so obese could have risen so far in the military. Surely gravity should have held him back? But, instead, the four-star general's career seemed to have advanced with the expansion of his gut. He wasn't a good advert for military discipline. He didn't seem physically capable of defending the land of the free. In Scott's mind, the only thing Kominski seemed capable of defending was his position in the buffet queue. 'Al-Boktorah's main distribution depot,' Scott said. Christ, Kominski was obtuse. Had he just zoned out for the last five minutes? The general was probably trying to get a rise out of him. He had to let it go. If his ego collided with Kominski's, the explosion would rock the capital. Scott jerked a thumb over his shoulder towards the satellite image of the building, little more than a clutch of dense black dots. 'Everything he moves across the Sahara goes through it.'

'Everything?' Kominski said.

'Everything. Guns, drugs, fuel, tobacco, fighters.'

'Pretty small warehouse,' Kominski said. 'Doesn't look right. What's that building next to it?'

Scott peered at the screen. 'A school, we think. Well, some sort of nursery anyway. Next to that there's a bakery. The two neighbouring buildings give the target cover. Lot of lorries and buses going by these buildings. Wonder why that is, hey? But you're right, General, the warehouse is way too small for the true scale of his operation. It's what happens underground that interests us. There's a load of bored-out caves. That's his real distribution depot, what's buried below, not what's above.'

'How deep down are the caves?' Kominski said.

Scott studied his notes. 'We reckon thirty metres.'

The general contrived a snort. 'Going to need some pretty big keys to open that door, then. Normal missiles aren't going to do it. We'll need bunker-busters. You'll hear them down in Jo'burg when they drop. Not sure how the Algerians are going to take to us blowing up half their desert. We have to work the back channels before we go anywhere near this plan. That will take time. The Algerians are going to want something out of this.'

Scott said nothing. He really could do without Kominski's hyperbole but he'd come to understand that four-star generals didn't do nuance. The way they spoke reflected their demeanour: blunt, aggressive, unyielding. God knew what they'd be if they weren't in the military. Hick farmers, probably, bossing livestock around just so they could feel powerful.

'You got a plan if this goes wrong?' Kominski said. 'I mean a proper, fully scoped contingency plan if this blows up in our faces?'

'It won't,' Scott said. 'Everything carries risk but we've studied this closely. This is the best chance we have of taking out Al-Boktorah and half his militia. Any day now he's going to kill the remaining fifty hostages. We don't have the luxury of waiting much longer. He's dictating the terms, not us. It's his clock we have to use.'

'How'd we find this location anyway?' Another voice. A woman's. Scott turned to Regan, the NSA's deputy director. Five of her could fit into one Kominski, he reckoned. Glacial. That was the word he'd use to describe her. Glacial and fucking scary, if he were asked for another two. Regan wore her intelligence heavily, asked too many unsettling questions for Scott's liking. Now, she really was a politician. She should be in charge of the Federal Emergency Management Agency, Scott thought. She'd be much better dealing with complex issues like urban flooding and storm damage rather than having to weigh up whether to bomb a terrorist back into the Stone Age. That sort of decision didn't require much in the way of thinking, as far as Scott could see. If they did nothing, the hostages died, and they would appear impotent. If they did something they could at least say they'd tried if it all went wrong. And this scenario was unlikely, given the intel provided by Raptor. Scott had studied all of the material Roscoe had handed over. Raptor had identified reams and reams of signals all coming from minuscule radio tags hidden in cigarette packets. They all centred on one location, now identified by satellite images. It was, Scott conceded, a genuine coup for Raptor, for Roscoe, for the ISG. It had done what no human could: it had found Al–Boktorah. Now there was only one choice to make: do nothing or pull the trigger.

'I mean,' Regan continued, 'this is just a photo of a building. How can we be sure the target's even there?'

'Good question,' Scott said.

'And?'

Scott reached for his glass of water. The hangover was really kicking in. 'An Agency initiative,' he said.

'Now I'm really intrigued,' Regan said. She stared hard at Scott. 'Do go on. I'm just wondering how the CIA has managed to locate a target that my agency has spent five years trying to hunt down but with no success. What's your secret?'

'We've been adulterating product with RFIDs,' Scott said.

Kominski swore audibly under his breath. He turned to two other defence chiefs sitting beside him, then back to Scott. 'In English? That too much to ask?'

Scott only just managed to stop himself shaking his head. He wasn't going to give Kominski that sort of cowed response. He wasn't some schoolboy, answering to a teacher.

Kominski needed to understand who was king. He needed to understand that those in charge of intelligence were calling the shots, not those who pulled the trigger. 'RFIDs,' Scott said. 'Radio frequency identification tags. We've been embedding them in packets of British-produced cigarettes smuggled into Africa and which the target was shipping across the Sahara. It's allowed us to track him and his people across the desert using satellites. All roads lead to the warehouse you're all looking at. We've been running the op for some time. Huge activity at night around that warehouse, according to the signals coming from the tags. We're sure he's there.'

'You got any visual confirmation on the target?' Regan said. 'You're putting a hell of a lot of faith in an unproven technology.'

Scott had been preparing for the question. 'Negative,' he said. 'But we do have secondary intel from a source that strongly suggests this is Al-Boktorah's HQ.'

'The source being?' Kominski snapped.

'One of the target's main fixers. He shared some intel with us.'

'What sort of quality?' Regan said.

Scott thought for a moment. The truth wouldn't be helpful right at that moment. To say Zetouin had died before he'd divulged what he knew wasn't going to help him win support. It was time for a necessary lie. An unimportant one. Raptor's technology was sound, he was confident of that. And Roscoe intimated that Zetouin had shared some intel before he'd died. It wasn't an outright fabrication.

'Good quality,' Scott said. 'He gave a positive ID of the target strike site that helped confirm our co-ordinates.'

Regan looked at Kominski then back at Scott. 'Well, that's good news.'

'Yeah,' Scott said. 'It is.'

'Never heard it done before,' Regan said. 'Those guys, the fixers, they don't tend to turn. Sure, you can board them but most of what they say then is just crap. No intel value at all. Just telling you what they think you want to hear.'

'We didn't waterboard him,' Scott said. 'We gave him the offer of a new life, for him and his family.'

'And how's that working out for him?' Regan said.

Scott cursed inwardly. He'd walked into a trap. It was clear that Regan knew what had happened to Zetouin. Jesus, the CIA couldn't even keep a secret from its own sister agency. 'The source died of a heart attack shortly after debriefing.'

'That's unfortunate,' Regan said.

'Unfortunate,' Scott agreed.

'This technology you've been using,' Kominski said. 'Where'd you get it from?'

'It's an ISG play,' Scott said.

Kominski laughed. 'Holy fuck. You got those jokers involved in this? Seriously? The shit they come up with is good for, I dunno, giving us a back door into systems to monitor emails or something but this, well, this is in a different league. You're going to target a drone strike based on what some nerds have built in their garage.'

'We're confident the technology works,' Scott said.

'Well, you'd better be,' Kominski said. 'Lot riding on this now.' He nodded at Scott, parting his lips to show some suspiciously white enamel.

Christ, Scott thought, did anyone have normal teeth in Washington? Even fat generals were sporting million-dollar smiles.

'Lot of reputations riding on this,' Kominski continued. 'Lot of doors going to slam shut if this blows up in people's faces. Careers going to get murdered before they ever really get going.'

Scott glared at Kominski. The stupid fuck. He promised himself that he'd personally ensure Kominski ended up somewhere like Yemen if he himself ever made it within a hundred yards of the White House. See how the fat guy would like living in that sort of arid, derelict country. See where his cynicism got him when the nearest buffet bar was in Kenya. 'Fifty lives,' Scott said quietly. 'That's what's at stake here. We've got to keep remembering that. I repeat: fifty lives. Around half of them Americans. Our job, our only job, is to protect the citizens of the United States of America.'

The khaki-clad warriors in the room seemed to give a collective shrug. 'This country loses twice that many people in RTAs in just one day,' Kominski said.

'And there's no guarantee that if you take the target out you're going to save them,' Regan added. 'Maybe you'll end up provoking him.'

Got you, Scott thought. It was time for another improvisation of the truth. 'Our source said there's no appetite to kill the hostages among Al-Boktorah's lieutenants. They just want to make money. They know the hostages are worth more to them alive than dead. Take out Al-Boktorah and we can negotiate with whoever replaces him. This is the only plan in town now.'

'That'll be the source who's no longer with us,' Regan muttered. 'You're asking us to trust the political views of a dead man. I don't trust people who are alive. Corpses, I don't trust at all.'

Scott studied her peroxide-blonde hair. He wondered

what her true colour was beneath the dye. He noticed that Kominski was shaking his head. The action was almost imperceptible but it was there, just a faint movement from side to side, a tiny act of defiance designed to be seen and yet not seen. So, then, neither side was going to make his job easy. The problem, Scott knew, was that neither Regan nor Kominski, nor anyone else present for that matter, had anything to lose by doing nothing. For those who'd made it into the room, maintaining their positions, their image, was everything. They didn't want to ruin themselves, their reputations, by taking risks. Scott felt a sense of unwanted kinship with Roscoe. He suddenly understood why Roscoe was so eager to genuflect before the altar of big business. Only corporations understood the intrinsic value that came from pushing things forward. Business was on the side of motion. Movement was progress. He took another glug of water, stared Regan and Kominski down. 'I say we've got enough intel to take out Al-Boktorah. We've got to use it. We have no choice. We've run out of options.'

Chapter 26

'The best thing about this place? Marrow bone. Got to be.' Ailes took his steak knife and stabbed it through the centre of the small oval bone until it oozed brown-grey jelly. He spread the viscous paste onto a thin piece of toast and nodded with satisfaction. 'You feel like you're eating the soul of an animal when you're eating marrow. You're ingesting another being. Not something you feel every day. You want to taste another life, suck on marrow bone.'

Roscoe contemplated his Caesar salad, wondering if he should have ordered a different starter. Croutons, Parmesan shavings, lettuce. No blood, no gore to gnaw on, just the shredded contents of a fridge's chiller cabinet. He hated his lunches with Ailes. They were something to be endured, not enjoyed. But they had to be done.

'You still eating here a lot?' Roscoe asked. He looked around the panelled dining room. If it were a person, he thought, it would be a centenarian. It would have arranged its funeral long ago. It would be waiting for the last act in some Florida retirement home. The place made him shudder. It was anathema to everything he believed in.

'Couple of times a week.' Ailes picked up a bone, liberated some brown goo with his knife. 'Good place to be seen.

Reminds my enemies I'm still alive. Allies, too. Same difference some days.'

'You got enemies? I wouldn't think that kind of knowledge would keep you awake at night.' Roscoe drained his
wine glass. He wasn't used to drinking at lunchtime. Come
to that, he wasn't used to drinking. The West Coast didn't
have a drinking culture, not the part he frequented anyway,
the profitable part, the part that ran the world, hurled it forward into the future, a bowling ball smashing down skittles.
But the East Coast, well, as far as Roscoe could make out,
parts of it still seemed to have barely moved on since independence. There were a lot of private clubs in Washington
inhabited by florid men talking politics. It was sort of quaint,
Roscoe thought. Sort of pitiful, too, really. All these men
thinking that politics was still important. He doubted
whether the next political elite would be so deluded. They'd
realize that the game was up, that they weren't calling the
shots any more, hadn't been for years. They would understand that politics couldn't keep up with technology and
they'd have to cut a deal with those who had the ideas, knew
how to exploit information, mine data, build solutions.
Politicians were becoming increasingly irrelevant in a net-
worked, outsourced, borderless world. Elites couldn't hold
the whip hand when technology was fragmenting traditional
power structures. In the future it was technology, not
politics, that would save hostages. Raptor would prove that
to the world. OK, there were some teething issues but they'd
be ironed out. The world didn't need to know about teething issues. It just needed to embrace the whole vision thing.

Yes, Roscoe thought, the likes of Ailes would be extinct
within a decade. In the power stakes the West Coast would
soon eclipse the East Coast. What was strange was that the

likes of Ailes couldn't see it coming. So much for the big beasts' fabled antennae. They couldn't see the storm clouds on the horizon. But right at that moment he needed Ailes more than Ailes needed him. It was better to flatter a dying king when he was still capable of passing a death sentence from his bed. 'I guess having some enemies is a good thing,' Roscoe said. 'Lets you know you're doing something right. Can't move forward without some kind of friction.'

Ailes beckoned a waiter. 'We'll have another bottle.' He pointed a finger at Roscoe. 'After all, we're celebrating.'

Roscoe played dumb. 'We're celebrating?'

'Oh, all right, you're celebrating,' Ailes said. 'Your Raptor IPO next week is going to be the biggest deal of the decade. Huge, huge buzz around it. Several of my clients, banks mainly, couple of venture-capital firms with close ties to the Pentagon, they're real pissed they're not part of it.'

'You could have been in on it,' Roscoe protested. 'You know we'd have given you some of the action if you'd wanted in. We could've used your banks to bring Raptor to market. They would have earned a lot of money when it floated. To be honest, I'm mighty surprised you sat this one out, given our relationship down the years. Of all the plays that have come out of the ISG, Raptor's the real nine-carat diamond. Raptor's going to be huge.'

Ailes studied his marrow bones, like they were chess pieces. He was sure a couple of them were still withholding some jelly. He probed the suspect pair with his knife. 'Yeah, maybe,' he said. 'But you can't win them all, right? And, besides, I guess a lot of people making money from the Raptor float need paying back. We can't all be in on it. You've got to keep your allies close.'

Roscoe stabbed a crouton with his fork. 'How d'you mean?'

Ailes took a deep gulp of his wine. 'Well, a lot of the names I see on the Raptor deal, it's no surprise to learn they've been funding certain personal action committees.' He flashed a nicotine smile. 'They're . . . How shall I put it? Sympathetic to a particular party, the one currently in power. They're at the dove-ish end of things. Not like a lot of my guys. Yep, it's going to be a big pay day for them when Raptor floats.'

Roscoe went back to studying his salad. 'I leave politics for other people. My job's just to get great technology out there, put it in the hands of the people.' He took another sip of his wine and tried not to grimace. It was French. Nothing good had come out of France, he thought. The revolution maybe, but that was all. He looked up and was alarmed to see that Ailes was having some sort of seizure. The lobbyist's face was bright red. Ailes was laughing at him.

'Jesus, Roscoe,' Ailes said, 'you've been spending far too long in the Valley. You sound like some sort of tech messiah. Way too evangelical to be sane. I mean, you almost sound like you really believe the horse-shit coming out of your mouth.'

Roscoe felt the anger rise within him. He forced himself to remember that he was talking to a dying species. Soon Ailes would be little more than a fossil or maybe some black gunk that people would remember had once powered a car. He stabbed another crouton with a fork.

'Tell me,' Ailes said, 'I take it that, as you asked to see me, it's because your new man Scott is still questioning the role of the ISG. You want me to keep putting him straight on a few things? Show him who's in charge? I met with him as we agreed but, well . . .' Ailes let out another deep laugh that seemed to roll in from somewhere south of the Mason-Dixon line. 'Let's just say we may have our work cut out there, Roscoe. Strikes me that he's maybe too ambitious to be reined in. Clear to me and anyone else in this great city that your man Scott sees the Agency as a stepping-stone to his own political career. Wouldn't be the first Agency director to run for high office. Won't be the last either. I'd be interested to learn his politics. Don't really think his sympathies are aligned with the current president. I got him pegged as more of a hawk than a dove. Guess we'll see soon enough where he stands on things.'

'What do you mean by that?' Roscoe asked.

Ailes dabbed his mouth with a napkin, placed the white linen with a stain the colour of blood back on the table. Almost every one of his fingers sported a ring, Roscoe noticed. It made him look like he was wearing a knuckle-duster.

'People talking,' Ailes murmured. 'Washington don't keep secrets well. Not from me anyway. That's why I'm the biggest beast in the jungle. Not because I got the biggest teeth but because I got the biggest ears. I can hear things coming a long way off. I predict something big's coming over the horizon just after Raptor floats. Something huge. I reckon it's going to be good news for its shareholders, good news for the Agency, good news for Scott, good news for the ISG, good news for you, good news for the president, good news for whoever in his party is chosen to succeed him, and good news for all his big backer friends. Washington is going to be drowning in good news real soon. It's like the city's water supply is going to be flooded with Prozac. Good for anything that's floating, I guess. Going to keep things real buoyant.' Ailes drained his glass, waved the waiter over to refill it. He stared hard at Roscoe then raised his glass. 'To good news,' he said. 'Long may it continue.' The two men clinked glasses.

'To good news,' Roscoe said uncomfortably. Ailes had him spooked with all his talk of good news. He was just bluffing, Roscoe told himself. The lobbyist knew nothing.

'I'm hungry for my steak,' Ailes said. 'You ordered the turbot, didn't you?'

Roscoe gave a half-nod. 'Yeah.'

'I'm mighty interested in seeing it on a plate. Been coming here almost a quarter of a century. Never seen anyone order fish.'

'I'm grateful. Seriously. I can't ask . . .' Kate wrung her hands apologetically. She tried again. 'I mean, I could ask, get it done by the guys Five use, but I just want to know if I'm right before I go around starting the Third World War. It could be that . . .'

The sound of electric drills tore through the police station's walls.

'It could be nothing,' she said flatly.

Sorrenson gazed at her. The woman standing in his office was so familiar, so alien. Fifty different emotions were threatening to pull him apart. He could make out the bandages under her blouse. What was the story behind those? What was the story behind her? Behind them, for that matter? Well, there was no point in asking her at the moment. He could read her face. He could see her desperation. 'No worries,' he said. 'I'm pleased you asked. Seriously.'

'Seriously?'

'Yes. Seriously.'

She couldn't help but smile at him. He was making it easy on her. He wasn't asking the obvious questions, drilling down to the nerve endings to extract a confession, an apology. He was trying to help. At that precise moment, as the world hurtled relentlessly through the twenty-first century and she was barely hanging onto it, she felt he was her only ally, the only one who could be trusted anyway.

The drilling started again. They waited for it to stop. Sorrenson picked up the small transparent plastic bag on his desk. 'Please,' he said, 'take a seat.' Christ, too formal. He felt like a bank manager meeting a client. 'Kate,' he began again, 'please . . .'

She sat down, still half smiling. 'You OK?' she said. 'You look tired.'

Sorrenson wondered what to say. 'No' would be the correct answer. But she clearly didn't need more weight on her shoulders. He decided to tell her a separate truth, one that had nothing to do with his current emotional state. 'Just staffing problems. One of my younger colleagues seems to have gone AWOL. Don't know where he is. Sleeping off an epic hangover, I hope. If so, the headache he has now will be nothing compared to what I'm going to give him.'

'Well, I hope you find him.'

'Me too,' Sorrenson said. 'We're short-staffed enough as it is. My colleague can be an idiot but he's a useful one most of the time, especially right now when there's so much going on.' He glanced at the bag in his hand, then held it out to her. 'This was an unusual request of yours. Normally these tests are done by the Borders Agency to help them determine the validity of an asylum claim. Lot of people get off a lorry in Dover with no passport and we have no way of knowing what nationality they are. The tests are pretty use-ful when that happens. We do forensic linguistic tests some of the time, too. Got a lot of people claiming to come from war-torn parts of the DRC when they don't. Their language betrays them. But these chemical tests we did on your sample are pretty infallible. Hair doesn't lie. God knows how it works but the tests clearly show where someone has been recently. These days, we're really only interested in whether someone is coming back from Pakistan, Afghanistan, Syria or Iraq, places where they're likely to have received terrorism training, but . . . Well, Williamson finished yours this morn-ing. I asked him to treat it as a priority. You made it sound pretty urgent over the phone.' He pointed at her bandage. 'You really don't look like you should be working.'

'I'm not. Not really. Supposed to be taking some time off. Got back a couple of days ago and, well, it's all a bit of a mess at work. I can't explain it. Mainly because I don't really understand it. Those emails you sent me, the ones you found on Carrington's computer, they were helpful. We got GCHQ to trawl deeper and we've picked up loads of seem-ingly disconnected threads. Nothing seems to bind them together, though.' She reached out, took the small bag from Sorrenson and inspected the lock of Fawcett's hair it con-tained. She contemplated the question she was about to ask. She didn't know what she wanted the answer to be. In many ways she'd rather not know where Fawcett had got his tan. It wasn't her job to investigate her own side. It wasn't her job to ransack the dead. But she'd pulled at the thread. The records showed he hadn't booked any time off work. Gaps needed to be filled. 'So,' she said, indicating the bag in her hand. 'What do the tests say? Where's my man been recently?'

281

'Biot,' Sorrenson said.

Kate frowned. It wasn't the answer she'd been expecting. She'd been wrong.

Sorrenson read the puzzlement on her face. 'It's an acronym: British Indian Overseas Territory.'

Now things made sense. It was the answer she'd expected, the answer she didn't want, the answer that would trigger a further thousand awkward questions for Five. 'Right,' she murmured. 'Figures.'

'You know much about the place?' Sorrenson said.

'Mainly what I read in the papers,' she said. 'Not much of it good. Most people wouldn't know it by its acronym.'

'What name would they know it by, then?'

Kate stared at the bag of hair. It was a bomb, really. It promised devastation. She could almost hear the ticking. What had a member of the British security services been doing in a part of the world that was about as accessible as North Korea? Whatever it was, it hadn't been authorized. 'Diego Garcia,' she said.

Chapter 27

They could probably tell that he'd pissed himself. He could smell it. They must be able to smell it too. It wasn't the fear that had made him lose control. The fear had been with him from the moment they'd whacked him as he'd bent over the Stag windscreen and peered inside the vintage car, but he hadn't lost control then. Now, two days into his ordeal, he had no choice. He was forced to relieve himself squatting on a metal stool behind a desk, legs chained to a sturdy metal trunk below, hands cuffed behind his back. Simm was practically insulated by his own piss, the liquid unable to escape his expensive motorbike leathers. He rolled his head from side to side on the desk, again tried to make out his surroundings. Some sort of single-storey building. No windows. Somewhere very quiet. The walls seemed to be extremely thick and muffled all sound outside. Almost all sound. Occasionally Simm could hear a sharp cracking. It would go on for three or four minutes. Crack, crack, crack. Then silence.

Footsteps. They were coming back. He tried to evade the thought that assaulted him every time he heard the men returning. *This is the last sound you will hear. This is the last sound you will hear. This is the last . . .* The two men padded into the building, neither saying anything. There was the now familiar grating sound of a key being turned in the handcuffs. Simm immediately started massaging his liberated arms, looked up at the two masked men. There was something about them, he realized, something almost familiar. It was their shapes. The men looked fit, athletic, even. They moved around him purposefully. Soldiers, Simm figured. Had to be.

One of the men broke open a cellophane-wrapped pack of sandwiches and thrust it at him. Another placed a bottle of water on the desk. Simm devoured the sandwich hurriedly. He was hungry, despite the fear. He tried to kick another thought out of his head. *This is the last meal you will eat. This is the last meal you will eat. This is . . .*

The two men stood looking down at him, still and silent. Simm sensed they were unsure about him. He'd disturbed them, traced their car from the respray garage to a small lock-up near Gravesend, forced them to develop a contingency plan right there on the spot. They'd come out of nowhere. An ambush. They'd clearly been watching him. One second they hadn't been there and the next they'd jumped him. The way they'd gone about neutralizing him had been impressive. Attacked, bound and deposited in the car's boot all within a minute or so. Simm had the impression that they weren't novices in the kidnap game. And yet, while their bodies seemed to act instinctively, the two men seemed uncertain about how to proceed. They didn't seem sure of what to do with him. He clung to the thought. It was all he had.

A spiral notebook was thrust in front of him and one of the men handed him a pen. Simm saw that several questions had been written in black capital letters on its top page. He studied them. Most could have come from any questionnaire. Name, occupation, that sort of thing. Only the last suggested something more sinister: what are you looking for? Simm took the pen and started writing down his answers. They must know the answer to half of them anyway, he figured. They'd taken his wallet. They would know he was a detective. Another thought assaulted him. *This is the last thing you'll write. This is the last thing you'll write. This is* . . . He took his time choosing his words. He was in no hurry to complete his answers.

'You want some porridge or don't you? I ain't asking a second time.' The hooded man walked up and down the lines of hostages, handing out small bowls of millet soaked in water. From somewhere nearby came the rumble of a truck. It seemed almost as if it were overhead. They were still getting used to not being in a cave. One by one the hostages nodded. They hadn't eaten for two days. They'd wondered if it was a sign that they were so close to death there was no point in wasting food on them. But, no, the porridge was back. 'You eat up, my little piggies,' the hooded man said. 'We going to take you to market.'

She approached Five's security doors, the knot in her stomach tightening all the time. There were going to be so many questions. Even more than during her debriefing two days earlier, when she'd returned from Belize in the same army transport plane used to bring Fawcett's body back.

She'd read somewhere that dead bodies were transported on most commercial flights. But, still, it was strange to fly on the same plane as a dead person she'd known. Stranger still to fly on the same plane as someone she'd killed, with only a couple of officers from Six and three embassy staff for company. She looked up at the dark, glowering building that housed the security service and felt the knot within her tighten further. She slipped her bag off her shoulder ready for inspection. Then she stopped. She needed a few minutes. She needed to have the momentary luxury of pretending the immediate future wasn't going to happen. Kate turned, walked back across the zebra crossing to the small park next to the Thames opposite Five's headquarters. It was an unusually hot autumnal day, just gone five o'clock. London seemed to be choking on diesel fumes. She could almost see the brown tinge in the air, a plague of carcinogenic locusts. She found a patch of grass under a tree, sat down, her back resting against the trunk, and closed her eyes. She counted to a hundred. Then she allowed herself another hundred.

When she opened her eyes she saw that she was alone in the park except for a young mother and her toddler daughter. Or was she a toddler? The child didn't seem able to stand on her own two feet. She was nearly there but, still, she couldn't walk without her mother's support. She would take a few steps and then her legs would buckle. It was only because her mother was holding her up that she wasn't falling down.

Both mother and child were laughing. They were making progress of sorts. The child was managing to take a few more steps each time under her mother's excited encouragement. Five steps, six steps, seven. Then the mother would remove her hands and the child's legs would start to fold underneath her. Instantly the mother would seize her daughter's arms and the dance would continue. Kate watched, mesmerized. The mother was completely absorbed in her child's actions. She was the moon to the child planet. The gravitational pull between the two was strong, unbreakable. All that mattered to the woman at that moment was the need to prevent her daughter falling.

Kate ordered herself to look away. But she couldn't. She found herself willing the child to walk, to break free from her mother's grip. Independence would bring autonomy. You didn't want to be dependent on anyone for your protection. That just made you vulnerable. It was true of children and it was true of countries. People forgot that. The citizens of free countries forgot that. But it was an unsettling knowledge for those who didn't forget, for mothers, for soldiers, for members of the security services. They knew how far they would go to protect something, someone. And this knowledge came with an attendant fear: that no matter how much they paid, they could never truly guarantee the protection of anyone or anything. Their best might ultimately not be enough. They would always live with the fear of future failure. That sort of knowledge was corrosive. They'd pay for it one way or another, the security obsessives. A broken marriage, a breakdown, an addiction, a crippling depression, a dependence on happy pills, a terror of having children. There were many ways it would take its toll. You spent your life trying too hard to save others and you risked losing yourself. But if you stopped trying, you stopped being human. Try walking that tightrope every single day, Kate thought. The only way was down.

She stood up, and willed herself to make the journey back through the fumes to the long, stone steps at the mouth of Five's headquarters. She glanced back at the mother and child and felt a profound sense of emptiness rise within her. She heard Fawcett's mocking voice. Was it worth it?

Chapter 28

You knew where you were with whores. Or, rather, you'd known. Ailes was once able to spot them a mile off in the Rayleigh, his hotel of choice in Washington. In the late eighties and even in the early nineties, when he'd had more enthusiasm for such things, the women stood out. Back then they were pictures of vitality. They exhibited a healthy glow that made them seem as if they'd just stepped out of the pages of *Sports Illustrated*. They tended to be in their early thirties, old enough to have something about them. Big hair, good teeth, naturally tanned skin. But now ... Well, go figure. For a start, they were no longer called whores, Ailes had learned. Today they were called escorts. Ailes wasn't big on semantics and rebrands. Wordplay interfered with his Manichean view of the world: defence was the best form of offence; man was born a hunter; the free market was God. But even he could see something had changed in the whore market since he'd been a regular customer. Half of them resembled his twenty-two-year-old estranged daughter. Pale and skeletal, they'd snap if you got too energetic with them. They scowled, affected boredom. They vaped. Most of all, they didn't seem fun.

Maybe he was just getting old, Ailes thought. Maybe he was just getting fat. Fatter. Hard to keep trim in his line of work. Networking involved so much grazing and imbibing. It was a double whammy. Not only was he consuming too much, the drinking and eating took up all of his hours and he had no time to burn any of it off. Well, he didn't care. One glance at the girls in the hotel lobby was enough to convince him that being thin, these days, wasn't much fun. Better to revel in excess. Stick your snout in that camp. At least then you knew where you wallowed.

The hotel manager escorted Ailes to his usual private booth just off the lobby, then hurried away to get one of his most important customers his favourite bottle of Johnnie Walker. Ailes nodded at the booth's other occupant. The man raised his glass of bourbon in greeting. Ailes sank onto a leather sofa that creaked under his weight. He consulted his watch. Just after noon. Hard to tell, though. Modern hotels seemed to exist in some sort of permanent cocktail-hour twilight, somewhere between seven and nine in the evening. 'So,' Ailes said. 'We live in interesting times.'

Jefferson caught the eye of a waiter, pointed at his empty glass. 'Sure do.'

'Raptor's floating in three days,' Ailes said. 'Massive buzz on Wall Street around it. Roscoe and his people are going to be ringing the opening bell first day of trading. Whole heap of publicity for them.'

Jefferson selected an olive from a bowl in front of him. 'Even Scott's interested. Hauled me in the other day, asked a lot of questions. Guess he's not immune to the hype. Difficult not to be when nearly every investment bank on Wall Street is in on the Raptor float. They've all got skin in the game. In their interests to talk it up. They say anything critical, they don't get a share allocation, they don't get a fat fee for floating the business, they don't get their bonuses. Their second, younger, wives lose interest in them, and hire expensive lawyers to contest the pre-nups.' Jefferson extricated the olive stone from his mouth, deposited it on a napkin. 'Sometimes I wonder if anyone on Wall Street learned anything from the dotcom boom and bust. Or maybe everyone's just got their bullshit detectors switched off, these days.'

'Well, these are lean times,' Ailes muttered. 'You can't attack the fatted calf. Doesn't pay to be a contrarian right now. So few mega-flotations around.' He reached for his Scotch from the salver presented by the waiter. 'Yeah, pretty soon the whole world will have heard of Raptor.'

'Raptor's going to save the world,' Jefferson said, raising his refilled glass. 'To Raptor. Nothing Raptor can't do.'

Ailes swirled Scotch around his mouth. God, it was delicious. He'd read somewhere about a company that embalmed cadavers in it. Or maybe he'd just dreamed that. He'd investigate it or invent it. It didn't seem a bad way to be preserved. He drained his glass. A waiter immediately brought him a fresh one.

'I saw Roscoe the other day,' Ailes said. His hand approached the olive bowl. Fat fingers seized a glistening green oval. 'Think he wanted me to get Scott off his back again. Make the case to leave the ISG alone. Well, I felt like telling him to quit worrying. No one will touch him soon. He'll be a leper.'

'The problem with Roscoe is that he doesn't know where he stands,' Jefferson said. 'He's been trying to reinvent himself as some sort of tech investment guru. The reality is he's just a spook. He's lost sight of that. He's dumb. He's forgotten who signs his cheques. He's forgotten that he works for the CIA.'

'Not for much longer,' Ailes said aggressively. 'His West Coast schtick's going to look pretty bankrupt when the blood starts flowing. A lot of grieving relatives going to want answers from him.'

'What do you think will happen to him?'

Ailes shrugged, reached for another olive, held it up for inspection. 'Same as you, I reckon. Truth'll get buried. Always does. There'll be a Senate investigation, a lot of public hearings. One day there'll be a heavily redacted report published that'll talk of intelligence failures. But no one'll really get blamed. It'll be usual. There'll be talk of systemic failures so no finger pointing at individuals. It'll be the structure not the agents that take the bomb blast. The public will understand. The Agency was trying to stop a mass execution. It had to act. It may inadvertently have pulled the trigger but it was Al-Boktorah who loaded the gun, put it in its hands. That sort of thing. Roscoe'll be long gone by the time any of this comes out. Reckon the ISG's made him enough money to live out a comfortable retirement up in Cape Cod or down in Key West or whichever rock he's planning to crawl under.'

Jefferson nodded. 'Zetouin? People are going to ask how Raptor got the co-ordinates for the strike so wrong. At some stage someone somewhere will mention Zetouin. He's in the files. When people work out Raptor's technology was a crock of shit, they might focus on him, ask if he was the real source for the co-ordinates. If so, they'll probably work out he sold the Agency a pack of lies.'

Ailes shook his head. 'Maybe, but who cares? It'll be old history then. People don't give a fuck about old history. It's too far in the past. You got a world whizzing forward, no one gives a fuck about what happened yesterday, never mind a decade ago. Zetouin sure was a dumb fuck, though. People should learn not to talk. You stay silent, you stay protected. You got to establish your position and stick with it. You can't move in the saddle mid-race. You can't go banging on the front door of one part of the CIA and start saying, "Get me out here," when you've just sold another part of it a massive lie. You've got to play it cautious, keep your head down for a while. Otherwise, one way or another, you're going to end up dead.'

'How much is our man making out of the Raptor float?'

Ailes thought for a moment. 'Twenty, I think. Around a quarter of what it's worth anyway. Around three billion will flow back to some investment houses who've been involved on the deal from the start. They know what to do with it.'

'And he's going to sell his stake the moment it floats?'

'Right, he's going to sell it all.'

'Share price'll take a battering.'

'He doesn't care. He'll be out of it by then.'

'He'll make a killing.'

'Two killings,' Ailes said. 'One on Wall Street, one in the Sahara.'

Jefferson drained his bourbon. 'It's going to be a fucking major mess to sort out. The consequences . . .'

Ailes raised a cautionary finger. 'Don't go flaking now, Jefferson. You know there's no chance of saving them. They've got only one future and it's in body bags. They're not coming out alive. You don't negotiate with Al-Boktorah. He dictates the terms. We're doing our best to exploit a very

293

bad situation. Nothing can be done for them. Only thing we can do is make sure another situation like this doesn't arise. And for that we need strong leadership. We're heading for a culture war and what we need right now, what the world needs right now, is a true warrior-in-chief. Someone not afraid to prosecute a war, rain fire down on all the psychopaths mushrooming across Africa and the Middle East. We need some regime change of our own before we start imposing it on others. That's what the three billion is for: bankrolling a new president. We got to change the colour of the political map. We need the hawks to take back control. Doves ruining this great country of ours. Time to tear their tiny hearts out. What we're doing now is not about shaping the next five years or the next twenty. This will shape things for centuries to come. In a culture war, you got to pick a side. You with us? Or you going to allow the enemies of freedom to thrive?'

Jefferson shook his head. 'You seem to be forgetting that we've been in on this from the start. We agreed this plan. Hell, we encouraged him to think big in terms of hostages. We are soaked in blood.'

'Horseshit. He'd been taking hostages long before we got involved. Think of this as Al-Boktorah's last stand. We get the right man in position in the White House and I guarantee his first act will be to hunt Al-Boktorah down and destroy him. Not like the flake we got in power now who's obsessed with staying out of things. So don't go getting concerned all of a sudden. What we're doing is just. What we're doing is right. You hear me?'

'I hear you. I just wish I didn't but I hear you.'

'Good,' Ailes murmured. 'Now is not the time to go deaf.'

Jefferson looked around the lobby. He performed a little circle motion with the index finger of his left hand. 'I don't know. I don't know anything any more. This place is changing. You remember when we used to come here? Am I imagining it or was it a lot lighter back then? At least, I think it was. Now it's like being in an aquarium or something.'

'Yeah,' Ailes said. 'Things change. Everything changes except for our line of business. People always need protecting. That's why what we're doing is the right thing.'

'The right thing,' Jefferson said, standing up. 'Not easy working out what that is right now.' He hesitated for a moment, looking down at Ailes. 'See you when it's all over.' He produced a packet of cigarettes and jammed one into his mouth, ready to ignite the moment he was outside.

Ailes nodded. 'Things are never over in our game, you know that. Got to keep moving to stay ahead. Stopping is fatal.' He watched Jefferson walk through the lobby, then allowed his eyes to rest on several of the women perched at the bar. He stood up and walked towards them. They weren't his type but he was vaguely interested in what his money could buy.

The banging was worse than the drilling. At least with the drilling there were long, calm silences. But the banging was almost relentless. Just how long did it take to reconfigure a police station? Sorrenson wondered. The builders had been there for months and there was still no sign of them finishing. Some Whitehall mandarin could approve the knocking together of a couple of police forces in the name of efficiency savings but they didn't get to experience the near-deafening consequences of their actions.

Sorrenson studied the blurred photos on the desk in front of him. He hadn't realized that Simm was a biker. He should have done, really. He had that look about him: a man in a hurry. Just as well, Sorrenson thought. Simm's alacrity had betrayed him. His Ducati had been caught on three separate speed cameras. It was a strange journey that his colleague had made. As far as Sorrenson could make out, it had gone from Kent up to the Midlands, the outskirts of Birmingham almost, then back down towards Gravesend. All in one day. What was Simm playing at? Why use your day off to make an epic journey that served little purpose? It couldn't have been simply to enjoy the ride. It was almost entirely motorways and dual carriageways. Sorrenson knew little about biking but he knew that such a journey couldn't be fun. If you wanted to enjoy your bike you headed for Northumberland or Yorkshire. No, Simm must have had a destination in mind. And then, when he'd got there, he'd turned back. Or almost back. He'd headed to Kent but not to his own part. So, Sorrenson thought, he'd found something in the Midlands that had sent him back the way he'd come.

The banging stopped. Instantly Sorrenson felt five years younger. His shoulders relaxed. He remembered Simm joking about the banging. He remembered his apology in the interview room. God, it seemed a long time ago. And they still didn't really have anything to show for their investigations. They had a handful of victims and no suspects. No leads either, except for his theory about the shoes. Sorrenson remembered Simm going on about the Stag. He'd become half fixated with it, convinced it was linked to the investigation. But, then, his colleague was a petrol head. Of course he was going to be obsessed by a rare car. Still, though . . .

The banging started again. Sorrenson opened up the laptop on his desk, typed three words into Google: West Midlands Stag. The noise from the builders was becoming intolerable. He picked up his computer and headed outside.

Chapter 29

She could tell from Callow's scowl that it was going to be worse than she'd feared. Now, that really was saying something. Kate hadn't thought she could dread the next few hours of her life more than she had been doing. She'd been mistaken. The urge to bolt from the sepulchral room in which she now found herself was all-consuming. For the first time in her life she felt truly claustrophobic. Cool and dark, the small office somewhere on Five's fourth floor made her think of a larder in a fusty house that hadn't heard laughter since the thirties.

She'd hoped that Callow would give her something to hold on to as she walked in. A nod. Some sort of apologetic shrug. But no. He remained implacable on the other side of the table, the constant rolling of his jaw confirming that he was engaged in a vigorous attempt to destroy nicotine gum. Callow should get a dog, she thought, looking at his sagging, crumpled face. He should get a bulldog. A woman sat next to him. She seemed familiar. She was clearly important. There was an air about her, a weariness that clearly came from great demands being made on her time. Another man sat next to her. He hadn't glanced up when Kate had walked in, she'd noticed.

'Sit.' Callow gestured at the empty chair in front of her.

He nodded at the woman next to him. 'Robin McKie, head of risk assessment. Next to her, Oliver Sumption, head of legal. We all know why we're here.'

Sumption hit record on a small digital machine. Callow threw some more gum into his mouth. McKie took a sip from a small bottle of water. And so it began. Question after question. Each one a test, a thrust, a jab from a different angle. They knew she was a killer. She'd confessed. But was she a murderer? Just who did they have in front of them? And whose side was she really on? Kate had to remind herself that they were just doing their job. If they'd really doubted her story, she wouldn't have been allowed to walk free when the plane had landed. True, they'd taken her passport but that was all – it was expected. Clearly they had stuff on Fawcett. The emails she'd seen, for a start. They were bound to have found out more since. But still the questions continued. It was inevitable. It was necessary. They had only her account of what had happened. They had to do right by Fawcett. They had to do right by a traitor: the law demanded it.

'Remind us why you were in Belize in the first place,' McKie said. Kate looked back at her female interrogator. She was a Muslim, Kate recalled. A white convert. Her husband was a prison imam. There weren't many like her in the service. She practically inhabited her own Venn diagram.

'I was tasked by the service with analysing patterns of trade in illicit tobacco. Much of this product was known to be ending up in the hands of terrorist groups, notably those operating in Saharan Africa, in particular the Al–Boktorah brigade that, as you know, is currently holding around fifty energy workers hostage in the desert.' Kate immediately regretted her explanation. Far too flippant.

'Please answer my question, Ms Pendragon.'

'I was interested in how the product, the illicit tobacco, was being transported from the UK to Africa. Five has been interested in this distribution network for some time. It clearly takes a lot of organizing.'

'And?'

'And the answer, at least a partial answer, was that a substantial amount of it was being moved by big container ships passing along the Thames estuary. It was being held on Maunsell Forts offshore, then loaded onto the vessels under cover of darkness.'

McKie frowned. 'Maunsell Forts?'

'Coastal defences designed to stop V1s and the Luftwaffe,' Callow muttered.

'Right,' McKie said hesitantly. 'You learn something new every day. And?'

'And it transpired the ships most likely to be carrying the illicit cargo were registered in Belize. I needed to inspect that country's shipping register to establish the ownership of the vessels.'

'Surely that could have been done with a simple phone call.'

'Normally, perhaps. But in this case it wouldn't have helped us very much. The register revealed the names of several companies but, as I'd suspected, they were all themselves registered in Belize, which, as I'm sure you know, is a tax haven. I needed to know who was behind the companies. I needed to examine their list of directors, their shareholders. I figured this might establish who was really running the tobacco-distribution operation, expose links to other interests.'

'I see,' McKie murmured. 'But, if I understand correctly, one can't simply inspect a list of the shareholders of companies based in tax havens. Directors, maybe, but not shareholders. They remain opaque for fairly obvious reasons.'

'Correct.'

McKie wrote something on a notepad in front of her. 'So the trail ran cold.'

'No. The service sanctioned the recruitment of an asset within Belize House. It holds Belize's shipping and companies registers. The asset provided us with useful information.'

'How useful?' McKie's pen hovered over her notepad.

'It still needs to be evaluated. The asset was due to deliver the information on the night . . . on the night that Fawcett died.' Kate took a deep breath. 'I mean on the night that I killed him. Six were able to approach her subsequently and obtain the information, but I have yet to run the names through our computers. An initial examination suggests that the directors and shareholders are listed simply as anonymous companies based in Tortola, the British Virgin Islands.'

'The BVI. Another tax haven. So now the trail does run cold.' McKie stared at Kate.

'I don't know. Like I said—'

'It still needs to be evaluated, yes, I heard you. I take it money was involved? The asset, I mean.' McKie looked across at Sumption, who seemed as if about to say something but then thought better of it.

'Correct.'

'So, in a nutshell, you went all the way to Belize to bribe someone.'

'I don't see it like that. I went to gather intelligence. Offering an inducement was necessary for the procurement of that intelligence.'

McKie turned to Callow. 'It is correct that the operation was sanctioned?' She waved her hand at some files. 'I know it's in here somewhere, but for the purposes of clarity, can we just confirm that?'

Callow nodded slowly. McKie wrote something else on her notepad. 'I see. And what was Mr Fawcett's role in all of this? Again, I know it's somewhere in these files.'

Callow scratched his nose. 'He was tasked with overseeing the operation. To provide support to Ms Pendragon.'

'She wasn't trusted to do it herself, you mean?'

Callow chewed his gum, considered his response. 'We thought this was the safest option.'

McKie offered up an empty laugh. 'Well, look how that turned out, hey? Case of more haste less speed?'

Callow grimaced. 'There are British subjects being held in the desert. At least twelve have been slaughtered so far. We have an obligation to do all we can to protect them.'

'No one doubts that,' McKie said. 'It's just the manner in which we're going about it that's in question.'

Kate had never wanted a run more in her life. She thought about the coast, about running her favourite trail between Margate and a Norman keep high on a crumbling cliff at Reculver. In the evening you ran towards the dying sun on a compacted road that edged salt marshes alive with birdsong. In her mind she started running. She could almost feel the sun on her face, smell the salt air.

The questions continued. Some gruesome: how many times did you hit him? Was the intention to kill him? Please explain why the skull was shattered so powerfully. Some perfunctory: did you stay at the same hotel? Where did you eat? Eventually McKie glanced at her watch, then put down her pen. She seemed mildly apologetic. 'We shall have to continue tomorrow. I must go. It's five pounds a minute if I'm late for the nanny.'

★　★　★

'He's real sick,' the hostage said. He crouched over the prostrate figure of his fellow hostage, wiped the man's face with a rag. 'Fever. Look at his brow. Soaking.'

The hooded man nodded. 'Yeah, he don't look too good, I'll give you that. Which one is he?'

'You call him Michael J,' the hostage said.

'Michael J?' The captor turned to two of his fellows. 'We call one of them Michael J?'

'Yeah,' one muttered. 'It's cos he's neither black nor white. Strange skin, bro. He's like Michael J.'

'Lame, bro, lame,' the hooded man said. 'Come and drag him over here.' The other two captors picked up the crumpled body of the sick hostage. They carried him into the middle of the concrete floor. The man made no sound. The other hostages watched silently, their backs pressed hard against the corrugated metal wall on the far side of the warehouse, as if trying to push themselves as far from their captors as possible.

'Seems he don't like his new surroundings,' one of the captors said. 'Got this big old underground warehouse for him and he's just not liking it. Maybe he prefers cave living.' The hooded man stared down at Michael J. 'Well, he's gone now. Nothing can be done for him.' He brought the butt of his Kalashnikov down on the man's skull.

'Fuck, bro,' another captor said. 'I mean . . . fuck.'

'Not going to waste a bullet, bro,' the hooded man said. 'He was gone anyway. Did him a favour. Pretty soon they all is checking out.'

Chapter 30

'I didn't have you down as the church-going sort, Callow.'

'Nice singing. Periods of contemplative silence. Free wine and biscuits. It's not all bad. Not that I take communion. Come here on Sundays and there's a bar after the service. Cheaper than going to the pub. One day my wife'll work that out. Hope it's not too soon. Only been coming a few months.'

Kate looked around the deserted church. 'Not sure you should make St Bride's your regular haunt, though.'

'You mean because it's the journalists' church? Worried matters of national security might leak out across the congregation?'

'Right.'

Callow laughed a smoker's laugh. Phlegm rattled in his throat. 'Wouldn't be anyone to leak to even if I wanted to. No journalists come here any more. They left Fleet Street aeons ago. There's a Christmas service for some journalists' charity or something, the odd funeral of some ancient pressman, of course, but that's it.' He examined the small wooden plaques marking the names of the newspaper proprietors who'd sponsored a pew. 'Fifth estate's gone the way of every other institution and I include the security service and the national cricket team in that assessment. It's on its knees praying for salvation.'

She looked at him curiously. In the flickering candlelight his skin was leathery and pock–marked. Smoker's skin. 'You praying for salvation, Callow?'

'Too late for me. Far too many sins.'

'Be serious for a moment.'

'I am.'

'So confess.'

Callow yawned. 'We should have gone to the pub rather than here. Still, this is more discreet. We need to talk.'

'McKie gave us a hard time.'

'It's what she's paid to do.'

'I know.'

'She's sharp, she asks the right questions. It'll all come tumbling out sooner rather than later.'

'What will?'

'Everything. The whole ugly everything.' Callow looked up at the crucifix on the altar, clasped his hands together and leaned forward in the pew. For one unnerving moment Kate thought he was going to pray. 'It was different,' Callow began. 'It was different when I started out with the service in the seventies. Fewer threats. Just one big enemy, the Soviet bloc. OK, there was the Irish problem, and I'm not trying to play it down but the Provos didn't have nuclear warheads. The Soviet threat seemed to be stitched into the country's DNA. Remember, this was a time of social unrest, mass strikes. The security service was more worried about the power of the trade unions to topple the government than the KGB.' Callow felt in his pocket, found some nicotine gum. 'It was . . . helpful to have assets in the trade union movement. If the NUM was going out on strike, we needed to know when exactly. A government could fall if the coal stocks were too low when the strike started. We needed the trains to run. We needed the national grid to keep humming. We needed things to keep moving. The threats we feared most were from our own citizens. It wasn't bombs that worried us, it was socialism. Seems quaint now, I know. But, well, a lot gets lost over forty years. You forget how quickly everything's changed.' Callow waved a hand at the plaques. 'Look at our papers. No one reads newspapers any more. It's all this internet gubbins. Who could see that coming, even in the early nineties?' He looked at Kate. 'No, don't answer that. You're probably just about young enough to make the case that you did.'

It was Kate's turn to yawn. 'I get the impression this is the part when you make your confession, Callow. You seem to be laying a very clear path.'

Callow sighed, popped some gum into his mouth and chewed for a few seconds. 'It was difficult to groom assets in the trade union movement, useful ones anyway, the ones who knew what the brothers were thinking. They weren't interested in money. They were just interested in power. So the service had to find other ways of . . . bringing them onboard.'

'Go on.'

Callow looked back at the crucifix. The candles beside it burned without a flicker. 'Well, you've probably guessed what happened. The service identified a few senior union officials as paedophiles. They were filmed. Various hotels, mainly in London. Third-party private investigators were used most of the time. They thought they were working for the papers. When the service got stuff on one they were offered a deal. Most played ball.'

306

'Most?'

Callow took a big gulp of church air. 'A couple threw themselves under trains, off cliffs.'

'Christ.'

Callow shot her a look. 'Remember where you are.'

'Says the blackmailer.'

Callow shook his head. 'It wasn't my op. I had nothing to do with setting it up back in the seventies. Before my time. But in the eighties I started to do some of the reconnaissance, check out suitable venues, that sort of thing. The problem was that it worked sort of too well. Not only did we gather some useful stuff on the leading lights in the union movement, we sucked up a whole load of their like-minded friends. We had intel on politicians, judges, embassy staff, businessmen, celebrities. At least two members of Six, if I remember correctly. It was a mess. It was in danger of getting out of control. We knew the Soviets were looking for this sort of stuff, too. They wanted some leverage over important people. We found out that they'd actually filmed one senior northern MP who had close links to the unions. In a phone box of all places. Hidden camera and a rent-boy. It was then that we decided to take steps to dismantle our operations, get rid of the material we'd amassed. If the Soviets got it, an entire tranche of the British establishment would be open to blackmail from an enemy state. Naturally, given some of my predecessors' sympathies towards the Soviet Union, we couldn't take any chances. So a lot of stuff got burned. Thankfully, most of those involved are dead now. You catch shadows of it every now and then. Somebody who'd been told something by somebody else pops up in the papers to make some sort of claim. But it's all pretty vague and, crucially, unverifiable.'

'And you're telling me this now because?'

'Because people in the service have long memories.'

'People like you, you mean.'

'Right.'

Kate gazed at the stained-glass window depicting Christ at the end of the church. She was conscious of the irony in her question. 'So you figured because it had worked in the past you'd resurrect it?'

'Pretty much. We scoped the company, scoped Carrington, looking for a way in. We needed someone who knew how terrorist groups were able to get their hands on massive amounts of tobacco. We needed to understand the supply chain. We got lucky with Carrington. Or, at least, we thought we did. Not only was he well placed, we found stuff we could use against him. Fawcett collected the evidence. Carrington wasn't an abuser himself. Just bought stuff over the net. I approved the op. We were able to bend Carrington quite easily. It really was something of a coup, like old times. He'd set up Smith and Webb's distribution network, remember. Carrington knew how product was being shipped all around the world to third parties so they could avoid tax and other ugly bureaucratic obstacles, like sanctions. He started supplying us with the names of front companies that were being used, offshore trusts, that sort of thing. We were close to following the flow of money all the way to accounts that were ultimately being run for the benefit of Al-Boktorah and quite a few other interesting parties. You'd appreciate our thinking behind it more than most. It was why we brought you in. We needed you to verify whether Carrington was providing us with solid intel. But we never got the chance to find out. A few months in and, well, you know what happened to Carrington. A lot of his files disappeared. Dead end.'

Kate ran her hands through her hair. She needed a shower. She felt smeared in the grime of the capital. 'I take it you suspect . . .'

'That Carrington was murdered because he was working for us, yes.' Callow rocked back and forth a little in the pew. 'If you're asking me whether we, the service, are responsible for his death, then here's my confession. Yes, we are. We signed his death warrant.'

'You can't be sure of that.'

'Those emails your partner found,' Callow said. 'They're from Carrington to Fawcett. They're quite curt, quite cryptic. But it's clear that, towards the end, Carrington was becoming uncomfortable about something. In one email he seems to hint that he's not prepared to be . . . "pliable" — that was the word he used — any more.'

'So he got cold feet. Thought he'd take a prison sentence over working for the service. That doesn't make you culpable in his death.'

'Do you know what Americanisms are?' Callow said.

'Are we on a new topic of conversation now?'

'No, stick with me.'

'Right, OK. Americanisms are American-style phrases and words. Like, I don't know, saying, "Go figure," or spelling "colour" without a *u* or calling "autumn" the "fall".'

'Correct. A British person rarely uses Americanisms.'

'Right,' Kate said.

'Someone pretending to be British rarely uses Americanisms. They don't want that to come out.'

'Figures.'

'But people "talk" differently on the internet and when they're using email. Stuff creeps in. They don't think they're being watched. They get sloppy in their grammar, in their spelling. It doesn't really matter, just as long as they get their message across.'

'So?'

'So we got some forensic linguists to study the emails between Carrington and Fawcett. We wanted to confirm it was actually Fawcett whom Carrington was communicating with. Fawcett's language betrayed him. He used a lot of Americanisms in his correspondence with Carrington. Turned out he also used a lot of Americanisms when completing his psychological assessments. To say this is all rather embarrassing is an understatement. A security service that can't establish the nationality of its own agents? If that got out, it would become a laughing stock. We're still trying to establish which rock Fawcett was under before he crawled out. Suffice to say we don't believe the story he peddled us is the full truth. Anyway . . .' Callow reached into his trouser pocket, pulled out a memory stick and handed it to Kate. 'The person who sent these emails from an encrypted server, the same server Fawcett used to communicate with Carrington, they also went heavy on the Americanisms. It seems pretty clear to me that the emails on this memory stick were also sent by Fawcett. Read them. I want to know just how much of a mess you reckon we're in.'

Kate examined the small, black plastic object in her hand. So much information, a library's worth, could now be packed into something so small. Three years from now a memory stick would seem clunky and antiquated. How long before they could build bombs the size of thumbs? 'Why are you giving me this?'

'Because, like I said, people have long memories. Because people remember how things got buried last time around. Because people fear that if it was left to those inside the service, they'd close ranks pretty quickly and the whole thing would be made to disappear.' Callow nodded at the stained-glass window. 'Because people want to atone.'

'But what do you hope to achieve? What good is it if all this comes out?'

Callow shook his head. 'Christ, I don't want it to come out. I'm not that idealistic. I don't particularly regret the operation. I just want us to acknowledge where we went wrong with Fawcett. Learn from our mistakes and move on. I think Americans call it closure.'

Jefferson hauled his giant frame through security and made his way up to Scott's office. He was struck by the CIA director's choice of venue. Scott tended not to spend much time at Langley, preferring to use the Agency's covert buildings scattered around Washington. If he was in the building then it was because he wanted to be seen and he wanted to be heard. Whatever he had to say was going to make waves.

Jefferson walked into Scott's office, found the CIA director examining a golf club. 'Thinking of taking it up,' Scott said, raising the club in greeting. 'When I get some free time.' He turned in the direction of the two men sitting on chairs behind him. 'You know Egan and O'Neill.'

Jefferson nodded. Interesting choice of company: the Agency's chief attorney and its senior State Department liaison officer. So Scott really was planning something significant. Jefferson started to feel nervous.

311

'We're bringing the Al-Boktorah drone strike forward to tomorrow,' Scott said.

Jefferson said nothing. He was conscious that Scott was studying his face. He was being read. He wondered why. 'OK,' he said. He completed the mental inventory of his jacket pocket. Yes, he'd put a fresh pack of cigarettes in there that morning. He was going to need a smoke very soon. Scott continued to stare at him. Jefferson realized that he was expected to ask a question. 'May I ask why?'

'Simple.' Scott bent over his putter and eased it forward, sending an imaginary golf ball to the far end of his office. 'Clock is ticking on the hostage situation. There is no point in delaying. Egan and O'Neill here have been doing the groundwork. Got the protocols established for the strike. Got the State Department to open channels to the Algerians, prepare them. They don't like it but they're not going to kick off too much. There's a lot of USAID coming their way soon.'

'You sure about this?' Jefferson said.

'Site's been scoped,' Scott said, straightening. 'We're good to go. President's been informed. We've shared our intelligence with him. He's been briefed extensively. He backs our chosen course of action. He's leaving it to me to decide when to push the button.'

So, then, Jefferson thought, Scott really didn't trust him. It should have been his job to brief the president's detail. But Scott had gone direct. What was the point of having walls and walls of bureaucracy if people were just going to ride roughshod over them?

'So you're going to go now,' Jefferson said. 'Two days before Raptor floats.'

Scott eased another imaginary golf ball down his office floor. 'Right.'

'Roscoe's going to be seriously pissed. ISG's been planning this flotation for months.'

Scott laughed. 'Roscoe's got to learn where he stands in all of this. There's fifty hostages in the desert somewhere about to be slaughtered and all he's worried about is making a name for himself on the NASDAQ.' He remained crouching over his club. 'You go tell Roscoe from me that we're bringing things forward.'

Jefferson turned and left the room, his hand automatically reaching for his cigarettes. So that was why he'd been brought into the loop: Scott wanted him to deliver bad news. Roscoe was going to explode when he heard the clock was being wound forward. He himself was being used as a human shield, Jefferson realized. Scott was going to hide behind him. It would be his body that would take the blast.

Chapter 31

'For one moment I thought I'd been burgled.' Sorrenson spoke softly. He felt like a hunter with a deer in his sights. One abrupt movement and she'd be off. 'Looked through the window and saw all these papers over the floor. Thought I'd become another crime statistic. Didn't fancy the police's chances of catching the offender. They're overstretched, these days.'

He drank in the scene. He'd half convinced himself he'd never see her in his house again. But there she was, kneeling on the floor of his lounge, dressed in running shorts and a vest, a bewildering amount of A4-sized pieces of paper scattered around the room. She offered him a smile, a big, genuine one. Sorrenson allowed himself to be dazzled.

'Sorry about your floor.' Kate pointed at the paper. 'Homework.'

'A lot of it.' Sorrenson knelt down. Printouts of emails mostly.

'I could have done this back at my place,' she said. 'But I wanted to be here.' She studied his face. 'I really wanted to be here. I could go if . . .'

Sorrenson shook his head. He looked at the gauze under

the strap of her running vest. 'No. No, it's OK. It's great to see you. The bandages are still there then.'

'They'll be off in a few days.'

'Can you talk about it?'

'One day. Not now. I want to. Something happened. Something went wrong. I'm not sure what exactly but I'm trying to put it right.'

Sorrenson hardly heard her response. He was too busy staring at her, willing himself not to think too much. He tried to distract himself. 'What are these?' He pointed at random to a sheaf of photocopies displaying dense, printed legalese and bearing several signatures.

She followed his finger. 'Company records. Company based in the British Virgin Islands.'

'Exotic.'

'They should be of interest to you. Professionally, I mean.'

'How come?'

'Ostensibly the company, Jepster Corporation, is a logistics business. It owns a number of vessels, including this one.' She held up a piece of paper displaying a photo of a large container ship. '*Capella*. Big container vessel.'

'And?'

'*Capella* was responsible for smuggling Smith and Webb's product to east Africa. All that stuff you found out on the forts, brought out by the late Mr Gaunt, it was intended for *Capella*.'

'Quite a breakthrough. So now you know who owns *Capella*. Your employer will be grateful for the information.'

'Former employer, and I doubt it.' She pointed at the documents. 'Think it might give them a headache when all this comes out.'

'How'd you mean?'

'Raises more questions than it answers. Jepster Corporation doesn't really show up anywhere. It's a brass–plate company. It has a registered address in the BVI. That's almost the only trace of it you can find. But it does surface somewhere, if you look hard enough, if you've got the sort of computers that can mine global databases, including the one operated by Eurocontrol.'

'Eurocontrol?'

'Aviation body. Logs all flights across Europe. Turns out Jepster doesn't just own boats, it owns planes. I'm interested in one of its planes in particular.' Kate scrambled across the floor, found another piece of paper and waved it at Sorrenson. 'This one. L3427V. Learjet. Here's its flight log.' She handed Sorrenson a thick wad of data. 'Look at its last recorded flight.'

'Diego Garcia to Egypt to Brize Norton.'

'Right. No commercial plane could have made that journey. Diego Garcia's one giant US military base. It's completely off limits to civilians, to anyone other than the US military. I suspect L3427V is a very rare plane, a ghost plane.'

'Ghost plane?'

'A plane operated on behalf of the CIA to move terror suspects around the world unseen.'

Sorrenson attempted to hone the question forming in his mind. It sounded preposterous. 'So, if Jepster's linked to the CIA, what's it doing running a tobacco–smuggling operation out of Britain?'

'Good question. Makes no sense.'

'Christ,' Sorrenson said, 'you go down that rabbit hole, it'll be difficult to come back up.' He looked at his watch. 'I have to go. Still hunting a missing colleague.'

'No joy finding him, then?'

'I have a lead. A thin lead. Will you be here when I get back?'

'I hope so.'

Whenever Scott ran along the Potomac he was reminded of the joke they used to tell about a former president. He'd forgotten which one, but it hardly mattered. The joke continued to amuse him: 'What does the President think of Roe v. Wade? He thinks they're both ways of crossing the Potomac.' Boom, boom.

Abortion, Scott thought, as he and his security detail ran through the Washington dawn. I need to establish my position on abortion. It was funny, he acknowledged, how his runs nearly always turned into political daydreams. His mind would wander as his limbs started to loosen up, found a comfortable pattern. Two or three miles into the run he'd envisage how his campaign for office would unfold. First stop secretary of state. Then VP. Then president. Three steps, a journey that would take at least a decade to complete. But it was a marathon, not a sprint, as the saying went. Scott ran marathons. He'd seen what happened to those who went out too fast, too early. They imploded by the halfway mark. By the end of the race they were just ragged, pitiful sights being passed by thousands. They were weak. Spent. That wasn't going to happen to him, Scott promised himself. He was going to finish strong. The glory would be all his.

He looked at his GPS watch. He was running seven-minute miles. He needed to speed things up a little now that, three miles in, his limbs were warmed up. He pumped his arms, quickened his gait. His watch told him he was running around 6:45 a mile. Not bad. Enough for a sub three if he could sustain that sort of pace over 26.2 miles. Any presidents run a sub three? He doubted it. Still, one for Google when he got back to the office. His security detail speeded up accordingly. It was clear some of them were struggling, Scott realized with satisfaction. He examined the small circle of fierce-looking men with buzz-cuts and wires running from earpieces down their backs. It was barely six in the morning yet every single member of the detail was wearing wraparound shades.

There had been objections at first when Scott had insisted on running in the morning. Originally his intention had been to run on his own. But he was persuaded otherwise. He was too much of a target alone, the Agency's risk analysts had explained. A phalanx of bodyguards provided a moving barrier between him and a bullet and afforded him a greater degree of protection. Still, you couldn't be too careful. Scott had to change his routes and running schedules each day to avoid routine, any sense of a pattern.

Five miles in and, mentally, Scott was accepting the nomination for VP. He saw himself somewhere remote, Iowa maybe, raising his hand in victory before a packed town hall applauding wildly. The soft slap of his running shoes against tarmac snapped him out of his reverie. He needed to focus more on his gait. Run tall, he told himself, run light. He checked his heartbeat: 154. Not bad.

They ran through a small park, little more than a strip of grass with an outdoor gym. Sometimes Scott stopped to use the equipment, installed by the District of Columbia authorities as part of their battle against America's obesity epidemic. A futile battle, in Scott's mind. He examined the street-food van looming into view ahead. With so much cheap, fattening junk on offer, the fight could never be won. When he became president the war on obesity was the one war he wouldn't even contemplate prosecuting. Better to stick to a more manageable one, like the war on terror. You couldn't battle against the bulge. People would revolt.

They were some twenty metres from the van. The Potomac was bathed in an early-morning glow that was spreading out across the city, turning its alabaster monuments pink. Scott was conscious of planes overhead, of traffic on the freeway nearby. Somewhere close a car was backfiring. Only it wasn't a car, Scott realized, as the screams started.

Too late he saw the three men clad head to toe in black and wielding automatic machine pistols jump out of the back of the van and begin shredding his security detail. Too late he saw the three bodyguards in front of him flattened by the spray of metal moving at high velocity. Four others in his security detail attempted to dive on him, put themselves between the target and the attackers. There were the sounds of call signals being shouted into microphones and of someone choking. Several of the bodyguards had pulled their weapons and were returning fire. But it was all too late. They had no cover. They were easy targets. They were picked off one by one as the three men walked calmly towards Scott, guns pointed at his head, their dark bodies silhouetted against the dawn. One guard attempted to raise his pistol only to be answered with a short burst of fire that all but took his head off. The massacre had been completed in less than a minute. The sound of shouting filtered out from the guards' earpieces, competing with the low, desperate moans from those whose lives had yet to ebb away.

Scott was trembling. The future, *his* future, was terrifying. He was going to become a hostage. He would be paraded

319

on the internet before they did God knew what to him. He would be—

Scott never completed the thought. Bullets scythed through every vital organ in his body. His GPS watch continued to flash its warning – danger: high heart rate.

Chapter 32

Sorrenson looked up and down the weed-ridden private road that ran alongside the high-speed rail line. On the other side of the track he could see fields, a small village and a church spire. If he turned his head forty-five degrees he could make out the towers of Canary Wharf some twenty-odd miles away. Behind him, some five or six hundred metres back, lay the Thames estuary, and beyond that the industrial netherworld that formed the Isle of Grain, a place of liquid-gas containers the size of circus big tops, ugly, low-slung electricity sub-stations, and derelict silos. It was a desolate place. A necessary place. A place that powered modernity. A place few would want to visit.

From his vantage-point, squinting into the late-evening sun, Sorrenson could make out the funnels of a large container ship protruding above a high grassy mound that blocked his view across to the Isle.

It was a strange location he found himself staring at. Not really countryside, not really coast. It had a nodding acquaintance with the city but its fields were little more than a flood-plain and were empty, save for scores of wading birds and a handful of rescue horses. With only nature for competition, the place had been claimed by the army. Sorrenson examined the football-pitch-sized field in front of the mound that was used as a military firing range. It seemed well maintained but even the army rarely visited now, although there was a major barracks just a few miles away. Ammunition was expensive. Every institution was having to make cutbacks. Those protecting the country were not immune.

There was no red Stag, no car at all to be seen. Sorrenson walked along the private road past a disused factory. Beyond it were a couple of two-storey buildings that looked as if they might still be serving some sort of function but there was a stillness about them that suggested they were rarely visited. Sorrenson checked the address on his iPhone. Yes, he'd definitely come to the right place. The Stag was registered to one of the two-storey properties, a square construction with a flat asphalt roof and peeling brown window frames. He peered through the venetian blind in the large window that dominated the building's ground floor. Yes, it had clearly been an office once. Probably something to do with the ships using the estuary. He spied a faded calendar on one wall. A dead pot plant stood in a corner. No one was using it as an office now. He was about to turn back when something caught his eye: there was post neatly laid out on the internal window sill. Sorrenson recognized the name. So the respray garage had told him the truth. This was the home of the Stag's owner, a former soldier who'd been stationed at the nearby barracks. This was what life was like for someone who'd left the army, Sorrenson thought. You joined up to escape working in an office and you ended up living in one.

Had Simm made it this far? Simm's mobile network had checked the location data of his phone. The company had triangulated its last-known signal against three different base stations. If Simm hadn't made it here, he'd made it to somewhere close by.

He should phone for assistance, Sorrenson thought. Get Forensics down and scour the place. It was clear that Simm wasn't there now but maybe they'd be able to establish that he had been. He started walking back along the road, away from the Isle of Grain, towards the strange, gleaming citadel on the horizon that was Canary Wharf. It was then that he heard the grumble of an engine. Sorrenson didn't know much about cars but he could tell from its growl that it was a V8. He pulled out his phone, hit speed dial and ducked into an alley next to the old factory. He felt faintly ridiculous. Him, a detective, hiding from a car with a powerful engine. What was he doing? But then he remembered the man with the golf-ball eyes and all the other cadavers that had invaded his recent dreams. He heard a voice at the end of his phone. 'It's DCI Sorrenson. Put me through to SCO19.'

Jefferson was experiencing a new and troubling sensation. He was no longer grey. He was vivid. He was defined in technicolour and all eyes were on him. For someone used to being in the shadows, his subjection to urgent illumination was painful, blinding. He had no choice but to endure it. He was no longer a Cromwell. He was a reluctant monarch forced to wear the crown.

It was Jefferson to whom the president had turned after Scott had been murdered. Castler, the CIA deputy director, was in hospital having a gall bladder removed. There were others more senior than Jefferson, but no one had his longevity. The president wanted someone who was CIA through and through. Someone who understood how it thought, how it healed, how it grieved. In the president's words, Jefferson was, at that precise moment, the right man for the wrong time.

'We need to respond,' the president told Jefferson. He was lying back in his chair, feet on the oval table. It was an attempt at nonchalance but Jefferson could see the sweat on the president's brow. Fear was seeping out of him. Fear of being seen to be powerless. 'We need to strike back,' the president continued. 'I've gone the best part of eight years trying to avoid escalating tensions, but the American public will expect, and deserve, a powerful reaction to this wanton act of terrorism. We need the world to understand that if you assassinate the director of the Central Intelligence Agency on American soil there will be urgent and devastating reprisals. I understand that we have a drone strike scheduled to take place in Saharan Africa tomorrow. That's a good start.'

Jefferson stared at the president. He'd never spoken to him before, never even been in the same room. But it was true what they said: the man had presence; he had charisma. You could see why he'd won two terms in office. And now he was going to bookend his glittering career by unleashing hell in arid lands far away, lands that most of his 265 million fellow Americans would be unable to point to on a map. The most powerful man in the world was as vulnerable as the rest of them, a hostage to events far beyond his control.

'Yeah,' the president mused, 'we need a concerted pro-gramme of reprisals. One after another.' He clapped his hands for effect. 'Boom, boom, boom. But we'll start with this drone strike, right? That will get things rolling.'

Jefferson gazed at the president, a man who was desperately trying to hold it together, who looked like his life depended on the urgent delivery of good news. 'Right,' he said.

★   ★   ★

They came out shooting. 'You can be Cassidy, I'll be the kid,' Robbie told Stevie. 'It'll be just like old times, down here on the range when we were at the barracks.' He did a cow- boy yee-hah, waved his pistol in the air, started singing an old country-and-western song. The gun was a Beretta, Simm saw. That made sense. He had read somewhere that thou- sands had been shipped to Iraq to equip the country's armed forces, following the overthrow of Saddam, only for most of them to go missing. Some had ended up as trophies in the hands of Coalition soldiers. Many had ended up in the hands of Al-Qaeda. For a second or two, Simm was convinced they were going to shoot him. The two ex-soldiers laughed when they saw the terror in his face.

'Relax, soft lad,' Stevie said. 'No lead for you. Not from us, at least. We're on the same side, ultimately. You should be protected in here, when it all kicks off.' Stevie nodded at the walls. 'This is a bunker, after all. Outside here's a firing range. Going to have some moving targets in a minute or so. See if the busies can shoot straighter than the squaddies, hey?'

They took the ammunition clips from their weapons and emptied them onto the floor. 'So,' said Robbie, looking at Stevie, 'we go down fighting. You could stay in here, if you want.'

'Surrender? No fucking way. This was how it was always going to end. We both knew that. I'd rather get mown down than spend fucking years banged up. It'd be just like being back in the army. Too many fucking soldiers inside as it is.'

They continued to ignore the muffled ultimatum from the police loudhailer outside. 'Must have traced the Stag.' Stevie scratched a few words on a piece of paper. 'Watched this place, followed us inside. I'm quite impressed. Plod's not as stupid as people make out. How do you spell "necessary"?'

Robbie told him.

'Ta.'

'Justified?'

'J–u–s–t–i–f–i–e–d.'

'Top man.'

They both looked at Simm. 'There's going to be a lot of questions flying around when this is over,' Robbie said. 'We don't expect people to understand why we did what we did but we do want to give our side of the story.'

'I've written most of it down here,' Stevie said. He stuffed a piece of paper down Simm's T-shirt. 'We're not mercenaries. We were paid, yes. But that's not why we did what we did. We were recruited to do a specific job, to take out bad people, protect others. We believed in the cause. There's a lot of sick fucks out there. People need to hit back. We hit back. The list you now got? That's the names of the killings we admit to, the ones who deserved it. Five of them. You've still to find one. A bint, no less. Would you believe it? I've given you the address. There you go, chief. You've got a full confession. Red-letter day for you. Promotion beckons.' He nodded at Robbie. 'Ready?'

'Ready.'

They ran out of the bunker guns levelled, shouting wildly. Simm heard the crack, crack, crack of sniper rifles. The absence of returning fire haunted him for years. It was confirmation of something terrible. The silence of men who knew they had nothing left to lose, men who were happy turning others into killers.

Chapter 33

She was confronted by too much information. She stared at the piles of papers littered across the floor. She needed to simplify, to see in abstract. Kate stared out through the retractable doors to the deck behind Sorrenson's house and the sea beyond. The sun was out but no one was around. She had an empty beach, a blank whiteboard, to herself.

She walked outside, padded across wet sand the colour of cocoa, found a thin piece of bleached driftwood. For several minutes she stood gazing out to sea. Its capacity to astonish her never diminished. Every day the shoreline remade and unmade itself. The ebb and flow would repeat for the next four billion years, until the sun died. It had shocked her to think of the world ending. But now she found it strangely comforting. Ultimately, there was only one story, only one narrative. Man could try to alter it but he would fail. The darkness would take them all in the end. Good, bad, evil, sane: they were all going to go the same way.

She dragged her gaze from the sea and used the piece of wood to etch Carrington's name into the sand. Clearly, he was central to it all. So she would start with him. A metre or so away, she wrote Fawcett's name. The emails confirmed that there was a clear connection between the two men.

Next to Fawcett she wrote 'Raptor'. That was what the two men had discussed, even if their conversations were cryptic and unilluminating. Using a dotted line she connected Fawcett to Jepster Corporation. There was no categoric link, but Fawcett had been in Diego Garcia and Jepster was about the only corporation that could have taken him there and back. Then there was the memory stick Callow had given her. It contained other emails that Five had found. They were believed to be from Fawcett to someone else. They didn't have a confirmed name for the recipient but the email traffic crossed a server that had been linked to some kind of security consultant called Matthews. The name sounded familiar, Kate thought. Metcalf had used a security consultant called Matthews, she was sure. Metcalf hadn't told her about him, in fact it was probably a company secret, but she'd traced payments to someone named Matthews via an account in Limassol. It was likely that it was the same man. But what was Matthews's connection to Fawcett? The emails were encrypted and not even GCHQ could shed much light on their contents. She needed Callow to pull everything Five could find on Matthews. His bank accounts, his phone records, his company files. Everything. Yes, she thought, work out Matthews's role and things would become a lot clearer.

She looked down at her work, then wrote '+4' next to Carrington's name. He was, after all, only one of five murder victims whose deaths were believed to be connected. But was that correct? Should she lump the dead together like that, especially given Callow's belief that Carrington was murdered because of his links to Five? Callow was seeing the present through the prism of the past. That could play havoc with perspective.

She stared at her handiwork etched into the wet sand,

turning from brown to gold under the autumn sun. Her efforts would not last. Within hours the tide would be back to claim it and her frantic attempts to make sense of things, to instill order into chaos, would be extinguished. Yes, she thought. Give anything a limited shelf life and it became rare, valuable. A ticking clock brought new pressures, made people do desperate things. Carrington's emails to Fawcett suggested a growing sense of urgency about Raptor. He wanted out but was it just a bluff? And what was so important about Raptor? It was just a cigarette-smuggling operation, an exercise in greed. She thought again. No, it was more than that. There was the strange technology, the radio transponders they'd found hidden in the packs and then, of course, there was Jepster's apparent involvement. A corporation linked to the CIA had supplied the vessels. Jepster. Jepster held all the answers.

She started walking back towards the house. There was a clutch of documents on Jepster that she had brought back from Belize but hadn't examined. The names of shareholders mainly, yet more anonymous companies based in tax havens that were linked to it. They would be a good place to start. Her mind swam. Some things made sense, then nothing did. The canvas she was painting was too vast to comprehend. It stretched halfway around the world and back.

Her phone rang. Sorrenson. 'Hi,' she said. 'You found your man?'

'Yes.'

'Is he OK?'

'He is now. He very nearly wasn't. I'll explain later but I think we've got something that might be of interest to you. I stress *might*. I'm still trying to get my head round it.'

'Shall I come down to the station?'

'No, the hospital. You can't miss me. I'm in the ward protected by ten armed police.'

'Come on, on your feet.' Music blared out from a mobile phone. The tinny sound of Rihanna filtered across the warehouse. It was the same song they played every morning: 'Disturbia'. Same rules, too. Anyone they thought wasn't dancing hard enough got a beating. Anyone who didn't dance at all got a beating and a bullet. It had become their favourite game. 'Like *American Idol*, innit?' one of the captors had explained.

Starving, dehydrated, sleep-deprived, the hostages stumbled to their feet. They looked at the hooded men in front of them and prayed for the roof to fall in. Anything was now preferable to the hellish repetition of their days. They had given up hoping to see daylight again. They were lost to their countries, lost to their families, lost to themselves. They were lost, even, to their own species. When they looked at their captors, at their hooded faces, they no longer saw them as human. Rather, they saw them as something else altogether. Some kind of predator that had learned to mimic their language. Something that had mutated far beyond them. Something that had skipped fifty thousand years of evolution.

Callow felt in his pocket for his nicotine gum. It wasn't there. He'd used it all. A whole pack, gone in just a morning. It didn't really matter. He knew there wasn't enough nicotine in the world to calm him down at that moment. Morphine might work, he thought. Maybe he could share it with Webster. He was going to need something to calm him down.

Callow took a deep breath, using ruined lungs that weren't up to the job of sudden excessive inhalation, and entered Webster's office. He wasn't surprised to see McKie was there already. She must have read the report. She couldn't fail to be aware of just how much was at stake.

Webster made a limp-wristed gesture for Callow to take a seat. On the television in the corner of the room Al Jazeera was reporting on Scott's assassination. Webster followed Callow's gaze. 'I got tired of watching it on the American rolling news channels. The coverage became rather uniform. It seems they've already decided it was the work of Islamist terrorists. There'll be massive pressure on the White House to retaliate. The administration must be mobilizing every drone above Africa and the Middle East. We need to issue an official communiqué. Public declaration of regret to show we stand with the Americans, that we mourn with them, that sort of thing.'

'I'll talk to the Home Office,' Callow said. 'We'll get something released to Reuters.'

'Good,' Webster said. He stared down at the paperwork in front of him and shook his head several times. He glanced back at the pair of them, then returned to the papers, as if unsure how to begin. McKie nodded at Callow.

'It's clearly the worst time to be doing this,' Callow said, 'but we have no choice. They need to know. Ultimately they will be . . . grateful to learn that one of our agents may have been operating without our authority in one of their largest, most protected overseas military bases. They'll need to do their own checking.'

'I know, I know, I know,' Webster said tetchily. 'Yes, yes, yes.' He bent his head down to his desk so that his forehead was resting on the backs of his folded hands. 'So,' he muttered, 'what are we to make of it all?'

McKie cleared her throat. 'I mean, honestly, if you want my opinion, it's that we can't share this intelligence. It's mainly unsourced, much of it unverifiable and, quite frankly, probably wrong. We push this the Americans' way, they're not going to thank us for it. I'm sorry but we can't listen to Pendragon. Not on the strength of what she's offered up so far. This could really stretch our intelligence-sharing relationship to breaking point.'

'Some of it checks out,' Callow said. 'The hair-follicle lab tests.'

'Oh, please,' McKie snapped, 'we've been over this. We have an agent who was possibly once in the vicinity of a British Indian Ocean Territory. It doesn't mean he travelled there or back on a CIA plane. You can go to Diego Garcia on a yacht. From what we now know of Fawcett, that seems quite plausible. I mean, we've learned that his father worked in US naval intelligence. Fawcett seemed to spend much of his youth being shunted around the globe behind him. He could easily have developed a love of sailing. He worked for our naval intelligence for a while, remember.'

Callow tried another approach. 'His background. He was basically an American. And, well, he'd hidden stuff about himself.'

McKie sighed. 'Just because he was born one thing doesn't mean he stayed that way. I'm a case in point. Not many Muslims in my family before me. So his father died, his mother remarried a British businessman and he ended up being sent to some school in Hong Kong where he was expelled for having an affair with a male teacher. It doesn't tell us much, other than that he was probably a bit lost as a young man. If we excluded him we'd exclude half the pay-roll. Perhaps that was why he tried so hard to pass himself off as the quintessential Brit. He was clearly uncomfortable with his past, tried to bury it all. I'm just astonished none of this came out in our security checks. There'll have to be an internal inquiry. Shows us how easy it is to slip through the vetting process. Next time it'll be some sleeper recruited by Al-Qaeda or Islamic State.'

'Fawcett's hardly the Cambridge spy ring,' Callow said. He needed to play it all down. He needed McKie to escalate the threat. It had to come from her. 'I mean, we're just talking one rogue agent, that's all.'

McKie snorted. 'Well, according to Pendragon, he was running a sizeable rogue tobacco-smuggling operation. For reasons that are still worryingly unclear.'

'Co-running,' Callow said quietly.

McKie stared at him. Webster's head tracked between the two of them, as if he was watching a ping-pong match. 'Sorry?' McKie said.

Got you, Callow thought. You walked straight into my crosshairs. 'Fawcett was co-running a smuggling op. We believe a second man was involved: Matthews, a former MI6 officer. We have found some . . . fresh information. It's complicated but we can prove that Matthews was working for a CIA front company called Jepster Corporation. We've traced hundreds of thousands of dollars transferred into his account from Jepster. It's the same company that runs the Learjets in and out of Diego Garcia, which we think were used to transport Fawcett. It's the same company that owns the cargo ships used to transport the large quantities of smuggled tobacco that ended up in the hands of Al-Boktorah. It appears Matthews and Fawcett were together both professionally and personally. We have no idea where Matthews is now. He has completely disappeared. No phone, no email, no money transfers. I wouldn't bet on him surfacing again.'

McKie's eyes flashed anger. Callow was clearly trying to bounce her. Just what else did he know? 'So,' she said, 'this is new news. Anything else you want to throw in?'

Callow shrugged, and reminded himself of what was at stake. He couldn't push the button yet. He needed to buy more time. They had to be sure. Everything was at stake. Fifty men in a desert. Tick, tock, tick tock, tick tock. 'Pendragon's still doing some checking,' he said.

Chapter 34

Was that the whore – no, the escort – he'd rented just the other day? Ailes wasn't sure. In the half-light of the hotel lobby she was scrawny enough, pale enough, bored enough. But it was impossible to be sure. Ailes could hardly recall the encounter less than a week on. It was understandable. He had a lot on his mind. Washington was a different place now compared to then. It was a scared city. A city of sirens and SWAT teams. 'Like downtown Mogadishu,' someone had remarked to him. As if they had any knowledge of what it was like living in such a fucked-up place, Ailes thought. But that was how people were thinking now. Failed cities, failed states were becoming the norm. The world was crying out for strong leadership. And only a superpower could provide that when a full-blown culture war was invading the capital of the free world, spilling blood on its streets. Scott's assassination had been a wake-up call to the complacent, those who had doubted the truth of things. It sure had given a fillip to the hawks. Ailes eased himself into his usual private booth just off the lobby, waved away the waiter rushing towards him. Now wasn't the time for drinking.

'So,' he said, to the booth's other occupant, 'here we are

JAMIE DOWARD

again. Twice in a week. There's a danger people might mistake us for friends.'

'Doubt it.'

Ailes peered at Jefferson. 'You OK? You look like you've lost a lot of weight since I last saw you.'

'I'm not sleeping,' Jefferson said. 'I'm trying to figure a path through all this shit.' He reached for an olive and gave up. He found a toothpick and held it between his fingers, like a cigarette.

'Well, let me help make things easy for you, Jefferson. Just stick with the programme. It's simple. Initiate the drone strike tomorrow as planned.'

Jefferson stared at him incredulously. 'Knowing what I know? That we'd be taking out fifty hostages on the strength of corrupted intel provided by an asset we know was planted deliberately to deceive the CIA? Fuck you, Ailes. I'm not giving you my head on a plate. It was different when Scott was in charge but I have sign-off on this now and things have changed.'

'How much?' Ailes said quietly.

'How much what?'

'How much do you want to stick with the plan?'

Jefferson shook his head. 'Nothing you could offer me would make any difference now. You can't buy everything, Ailes.'

'Maybe, but we don't have to talk money. Some people prefer to talk power. Tell me, you like your new job?'

Jefferson said nothing. He resisted the urge to use the toothpick as a cigarette.

'Think a lot of people I know could make a powerful case for you to get the position permanently, when the next president comes in,' Ailes said. 'When we get the regime change we've both agreed is necessary.'

The toothpick snapped between Jefferson's fingers. 'I'm not sure people will think it's a good idea to make someone who was responsible for the deaths of fifty innocent hostages the next head of the CIA.'

'You know our man will be very disappointed if the strike doesn't happen. This was what was agreed with him at the start. He'd send in Zetouin, set the hare running, and we'd ensure the drones did the rest. Both sides get something out of this, providing everything stays the same.'

Jefferson stared at the broken toothpick between his fingers. 'Everything's fucked. Everything's changed.'

'Nothing's changed,' Ailes growled. 'What happened to Scott just confirms we need to win the defence argument. This should just strengthen our resolve.'

'That's crap,' Jefferson hissed. 'You know Scott wasn't taken out by some Islamist cell. Someone was activating an insurance policy. Someone didn't want Al-Boktorah killed by a drone before the Raptor float. They knew that Raptor wouldn't get any of the credit for finding him if that scenario played out. But do it when its TracknTrace technology has floated and people are patting it on the back and buying the cigars and then its shares are going to soar. That way the drone strike becomes one massive PR event for Raptor. Not saying it was Roscoe who pulled the trigger on Scott but it could have been. He would have been just one of many investors leading the stampede to have the strike pushed back.'

Ailes shrugged. 'What's it matter who killed Scott anyway? We both agreed this needed to be done to protect the long-term future of the CIA. We need to change the Washington mood music. We need a strong commander-in-chief. You're an Agency man, Jefferson. You want someone running this country who understands the importance of intelligence, who's not going to slash the Agency's budgets but pledges to give the CIA what it needs and not fold on it when things get awkward. You need regime change. The Agency needs regime change. America needs regime change. It's a simple choice. You got to decide. Either you want to protect the United States of America or you don't.'

Jefferson reached for another toothpick. Christ, he needed a cigarette. 'If this goes down I'll be obliterated,' he said.

'No, you'll be looked after. I'm sure our man will ensure you're very comfortable. Come on, Jefferson. We've got this far. You can't flake now. You're a hawk, not a dove.'

She held up a photocopy of Fawcett's passport. 'Do you know this man?'

The former soldier stared at her blankly and shook his head. 'Like I told you yesterday, ask my fellow patriot.'

'You know that's not possible right now,' Kate said.

Robbie attempted a laugh. 'Well, when he comes out of his induced coma, then.'

She looked around the windowless room. It was barely big enough to house a patient, especially one the size of the man handcuffed to the bed in front of her. Two armed police guarded the door. 'You believe that, that you're patriots?'

Robbie attempted a shrug. 'You can think what you like but we did our country a service, taking out that trash.'

'How exactly? I mean . . .'

Sorrenson entered the room, dragging a chair. He sat down. 'Sorry to interrupt. Do continue, Mr Armstrong.'

'It's all there,' Robbie said. 'We wrote it down before we got shot.'

'How's the leg?' Sorrenson said.

'You should have gone for a chest shot.'

'Not SCO19's way,' Sorrenson said. 'If they can disable a person without using fatal force then they will.'

'Well, I reckon they were just lousy shots.'

'I've read the note you left,' Kate said.

'Stevie wrote it.'

'OK, I've read the note Stevie wrote. You confess to murdering five people — all paedophiles, apparently.'

'Right.'

'How d'you find them?' Sorrenson asked.

Robbie said nothing.

'How could you be sure they were paedophiles?' Kate pressed.

Silence from Robbie.

Sorrenson handed her a small brown envelope from which she removed a photograph. 'Do you know this man?' She showed Robbie a photograph of Matthews. Still silence. 'Because he knows you.'

'You can't prove that.'

Kate leaned forward. 'I couldn't a few hours ago, no. I didn't know very much about Mr Matthews and I knew nothing about you. But you, Mr Armstrong, you're the missing link. You join all the dots. We've done some checking. We have proof that money from an account in Limassol, Cyprus, controlled by him, was paid into your account. Tens of thousands of pounds.'

'No idea what you're talking about,' Robbie grunted. She was a strange copper, the woman. Sounded more like an accountant.

'I suspect Mr Matthews met you when you were posted overseas,' Kate persisted. 'Iraq, possibly, or Kenya, more likely. We know you were out there helping train troops on the Somalia border. Mr Matthews once worked for the intelligence agency, MI6. But you probably know that or believe that's who he still works for. He kept in touch with you when you returned from your tours. You got chatting on protected email systems, and he explained that there were some unsavoury types out there who were beyond the law. Types the nation would be better off without. How am I doing so far?'

Robbie tried to roll over on his side away from the woman with the nagging questions. 'Don't have to talk to you.'

'Well, arguably you do. But let's not debate that right now. Do you know what a proxy war is?'

Robbie shook his head. 'Fucking leave me alone.'

'Well, you've been fighting one, Mr Armstrong. Mr Matthews was using you to fight another battle. His own. One that was making him pretty rich. Five murders, that's a lot of dead people. All connected. Paedophiles. They had it coming. Few will cry. But what if four of those murders were committed to hide the real reason why the other one was killed?'

'As if. You fucking—'

'Careful,' Sorrenson said. 'We don't mind the swearing but the walls here are pretty thin.' Robbie rolled his head from side to side. Sorrenson scratched his stubble. 'I'm an amateur astronomer, Mr Armstrong. I like picking out a star and using it to help me find others. So, say you find Merak, part of the Plough, you know you can use it to help find Polaris, the North Star, because there's a pattern up there, if you can just remember it. That's pretty useful. But what I'm learning now is that although patterns help simplify things they can also confuse. Detectives need to remember that. There's a danger you establish a common motive in a series of murders and you think, Job done, so you stop looking. Sometimes, just sometimes, people want you to see patterns because they want you to stop looking. They want you to think you've found the links.'

Robbie looked at the detective and then at the woman. The one thing he'd had, the one certainty he'd been able to cling to, that the war they had waged had been just, was in danger of shattering. 'Water,' he said. 'Water.' Sorrenson poured him a glass from a plastic jug on a table beside the bed.

'Mr Matthews left MI6 several years ago,' Kate said. 'He had an undistinguished career, I gather. These days, Mr Matthews actually runs his own private security consultancy, which ostensibly had just one client, a tobacco company called Smith and Webb. His work for this company made him privy to a lot of interesting things, so much so that we're pretty sure he became of interest to various foreign actors, including an outfit that appears to have close links to Chinese intelligence. Whether Mr Matthews ever worked for any of these foreign actors we just don't know. But we can prove he ended up with a company called Jepster Corporation, which is wholly owned by an outfit known as the ISG, or the Intelligence Support Group, to give it its full name.'

Robbie took another sip of water. She was using way too many initials. 'What does this . . . what's it called? . . . IGS thing do?'

'ISG. It's effectively what investment banks call an incubator. It takes technology, in this case technology developed by the US military, and scales it up, finds new applications for it. Sucks in lots and lots of investors, who pump money into its start-up costs. Then it floats the start-up and a lot of people get very rich. The ISG was set up as a distinct arm of the US Central Intelligence Agency. It appears not many in the Agency know about it and fewer still have any influence over it.'

Robbie wished there was a window he could stare out of. He closed his eyes. They were scum. They'd deserved what they'd got. It was graphic and it was grotesque but it had served as a warning. Others would think twice the next time they thought about sharing stuff online. Whatever the woman was going on about, it had nothing to do with him.

'Have you ever been to Belize?' Kate said. Robbie shook his head. She was doing his head in. Her questions were scattergun. Typical bint.

'A few years ago, the army might have posted you over there,' Kate continued. 'But I guess cutbacks have changed all that. I was there recently, collecting some corporate information. I was gathering intelligence on a business called Jepster Corporation, the company that employed your friend Mr Matthews.'

Corporate information, Robbie thought, what the fuck was she on about?

Kate held up a piece of paper. 'I found this while I was over there. It's a list of investors in a start-up called Raptor. Jepster's one of the big investors. Raptor makes highly specialized, super-powerful, microscopic tracking devices. You plant one of their tags on something – maybe one day someone – and you can find it anywhere in the world. I believe the company has been road-testing the technology by following packets of cigarettes being smuggled around the world by terrorist organizations. Clever thinking, really. Follow the packet and you'll find the terrorists. Only there's a problem. We suspect that the technology doesn't actually work yet. It probably will, one day, but no one's sure how well or when exactly. One of the men you murdered, Mr Carrington, he was being blackmailed, forced into helping run the cigarette-tracking operation. We know that he became very concerned about the way he was being used. So much so that he wanted to blow the whistle on the whole thing. It's not a huge jump to surmise from this that someone would have wanted to stop him talking. Only that would bring a whole new set of problems. Simply killing Mr Carrington wouldn't be enough. People might ask difficult questions. Just what did he know?' She nodded at Sorrenson. 'But, as my friend here has just been pointing out, you bury people in a pattern, make them one murder among many, then others are going to leap to very different conclusions. You, Mr Armstrong, helped them make that leap. You buried Mr Carrington in a pattern.'

She'd lost him. The woman was unhinged. Robbie found himself looking at the detective, hoping he'd bring some sanity, but the big man remained mute. The woman held up a pink newspaper. 'According to my copy of today's *FT*, Raptor is going to float on the NASDAQ tomorrow.'

'Nas-what? Talk sense,' Robbie muttered.

'The NASDAQ. The US stock market for tech companies. The Raptor float is going to make tens of billions of dollars for its investors. The hype around its TracknTrace technology is huge. People talk about it in the same way they once talked about the biggest internet plays to come out of Silicon Valley. Makes sense, I guess. Tracking products is just the start. These tags, they'll be embedded in everything one day. They'll be as common as salt. They'll communicate with everyone and everything. They'll connect every person to every machine. Their potential is almost unlimited.'

'You fucking lost me ages ago, lady.'

Kate nodded at the newspaper. 'Interesting to note who's been investing in Raptor, who stands to make billions. According to the documents I found in Belize, the second biggest shareholder after Jepster is a trust called Faversham, based in the Turks and Caicos. That in turn is owned by a company called Firestarter, based in Nassau. Bear with me here, it's pretty complicated, which, I assure you, is the point. Firestarter is owned by a trust called Brex47 based in Liechtenstein. Brex 47 is owned by a Bermudan shell company called Treefer1987, whose major shareholder, it transpires, is the Polaris Trust based in Grand Cayman.' She pointed at Sorrenson. 'My amateur astronomer friend here might find that name significant although it won't mean much to most people. But guess what? Four years ago the US Treasury blacklisted Polaris, issued a special notice preventing it operating or investing anywhere on American soil. Do you want to know why they did that, Mr Armstrong?'

Robbie didn't want to know anything.

'Because the US government believed that Polaris was being used to finance a major terrorist organization.'

Robbie wanted to say something but he couldn't form the words.

'You want to know which one?'

Robbie resisted the urge to nod.

'The Al–Boktorah brigade.'

Robbie felt like he'd been shot a second time. Kate pulled her chair a little closer to his bed. 'Mr Armstrong, you've been killing for the world's most wanted terrorist. All those murders? Turns out they weren't to get rid of paedophiles.

They were to stop people crawling all over Raptor, discovering its technology doesn't work. Just so a lot of other people, including a man who is holding fifty hostages in the desert and has already killed fifty others, can make a killing on the stock market. So tell me now, do you still think you're a patriot? Do you think it's all been worth it?'

Robbie struggled to get his words out. They were playing him, messing with his head. It was probably all bullshit. 'I've confessed to the murders, for fuck's sake. There's nothing else to say.' He stared at them. His eyes were pleading.

Kate looked at Sorrenson, nodded a couple of times. 'My colleague here, he's interested in the murders. Me, not so much. I'm interested in money, Mr Armstrong. That's what I do for a living. I follow money. And sometimes I try to stop it moving. That's what I'm trying to do now. I really need to stop some money moving very, very urgently.' She reached down and pulled a document from her handbag. 'I get the feeling you'd rather I wasn't here. Sign this document and I promise you I'll leave this room immediately. You'll never have to see me again.' Kate delved back into her bag and retrieved a pen.

'What is it?' Robbie mumbled.

'Just a declaration that you'd be willing to give the Inland Revenue outlining your tax position.'

Robbie wondered if he'd heard correctly. 'Tax position?'

Kate nodded. 'I need you to confirm that you have no intention of declaring any of the money that was paid to you from an offshore bank account located in the tax haven of Cyprus.' She held the pen towards him, with a smile. 'Your signature, that's all I need to disappear.'

Chapter 35

'Sir, you have a call.'

Jefferson wondered if he'd heard right. Now was not the time to be presented with an encrypted cell phone by one of his security detail. Show some respect, for Christ's sake. He stared at the hundreds of mourners snaking into the small cemetery on the outskirts of Washington. With half a dozen Stars and Stripes flying at half-mast, the pristine patch of grass was a boneyard for dead warriors. It housed four deceased generals, a handful of Navy Seals, a defence secretary and battalions of marines. Beyond its ivy-clad walls, scores of stretch limos vied with the television vans for parking spaces.

'Sir, you really do need to take this call. It's the head of the British security service. Says it's extremely urgent.'

Jefferson swore under his breath, reached for the cell. The fucking Brits. Everything was urgent with them. Look where that urgency had got Scott. Six feet down, a grieving widow and two fatherless kids. No, what the world needed now was a little less urgency, Jefferson thought. What it could really do with right at that moment was slowing things down dramatically.

He walked towards a quiet corner of the graveyard, studied the rows upon rows of stones, thought about the immediate future. He thought about fifty grieving families. He thought about what Ailes had said: you can't save the hostages, you can only exploit their deaths. He heard Ailes's Texan twang: hawk or dove? He looked at his watch. Almost four in the afternoon. Raptor would float in a little over twelve hours. Shortly afterwards Al–Boktorah would sell his entire stake in the company, and the US government would inadvertently murder fifty energy workers in a drone strike on the strength of flawed intelligence that would be blamed on a flawed technology. Voters would have their vengeance, come the election. There would be no mercy. The president's party wouldn't survive the fallout. It would be smashed into a hundred pieces. It would have no chance of building a mandate for decades. Voters wouldn't back anyone who couldn't keep them safe. The one thing, the only thing, a president had to promise his people was that he would protect them. But once that promise was shown to be an illusion, the hawks would take back Washington, and the defence budget would start pumping again. The Agency's long-term future would be secured. It was just fifty hostages, Jefferson told himself. Half the number of people who died in road traffic accidents in just one day. It was a necessary trade.

'Yeah, this is Jefferson. Shoot.'

Across the cemetery came the haunting sound of a solitary bugle. Jefferson tried to block the thin, tragic notes out of his head but he couldn't. There were just too many of them.

She'd seen the bank's headquarters up close several times before. But only as she ran past it on mile nineteen of the London Marathon. For some reason her GPS watch would always get jammed on that section of the course. It played havoc with her pacing when she came out of the long underpass running under Canary Wharf and entered the final quarter of the race, the mad, desperate dash for the finish when she had little left in the tank but fumes.

Now, standing outside JM Global, gazing up at its hundred-plus storeys, Kate could understand why in some photos its summit was often encased in cloud. It was a postcode in its own right, a vertical city that never slept. Even at four thirty in the morning every one of its floors was lit up.

She turned to Callow standing beside her. 'Your future's tied up in there, you know. JM Global runs the service's pension fund.'

Callow lit his third cigarette of the hour. 'Waste of carbon, all those lights being on.' He turned to the tall thin man standing next to him. 'They all do this with their lights, Miller?'

'The banks?'

'Yes.'

'Don't know. Never stood outside one at this hour before.'

'Well, now you have,' Callow muttered. 'How long have you been running your unit in HMRC?'

'Nearly three years.'

'What were you doing before?'

'Immigration.'

'Christ,' Callow said, 'you get all the fun jobs.' He looked at the eighty or so police officers massed in ranks behind him. 'Still, should be good overtime for them, I suppose. SFO?'

Kate shook her head. 'You need to have a fraud worth more than a million pounds before the Serious Fraud Office get involved. This is small fry.'

'It doesn't fucking feel like it,' Callow grunted. 'This feels like very big fry where I'm standing. Got Webster on the phone every ten seconds demanding an update. We're about to throw a grenade into the middle of a rogue CIA op. Fuck knows how this plays out.' He gestured at the figure walking towards them. 'Aye, aye. We'll have half the service here at this rate.'

'Morning,' McKie answered. 'If that is indeed what this hour is.'

'Would have thought you'd be used to getting up at this time, what with you having two young ones,' Callow said.

'My husband gets up with our children during the night,' McKie said.

'Good of him.'

'It's called shared responsibility.'

Callow drew heavily on his cigarette. 'Right.' McKie grimaced as the smoke wafted over her.

Kate checked her watch. 'Nearly time. Where's the lawyer?'

Callow pointed at a small figure some ten metres away, a phone clasped to her ear. 'Think that's her.'

Kate nodded. 'Yes, it is. Constance Ekowondu. Tiny but she's got massive teeth. They call her the piranha at the Financial Conduct Authority.'

'They can call her what she wants but she's still a minnow,' McKie murmured, 'given how flimsy all of this is. JM Global is going to eat us alive. I don't know why Webster's sanctioned it.'

Kate said nothing. McKie was right: the whole thing could crumble at any second. They just needed to get through the door, create a bit of chaos, that was all. She thought of fifty frightened men somewhere in a desert. The

349

clock was ticking. What they had was all they had. One shot. One tiny sliver of opportunity to make someone angry. People behaved rashly when money was at stake. When billions were at stake they behaved very rashly. She looked at her watch again. 'Let's go,' she said.

Chapter 36

Roscoe was troubled. There was nothing he wanted. That didn't feel right. It was just gone two in the morning and he was sitting in the boardroom of JM Global, giving final approval to the press releases and investor-relations packs that would be released in a few hours' time when Raptor floated. A clutch of the bank's most senior executives were lounging around in party mood. Vials of laughing gas and helium were scattered around the room. There were regular visits to the restrooms. If you wanted to save the Amazon rainforest, one good place to start would be persuading Wall Street to go easy on the white stuff, Roscoe thought. It had become evident to him that the nostrils of most senior bankers had to be responsible for vast amounts of deforestation.

He just didn't get it. Roscoe didn't do drugs. In fact, he had no discernible vices. When some of the bankers had disappeared from the boardroom to avail themselves of the services of the high-end escorts the bank had hired for the night, Roscoe had remained resolutely in his chair. He wasn't even interested in money. Not that he could let on. Someone had asked him what he'd do with the millions he was about to make from the Raptor float and he'd struggled to come up with an answer. 'A watch,' he'd said lamely. 'I'll buy an antique watch.' But the truth was he didn't want a watch. He liked the one he was wearing. His grandfather had worn it in Korea and it was about the only thing he liked that was older than him. No, Roscoe wanted nothing material. He just wanted Raptor to float and the ISG to become ever more powerful. He was building an empire. He wasn't interested in shopping. Power was a commodity and it trumped money every time.

He poured himself another coffee. Five hours' time and he'd be a multi-millionaire. He eyed the bottles of champagne nestling in ice buckets, thought about raising a glass to himself. Maybe it was the over-brewed coffee, but he couldn't summon the enthusiasm for such a toast. He pointed to a painting on the boardroom wall. 'Who did that?' he said, to one of the bankers sporting a chemically induced smile.

The man smirked. 'Freud, I think. British guy. Self-portrait.'

'Right,' Roscoe said. The name meant nothing to him. He looked at the face staring down at him, imperious as an eagle. He felt like he was being judged. If he was going to buy art with his money, it wouldn't be portraits, Roscoe decided. He'd buy Pollock or Rothko. He didn't want someone watching him. He wasn't good with scrutiny, with people poking their noses in. Just ask Adams and Scott.

Lord Greville Rayner was expensive. His hourly rate was in excess of three thousand pounds, but for call-outs in the middle of the night, it was double. As a former chair of the FCA, and now one of the world's leading commercial barristers, legions of anxious banks beat a path to his door whenever they were in trouble. Rayner knew the loopholes and how to exploit them. He knew how ill-equipped public prosecutors were when it came to taking down his clients. Sometimes it didn't seem fair, he thought, the asymmetry of it all. His opponents had such pathetic weapons. Still, so long as his clients kept writing the cheques . . .

Rayner studied the search warrant that had been thrust under his nose by an alarmed VP as soon as he'd walked through the doors of JM Global shortly after five that morning. 'You just have to be joking,' he said. 'No, this will not do. This will not do at all. This is a perversion. This is . . .' His head jerked up at the slap of brogues on the bank's polished marble floor. Millington, the head of the bank's London division.

'They are going to fucking hang for this,' Millington said quietly. 'I assure you. Every single fucker crawling over us right now. Forty fucking thousand pounds. Are they out of their fucking minds?' He pointed at the police officers swarming around the bank's capacious atrium. 'We're a fucking bank, not a fucking paedo-ring.'

Rayner approached the small bird-like woman who seemed to be directing operations. 'I take it you're responsible for this debacle.' Ekowondu shook her head and nodded at Kate. 'And who are you?' Rayner asked.

Kate handed him a business card. 'Pendragon. I work for the Treasury's Financial Intelligence Unit, currently seconded to MI5.'

'Let me get this straight,' Rayner said. 'We have half of Scotland Yard in this bank because there are suspicions of illegality involving the misappropriation of forty thousand pounds.'

'We believe it may actually be around fifty thousand in all. And it's not misappropriation. We believe the payment, from an offshore account, may have constituted a bribe.'

'What fucking offshore account?' Millington screamed. Rayner placed a placatory arm on his shoulders. 'I mean, we're talking fifty grand,' Millington hissed. 'This is fucking ridiculous.'

'The money was paid by someone working for a JM Global client, Jepster Corporation,' Ekowondu said. 'We have a signed affidavit that there is no intention to declare the money to the Inland Revenue. We believe the contorted nature of this transaction may be because it was considered by both parties to be a bribe. As I'm sure you are aware, we have a duty to investigate under the Bribery Act of 2010. Unless, of course, your client has another explanation, which we would be only too happy to hear.'

Millington shook his head. 'You have a duty to be fucking sane. You won't find anything. You know that. We've had auditor after auditor give us a clean bill of health.'

'Auditors have been known to be wrong,' Ekowondu said. 'There are some notable examples. Enron, WorldCom . . . I could go on.'

Through the bank's revolving doors Kate could make out at least three news vans. Good. The exposure would be welcome. She turned back to Millington, who was almost visibly melting with fury. 'This is just an interim measure,' Kate said. 'Until we've established the correct picture, we're instructing you to suspend any accounts or dealings with Jepster Corporation, its associates or vehicles in which it has financial interests, or which in turn are invested in it, both in this country and the rest of the world. This is a legal notice to inform you that, with respect to Jepster, you are now in lockdown. You are reminded that, under the Bribery Act, you, your bank and its board could be subject to serious criminal penalties if it is demonstrated that you helped facilitate an act of bribery either by a client or an agent acting on behalf of that client.' Ekowondu handed Millington a thick wad of papers. He glanced down, read the first page of the documents.

'You cannot be remotely serious about this,' Rayner said. 'You cannot give notice that you're putting Jepster's banking facilities in lockdown. It's the major investor in an eighty-billion-dollar company that's about to float in New York in a few hours' time. If we have to declare to the market authorities that Jepster is now the subject of bribery allegations, the float will have to be pulled so that due diligence can be performed. You must be aware that this is a completely disproportionate interpretation of the Bribery Act. You cannot buy a decent car for fifty thousand pounds yet you're about to destroy one of the great technological innovators of the twenty-first century. We have a prima facie case that the security services are acting out of malice against my client. The damages will run into millions.'

Rayner represented everything Kate hated. It wasn't his arrogance so much as his lack of wit. He'd earned a fortune exploiting the wealth of his clients, using their formidable financial firepower to cow critics and regulators. All of his life he'd benefited from a massive imbalance of power and the one time it had swung against him he'd cried foul, complained about the rules of the game. She moved towards him, brought her face close to his.

'Is that all you've got?' she whispered. 'Is that really all you've got? Whatever they're paying you it's too fucking much. They're going to rumble you. Your clients. They're going to work out that you're just not worth it.'

Rayner was trembling with rage. With a supreme effort, he twisted his mouth into a smile. He bent his face close to her ear. 'Cunts like you never last,' he whispered. 'So many of your sort think they can blaze a trail. But you don't. You fucking burn in the end. Whoosh, one big fireball. Hope you think it was worth it.'

Kate stepped back from him. She saw that his hands had curled into fists. She thought about fifty men in a desert. She thought about a small child in a park. She thought about tiny pinpricks of light in the darkness above. 'Yes,' she said to Rayner. 'The answer is yes.' She turned to Millington. 'We've informed the US authorities of our concerns. They take bribery allegations very seriously and we've promised to liaise with them closely.' She looked at Ekowondu. 'You OK to carry on?' The lawyer nodded. 'Good,' Kate said. 'Then I'm done here.' She turned to Callow, who was talking to a small, wiry man in jeans and Timberlands. 'You coming?' Callow said something to the man, then followed her outside to a London just waking up, a chaotic, roaring, uncontrollable capital bathed in the half-light of a million streetlamps that burned black pavements grey, dark skies silver.

Kate stared at the angler in the painting on the far wall of Webster's office. It really was truly terrible art, presumably chosen by some civil servant on a tight budget long ago. Poor Webster, she thought, having to put up with something so bland and inoffensive every day of his working life.

'GCHQ are monitoring traffic across the submarine cable

coming out of Land's End,' McKie muttered. 'We're not hearing anything so far. Getting much from the Americans?'

'Still heard nothing since you asked me five minutes ago,' Callow said. 'Gallahue said he'd be in touch as soon as.'

'Gallahue?' Webster said.

'CIA's point man on the op,' Callow said. 'He was there this morning. Typical CIA spook. Jeans, boots, buzz-cut. There was a few of them like that, hidden among our lot. Not sure whether they were there to observe or to bury things. People find out that a rogue arm of the CIA nearly helped the world's most wanted terrorist float a company, it'll get torn to shreds.'

'Not sure they'll be able to bury this,' Webster said. 'Our station chief in Washington says arrests have already been made. Some high-profile lobbyist. There's a suspicion that someone has turned whistleblower. Rumour is it's someone very high up in the Agency. It appears certain people in Washington have been working with Al-Boktorah for some time. There seems to have been some sort of collusion over the fate of the hostages, a plot to turn them into targets for drones. It's all rather opaque at the moment but I guess things will become clearer very soon. Perhaps your new acquaintance Gallahue was collecting evidence that may one day end up being used against his employer.'

'Christ,' Callow said, 'let's hope it's not catching. All we need is someone marching our skeletons in front of the ISC.' He hunted in his pocket for some nicotine gum but found only the remnants of a vaping kit. He took the pieces out and stared at them in disgust. 'It was Gallahue's friends, the ones we didn't see this morning, who are more interesting to me,' he went on. 'The NSA had four vans parked around the bank sucking up anything coming in or out of it. They'll be tapping the fibre-optic cables out of London and Frankfurt, too. Someone in the bank would have made a call to Al-Boktorah's people to let them know that the float was being pulled. I just hope the NSA's computers can track it in such a short window. Otherwise they've just lost the best chance of finding their man that they'll get for years.'

'Well, I won't hold my breath for the Americans to make contact,' Webster muttered. 'It's been more than twelve hours since we raided the bank. They've had half a day to fit all the pieces together. That's a lifetime in the intelligence world, these days.' He looked at the clock on his desk. Tick tock, tick tock, tick tock. 'You know how they think. They'll tell us only after it's done. Whatever it is exactly. We'll probably hear about it on CNN before they get in touch.'

'If they've got a location for the hostages they'll be looking to get boots on the ground about now,' Callow muttered. 'Going to be flying them in from ships off Italy, I guess. Need to wait until dark. They'll launch some sort of limited drone strike to create confusion and then the special forces will go in.'

'I can't believe they'll use a drone,' Kate said. 'For all they know there's fifty hostages under those co-ordinates.'

'From what's coming out of Washington, I rather think that was the intended scenario,' Webster said. 'At least this way any strike will be targeted, rather than some sort of blanket bombing.'

'But think of the risks,' Kate said. 'It could be a disaster. I mean—' She broke off. There was nothing to be said. The impossibility of the situation made words useless.

'They've got no choice,' Callow said, yawning. 'It's not going to be clean whatever happens. But at least they'll have a chance of saving some lives. Probably use a drone piloted from here.'

Kate shook her head. 'Seriously? The US operates drones from here?'

'Some, yes,' McKie said. 'We never know which ones but they have at least three sites in the UK that they use. We obviously don't like to publicize it. Every drone strike creates martyrs. And where there are martyrs, recruiters aren't far behind.'

Kate glanced at her watch. There was no point in waiting for something to happen that she couldn't control. She needed to be somewhere else, somewhere below a tar-black sky with a man who knew the names of stars. She needed to understand the irrelevance of it all, to be confronted by a universe that could be measured only in light years. There would be more drones, more killings, more terrorists . . . It was an endless cycle. 'I'm off,' she said.

'Do you want to be informed when we hear anything?' Callow said.

She took a final look at the painting on Webster's wall, walked towards the door. 'No,' she said. 'It can wait.'

Chapter 37

From the rooftop garden of JM Global's New York head-quarters she had a view of Manhattan enjoyed by only the very few. So, she thought, this is the perspective that bankers can afford. This is what it's all about. You could see for more than thirty miles, she reckoned, to a point in the far-off distance where land ceded to sky. The escort stubbed out her cigarette, drank in the 360-degree vista for a final time. Reluctantly she started to make her way back inside. The party mood in the bank had soured hours earlier and she was in no hurry to make her descent. The building resembled a hospital. It seemed to be populated exclusively by sick men preparing for doctors to tell them the worst. The ashen-faced bankers held whispered urgent conversations in corridors, their faces turned away from the internal CCTV cameras, their shaking hands fumbling for cigarettes. Everything had changed so quickly, like a virus had ripped through the place, devoured everything in its path. The escort had hung around for a while, waited to see if things were going to improve, but the atmosphere had become increasingly funereal. It was when the squadrons of police cars had pulled up and the bank had been swamped with FBI that she'd headed towards the roof for air. She'd walked through vast, open-plan offices denuded of staff, past television screens showing breaking financial news from around the world. The oil price was moving, the screens informed her. Something to do with an incident in the Sahara. Twenty-five hostages freed, twenty-two dead, three unaccounted for. She'd continued walking upwards, preferring the quiet stairwells over the frantically moving lifts. Now, a safe distance from the turbulence below, she was pleased that she'd made it to the calm of the rooftop. The view of her adopted city had been worth the journey. Her day hadn't been entirely wasted. She was about to enter the stairwell, return to the lifts, when she saw the man standing on the ledge. His hands were clasped behind his back and he was swaying slightly, as if being bent by the evening breeze. He caught sight of her, shouted something that she didn't catch. Roscoe fumbled with his wristwatch, threw it towards her . . .

And then he was gone.

Acknowledgements

Thanks to Clive Hebard, Krystyna Green and Grace Vincent at Little, Brown; Peter and Rosie Buckman, Hazel Orme and Edie Reilly for much needed help and advice in making this book come to life. And thanks to L, Bill Berry, George, Bernard, Emily and Sophie for all the laughter along the way.